BROOKS &SMITH

DETECTIVE TALES, VOL. 1

Printed in the United States of America.

ISBN (print): 978-1-958245-01-9

ISBN (e-book): 978-1-958245-02-6

Fonts: Riverside (lic. from Creative Market), Garamond.

Visit the author's website at www.martina-fetzer.com.

Cover and illustrations by okdoodle.net.

Proofread by: Alex Blachernae (Bread).

BROOKS &SMITH

DETECTIVE TALES, VOL. 1

BY: MARTINA FETZER

INTRODUCTION

The idea for this collection came about while I was writing *Time Binge,* the first novel in the *Brooks & Smith* series. It's a silly book set in a silly universe, and it's about a pair of paranormal detectives who struggle more with ennui than with any of their cases. Because *Time Binge* is a time travel story, I ended up writing a *lot* of flashbacks. Most of them involved drama between the two detectives, and when it came time to edit, they were the first thing cut because ~~I seek validation from others and comedy is one of the few things I've ever received positive feedback on in my life~~ I'm trying to make people laugh.

What did make it into that story (and its sequels) were offhanded references to Brooks and Smith's prior cases—most of them quite stupid. The ideas started mixing together in my mind, along with a notion I've always had to write a collection of short stories. After years of fiddling around between larger projects, I had enough material for a book.

These are the early adventures of detectives Brooks and Smith (thus "Volume 1"). This collection contains thirty short stories and vignettes that take place in chronological order, spanning from 1997 to 2014. Some are super short. Some are illustrated. Some aren't stories at all. Just putting that out there now. Anything goes here, but it all adds up to tell a bit of a story of its own.

No prior knowledge of the universe is necessary. Whether you've read any of the other books or not, I recommend reading from front to back. It makes more sense that way, and it's especially important if you're new.

Whoever you are, grab a cup of your preferred beverage and get ready for silliness, dark humor, a touch of drama, a bit of mystery, a smidge of genuine horror, a pinch of queer romance, and a boatload of questionable decisions by both the characters and the author. This book is what businesspeople call a "loss leader." When you're done, you'll either want to dive into the novels (yay!), or dive into the nearest pit of knives so you never have to read anything like this ever again (sorry, no refunds).

CONTENT NOTE

These stories are meant to be funny, but they do contain plenty of foul language, casual gore, sexual content, drug use, and references to horrid acts of violence. Nothing is described very graphically, but if you're sensitive to anything in particular (and don't mind mild spoilers), content warnings for each story are available at the author's website: martina-fetzer.com.

TABLE OF CONTENTS

Pretend this is some sort of deep quote.
- Someone respectable

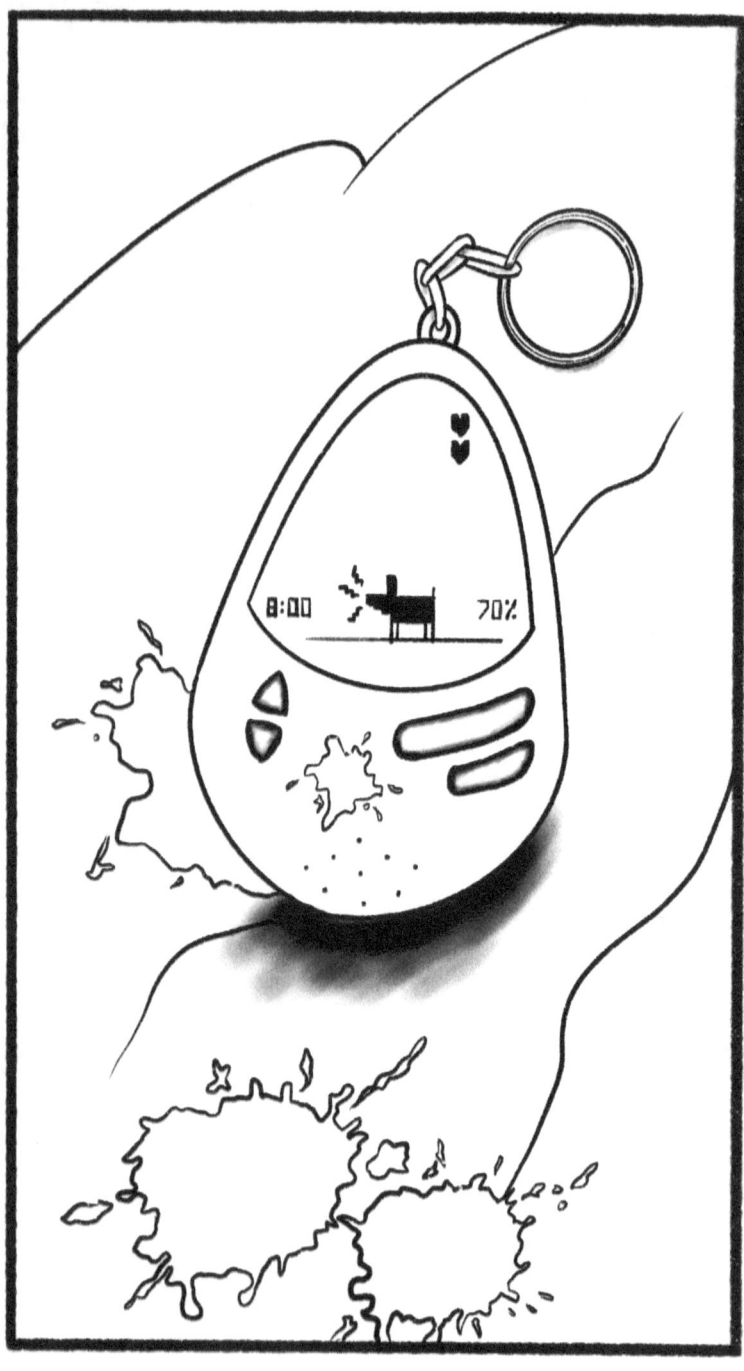

MIRUKUTCHI ON 34TH STREET

In 1997, New York City was neither the crime-ridden wasteland it had been in the 1970s nor the family-friendly tourist destination it is today. It was just a place—a place where people did typical 1997 things like listen to Jewel and rent VHS tapes from Blockbuster Video.

As he got ready for work, Edward Smith, age twenty, assumed it would be a typical 1997 day. Like many pasty men of the time period, he had tragically limp, dirty blond hair that fell just below his ears. He brushed it out of the way for the fourth time in three minutes so he could check his reflection in the bathroom mirror. If he ignored the mixed pile of towels and clothes in the background, everything looked fine. Good even, considering it was six o'clock in the morning and he was running on almost no sleep. His cargo jeans were nice and baggy, and a bowling shirt hung loosely over a studded belt with a chain wallet. A pair of Airwalks completed the ensemble.

Edward—*never* Eddie—grabbed his black Jansport and tossed it over his shoulder. It was heavy with the weight of the wares he'd soon be selling, and he grunted as he barreled out the bathroom door and through the rest of his studio apartment. To put a little pep in his step, he chugged what remained of a warm bottle of Surge soda. Like his hair, it was flat. Just before heading out the door, he grabbed a pack of cigarettes and stuffed them into the most gigantic pocket of his gigantic pants.

He didn't need to dodge his landlord demanding rent, for once. Edward was paid up for the time being. How long that would last grew more uncertain by the month. Washington Heights was on the cusp of gentrification, and though he'd only been living there for two years, he was damn close to getting priced out. Edward wished for a rise in crime, if for no reason than to avoid having to put in the effort of packing and moving to a shittier neighborhood.

The hassle of moving aside, he knew his neighbors. He didn't like any of them, but he knew them. There was Melon Guy, who always seemed to be carrying a melon. There was 3 AM Pisser, who lived directly above Edward and urinated at the exact same time every night.[*] And there was Pigeon Lady, who once wore a shirt with a picture of a pigeon on it, but was otherwise unremarkable. Edward knew who had the good cocaine, who had the bad cocaine, and who had no cocaine at all. It was home enough, and infinitely better than anything he'd ever had in Indiana.

He walked past all the homeless people who knew he had no money to give them, down into the subway station. Without incident, he boarded the 9 train toward Lower Manhattan.

Nothing with Edward Smith was ever 'without incident' for long.

It was standing room only. That was fine. He could physically stand. What he couldn't stand were the dulcet sounds blasting from a nearby set of headphones. They were nestled around the neck of a well-groomed Columbia student, instead of over the man's ears where they belonged. For what seemed like the thousandth time this week, candles were in the wind, courtesy of Sir Elton John.

---

* 4 AM. Edward's clock was off.

"Jesus Christ," Edward muttered to himself—a little too loudly, and intentionally so.

The student turned his head and spoke like angry New Yorkers do. "You got a problem?"

Edward scoffed. "Listening to schlock's not gonna bring the bitch back from the dead."

'That bitch' in question was Diana, the late Princess of Wales, and the man on the train made an accurate assessment:

"Rude."

"Not sorry," Edward said. "I'm so sick of that fucking song. I don't see why anyone this side of the Atlantic gives a shit."

"Her work on landmines? What she did for the gay community?"

Edward rolled his eyes, hard. "Oh, do tell me what she did for me."

"You're gay?" The Columbia student eyed him up and down.

Edward shrugged. "Sometimes."

"Oh." The student harrumphed. "One of *those*. No wonder you had to bring attention to yourself."

"I just wanted to complain under my breath. You're the one who made it weird."

"Whatever." The student put his headphones on, properly this time. "*Asshole.*"

For the next fifteen minutes, Edward rode next to the annoyed monarchist, who replayed the same song four times, loud enough to be heard even with the headphones on his ears. After the young man exited the train with a sarcastic smile and wave, Edward rode another thirty minutes in silence to Battery Park. With its carousel, miscellaneous statues, and boat rides to the Statue of Liberty and Ellis Island, it was a prime spot for hawking goods to tourists.

Edward Smith had some of the best goods around.

Tamagotchi virtual pets sold for $17.99 retail. Mirukutchi virtual pets, their off-brand cousins, were twelve for a dollar in Chinatown, and ignorant tourists happily paid $10 each for them. Sometimes—if they insisted on haggling—Edward would give them a bargain and sell the egg-shaped keychain toys for $5, pretending he was doing the tourists a favor and that some mysterious boss would be furious at him for letting the toys go at such a low price. In reality, these knockoff virtual pets tended to experience total hardware failure within days of purchase, but it didn't matter. Due to the nature of tourists, no one who bought one ever showed up to return it.

Edward claimed his favorite spot, between a trashcan and Lois Row, which was not a street but the name of a person and the closest thing he had to a friend. She, unlike anyone else in New York, acknowledged his existence with something other than disdain.

"Nice spread today," Edward said, eyeing her Teenie Babies, a collection of off-brand beanbag animals.

From her folding chair, Lois replied with a simple, "Mmmhmm."

Edward unzipped his backpack. First, he removed and unfurled a coffee-stained sheet on the sidewalk. Atop it, he scattered dozens of Mirukutchi in no particular order, and adjusted them in a way that didn't make them any more appealing. Spread across the mint green sheet, the colorful plastic eggs could have resembled a nicely arranged Easter basket. Instead, the visual was more akin to a rabid hen having fucked a clown and spasmed out a bunch of its eggs before dying in a puddle of its own piss. A passerby nearly stepped on one Mirukutchi—a pet dwarf goat—and Edward mumbled something as he pulled the whole lot in closer to the sidewalk's edge.

"Would you quit being stubborn and put those Miru-whatsits on the cart already?" Lois had offered to share her space on dozens of occasions.

Edward declined every time, in the same way. "I don't need your help."

Everything about him screamed otherwise, especially the fact that he always set up shop in the same spot, but Lois acquiesced and changed the subject. "You watch that new cartoon I told you about yet?" She meant *South Park*, because it was 1997.

"No. Not yet."

"I really think you'd like it," Lois said.

He scoffed. "I don't like *anything*."

"Sure you do." Lois smirked. "You like being obstinate."

Edward continued fidgeting with the Mirukutchi. "I don't even know what that means."

Lois tutted. While her goods weren't legitimate, her business was. The retired teacher and widow had a vendor's license, a little cart, and a relaxed demeanor. She wasn't there for survival, but pleasure. This was how she chose to stay engaged with the world, and one of her favorite things to do was continue teaching wayward youth, however informally.

"It means stubborn," she said.

Edward was busy tapping at a giraffe pet whose screen had become frozen. He stopped and stared at her. "What?"

"Obstinate," Lois said.

"Oh." He nodded. "Yeah, that tracks."

Edward stood up from his display and scanned the area, squinting his normally bulging green eyes. Like he was looking for something.

"You all right?" Lois asked.

"Where's Sean?" Edward asked.

Sean was a twenty-one-year-old college dropout who sold CD singles of "Candle in the Wind" that he burned using his cousin's brand-new CD-RW drive. They weren't friends (see above re: friends), but Edward enjoyed looking at him while he worked every Tuesday and Thursday. Except this Thursday.

"Maybe he's sick," Lois suggested, before contorting her face into a smirk. "Why do you care?"

Edward leaned against her cart. "*I don't.* I just think it's weird we've lost half a dozen regulars in the last week."

In addition to Sean, the missing included Brandy, who hawked Tickle Me Elmos left over from the previous holiday season and Cenk, who'd just up and abandoned his expensive kebab cart. Edward had never learned the names of the others, but there were definitely more people missing.

"It happens a lot. Lotta troubled people down here," Lois said.

Edward resembled that remark, and he scowled.

A passerby who'd been eyeing the Mirukutchi caught the scowl and turned away. First missed sale of the day.

"Goddamn it." Edward focused up, straightened his bowling shirt, and tried making eye contact with pedestrians as they passed.

Most people looked away, trying to avoid harassment.

One man in a long, brown trench coat didn't manage to avoid his gaze. Their eyes met.

Edward's lips opened. Before he could get a word out, the businessman raised a hushing hand toward him. "Don't fuckin' talk to me."

Second missed sale of the day, and the interaction left a bad taste in Edward's mouth. Worse than the Surge he'd had for breakfast. But the show had to go on.

A pack of students who, according to their jackets, were from Saint Ælfheah High School (Go Vikings!), spoke loudly as they passed. Something about a new Mariah Carey album. It didn't matter. One of them came within centimeters of the fake Tamagotchis.

Edward snapped. "Watch where you're going!"

The teen turned around, unafraid to confront the man who'd yelled at him.

"I didn't touch any of your crappy knockoffs," the teen said.

"You want to? They're only five bucks," Edward said, reducing the price.

"Do I look stupid?" the teen asked.

Edward sized him up and took note of the varsity jacket. "No. But you're from Staten Island, so I wouldn't be shocked."

"Ugh. Whatever. At least I'm not an old dude selling fake Tamagotchis." The younger man sneered and walked away.

Edward raised a middle finger for his departure.

"That chip on your shoulder's the size of an anvil today," Lois said.

He replied with zero emotion. "Fuck off, Lois."

She ignored that, as she always did. "Long night?"

Edward pulled a cigarette from his giant pocket and lit it. "Didn't sleep."

"Didn't or couldn't?" Lois asked.

He exhaled. "What's the difference?"

Lois explained. "'Didn't sleep' is for when you stayed out late having a good time. 'Couldn't sleep' is for when you laid in bed all night trying to sleep and your brain wouldn't let you."

Edward corrected her, drolly. "I was lying on the *couch*."

That was a fib since he had no couch, but it sounded

better than tossing and turning on a recliner that had long lost its ability to recline.

"What was on your mind?" Lois asked.

"Mostly how much I hate the new version of goddamn 'Candle in the Wind.'"

"It's a beautiful song. We should all be so lucky when we go."

Edward rolled his eyes. "Oh, here we go again."

"*Again*?" Lois asked. "How often do you get into arguments about a harmless song?"

"More often than you'd think," said Edward. He took a deep drag.

"You really try as hard as you can to alienate people, don't you?" Lois asked.

Edward grumbled through his cigarette. "I don't have to try."

"One of these days, we're gonna get coffee and you're gonna tell me your life story," Lois said.

"No offense, but you'll be dead before that ever happens," Edward retorted.

"I'm only sixty-three," she noted.

He shrugged. "That's three times as many as me."

"Eddie—"

"—ward."

"You keep living the way you do and you're going to be dead before I am," Lois said.

He rolled his eyes, harder this time to make it obvious. "Wouldn't that be a shame."

"It would." She poked a finger at his chest. "There's a good person in there."

"Yeah? I've never met him."

"I have," Lois said. "Any time one of those beanies falls off my cart, you pick it up before I can even get up off my chair."

He tossed his cigarette butt to the ground and pressed it with his shoe. "That's not being a good person. That's just what you do."

"That's not what everyone does," Lois said.

"Whatever. No one gets a 'Candle in the Wind' for picking up Teenie Babies." Edward looked for an exit from the conversation. "I gotta piss. Can you watch my 'kutchi?"

Lois nodded.

Edward didn't make his way to the restroom in the ferry station, or to any restroom. Instead, he headed for the nearest alley. In the shadows between two skyscrapers, it almost felt like nighttime.

Desperate to turn this day around, he dug deep in one of his many jean pockets to pull out a tiny Ziploc bag with a scant amount of white powder settled in its bottom. He heard something—footsteps, maybe—and stuffed it back down.

"Someone there?" he asked.

No one replied. He looked around for signs of cops and decided what he heard was probably a rat.

"Whatever," he muttered.

Edward reached back into the pocket and pulled the baggie out. There wasn't much left, but it was enough to do a quick bump off his hand and feel *something* other than contempt.

"Good person." He scoffed. Then he sniffed.

As his heart began racing, a deep voice called out from within the alley's shadows. It didn't have any accent, but it had an affectation that made it sound regal—the sort of voice that in 1997 could have sold Viennetta ice cream or Grey Poupon mustard over the radio.

"You have something I want," it said.

Edward turned. His dilated pupils couldn't make out a face. A figure—human, presumably—stood further down the alleyway, enrobed in shadows. He squinted, and spoke to the nothingness. "Sorry. I'm not holding. If you want a Tamagotchi, though—"

"I don't want your cocaine," the voice said, "or your virtual pet."

The figure came closer, but remained a shadow.

Edward, becoming wired, spoke quickly. "I usually don't go for that, but fuck it. I'm broke. Fifty to suck, hundred to fuck."

The shadow came closer. "I don't want your body."

"Okay, you wanna spit out what you do want sometime today?" Edward tapped at his wrist as if he were tapping a watch.

"I want your blood."

As those words emerged, the voice gained a face. It was a pale, masculine one, with sharp edges all over. Grim, but strangely desirable in spite of its dry, cracking lips. A long, black cloak obscured the rest of its body, but it loomed large, towering over the six-foot-tall young man. For just a moment, the creature's eyes seemed to glow yellow.

"Uh... what?" Edward asked, certain he'd imagined the last part.

"*Your blood*," the creature repeated.

"'Kay. Have a nice life, weirdo." Edward turned to leave the alley.

Softly—almost seductively—the voice called out again. "I know what *you* want."

Edward was used to addicts and homeless people saying bizarre things. This was different. Something in the voice physically compelled him to turn back and remain in the alley. He looked down at his Airwalks and tried to persuade them to leave, but his feet wouldn't budge. His body became warmer. His eyes shifted from side to side in paranoia and confusion. Some of this was the cocaine, of course, but a greater part of it was the creature's thrall.

"I wanna leave," Edward said. His body was teeming with energy, and it was screaming at his brain to let it expend some.

The creature pointed a bony, sharp-nailed finger at him. "That's not what you *really* want."

"What do I want then?" Edward swallowed deeply, trying to calm his twisting insides.

The creature ran the long, cold finger along Edward's jawline, leaving a shallow scrape.

"I'll show you," it said.

Edward didn't understand, and he didn't want to. He managed to get one pleading word out from under the thrall. "Don't."

The strange creature moved in close, until their faces were nearly touching. So close that Edward could tell it had no breath. He tried to turn his head to the side, away from the monster whose cold, dead lips were too close to his own. He couldn't. He shut his eyes.

The creature took a step back. "If I were to end your life right now, would anyone mourn you?"

Edward opened his eyes and put every bit of his willpower into responding sarcastically. "My landlord would miss the check."

"No one would miss you," the creature said, as if it were a universal fact.

"You don't know me," Edward replied.

"I don't have to. I'm sensing your thoughts."

"Like—?" Edward stared in confusion.

"Like maybe this is it. Maybe this is the day your life ends, and you no longer have to force yourself to endure it. The day you no longer have to pretend."

"I'm not pretending anything," Edward said. "Except pretending to care what you have to say."

The creature flashed its sharp teeth as it explained. "You most certainly are. Pretending you're above caring. Pretending it doesn't hurt every time one of those tourists looks at you with contempt. Pretending you can overpower their scorn and indifference with your own. You can't. You never will. Your life ends in misery now, or it ends in misery later."

"That's... your opinion," Edward said, fighting back his own feelings.

"That's the truth."

Trying to focus on something—anything—but his existential dread, Edward noticed something around the creature's neck: a necklace that had belonged to Sean. His favorite CD vendor was certainly dead. It didn't matter. He'd soon be dead too. His eyes welled, partly in fear and partly in relief.

The monster moved its fangs to Edward's neck and spoke softly. "You're no longer under my thrall. You can leave at any time, if you wish."

Edward didn't leave.

"I thought so," said the creature. "I'm going to drink from you now."

Edward remained perfectly still as two sharp teeth pierced his neck. The fangs felt no more painful than getting a tattoo, though that may have been thanks to the cocaine.

His neck became warm and wet as his blood flowed into the vampire's mouth. As violent as the act was, the creature held him gently as it sucked the life from him. It was—for a moment—the most peaceful he had felt in his short life. Also the horniest.

Before Edward could lose enough blood to collapse, the creature jerked away from him and let out a violent, catlike hiss.

Edward stumbled backward and was soon leaning against a brick wall, pressing a hand to his neck wound. "What the *fuck*?"

The creature coughed and spat blood all over the alley. "Disgusting."

"What—"

The monster dropped the regal act, and his voice changed to that of a regular New Yorker. "Your blood. Nicotine, cocaine, *and* benzos?" He spit some more. "*And Surge*? Are you trying to kill me?"

Edward stared, dead-eyed. "I'm not good enough to *eat*?"

"Hey, it's not like I expected you to be kosher or somethin'. Just not... blech. I can still taste it."

Edward dropped to his knees, still holding his neck. The sounds that emerged from him were half sobs and half laughter. "Fuck me. I can't even get murdered right."

"Oh, I'm still gonna murder you," the monster said.

Edward brushed his hair out of his face. "Well, hurry up."

As the creature moved closer, it became apparent that something was very wrong. Its lips had swollen to three times their original size, more around the fangs. It swayed a little, and staggered.

Edward squinted. "Are you allergic to something?"

"No... but your blood..."

The monster lost the ability to complain as it collapsed to the ground, still retching.

Some sense made Edward's eyes dart around the alley. He could have sworn he saw another shadow moving. Then again, it could have been the cocaine.

It definitely wasn't the monster at his feet, which had stopped vomiting. It had stopped moving altogether and come to rest on its stomach.

Edward knelt down to roll it over.

"Fuck," he said, gagging.

The creature had withered to the point that it looked like a skeleton. Only dehydrated, crusty skin remained, pulled taut over its bones. He regretted the boner he'd gotten earlier.

"Nice work," said a female voice.

Edward had been right. There was something else in the alley. He twitched a little as he rose to his feet looking for it.

"Was that a vampire?" he asked, addressing the other shadowy figure.

"That was a vampire," the voice confirmed. "A master vampire, in fact. I'm surprised you were able to resist its thrall."

"Yeah..." Edward changed the subject. "You a vampire?"

"I'm just a person." A feminine figure stepped into the light. She was 5'9", but almost matched his height thanks to a set of tasteful heels. With flat brown hair and not-striking brown eyes, she looked like the default model in a video game's character designer, except that she was a woman.

"You got a name?" Edward asked.

"Erin Burroughs," she said.

"What are you doing in an alley chasing vampires?" Edward asked.

"I work for The Reticent," she said.

"The drug company?"

"Yeah. It's a front for paranormal investigation." She was pretty blasé about it.

Edward shrugged. "That's... not the weirdest thing I've learned today."

"Listen. If you can resist a master vampire's thrall, we

could use someone like you."

"No thanks. I've got a uh... good thing going," Edward said.

Erin Burroughs didn't remark on the obvious lie, but extended a hand. "Here's my card if you change your mind."

"Uh huh." He took the card without looking at it and hurried away, promising himself never to return to that alley—or, if he had to, that he would only do so for the choicest cocaine.

Edward made his way back to Battery Park and his Mirukutchi. When he was about twenty feet from his destination, he knew something was wrong.

The toys were gone. His entire display was gone, even the sheet.

"What the fuck, Lois?" Edward asked the air.

He picked up his pace to find out what the fuck.

Lois lay slumped behind her cart, which had been looted of Teenie Babies. She looked peaceful, like nothing untoward had happened. A natural death, one that made him genuinely sad.

Edward eyed the business card in his hand, then Lois. Even as he grieved, his twisted mind cued up the twinkly piano intro to "Candle in the Wind." She deserved it.

Goodbye, Lois Row
Though your Beanies weren't real at all...

SIRENS OF BRIGHTON

Every Wednesday evening, the Women's Empowerment Working Group met in the second cafeteria of Reticent Headquarters in lower Manhattan. It was smaller than the main cafeteria and had pink chairs. Very empowering. On the agenda were diversity initiatives and sensitivity surveys. Some women attended to ensure their voices were heard by higher-ups. More attended because they feared higher-ups regarding them as 'not team players' if they didn't.

Erin Burroughs attended solely to talk shit about men. After the corporate nonsense was over, she led her three closest work friends to the martini bar across the street.

It was noisy, in a pleasant way. Not like a pub or sports bar, just a steady stream of low-volume chattering and fancy glasses clink-clanking. Thick purple curtains and $15 cocktails abounded.

Sitting around a high-top table with Burroughs were Agents Anna Cook, Sofia Smirnova, and Delia Foster. All four women were in their mid-to-late twenties. All four were having a great time.

"How's the new partner?" Cook asked.

"He's an idiot," Burroughs said.

"Didn't you recruit him?" Foster asked.

Burroughs sighed. "*Yeah.*"

They all laughed at her misfortune, together.

"What did he do?" Smirnova asked.

Burroughs set down her drink. "For starters, he won't

stop hitting on me—"

There was a collective groan. They'd all been there.

"—And then... did I tell you about the sirens?"

Cook went wide-eyed. "No, but you're gonna."

Burroughs explained. "A case came across our desks. The file said there were sirens on Brighton Beach."

"Honest-to-God sirens?" Foster wondered. "You're shitting me."

"I'm not. Sexy ladies with bird wings, the whole deal. Supposedly they were luring kayakers to their deaths. I started gathering names, getting ready to interview the family members and whatnot..."

"Sure. Sure." Cook nodded along.

Burroughs continued, her eyes constantly in various stages of rolling. "Ed—Agent Smith immediately calls up a kayak rental stand and *books us a tandem kayak*."

Smirnova's face scrunched. "Did he want you both to get murdered by sirens?"

Burroughs put her hands up in a thank-you gesture. "Right?"

"You told him what they do to men, right?" Foster asked.

"Oh yeah. I told him they're irresistible. I told him they would *literally eat him alive*. He didn't care. Said he was fine dying quote 'at the hands of some hot chick' and it wouldn't be a problem for me, so what was I worried about?"

"Did you do it?" Cook asked. "Did you go on the kayak?"

Burroughs lowered her head in embarrassment.

"*No*," Smirnova and Foster said at once.

"I know," Burroughs said. "I know."

"Then why do it?" Foster asked.

"He's... weirdly convincing," Burroughs said.

The other women exchanged devious glances.

Burroughs continued her story. "So we get on this kayak, and... he doesn't even know how to kayak... has *never kayaked before.* I try to explain that his giant ass needs to be in the back for balance, but he's already sat up front and won't move. It's basically impossible to get this thing moving. He's splashing me with the oars every three seconds. Water is filling the whole boat. I'm thinking we're going to sink before we ever get lured in. But somehow we don't. We just paddle around for *two and a half hours.*"

"Sounds miserable," Foster said.

"It *was* miserable, and we never heard a siren. I got him to abandon ship, and then we headed over to a bar by the shore," Burroughs said.

Before Foster could say something snarky about them going on a date, Smirnova finished Burroughs's thought. "To do the investigation like you should have in the first place."

"Right," Burroughs said, shooting Foster a glance. "So anyway, this place is all Eastern Europeans in tracksuits." She looked directly at Smirnova. "No offense."

"None taken. It's a horrible look," Smirnova said.

"Yeah. You know what else is a horrible look?" Burroughs took a dramatic sip of her drink, then set it down. "Flirting with every Tom, Dick, and Vladimir in the place."

"I thought he kept flirting with you," Foster said.

"He flirts with anything that moves," Burroughs replied.

Cook raised her brow. "Should you report that to HR?"

"Should I? Maybe. But I definitely don't want to interact with the witches in HR," Burroughs said. She wasn't being catty; many of them were literal witches.

"You think he's cute," Smirnova teased.

"No," Burroughs said, definitively.

"Oh my God. You're sleeping with your partner,"

Foster said.

"No. I'm not."

"Yet." Smirnova smirked.

Burroughs crossed her arms. "Can I finish the story or not?"

Smirnova and Foster exchanged mischievous looks before nodding to let her continue.

"*Thank you.* Anyway, in the middle of our investigation, he left the bar with one of the tracksuit guys," Burroughs said.

Cook didn't get it. "To investigate further, or—"

"To investigate what was inside his pants," Burroughs said. "One minute, they're at the bar flirting. The Euro guy is super touchy-feely about it. Then they're gone. Out the door."

"Did you go after him?" Cook asked.

"No. I *did my job.* Kept talking to the other patrons. It was mostly nothing, until... one of them told me a story about Rusalka."

"Ohhh," Smirnova said.

"You've heard of them, I'm sure," Burroughs said.

"Of course. Where my family is from, we call them Vodyanitsy." While the others looked on in confusion, Smirnova explained. "They're women who drowned, either by murder or suicide. They seek revenge by drowning the men who broke their hearts, or by tickling them to death."

"Wait," Foster said. "I followed you until the tickling."

"It's said to be a painful way to die." Smirnova shrugged.

Burroughs continued her story. "Exactly. They had their hearts broken, so they tickle men until their hearts literally break. We're not exactly dealing with sirens. But you know what all of the people who were found drowned had in common?"

"What?" Cook asked.

"They all left that bar with someone the night they died," Burroughs said. "Like my idiot partner just had."

"But you said Agent Smith left with a guy in a tracksuit," Foster said.

"Ohhh," Smirnova said.

"Mmmhmm..." Burroughs encouraged her to continue.

Smirnova obliged. "It's said by some that Rusalka can change their appearance to suit the tastes of the men they seduce. I've not heard of one changing to look like a man, but I suppose anything is possible..."

"It *is* possible. I ran out the door and... thank God Eastern Europeans are homophobes." Burroughs stared directly at Smirnova again. "No offense."

"No, it's true," Smirnova said. "Many of us are very bad about it."

"Well, *everyone* could point me in the direction they went. So I followed their directions to an old warehouse right on the ocean. I've got my gun ready. I've got a knife in my hand. I go through the door, ready to fight something." Burroughs moved her hands around like she was holding weapons.

The women set their drinks down and waited in wide-eyed anticipation.

"My partner..." Burroughs shook her head. "...was buck naked on the floor, consoling a naked Rusalka about its performance anxiety."

"What." Foster squinted in confusion.

"Apparently... this thing took Ed—Agent Smith back to its lair, got him undressed, started the whole weird thing with the tickling and just... stopped. Couldn't keep tickling."

"Why not?" Smirnova asked.

"Oh, I'm getting there." Burroughs spoke with disbelief at her own story. "Rusalka had their hearts broken, so they want to break hearts, right? This one said it realized that—you can't break a heart that's already broken. And since my partner doesn't believe in love, his heart is *metaphorically* already broken."

The other women groaned.

"That's such bullshit," Foster said.

"Right?" Burroughs said. "This idiot should be dead, but he gets off on a technicality because he's a loveless scrub?"

Smirnova rolled her eyes. "Men can get away with anything."

The women simultaneously drank to that.

"What did you do with the Rusalka?" Cook asked.

"Oh. You'll love this," Burroughs said. "It got so depressed about its performance issues that it killed itself."

Foster nearly choked on her martini. "*What?*"

"I don't know. Maybe when it became a man, it started thinking like a man," Burroughs replied. "All I know is, Agent Smith is the luckiest idiot on the planet."

"I'll say," Cook said.

"It's infuriating." Burroughs finished, "And on the way out the door, he took the damn tracksuit. I don't know what for. I don't want to know what for."

"Probably something kinky," Foster said.

"I don't want to know," Burroughs repeated.

"I think you do," Smirnova teased.

The others laughed.

Foster shot Burroughs a sly look. "You gonna let him tickle you?"

Burroughs responded so enthusiastically that she spilled a bit of her drink. "No!"

"Come on," Smirnova said. "Everyone breaks Rule 1.14.9."

"Not *everyone*," Cook offered.

"I haven't!" Burroughs insisted. "And if I were going to,

it certainly wouldn't be for a maniac who sleeps with Russian tickle monsters."

No one found her protests convincing.

CODE FOURTEEN

Date: 3 August 2004

This transcript has been compared with the audio recording submitted and is an accurate transcription. Signed, Agent Keiki Harris.

Q1: Agent Aaron Moreno (ID#6213459)

Q2: Agent Lori Griffin (ID#6994127)

A: Agent Edward Smith (ID#7717812)

==BEGINNING OF RECORDING==

Q1: Agent Smith...

A: It's about god**** time someone showed up.

Q2: There's no smoking in here.

A: I've been sitting here for four hours.

Q1: Is it going to bother you?

Q2: Not really. You?

Q1: No. We'll let it go, I guess... Agent Smith, you reported a Code Fourteen taking place the evening of August 4, 2004. Correct?

A: That last night?

Q1: Yes.

A: Then yeah.

Q2: You understand that the information you're going to share with us cannot be shared outside of this room. Correct?

A: Yeah. I know. I'm not f***ing stupid.

Q1: Tell us what you saw.

A: I was on my way back from Trenton. Got the call for Willowbrook Park, so I headed over.

Q2: What were you doing in Trenton?

A: None of your business.

Q2: Not making a drug deal?

A: (laughing) I don't have to go all the way to god**** Trenton for drugs. Anyway, the wraiths were pretty much under control by the time I got there. I think I got to kill three... four, maybe? Saved one twink.

Q2: Arturo Brooks?

A: Are those words?

Q2: That's the name of the man you saved.

A: Sure. If you say so. In any case, the wraiths were a total waste of time. But then I saw a Code Fourteen.

Q1: Explain.

A: Everyone was doing cleanup and I f***ing hate that s***. I saw a few survivors in the distance, so I headed that way. Then they were me.

Q2: I beg your pardon?

A: I saw two guys. One of them was me.

Q1: And the other?

A: Didn't know him.

Q1: Can you describe him?

A: He was dead.

Q1: Anything else?

A: It was night. I couldn't see s***.

Q2: But you're sure the other man was you?

A: Yeah. Turns out it's pretty easy to identify yourself.

Q1: Can you be more specific? Was the other you the same age as you? Older? Younger?

A: Older. Future me, I guess.

Q2: What was he doing?

A: I don't know.

Q2: How can you not know?

A: I skedaddled because it's a Code Fourteen. Time travel. Oooga booga. You drill it into our heads that there's s*** we're not sup- posed to see. Now you're surprised I didn't want to see it?

Q1: Agent Smith... you have a reputation for bending rules. I find it difficult to believe that you'd follow them to a tee in this one specific instance.

A: Well, I did. I don't know what to tell you.

Q2: Why?

A: Why what?

Q2: Why follow them this time?

A: Because it's freaky s***. Someday I'm gonna time travel? No thanks. I've watched enough sci-fi. I know not to meet myself.

(Brief silence)

Okay. Fine. The other me said not to talk about it.

Q1: You spoke to him?

A: Not exactly. I saw him, said "what the f***." He saw me. Said not to tell anyone I saw him.

Q1: Were those his exact words? "Don't tell anyone"?

A: What am I, a tape recorder?

Q2: You just finished a cigarette.

A: Yeah, and now I'm starting a new one.

Q2: Are you nervous about something, Agent Smith?

A: Why would I be nervous? Because I saw something I shouldn't? Because Reticent agents sometimes... disappear?

Q1: Nothing's going to happen to you. You've been with us for six years, and in spite of your... everything... you're one of our better agents. We just need a complete record of the incident.

A: Cool. You have it. Can I go?

(Unintelligible)

Q2: Do you think the man you saw with your future self might have been Arturo Brooks?

A: I'm really not good with faces.

Q1: Even ones you've just met?

A: Even your mom's.

Q2: Is there anything you're leaving out?

(Brief silence)

A: No.

Q2: Then you can go.

(Shuffling, door slamming)

Q1: Think he knows something he's not telling us?

Q2: I know he is.

==END OF RECORDING==

WILLOWBROOK PARK

Arturo Brooks had never been to the SUNY Staten Island Counseling Center, but his grades were slipping and an academic advisor assured him that seeking counseling could help him get a mulligan on the fall semester and preserve his 4.0 GPA. The young man let out a loud sigh, then extended a hand to pull open the heavy door to the basement-level waiting room.

The room was empty of people, but full of peeling vinyl chairs and chipped end tables—each covered in staple magazines like *Vehicles*, *Wine Aficionado*, and *Pretend You Like Sports*. Stock photos on the wall featured diverse people smiling in fields, eating salads, and giving each other high fives in a library. Each photo was faded, thanks to years' worth of exposure to buzzing fluorescent tubes. In short, it was a pretty depressing place for a place that treated depression.

Arturo approached a reception window. It slid open with a HRRRRCH, bringing him a depth of plexiglass closer to a smiling, chubby receptionist in oversized, purple-framed glasses. He was tall and she was seated, so he bent down a bit to make eye contact.

The receptionist's fingers hovered over the keys, ready for action.

"Name?" she asked.

"Um... Arturo Brooks."

She spoke as she typed. "Do you need a Spanish

language counselor today?"

"No." Arturo squinted. "Not sure why you'd assume that."

"These are just standard intake questions," she said.

Arturo wasn't sure he believed that, given his name and tanned complexion. He responded with a curt "'kay."

"Do you need to speak with a gender and sexual orientation specialist?" she asked.

"Um. No."

"Are you sure?" she asked, with a serious look.

Arturo tilted his head. "*I'm sure.*"

"What can we help you with today then?" she asked.

Arturo didn't know the best way to explain. He settled on, "I was at Willowbrook Park."

The receptionist seemed to understand. "I'm sorry to hear that."

"Yeah. *Everyone is.*" Arturo's response came out bitter.

A clipboard slid through the window, with a pen attached by a springy plastic string. Arturo took the board and glanced down at the paperwork. Primary Care Physician... allergies... emergency contacts...

"I... uh... I don't have any," he said.

"If you don't have a Primary Care doctor or allergies, just leave them blank."

"I mean any of it..." He slid the clipboard back through without writing anything.

The stock photo salad eaters looked on, judging him. Arturo took a squeaky seat and buried his head in his hands, unable to pretend he liked sports. Three months earlier, everything had been fine. The young man hadn't had plans for his life, and he hadn't needed any. But his live-in-the-moment attitude became untenable in the face of death. Several faces of death. Dozens, actually. He looked through his fingers at the people eating salad, and his mind distorted the image. They were pale monsters. Their salad was human skin. He stopped looking and buried his head deeper.

It didn't take long for Arturo Brooks to be welcomed into the office of Dr. Wendy Santos.

Her voice beckoned. "*Ven, for favor.*"

Arturo entered with a sigh. "*Dije que no necesito un hispano-hablante.*"

"Sorry. Our receptionist is a little racist," Dr. Santos said.

Arturo sighed again, then took a seat in a slightly inclined armchair that he'd definitely seen at IKEA. Kläppsta or Klackbö or something like that. It wasn't comfortable. He would have nervously tapped his fingernails on the end table next to it, if he had any fingernails left.

Dr. Santos's office was still in the basement, but at least the lighting came from a warm lamp on her laminate desk. Instead of stock photo people, there was abstract art. Instead of sticky magazines, a fake potted plant. It was an office that said, 'I'm trying my best on a state school's mental health budget.'

"What's going on?" Dr. Santos asked.

"I'm probably going to flunk out." Arturo despaired. "I don't know why I care. Nobody else does. My dad did, but..."

The doctor waited for him to finish. When he didn't, she asked, "He doesn't care now?"

Arturo explained. "He's dead. Willowbrook Park."

"I'm sorry," Dr. Santos said.

Arturo shut his eyes and pinched the bridge of his nose. After a moment, he opened his eyes and ranted to the doctor's face. "No offense, but I am *so tired* of hearing people say they're sorry. Or that it'll get better. Or that they understand what I'm going through. And then I never see them again because they don't want to hang out with someone who's a bummer, or we were never that close in the first place."

She acknowledged that. "You feel like you're alone."

"I *am* alone. My mom is dead. My dad is dead. My sister is dead. And I have to go to work and pass biochem and pretend I'm fine," Arturo said.

"Why?" she asked.

"Someone has to, but... I'm only twenty-two. I don't know what to say to... to funeral homes, or insurance agents, or... debt collectors..." His voice became bitter. "I shouldn't have to know." Arturo sank deeper into his seat. "I don't know how to give a eulogy to a room full of people I barely know. I'm... I'm living in my childhood home, and it's just me. And I don't even know how to make the stupid kitchen sink stop dripping. Or who to call. Or how to pick up enough hours between the student union and Subway to pay the bills until the insurance people do whatever they do. And... and if I even find the time to study, I can't focus. I can't even bring myself to set foot on campus because Willowbrook Park is *right there*. Just behind the treeline." He made a vague gesture toward the wall, which became a vague gesture at himself and the tears that were now flowing from his eyes. "*I do this now*. All the time."

"You have a lot to deal with," Dr. Santos said.

"You think?" Arturo shook his head. "Sorry. I just... don't know how long I can do this. The grades are the first thing to go, but it's... there's gonna be more. I can't do everything. Either the house, or my job, or I'm gonna starve to death because I can't eat without thinking about *crunching noises*." His left eye twitched as he remembered something from that night.

"It's good to recognize your own limits," Dr. Santos said.

Arturo sniffled. "What am I supposed to do?"

"That's the question, isn't it? You know all the things you want to do, and you know you don't have time or energy for everything. Only you can choose what to prioritize."

"Super helpful," Arturo scoffed.

"What do you value most? Is it school? Your childhood home...?"

Arturo pondered that. "My sister and I were gonna be the first generation of our family to earn a degree... that's all on me now, but... I don't really care. I mean, my dad's not here to care, so who am I doing it for?" He bit his lip. "I don't want to live in that house. It makes me feel miserable. But I don't want to clean it out either, because then I'd have to throw their things away. What I really want..." He trailed off.

"What?" Dr. Santos asked.

"I want revenge," he said.

"That's understandable, but—"

"But I can't," Arturo said. "Because they're dead. I mean, they were already dead when they attacked, right? Now they're super dead—"

Dr. Santos tried to keep her face neutral. She failed, and her eyes narrowed. "Arturo..."

"*What?*" he snapped.

"Do you ever see things that aren't real?"

Arturo glowered. "No."

"It's okay if you do. There are ways to manage that."

"*I'm not crazy.* I watched entire families get murdered, and now you and everyone else are pretending like I wasn't there. Like I didn't see what happened."

"What happened?" Dr. Santos asked.

Arturo leaned forward in his seat, and his voice took on a ranting quality. "There were monsters. They looked like dead people. Like skeletons. Their skin was so thin you could almost see through them. They moved like wild animals, and they had razor-sharp teeth. I mean, they tore people apart like it was nothing. Their eyes were glowing yellow. Once it got dark, that was the only thing I could see..." He saw her scribbling something on a notepad. "You don't believe me."

"I believe you believe it," Dr. Santos said.

"*No.*" Arturo clenched his fist. "There's an objective reality. *There is.*"

"Did you have anything to drink that evening?" Dr. Santos asked.

"Maybe two beers," Arturo said, and he countered her insinuation. "I wasn't drunk."

"Have you ever used any psychedelic drugs?" the doctor asked.

"What? No. *Never,*" Arturo said, with scorn.

At just the wrong moment, something on the doctor's desk caught his eye. A staple remover, lying there with four ultra-sharp prongs facing him. He fell back in his Kläppsta and gripped the chair's arms, tight. "Monsters got *everyone.*" The fangs glistened in the glow of her lamp. "They're gonna come back and get me."

Dr. Santos dismissed that. "The people who attacked were on bath salts. Every one of them was either killed or arrested, Arturo."

Arturo was no longer focused on her. He could see the fangs, hear the crunching. He was pulling his sister by her hand until he was holding nothing but half an arm. Gunshots fired all around. People screamed. Bodies. Blood. Screaming. Fangs. Crunching. Over and over.

Half aware of where he was and half reliving the worst day of his life, Arturo snapped. "Everyone's acting like the world is normal, and it's not. It's not! How can it be? If there are wraiths, who knows what else is out there? There could be aliens. There could be demons. And I'm supposed to focus on *biochem*?" He leapt from his seat and began pacing. "People should be arming themselves. The government should be doing something. *Why isn't anyone doing anything?* There's *one pharmaceutical company* handling all this? What the hell is wrong with the world?"

"A lot," said the doctor, with a tone that seemed almost pleased about it.

Arturo stopped pacing and looked at Dr. Santos. At the sight of her face, he took a step backward. The woman's eyes had gone completely black, and thick, black tears oozed from their corners.

"What are you?" Arturo asked. "What's going on?"

The doctor pushed a button under her desk. Behind him, a door locked.

Arturo awoke in his own bed, in his family home, with no idea how he got there and no idea why it smelled like cigarettes. He shot up into a seated position to find the shadows of a man and woman sitting at the foot of his bed, observing him. He reached toward his nightstand and flicked on a lamp, revealing the college dorm-style posters tacked to his walls as well as the identities of the two people.

They'd met before. Two of the Reticent agents who did cleanup at Willowbrook Park.

The man—Edward Smith—spoke first. "Hey, kid. Haven't seen you since—"

"Since my family got massacred?" Arturo wondered.

"Yeah. You look like you've done time at Auschwitz," Smith said.

"Haven't been eating well. Thanks," Arturo said.

Smith reached down into a pocket and handed over a granola bar that—judging from the wrinkles on its wrapper—had been in that pocket through at least one wash cycle. "Here."

"I'm not hungry," Arturo said.

"Either you get hungry or I'm gonna shove it down your throat," Smith said.

Smith's partner—Erin Burroughs—didn't like that. Her voice took a condemnatory tone. "*Agent Smith*—"

Though she didn't like it, Smith's threat had worked. Arturo nibbled at the stale granola bar, but the crunching nauseated him. He set the bar down, as if he'd come back to it. "What are you doing here?"

"Keeping you from being murdered by an Oizysian," Burroughs said.

"An oh... what? Like the Greek goddess of misery?" Arturo asked.

Smith made a quick jerking off motion at this display of knowledge.

Burroughs's face lit up. "Yeah, actually. They're monsters that consume negative emotions."

"And livers," added Smith. "Never trust a shrink."

"Have you been *spying* on me?" Arturo asked.

Smith scoffed. "You're welcome. If we hadn't been, you'd be misery chow."

Arturo couldn't even articulate his confusion. "Wha—"

Burroughs reached across the bed with a Reticent business card.

"I have one of those. Thanks." Arturo waved it off.

Smith stood to leave. "He doesn't want it. *Let's go.*"

Burroughs raised a finger to hush her partner. With her other hand, she pushed the card toward Arturo a second time. "You don't want to be in school anymore. You don't want to be here in this house. You're right that revenge is off the table. You can't do anything to the monsters that took your family, but you can stop something like that from happening to others."

Arturo mumbled something to himself.

"What?" Smith asked.

Arturo griped. "The website said sessions were confidential."

"Nothing's confidential unless you keep it to yourself," Smith said. This was taking too long, and he lit a cigarette. That explained the smell.

Arturo shook his head. "Can you *not*?"

Smith rolled his eyes, then put the cigarette out against his shoe. When it was no longer a fire hazard, he let it fall to the otherwise pristine wooden floor.

Arturo turned to Burroughs. "So what? You're supposed to offer me a sense of purpose?"

Burroughs nodded. "Something like that. Along with excellent health care benefits, and a retirement plan—"

"Go away," Arturo snapped.

Smith was already halfway out the door when the demand took a turn...

"I want to talk to him." Arturo pointed at Smith.

Burroughs gave Smith a suspicious glance on her way out the door.

He shut it behind her.

"What do you want?" Smith asked.

Arturo responded with another question. "Do you think I should join?"

"I don't care what you do," Smith said. "I just know I have to surveil your crazy ass for six months 'cause you're a loose end on Willowbrook Park."

"You mean I'm the only one not buying the bullshit about bath salts," Arturo said.

"Yeah." Smith reseated himself on the bed.

Arturo wanted a better read on the cold blond seated next to him. "Why did you join?"

"Had nothing better to do," Smith said, looking away.

Arturo eyed him from top to bottom. "Are you happy there?"

Smith glanced back and scoffed. "I'm not happy anywhere."

"Why are—"

Smith cut him off. "Why'd you punt Agent Burroughs from the room?"

"She's nice." Arturo shrugged. "I'm tired of people being nice."

Smith developed an impish smirk. "Want me to call you names and pull your hair?"

"I mean... maybe, but... no. Just be honest," Arturo said.

"I don't think anyone should work for The Reticent," said Smith.

"Not even you?" Arturo wondered.

"I have no skills, no better options, and a death wish," Smith said. "If there is *anything else* you can do, you should do it."

Arturo heard that, but doing what he'd been told to do had led him here.

It was time for a change.

MANDATORY TRAINING

For what must have been the dozenth time, Arturo Brooks raised his hand high above the sea of bisque classroom desks. For emphasis, he gave it a little wave.

"Yes... Mister Brooks..."

Each time the instructor said his name, it was with more annoyance.

Nevertheless, Brooks answered the question.

"The Reticent was founded in 1693." He emphasized the word 'the' to show he'd been paying attention to the part of the lecture about definite articles and trademarks.

"Yes. And does anyone remember why?" The instructor's eyes pleaded for someone else—anyone else—to answer.

Brooks's hand shot up again.

The instructor sighed. "Mister Brooks..."

"Because the Salem Witch Trials missed all the real witches," Brooks said.

"Correct," the instructor said.

Surrounding Brooks were ten other new recruits, each sitting at a desk with their eyes glazed over, completely zoned out from the lesson. Three dull hours into onboarding day, they didn't care enough to be bothered by the overzealous young man answering every question.

The instructor silently walked to the back of the room. He returned to the front with a rolling projector that screeched and squeaked for the duration of the journey.

"Everyone please bring your attention to the front of the room. This video is a little outdated, but HR requires I show it to all of you." He turned it on, then walked across the room and flipped the light switch.

The projector made a sound like BRRRRRRRRR TRPTRPTRPTRP. Over and over.

One student immediately fell asleep. The others watched as a training video from the 1980s came into focus. It opened with a mellow synthpop jingle as a series of point-less shapes—teal triangles, lime green rectangles, pink semicircles, and yellow squiggly lines—bounced around the screen over a grey background. A title appeared: 'The Reticent & You.'

Then, the song developed lyrics. A peppy, Cyndi Lau-perian voice greeted the recruits.

It's your time
To do what we do
To be the best
To see the job through

As she sang, flashes of Reticent agents appeared on the screen, each in a sharp black suit with massive shoulder pads. They were pleasantly diverse, but not diverse in their pleasantness. Each one had a wide grin as they staked vam-pires, shot werewolves, and held Erlenmeyer flasks. At the bottom of the screen, an asterisk marked the statement 'Not real agents.'

Helping people
It's what The Reticent doooo

A booming, disembodied voice spoke to the students with authority as the video cycled through generic shots of an office building. "Welcome to The Reticent. You've made the first steps of an incredible journey. Working here can be as fulfilling as you want it to be. Let's take a look at some bad behaviors that could put a blemish on your time here, in order to avoid some easy mistakes."

On screen, the word 'Reticent' appeared vertically, comprised of corporate sloganry:

R – Responsibility
E – Engage
T – Take Charge
I – Integrity
C – Commitment
E – Expertise
N – Never Give Up
T – Tomorrow

Responsibility became bold, and the video transitioned to a fake scenario.

A Reticent agent in a city park, minding his own business and eating a hot dog. Across an expanse of lawn, a small child was being chased by a large figure in a black cloak.

"I'm off tonight. That's not my problem," the agent said in a thick Bronx accent, before gripping his wiener tight and walking away.

The video responded to itself with a harsh BZZT sound.

The word NO stamped across the screen, in red.

Disembodied Voice explained. "As a Reticent agent, you should always be ready to handle a paranormal situation. By ignoring the child, this agent just allowed it to be sacrificed to a goat god in order to open the door to a demon dimension. That's not good. Let's try it again."

The sound of a rewinding video tape played as the scenario was revisited. This time, the agent sprinted across the lawn and tackled the cloaked figure.

The audio went PING. The word YES appeared on screen, in green.

"On or off the clock, you are always *responsible* for handling a paranormal event," said Disembodied Voice.

Back on the RETICENT screen, the word **Engage** boldened.

In a dark alley, at night, an agent staked a vampire. It fell to the padded stage cement and was replaced with a still photograph of dust. The agent then looked down at two people cowering against a wall.

"Bye," said the agent, unceremoniously.

BZZT. NO.

Disembodied Voice tutted. "Victims of paranormal events are often traumatized. Remember to *engage* with them. Talk to them. If possible, convince them that what they saw wasn't paranormal in nature. It'll help them sleep better at night."

The tape rewound. Back to the alley. This time, the agent was cheerful and approached the civilians. "Sorry about that. They were supposed to clear the alley before we filmed this scene."

PING. YES.

Disembodied Voice beamed with pride. "Good job, Agent Wing. The Hollywood explanation is a classic, and it works sixty percent of the time."

Take Charge was the next text to bolden.

The scene was inside a bank being robbed by an orc. As the giant, green creature (played by an actor in a felt costume) loaded gold bars onto a cart, humans were all around the room cowering, their hands behind their heads.

"Everyone stay on the ground," the orc said.

On the ground, one civilian turned to a Reticent agent.

"Someone's gotta do something," the civilian said.

The agent responded with a cold, "Knock yourself out, pal."

The civilian stood and ran to the orc, who snapped him in half in a low-budget animated effect.

BZZT. NO.

"Sometimes, civilians will try to take the initiative. That can get them killed. *Take charge*, even if you have to knock someone unconscious to do it."

The scene rewound and repeated. Back in the bank, the agent put a hand across the civilian's mouth and pinched his nose. This instantly knocked him unconscious.

PING. YES.

"That's the way to do it!" Disembodied Voice cheered.

Another bold word. **Integrity**.

Two Reticent agents chatted next to a water cooler, in a bright break room full of vending machines packed with healthy snacks.

"I heard Agent Evans had sex with a werewolf," one agent said.

"I heard it was a werefox," said the other.

BZZT. NO.

Disembodied Voice was filled with disappointment. "Nobody likes an office gossip. If you suspect another agent is up to no good, don't whisper about it. File a report with your direct manager."

Back at the water cooler, the first agent made the same declaration. "I heard Agent Evans had sex with a were-wolf."

The other agent replied like he was reading from a hand-book. "If that's true, you need to file a report. If you don't feel comfortable reporting to your direct manager, file an anonymous report on the corporate Reti-net."

PING. YES.

"That's right. Act with *integrity*." Disembodied Voice

proceeded to alliterate. "Proper procedure prevents piss-poor paranormal probes."

Commitment went bold next.

In another dark, padded alley—identical to the one before—a werewolf with a zipper down its chest approached a Reticent agent. The creature held a stack of hundred-dollar bills and spoke like a stereotypical mob boss. "Listen... I know you got a job to do and whatnot, but uh... it's a lot easier for me if I don't gotta spill blood, y'know. I bet it's easier if you don't gotta fill out paperwork. So how 'bout we make this go away?"

The agent smiled, accepted the werewolf's money, and walked away.

BZZT. NO.

Disembodied Voice explained. "Always remain committed to your mission, especially when it's hard. Monsters may offer money. Cults may claim they can cure cancer. They're usually lying, or there's a twist they aren't telling you about. Just say no."

Back in the alley, the werewolf asked again. "How 'bout we make this go away?"

"The only thing I'm making go away," said the agent, "is *you*."

The agent drew a gun and fired a silver bullet at the werewolf's heart.

PING. YES.

Disembodied Voice reiterated. "Be *committed*. Murder evil. Don't make deals."

Expertise, in bold.

A Reticent agent stepped into another agent's office. "Hi, Agent Murray. I heard you defeated a leprechaun last week and I just got assigned a case with one. Do you have any pointers for me?"

"Sorry. I'm busy," Agent Murray said.

BZZT. NO.

Disembodied Voice sighed. "Always share your knowledge. If you learn something new, everyone needs to know. There's no bonus for being a smarty pants—or anything else—and your information could save a fellow agent's life."

The agent tried again. "Do you have any pointers for me?"

"I do," Agent Murray said. "I'm busy right now, but how about you come back at 2:30 and we'll go over everything?"

"Sounds great!"

PING. YES.

"Be a good expert. Share your *expertise*," Disembodied Voice said.

Never Give Up.

For this scenario, the camera zoomed on an agent crying in a bathroom. On the wall was a posted sign: 'All Employees Must Stop Crying Before Returning to Work.'

"I don't think I can do this anymore," the agent sobbed.

BZZT. NO.

Disembodied Voice offered a tip. "Emotions are great, but set aside any that hinder your performance. If you're not with us, you're with the monsters. *Never give up*."

The agent in the bathroom looked at the sign and steeled her resolve.

"Not today, feelings," she said.

PING. YES.

"Atta girl," said Disembodied Voice.

The last word on the screen went bold. **Tomorrow**.

Two agents, bloodied and bruised thanks to some B-movie makeup, stared at a ticking bomb that counted down seconds. The room around them was filled with poison gas, identifiable as such because it was green. Twenty to go. Nineteen. Eighteen...

"We have to disarm this thing," one said.

"Who cares? We're dead either way," said the other agent.

BZZT. NO.

"Your actions aren't just for you. They're to protect future generations from apocalyptic conditions. Remain future-focused. You may not live to see it, but strive for a better *tomorrow*."

The camera returned to the agents, lying dead over a disarmed bomb.

A new agent appeared, proud. "They sacrificed their lives to save everyone. They were heroes."

PING. YES.

"A death for our cause is a meaningful death," Disembodied Voice said.

The cheery pop song kicked in again.

Helping people
It's what The Reticent doooo

Finally, Disembodied Voice revealed his body. He was a stern sixty-something—with a full head of white hair and a serious mustache—who stood in dramatic, noir lighting.

He signed off. "With the knowledge you've just gained, you are now ready to join The Reticent. Save some people, have fun, and remember: Unions are bad. If any of your coworkers try to talk to you about forming a union, let your HR representative know."

BRRRR TRPTRPTRPTRP. The projector stopped.

The lights in the room flicked on. Most students reacted like vampires, shielding their eyes from the light and groaning at the instructor.

Not Arturo Brooks. He'd fallen asleep.

HARMFUL PIRATE STEREOTYPES

Reports of a ghost ship kept coming in. Dozens of them (reports, not ghost ships). They came mostly in Long Island accents, the ten-time winner of the Van Der Beek Society's award for World's Least Attractive Accent.

"It's awwwful," said one voicemail. "I was out wawkin my dawwwg and I start hearin' this spooky sowwwnd. It wasn't coming from no yooman, so I go dowwwn to the dawwwk and there's a ship in the fawwwg that don't look like no ship I ever seen before. It was like *Pirates of the Caribbean* or something. And then it just disappeayahd. Poof. Right inta thin ayah."

Agents Burroughs and Smith sat in the front of a company-provided Pontiac Aztek, listening to that voicemail and chugging coffee—spiked coffee, in Smith's case. They were rejoined by Arturo Brooks, who'd been poking around the dock and now eagerly jotted down notes on a notepad from the backseat. He wasn't yet a full agent. He was shadowing as part of his probationary period, and he was so wired from the excitement that he didn't need any coffee.

The group was parked at Northport Harbor, Long Island. Windows down, ready for action. EMF readers sat on the dashboard, pointed at the water, but they hadn't made a peep in over two hours. As the sightings had all taken place between eight and eleven o'clock, they were running out of time.

Brooks cleared his throat to get his mentors' attention. "Are they ghost pirates or pirate ghosts?"

"What?" Smith whipped his head around and stared.

Brooks explained his rationale. "A ghost pirate would be a pirate who died and became a ghost. A pirate ghost would be a ghost who later decided to become a pirate after death."

"*Jesus Christ.*" Smith scoffed and turned back around to face the water.

Burroughs slapped her partner's shoulder, then turned back to Brooks. "That's a smart distinction, but I don't think it matters in this case. *If* there are ghosts, we just need to bash 'em with some iron and do a little chant, not figure out their motive."

"*If?*" Brooks wondered. "There have been twenty-seven reports. You think they're all crazy?"

"It's almost never ghosts," Smith said.

"What else could—"

The full agents didn't let him finish the question.

"Projected image," Burroughs said.

"Illusion magic," Smith added.

"Drugs in the water," Burroughs offered.

"High schoolers pulling a prank," Smith said.

"Literally just fog hitting a boat the wrong way," Burroughs said.

"Some rich asshole with fog machines on his yacht," Smith said.

"Mass hysteria," Burroughs said.

Brooks got the point. "Okay. I guess it could be a lot of things. But... where is it? I didn't find anything out there."

They all watched the water and saw nothing. It was foggy, all right, and full of boats. But they were sailboats, yachts, and the occasional fishing boat. Nothing that met the description of a large, wooden pirate ship. No spooky sounds, either. Just the occasional BLORP or SPLISH when a wave hit the dock the right way.

Eventually, Smith made a dramatic declaration. "I'm bored."

He hopped out of the car, leaned on the hood, and lit a cigarette.

Brooks followed, notepad in hand.

"Settle down," Smith said. "Just havin' a smoke."

Brooks stepped toward him. "I could stand to stretch my legs."

"You were just outside..." Smith—having had his personal bubble invaded—took a few steps toward the water.

Brooks followed.

"Really not good with hints, are you?" Smith motioned toward the car. "Go away."

"I still have two weeks left shadowing you two," Brooks said. "I think we should get to know each other."

"I don't really care what you think," Smith said.

Brooks tucked his notepad into his pocket and frowned. "Did I do something to piss you off?"

Smith's eyes shifted as he pondered that for a second. "No?"

"Then why are you being a dick to me?"

"He's a dick to everyone," Burroughs said, joining them.

Smith ignored her and watched the water. It BLORPed and SPLISHed, but there were still no pirate ships.

Brooks looked from Smith to Burroughs. "Why?"

Burroughs answered on her partner's behalf. "Didn't get enough hugs as a kid or something."

Smith turned back and scowled at her.

Burroughs returned the look. "A word, *Agent Smith*?"

Smith huffed, and directed Brooks not to follow as he went with Burroughs to be chastised a few yards away.

"You're being really hard on him," she said.

"*And?*" Smith asked. "If he can't handle me being a big meanie, he can't handle the job. Period. Might as well find that out now."

"What's going on?" Burroughs asked, sincerely.

"Haven't slept great the last few nights," Smith admitted.

"Me neither," Burroughs said. "Ever since that erlking. But that's no reason to take it out on him."

"Sure it is. He's gonna get himself killed with The Reticent."

Burroughs didn't follow. She tilted her head in confusion.

Smith took a deep drag of his cigarette. "Fuck. I don't know, Erin. It just feels a little weird to save someone's life then throw them back in danger. That's all. Like I need another goddamn thing to feel guilty about. They could have had him shadow any other fucking agents—"

"Well, they didn't," Burroughs said. "Try and be nice?"

"I make no promises."

They made their way back to Brooks, who was retracing his own steps with an EMF reader, just in case he'd missed something.

"Hey, nerd," Smith said. "We're about ready to pack it in."

Burroughs shot him an annoyed glance.

"It's still twenty 'til eleven," Brooks noted.

"I think it's safe to say we got got," Smith said.

Brooks objected. "Proper procedure is to stay until—"

Smith spoke through clenched teeth. "*Erin.*"

"Don't look at me," Burroughs said. "He's right." She developed a grin. "Why don't we spend the last twenty minutes getting to know each other?"

"I hate you so much," said Smith.

Brooks loved this idea. He turned to Burroughs. "How

did you join The Reticent?"

"My neighbors started acting weird. One day I saw green goop leaking out of one of their ears. Turns out, there was a colony of quidrils in the dumpster outside my apartment," Burroughs said. "A few agents got there as I was killing them with a lighter and some hairspray. Now I'm here."

Brooks turned to Smith. "How about you? How did—"

Smith groaned loud enough to drown out his question.

"Stop being rude," Brooks snapped.

"Tell you what," Smith said to Brooks. "I'll be nice to you when you're anything more than a useless nag full of stupid questions."

Brooks didn't say anything. He looked out at the water, obviously hurt.

Smith searched the deepest recesses of his mind for some empathy. "Nothing personal, okay? I feel like shit and I don't want to be here. The sooner we get off fucking Long Island, the better."

Brooks absorbed that. "Anything you need to talk about?"

Smith shot Burroughs a look of can-you-believe-this-shit before mocking Brooks. "Kumba-fucking-ya. Let's all talk about our feelings." He huffed. "Fucking christ."

"*Este puto pendejo*," Brooks muttered under his breath.

"*No es personal*," Burroughs said.

Brooks and Burroughs continued conversing in Spanish. Fifteen minutes to departure became fourteen minutes became thirteen minutes. That was long enough to annoy Smith.

"Knock it off," he said.

"Why? Does it hurt your *feelings*?" Brooks retorted. "You want to talk about it?"

Instead of angering Smith, the backtalk made him smile

for the first time all evening. He shook his head. "I'll give you that one."

Brooks saw the attitude shift as an opportunity to get to know the other agent better. "Just out of curiosity... do you live alone?"

"Holy shit," Smith said.

"I didn't think it was that invasive a ques—oh." Brooks noticed what Smith had: a pirate ship, about a hundred yards away. "Oh!"

It appeared from the mist, docked. The wooden hull was green with algae and broken by scores of cannonball holes. The ship's masts were bent and broken, and only one had a sail, which was tattered and dropped sadly onto the deck. It looked like a boat that sank decades ago. But there it was, fully afloat.

Smith pressed his cigarette butt into the ground with his shoe. "Think we can climb aboard?"

"You think that's a good idea?" Brooks asked.

"No. It's not," Burroughs said. "We should try and scan it from afar befo—"

Smith was already halfway down the dock and didn't hear her.

Burroughs sighed and followed him.

Brooks sighed and followed her.

BONK BONK BONK went the dock, as three pairs of feet plodded across it. If pirate ghosts had functioning ears, they definitely heard the group coming.

Sounds came from the ship, in response. Haunting sounds.

BOOOOOO. BOOOOOOOOOOOOO.

Smith skidded to a stop.

Worried he'd seen something serious, Burroughs and Brooks sped up. When they caught up with Smith, they found him laughing.

BOOOOOOOOOOO.

Burroughs started chuckling along with Smith.

"What?" Brooks asked.

Smith spoke through laughter. "Did the boat just fucking *boo*?"

"Ghosts don't boo?" Brooks asked.

"Ghosts don't boo," Burroughs confirmed.

"Told you it wasn't ghosts," Smith said.

Brooks stared at the decaying hull. "But the ship..."

BOOOO. BOOOOOOOOO.

"It does sound kind of fake," he admitted.

Smith stepped over to the ghost ship's rotting wooden gangway. He put one foot down on what should have been a creaking board. CLANG.

"Metal," he announced.

Next to the first plank was a missing plank. Smith looked through the hole, down at murky water with fast food wrappers floating on top. He put his next foot down in the center of the hole. Instead of falling through and needing a tetanus booster, he created another CLANG as he appeared to stand in mid-air. Smith bounded up the rest of the gangway—CLANG CLANG CLANG—and slapped the ship's hull. CLAAAAANG.

"All metal," he announced again.

"Who cloaks their ship as a ghost pirate ship?" Burroughs wondered.

"Let's find out," Smith said, climbing aboard. Then, to Brooks, "You stay there."

"Isn't protocol to—" Brooks's objection went ignored, so he ignored Smith's direction and followed Burroughs up the gangway.

One by one, the group stepped through the ghost ship visage, passing through a curtain of light. On the other side was a modern vessel—a bit rusty and worse for the wear, but with GPS, satellite phones, and all the other things one would find on a seaworthy ship. Its most advanced piece of equipment sat on the deck—a tangled mess of wires, prisms, speakers, and laser beams loosely contained in a black plastic crate—projecting images of a haunted ship and emitting ghostly boos. Across the front of the crate was a label: Spirit Halloween.

The vessel was also equipped with a loud, angry crew whose loud, angry noises got closer and closer. The agents didn't get much chance to look around before they were confronted by a group of eight camouflage-clad young men carrying AK-47s. The men exchanged words in a language that wasn't English, Spanish, or Klingon and was therefore incomprehensible to Smith, Burroughs, or Brooks. Luckily gun pointing was a universal language.

"Oh no," Burroughs said.

"*Actual pirates?*" Brooks couldn't believe it.

Smith could. "I told you to stay behind." He sighed. "I didn't expect to get raped and murdered today, but I guess life's full of surprises."

Brooks eyed him with concern.

Guns are an effective way to get people moving, and the pirates used theirs to direct the trio below deck. There, an English-speaking pirate greeted them from the comfort of a tiny, U-shaped couch that surrounded a coffee table. He wore camo like the rest, but offered a big smile. The only thing shinier than his teeth was his bald head, which glistened under a swaying lighting fixture.

"Have a seat," the pirate said.

The three agents scooted in across from him, on one of the non-bendy parts of the U.

"You're government?" the pirate asked.

The group exchanged looks, not sure what the right answer was.

"If you're not government, we have no use for you..."

They still weren't sure.

"Do we want him to have a use for us?" Brooks whispered.

Smith made a decision. "Yeah. We're government."

Brooks and Burroughs stared at him, wide-eyed.

"Good," said the pirate. "Then you can do something for us." He leaned forward and spoke with complete seriousness. "You can stop Hollywood from making those *Pirates of the Caribbean* movies."

The detectives simply stared at him.

"We are sick of them," said the pirate with fierce gesticulation. "Every time we go to steal a ship, it's 'they aren't like the pirates in the movies at all' or 'are you going to make us walk the plank?' or... OR! These tourists have the nerve to look at me and ask 'why's the rum gone?' We are *intimidating*." The complaining made him decidedly less so. He slammed a fist down on the coffee table.

"Aaah," Burroughs said, feigning fright.

"Thank you," said the pirate. "Now you'll kill these movies for us, and we can go back to regular scary piracy instead of scary ghost piracy."

"We can't really do that," said Smith.

Burroughs nodded. "It's kind of a free country thing..."

The pirate scowled in anger.

"I agree!" Burroughs said. "The movies are terrible and they should go away. I'm just not sure we can, uh... do that."

The pirate raised a hand, gesturing to his armed goons. "They're worthless. Shoot them and throw the bodies overboard."

"Can we rape them first?" asked one goon.

"You're pirates. Don't ask. Just rape," said the pirate.

The pirate goons approached menacingly, pointing their

AK-47s and their dicks.

In a quick burst of survival instinct, Brooks blurted, "I know how we can help."

Burroughs and Smith stared at him.

"Um..." Brooks improvised. "I'm a little embarrassed to say I read gossip rags, but I do... do that. Um... Some of them say Johnny Depp is abusive and whatnot... We could do the research and leak some things to ruin his career?"

Smith nodded. "Can't have the *Pirates* movies without him."

"Exactly," Brooks said. "So, um... don't do the raping and murdering, and we'll go use our *government connections* to hack his phone and computer..."

The pirate pondered it for a moment. "I need assurance you'll do this."

"What kind of assurance?" Burroughs asked.

The pirate held his hand to his chin, thinking. Then he got it.

"Nudes," he said. "We get nudes of you three, and if you don't leak the Depp tapes, we leak those instead."

"Deal," Smith said on everyone's behalf.

The trio disrobed and took part in what the pirates considered an erotic photoshoot. Highlights included lying spread eagle on a giant Jolly Roger, using what they hoped were plastic skulls to cover their genitals, and pointing AK-47s at each other's butts.

When it was over, the group put their clothes back on and headed toward the gangway.

"At least I wasn't underaged this time," Smith remarked.

Despite the joking tone with which that was said, Brooks found it alarming. He kept an eye on Smith as all three disembarked from the boat, embarrassed and a little emotionally scarred but physically unharmed.

"Good job getting us out of being murdered,"

Burroughs said.

Brooks beamed. "Thanks. Sorry you had to get naked."

Burroughs shrugged. "It could have gone a lot worse. I *am* going to have to learn to hack computers, though... Johnny Depp? Really?"

Brooks shrugged. "That's the word on the street."

While Burroughs walked ahead of the men toward the car, Brooks pulled Smith aside.

"You can't say anything nice?" Brooks asked.

Smith squinted. "You want a medal or something?"

"A little feedback, maybe? I kind of got us out of being brutally murdered..." Brooks crossed his arms. "You said you'd be nice if I did something useful."

Smith snorted. "Keeping me alive isn't useful."

Brooks could tell that Smith liked being contrary, and he decided to catch this fly with honey instead of vinegar. "Are you okay? You said you were having a bad day before, and it only got worse."

Smith didn't know what to do with that, so he dismissed it. "Yeah. Sure. Whatever."

"I just... get the impression you don't have a lot of friends," Brooks said.

"*And?* What's your point?" Smith asked.

Brooks wasn't sure. "My point is... if you ever need someone to talk to—"

Smith laughed. "If I did, it wouldn't be someone who's fucking doomed."

"What does that mean?" Brooks asked.

"It means you got lucky today. You won't always."

"Then maybe you should be nice to me," Brooks said. "While you can."

To Smith, that made about as much sense as the ghost pirates.

SHAMULET

Brooks stood in the doorway of the office Smith and Burroughs had shared for years, his arms folded and his mind agitated. Joining The Reticent was supposed to help him get revenge on the kinds of creatures that killed his family, but for nearly three years he'd spent most of his time filling out paperwork and chasing leads that went nowhere. He was good at the paperwork, but he hadn't even seen—let alone vanquished—a single monster. It wasn't fair, and he was ready to explode.

The office, meanwhile, looked like it had already exploded. Packed boxes were scattered everywhere, and Brooks had to peek behind one to locate his new partner.

"I thought we were supposed to meet upstairs," he said.

Smith didn't look up from his computer. "Yeah, we are."

"Forty-five minutes ago."

"*Shit.*" Smith stood and grabbed his coat. He needed a few more minutes to finish what he was working on, but the crossed arms rebuked him. "Yeah, let's go."

It was a decently long walk to Battery Park, even at their hurried 'It's March in New York and I'm going to freeze to death' paces, and the two conversed as they walked it.

"You're in a weirdly good mood. You haven't insulted me once," said Brooks.

"Don't get used to it," Smith said, pulling a flask from his coat pocket.

Brooks   stopped   in   his   tracks   for   a   moment, flabbergasted, before shuffling to catch back up. "Are you drunk on the job?"

"No," Smith said, "I'm *drinking* on the job."

Brooks didn't have a response for that.

Smith took a sip and tucked his flask away. "So... Reticent working out for you?"

"I guess..." Brooks didn't sound so sure. "But why am I here? Your partner wasn't working out?"

Smith's mouth tilted. "I wouldn't say that."

Brooks let out an exaggerated gasp. "You didn't."

"If you're insinuating that I violated rule 1.14.9 with my partner, you are correct. If you're thinking it happened in our office, you are also correct. If, by some chance, you're suggesting that I did a thing that she really didn't like, which led to her shouting at me, which led to our boss finding out and ending our partnership... Yeah. That happened."

"And neither one of you was fired?" Brooks asked, in disbelief. There was something strangely attractive in how nonchalant his new partner was about the whole thing.

"*Demoted*," Smith said. "That's why I'm babysitting you instead of partnered with somebody who knows what they're doing."

Brooks was at the very end of his initial probationary period. If he could manage not to do anything stupid for the next few weeks, he'd get better, less paperwork-heavy assignments. Under his new partnership, the odds of him not doing anything stupid had just decreased tenfold. He didn't know the exact odds, but he did know he was in trouble when he found himself far too distracted by Smith's eyes. He'd only ever seen them at night, but in the light of day, they were a vivid, almost mesmerizing green.

Smith noticed him noticing. "What's your deal? You got a boyfriend?"

Brooks, stunned, failed to respond.

"Girlfriend?" Smith asked, perplexed.

"No, you got it right the first time. But no. There's nobody." Brooks paused. "How did you—"

"Please. You're too gorgeous to be straight. Also, you keep staring at my eyes like we're in some Fabio-covered romance novel." Brooks turned bright red, and Smith winked. "Lucky for me."

And just like that, the conversation became tense, even as it turned to the mission.

Brooks pretended to focus on the work. "Sooo... this guy in Battery Park..."

Smith explained. "He sells potions, plastic amulets, and whatnot. Six days a week. Huge hit with the tourists."

The Reticent suspected that the potions and amulets were, at least in part, real magical artifacts. That was a problem, and it was why the pair were investigating.

"I read the file," Brooks said. "I was gonna ask if you know how late he works."

"He's usually there all day, 'til six at least. Why?"

Brooks looked at his watch. It was only two o'clock.

"You want to get something to eat first?" he asked.

Smith came to a halt, very nearly causing a woman walking behind him to rear-end him. She muttered something explicit as she dodged him at the last second, but Smith was too startled to hear it. He pressed his back against a building to get out of the way and Brooks followed.

"Are you hitting on me?" Smith asked.

Brooks shrugged.

Smith bit his lip. "I was just demoted for workplace relations—"

"Yeah, so obviously you're up for some," Brooks said.

"Holy shit." Smith grinned.

"Have you been to Bar-B-Cute?" Brooks asked. "They

make this pork sandwich that—"

"I'll take a raincheck on lunch," Smith said, taking his new partner's hand and pulling him into a narrow alley. "But if—"

He didn't have time to finish the sentence. Brooks pressed him against the wall and, with no warning, they were kissing. It was the second most intense make out session of Smith's life, and who could ever compare with Mick Jagger? With less than no warning, Brooks dropped to his knees. His breath made a thin stream in the cold air. Then there was the sound of a zipper, and Smith was treated to a much better sight than condensation.

Things had escalated quickly. When the men had recomposed themselves, Smith tried to think with the head between his shoulders.

"So... amulets," he said.

Brooks—fresh off the most excitement he'd had in three years with The Reticent—was still thinking with other parts. "What's the rush?"

Smith couldn't come up with anything compelling. Their vendor would be around well into the evening. He stumbled. "We should... do our jobs?"

"Lunch," Brooks insisted.

"Hey, I appreciate a classy alley blowjob as much as the next guy, but..."

"Save it. You're going to get lunch with me."

"I..." Smith didn't know how to react to the pushback.

Brooks folded his arms and stared.

"...Okay." Smith shook his head as he followed Brooks to Bar-B-Cute.

☙

Bar-B-Cute was a hole-in-the-wall joint with only four booths. Even for those who managed to grab a table—as Brooks and Smith had done—food was served in Styrofoam takeout containers. The divided kind, like a school cafeteria would use.

The pair settled in over a checkered vinyl tablecloth. They poked at their lunches with plastic forks as they made an earnest attempt at conversation.

"I gotta say… I'm surprised," Smith said. "You seem pretty by-the-book, but… first the beej and now you're delaying the shit out of this case for pulled pork."

"It's good pulled pork," Brooks said.

"Uh huh," Smith said, suspect.

Brooks posited a theory. "Maybe watching your whole family get murdered makes you take a few more risks. What's the worst that could happen?"

"You get fired?" Smith wondered.

"And then what? I don't get to *not* hunt any monsters? I'm already doing that."

"What made you think I'd agree to this anyway? I'm not agreeable," Smith said.

"Yeah, I get that, but… the handful of times we've seen each other, you've given me this look."

"I have a look?" Smith asked, avoiding eye contact.

"Yes." Brooks pointed at Smith with his fork. "*That one.* You're doing it *right now*. You stare at me, and then when you realize I'm looking at you, you look away like you're embarrassed."

"I don't do that," Smith said. He made a V with his fingers to point at his own eyes, then pointed at Brooks. "Boom. Eye contact."

Brooks rolled his eyes. "Whatever. You like me, I like you. So… tell me about yourself. Where are you from? How did you get tangled up with The Reticent?"

Smith eyed his empty tumbler. "There isn't enough booze in Manhattan."

Brooks frowned. "That bad?"

"Pretty bad." Smith didn't elaborate.

Brooks cringed a little, but forced confidence on himself. "Well, you sound generic."

Smith squinted. "Thanks?"

"I mean your accent. It's Midwestern. Ohio?"

"Indiana," Smith corrected. "You're obviously from Staten Island."

"I could have moved there," Brooks said.

"Nobody moves there," Smith said.

"Yeah. Born and raised."

There was a brief lull in the conversation.

Smith ended it by blurting, "Your name doesn't make any sense."

Brooks shrugged. "Mexican mom. White dad. It's not that complicated."

"And—"

"Oh no," Brooks said. "It's my turn."

"No, it's not," Smith objected.

"Yes, it is. I asked where you're from, then you asked where I'm from, then you asked about my name. It's my turn," Brooks said.

Smith shook his head. "I didn't *ask* where you're from. I made a statement. First *you* asked how I joined The Reticent, then *you* asked where I'm from, then *I* asked about your name. By my count, I've got another question."

Brooks glowered. "Well, if we're going to come up with a bunch of technicalities, you didn't answer the first one, so we're even."

Smith was not one to let someone get the upper hand. "I got attacked by a vampire while I was doing a line of coke in an alley. That's how I found The Reticent."

Brooks blinked. "Okay..."

"My parents were meth-heads who blew up our house, so I grew up in foster care. Though 'care' is really... not the word I'd use." Smith continued his tirade of facts. "My middle name is Lock. I dropped out of school. I've never been in a real relationship. I've never been happy in my life, and I have a good feeling I'm not gonna live past forty. Probably why I took this job." He breathed. "That enough answers for you?"

For a good thirty seconds, they sat in silence.

Brooks broke the tension. "Your middle name is *Lock*?"

They both started laughing.

"So... you're fucked up." Brooks shrugged. "Me too."

"Because you give people you don't know alley blow-jobs?"

"No. No regrets there." Brooks inhaled deeply. "I tried to go back to Staten Island last month for my cousin's graduation party. I haven't been there since... you know."

"And?"

"I had a total meltdown on the ferry. I mean, full on... I was screaming at people to evacuate. Cops tried to commit me to a hospital, but The Reticent got me out. I thought they'd fire me, but... apparently not."

"No, we actually encourage lunatics to work for us," Smith said. "The kind of people who can't work anywhere else are the kind of people who'll do whatever you ask them to."

Brooks considered the 'whatever you ask them to' aspect of that. "What's the worst thing you've seen working for The Reticent?"

"Dunno." Smith went deep into his own thoughts. "Willowbrook Park barely cracks the top ten..." He got quiet and focused on his food.

Having the good sense to drop it, Brooks asked, "How

about the weirdest thing?"

Smith bit his lip in thought before settling on an answer. "Fuck psychic."

"You fucked a psychic?" wondered Brooks.

"No," Smith said. "There was this chick who could read people's futures, but only when she fucked them."

"And you didn't...?"

"No," Smith said.

"Why not?" asked Brooks.

"Just because I'm *willing* to fuck anyone doesn't mean I want to fuck *everyone*."

Brooks shook his head. "I know, but I mean... I'm gay and even I'd be tempted to suck it up just to get that info. You're not interested in your future?"

"Not really," said Smith. "Did you miss the part about 'dead by forty'? I assume it's gonna be a lot of bullshit until eventually something eats me. That's the life you've chosen too, pal. Not sure what you think you'd find out from a psychic."

Brooks explained. "I'd want to know... am I ever going to do something that matters?"

"Nothing matters," Smith said, as if he were a Goth teenager and not a thirty-year-old man.

"You saved my life. That mattered," Brooks said.

"Did it?" Smith asked. "We all take a dirt nap one day or another."

"Wow," Brooks said.

"Am I wrong?" Smith asked.

"*Technically*... no. But yes. You're wrong." Brooks became impassioned. "Just because time's short, that doesn't mean it doesn't matter. If anything, that means it matters more. If I were going to live forever, what's one day? But I'm not, so... today matters to me. I won't forget it."

Smith stared at him.

"What?" Brooks asked.

"You're really hot when you get worked up about something," Smith said.

"Oh my God," Brooks said, realizing his heartfelt plea for life's meaning had only made his new partner horny.

Smith reached a hand across the table. "I'm gonna be in the bathroom, if you want another moment you won't forget—"

Brooks bit his lip as he watched Smith walk away.

It was after five o'clock and getting dark out when the detectives finally arrived at Battery Park.

Smith took a look around. "We *really* should have come sooner."

"I don't know. I think we came at the right time," Brooks said.

Smith looked at him and smirked.

Battery Park started each day well-kempt and sunny, and ended each day covered in trash as the sun set and obscured all the drug needles from view. The pair watched as bootleg vendors put their goods away, into duffel bags and backpacks, and counted their cash earnings.

"Ah, the sweet smell of desperation and despair," said Smith.

Brooks looked around at the trash-strewn lawn and the sketchy vendors all over it. "Do they not know they can get real jobs?"

Smith's uncharacteristic good mood turned. "Wow. You're real fuckin' judgmental for someone who blows strangers in alleys."

"Look around," Brooks said.

"Yeah. *I am.*" There was audible anger in Smith's

voice—more passionate than his general disdain for everything and everyone.

Brooks stopped walking and grabbed Smith's shoulder to get him to do the same.

"You were just joking about the smell of despair, but you're mad at me?" Brooks asked.

"Yeah. I am." Smith spun to face Brooks, and snapped. "Because it's never been you on the ground getting sneered at by yuppie pricks."

"You don't know anything about me," Brooks said.

"I've met *enough* people like you. Middle class. Loving family. Probably did some school sport. God help me if it was lacrosse. I bet your favorite movie is some basic shit like *Scarface*."

"Soccer and *Top Gun*," Brooks said. "And who's judgmental now?"

Smith shrugged. "I wasn't wrong."

"No, but... I know your type too. You think just because your life has sucked that you get to be a dick to everyone. That you're better than them because you suffered more. Well, guess what? You don't have a monopoly on pain."

Smith sneered. "I don't think I'm better than anyone."

"You sure?" Brooks asked.

Smith resumed walking.

Brooks huffed. "Now you walk away."

"I'm looking for our guy. You know, the job? The one we should have been doing *hours ago*?" Smith stopped, turned, and retraced his steps. "He should be right here."

"Maybe he moved?"

"Reggie never moves," Smith said.

"You're on a first name basis?" Brooks got a slack-jawed look as he realized something. "Did you—"

"Used to work down here? Yeah. Good job, *detective*." Smith continued walking the same path, back and forth, over and over.

"I'm sorry," Brooks said, completely earnest.

"I don't care."

Something caught Smith's eye. A glimmer behind a bush. He walked toward it.

The glimmer was Reggie's bootleg Ralex watch. The fifty-year-old vendor lay dead at the center of a ring of shrubbery, his trench coat spread around him like a drop shadow laid there by a late-1990s website designer. Blood stains spread across his white t-shirt from four or five central points.

"Fuck," Smith said.

"Is that—"

Smith nodded. He knelt and started rifling through the trench coat. Nothing. "All his amulets are gone."

"Random mugging, or—?"

"Random mugger would have taken his watch," Smith said. He unlatched the Ralex and pocketed it for himself. "Whoever shot him wanted the potions and amulets. Fat lot of good it'll do them. I guarantee you everything he sold was fake. That's why I wasn't in a hurry to get here..."

Brooks looked at his partner with disgust. "Are you *stealing* from the dead?"

"Something to remember him by," Smith said. "You'd rather the city have it?"

"What about his family—"

Smith broke into a cackle.

Brooks stared at him.

"You're serious?" Smith laughed harder.

"You don't know he didn't have any—"

"*Yeah I do*," Smith said. "Anyway, he's still warm, so it didn't happen too long ago. There might be someone around who saw somethi—" Smith shut up when he himself saw something. Among the vendors packing up their wares and dissipating crowds were a man and woman in black suits. Not the stockbroking kind. The Reticent kind. One of them carried a tote bag that sagged under its own weight. He took a deep breath. "We took too long. Reticent took care of it."

Brooks's eyes widened. "Are you saying our employer would order someone killed without any proof they did anything wrong?"

"Didn't necessarily have to *order* anything. There's plenty of trigger-happy asshole agents." Smith took a deep breath. "Anyone asks what held us up, we ran into a vampire."

"O... kay..." Brooks was still processing the wanton murder, and pondering what exactly he'd gotten himself into.

Smith eyed Reggie's body again, and frowned. It bothered him, but so did something else. Something from earlier. He lit a cigarette as more Reticent agents arrived, dressed as cops. There was something he needed to say before he and his partner parted ways for the evening.

"Just so you know... I don't think I'm better than anyone," he said.

Brooks shook his head. "Things got heated earlier. I'm sorr—"

"I think I'm worse," Smith said. "Also... you were right. I shouldn't have judged. I don't know you." Brooks started to say something, but Smith wouldn't let him. "I don't *want* to know you. Reggie's dead because I couldn't keep my dick in my pants."

"That's not on you," Brooks said.

Smith didn't believe that, but he couldn't be bothered to argue the point. "It doesn't matter. Nothing good's gonna come of this, so... from now on, let's keep it professional."

"Little late for that, don't you think?"

Smith did the thing he always did; he avoided eye

contact.

Brooks grabbed him by the shoulder and forced their eyes to meet. "You like me. I like you."

"Yeah." Smith pulled away. "And Reggie liked amulets. Look where it got him."

PRO/CON LIST

Pros:

Cute

Funny

~~Good~~ Great kisser

Those eyes

That dick

Saved my life

Unpretentious

Honest

Empathy for poor

Cons:

~~Kind of~~ <u>Really</u> a dick

Messy

Smokes

Immature

Dragon tattoo

Emotionally stunted

Bad grammar

Moody

From Indiana

PONDTERGEIST

Smith stepped out of his Pontiac Aztek into a sludgy puddle of mud and horse shit. He and Brooks had driven separate company vehicles to Lititz, Pennsylvania. It was expensive and illogical, but Smith wanted nothing to do with the kinds of lengthy discussions that accompanied three-hour road trips. The relationship between him and his new partner was to remain strictly professional, with as little interaction as possible. He wouldn't even address Brooks by his first name. He was "Agent Brooks" only. *Strictly professional.*

Just outside the city—if it could be called one—was a rock quarry where workers had reported a series of unusual happenings. A few quarry workers had gone missing, and there were murmurings of ghost activity. Word had gotten so loud that television's *Spook Seekers* had even shown up to investigate.

A second Aztek approached the quarry manager's office: a rusting trailer on a concrete pad in a vast expanse of gravel, dust, parked vehicles, and machinery.

Smith stepped out of the sludge pile and wiped his shoes on the pad, sneering the entire time.

"You almost lost me back there," Brooks said, hopping out of his car onto some gravel.

"That would've been a shame," Smith said.

"You realize we hit *ninety-five* on the interstate?"

Smith stared at him with contempt. "*So?*"

"That's reckless endangerment," Brooks said. "If we'd been pulled over—"

Smith rolled his eyes and approached the manager's door. "Wait 'til you find out I wasn't wearing a seatbelt."

Brooks was appalled. "Are you serious? That's—"

Smith tuned him out and gave the thin metal door a few taps, which caused it to rattle.

No one answered.

"Parking lot's full," Smith noted.

"Maybe the ghosts got him," Brooks said.

"Him *and* all the workers?" Smith spread his arms wide to note the nothing. All the quarry equipment was unmanned. The place was silent. "There's no one here."

"Except ghosts," Brooks said, deliberately annoying his partner.

"*There aren't any ghosts,*" Smith said.

"There could be," Brooks said.

"You read the file?" Smith asked, already knowing the answer was yes. "Nobody's seen any specters. No EMF activity. It's just a bunch of hicks making wild accusations."

As he tapped at the door again, a voice came from behind them.

"You fellas lookin' for a ghost?" it asked.

Brooks, still new to field work, jumped a little.

Smith drew his gun, whipped around, and pointed it at the source of the voice. An old man in a straw hat stood at the end of the concrete pad, unfazed by the gun.

"You've gotta be kidding me." Smith tucked his weapon away. "You the manager?"

The old man—who would have looked perfectly at home on a rocking chair—shook his head in the negative and blathered on. "Lotta folk come 'round here looking for a ghost. You two look like you're from the city."

The city the old man meant was Harrisburg (population: 48,950).

"Where would we find a ghost?" Brooks asked, to Smith's eyerolls.

"If it's a ghost you're lookin' for, check the quarry pond." The old man pointed to a break in the treeline at the edge of the gravel. "I wouldn't go over there, though. Lotta bad history at that pond. Just last week, Leewood Tankle drowned out there. Six-time county swim champion and he just up 'n' drowns in not much more'n a puddle. Ain't right."

"*One event* is a lot of bad history?" Smith asked, like a smartass.

"Thanks," Brooks said, pulling his partner away from the old man and toward the treeline.

The old man droned on about the town's history, but the detectives were well out of earshot.

Beyond the treeline was another gravel expanse. Sure enough, this one contained a pond. An unimpressive pond, at that. Maybe ten feet in diameter and three feet deep, composed of grey pebbles like the ones that surrounded it. Brooks and Smith circled it for ten minutes and found nothing. No remnants of Leewood Tankle. No EMF activity. No evidence of a pirate ghost or a ghost pirate. Nothing.

On a flat, pebbly area, Smith began pulling his shoes off. Then his mismatched socks.

"What are you doing?" Brooks asked.

"I'm gonna check the pond," Smith said, removing his belt.

"You think it's a good idea to walk into a *haunted pond*?"

Smith, top half in a suit and bottom half in nothing but worn-out boxers, stepped into the pond and made a declaration. "There are no ghosts."

Almost immediately, the water in the pond disappeared into thin air and he was standing in an empty gravel pit. Smith took a step back and looked down at it, scowling.

Brooks crossed his arms. "*You were saying?*"

"There *might* be something fucky," Smith said, "but it's not a ghost and it's not in this pond."

There was nothing in the pond. No twigs, shards of glass, or used needles. Nothing but pebbles. It was the cleanest pond Smith had ever seen.

"We should head back to the office," Brooks said. "See if that old man's seen any workers or—"

"Yeah." As soon as Smith's feet left the pond, its water reappeared. He squinted at it. "That's fucking weird... but it's not a ghost." He wiggled his EMF reader at it. "Nothing."

"I guess not," Brooks said. He still sort of thought there was a ghost. Mostly he thought about what a shame it was that Smith was putting his pants back on.

When they got back to the quarry, the old man was nowhere to be found, and all of the employee cars were gone.

"Apparently quarry work stops at five on the dot," Smith said.

Brooks shook his head. "*What work?* There was no one here."

"There's definitely a case," Smith said.

"We're going to have to stay overnight," Brooks said, with a sly smile.

Smith didn't acknowledge it. "I'll meet you here at eight tomorrow." He then remembered he could set his own schedule. "Make it nine. Ten, even."

Brooks curled his lip. "We're the only two agents out here. You don't think we should hang out and do some research? Two heads better than one and all that? Who knows, we could even get food."

"Do your own research. I know what your idea of *food* is." Smith opened his Aztek's door.

"Drinks?" Brooks wondered.

"Do whatever you want," Smith said. "I'm gonna rent a room at the Ramshackle Inn and eat chips for dinner like a fucking deviant while I read about pond monsters."

"There's nothing to do out here," Brooks complained.

"Exactly." Smith shut the door and drove off.

Smith wasn't alone in his one-star hotel room for long. One bag of Amish kettle chips and a hardcore porn rental later, there was knocking at his door.

"No room service!" Smith shouted, fumbling to cover himself with a duvet.

"It's me," Brooks said through the door.

Smith grabbed the remote and quickly flipped to the Sci-Fi Channel. He threw on some pajama pants and cracked open the door. "*What?*"

"There's only one hotel in this town," Brooks said.

"Okay... *and?*"

"I went to a bar first, and by the time I got here, it was full," Brooks said.

Smith squinted at the parking lot. "It's *full?*"

"Cheese convention," Brooks said. "Can I crash here?"

"It's a single," Smith said.

"I can sleep on the floor," Brooks offered.

Smith rubbed at the inside corners of his eyes. "*Fine.*" He opened the door wide.

Brooks eyed the older man's low pajamas and made an even lower chuckle. "Can we talk about the dragon tattoo?"

Smith pulled his pants up to his waist. "I was seventeen."

Brooks stepped into the room and noticed half a dozen empty beer bottles on the nightstand. "You didn't want to get drinks, huh?"

"Sure didn't," Smith said.

"Yeah, okay—" Brooks eyed the TV "—and that's research?"

Smith flopped back onto the bed. "You've sure got a lot of complaints for a freeloader."

"Yeah. Okay..." Brooks seated himself on the edge of the bed. "So, like I said... I went to the bar, and... everyone there had a ghost story."

"For the love of—"

Brooks held his palms out to tell his partner to settle down. "All of them described the ghosts differently. Some of them saw dead Victorian kids. One of them claimed they had sex with a ghost, which... definitely didn't happen. I think you're right about them being full of it."

"I know I am," Smith said.

"So... we have... six missing quarry workers, one drowned swim champion, a disappearing old man in a hat, and a bunch of liars. What do we do with that?"

"My best guess? Illusion magic. But there's nothing to do until we can talk to the quarry guys tomorrow," said Smith. "Whatever's going on, it involves them."

"We could go talk to them at home now. We could go talk to more townies," Brooks said.

"Yeah," Smith said. "You know what people love? Being harassed at home at ten o'clock at night."

"But if they're already out in public—"

"Quit being a go-getter. My report on you is gonna say 'adequate' either way."

Brooks grouched. "*Wow.* Thanks."

An hour later, he found something else to grouch about.

While Smith reclined in comfort, watching *Quantum Leap* reruns atop a pile of four pillows, Brooks folded awkwardly in the space between the bed and the wall, browsing Reti-net on his laptop. His back, which was too young to hurt, hurt.

He eyed the king-sized bed. "The floor is harder than I thought it would be."

"I'm not sharing," Smith said.

"Please?"

Smith turned up the volume. "Nope."

Brooks tugged at the comforter. "Come on."

Smith looked down at a pair of pleading brown eyes. Part of him wanted to crank the volume even higher and flip his partner the bird. Another part felt the smallest twinge of affection.

"*Fine*," he said, tossing one pillow to the other side of the bed.

Inside, Smith raged at himself for being a pushover. To keep his pride and his distance, he scooched himself as close to his edge of the bed as possible.

Brooks didn't do the same. He settled in the middle of the bed and—despite bringing his laptop with him—fell asleep in an instant, making the occasional assault on Smith with an errant arm or leg.

Hours later, one egregious bump woke Smith in the middle of the night. It had been hard enough for him to fall asleep in the first place, and he prepared to shove the other detective across the mattress and yell at him. For some reason, he didn't do either of those things. He just lay there, watching Brooks sleep, thinking about Willowbrook Park, and repeating a mantra:

He's cute, but he's doomed.

The next morning, the quarry buzzed with activity. Loud equipment beeped and slammed rocks. Workers shouted in order to hear each other through their noise-blocking ear muffs. Plumes of dust filled the air. Brooks and Smith pulled up in their Azteks and began interviewing everyone they could find.

None of the workers had any idea what the men from New York were going on about.

"I was here all day yesterday," one worker said.

"We were here at four o'clock," Brooks said. "The parking lot was full, but no one was here."

The worker shrugged. "I was here. I don't know what to tell you."

"Tell us about the pond," Smith said.

"What pond?"

Brooks pointed in the direction of the pond. "The one over there. Maybe two hundred meters?"

"That pond's been empty all season. Drought, y'know."

"We were just there *yesterday*," Brooks said. "It was a pond."

"Leewood Tankle *drowned there*," Smith noted.

"He may have drowned *at* the pond," said the worker, "but he couldn't have drowned *in* the pond. I'm telling you it's been dry all season."

Brooks and Smith led the worker back to the pond, only to embarrass themselves.

The pond was empty. Smith kicked at it, hoping the pond would respond to him. It didn't.

When they returned to the quarry, the dust had settled. The noise was gone. The only cars in the parking lot were the Azteks and an old Camaro belonging to the agents' tour guide.

"Shit," said the quarry worker. "Where'd everyone go? If they're not working, I'm not." He ducked into his

Camaro and sped off, leaving the detectives in a cloud of dust.

Brooks and Smith continued poking around the quarry all afternoon. As far as they could tell, it looked like a quarry. There were rocks everywhere, and an empty pond. No corpses. No EMF. With nothing to go on, they did what any sensible person would do and made their way to a local tavern. They claimed a high-top table near the bar, where they could overhear everyone in the room.

"Ever heard of a ghost pond?" Brooks wondered.

"Pondtergeist," Smith offered. "And no. There's no ghosts, and that includes the goddamn pond."

"Maybe the workers are turning invisible together," Brooks suggested. "And if one of them is away from the quarry, they don't get turned."

"So they come back and it looks like everyone else is gone, but everyone else is just invisible?" Smith thought on it. "That's dumb. Won't rule it out. But the cars disappeared too."

"Our cars didn't disappear," Brooks noted, ruining his own theory.

As they thought on it, a server brought out the abomination Smith had ordered. Knot-chos were like nachos, but instead of chips the base was a pile of sourdough pretzels. They were topped with liquid cheese product, jalapeño slices, olives, bacon bits, and a glob of sour cream.

Brooks eyed the mess and winced. "How are you still alive?"

"I ask myself that every day," Smith said, before devouring a knot-cho.

Brooks regained his focus. "How could Leewood Tankle drown in an empty pond?"

"Suicide?" Smith suggested.

"It was a rhetorical question," Brooks said.

"This is why I hate working small town cases," Smith said. "No one's stories ever line up and it almost always turns out to be some group of busybodies dicking around."

Brooks eyed Smith's knot-chos. "Can I try one of those?"

"Sure." Smith slid the plate toward the center of the table. "They're terrible."

Brooks grabbed one and popped it into his mouth. He rendered his judgment. "Awful."

"Told you," Smith said.

"But weirdly enticing..." Brooks grabbed another.

"The power of salt," said Smith.

Smiling between bites, they made quick work of the knot-chos, which were nearly gone by the time their server returned with an apologetic face.

"Um... my manager told me you two are making other patrons uncomfortable, so I'm supposed to ask you to tone it down..."

Brooks's eyes shifted from side to side. "You sure you have the right table?"

"Yes." She not-so-subtly slid Smith's plate back toward him.

Brooks took a sip of water, so the cheese goop couldn't impede his ability to complain.

"We didn't do anything," Brooks said, "but if you're going to give me that attitude, we will."

Smith gulped down a knot-cho. "We will?"

Brooks hopped off his seat and stepped around the table, with a look that sought consent.

Smith gave a quick nod, and Brooks leaned in to kiss him. Nothing too outrageous. Soft mouth-to-mouth action with only the slightest bit of tongue. When Brooks pulled away, Smith's mouth trailed toward him, like he was a cartoon character floating through the air in pursuit of a pie. He shook it off and resettled himself.

Brooks turned back to the server. "Tell your manager they don't have to like it, but they can deal with it." She scurried off, and Brooks reseated himself, huffing. "All we did was *share a plate*."

Smith—trying to hide his fluster—gave his partner the side-eye. "Why do I feel like that was a thinly veiled excuse to kiss me, *Agent Brooks*?"

"Don't *Agent Brooks* me," Brooks said.

"That's the *only* way I'm gonna name you," Smith said. "*Because we're keeping it professional.*"

"Yeah, we'll see..."

One by one, a circle of patrons formed around Brooks and Smith's table. Muttering and whispering amongst themselves, they gave off angry mob vibes. The detectives found themselves surrounded, and they readied themselves for a fight. For Brooks, that meant mentally reciting Reticent fighting tips. For Smith, it meant loading up on carbs.

Instead of attacking, a woman with a speak-to-the-manager haircut reached for Brooks's hand and gave it a friendly shake. "Hi. We all just wanted to say... how brave it is for you two to express your love here."

Smith almost choked on the last knot-cho. "Our *what*?"

"Kudos to you," said another local, who sported a mullet.

"Um... thank you?" Brooks said. "What are—"

The circle mumbled a few words of encouragement, then dispersed as the detectives' server returned to announce that their food and drinks had been comped.

"My manager had a change of heart," she explained with a smile.

Things were really starting to feel amiss.

"What just happened?" Brooks asked.

Smith didn't have an answer for him; he was busy reminding himself of his new mantra.

He's cute, but he's doomed.

~

Back at the hotel, Smith hung his jacket on a peg near the door as he made a proclamation. "Today was a bust." He clutched his side. "And I'm pretty sure the knot-chos are killing me."

Brooks—still fully dressed—leapt onto the bed and sprawled out, exhausted.

"You're somehow taking even more space than you did yesterday," Smith said.

There was an incomprehensible, sleepy mumble.

In the forty seconds it took Smith to change into his low-rise pajama pants, Brooks passed out. Smith tucked into the sliver of bed that had been set aside for him and shut his eyes.

Said eyes sprung open to another bump in the night. But it wasn't an errant limb this time. Brooks had moved his whole body over and made it conform to Smith's. It was far too cozy and warm for someone unused to being either, and Smith readied a complaint.

He tapped Brooks's shoulder, but the younger man didn't rouse. He aimed his finger again, but something came over him. Instead of prodding for more space, Smith ran his hand down the side of Brooks's body, threw his arm around him, and pulled him closer. Just as this made him feel like a creep and he prepared to retract his arm, Brooks grabbed it and pulled it tighter.

"You're awake?" Smith asked.

Brooks said nothing.

☙

Door by door, citizen by citizen, Brooks and Smith got a complete picture of Lititz. It was a boring picture, and only a few houses had information of note...

Ms. Carpenter (née Wilson). Age 58. Widow. After her former husband won the lottery, he skipped out of town, attempting to leave her without the fifty percent she was owed after a quarter century of marriage. Thankfully, he died almost immediately, and she inherited every cent. For some reason, she remained in Lititz.

Mr. Tucker. Age 23. Some kind of IT worker. House full of anime posters. He smelled like beer, nachos, and body odor. He was, in Smith's words, "absolutely unfuckable." And yet, he had a girlfriend. One who was, in Smith's words, "reasonably fuckable." It didn't make sense.

Mr. Abrams. Age 72. Retired quarry worker. The state of the quarry was so bad that—despite his age—he received a call every morning begging him to come back to work. There weren't enough experienced quarry workers, it said. There weren't enough workers, period. He'd declined each day, citing his bad knees.

That was it, and that information wasn't all that notable or reliable.

While leaving the last house of the day, Brooks and Smith noted a suspicious white panel van parked across the street. They walked over to it and knocked on the back door.

It opened with a screech to reveal a female face, instantly recognizable.

Clarity "Claire" Voyant, one of late-night television's most famous ghost hunters. Claire—along with Sam Cork and Rhonda Lona—was part of the ghost-hunting trio that starred in *Spook Seekers*. Everything they presented to the public about ghost hunting was completely wrong, from their imprecise EMF readers to their insistence that ghosts were cold. Off-screen screams and slamming doors were obviously fake, set up to lend more credence to their work.

Brooks recognized her from many a late-night viewing mistake. He groused. "Claire Voyant."

"Where are the rest of the three musketeers?" Smith asked.

Claire's coils of red hair bounced as she enthused. "They went to Radio Shack to get more memory. We've gotten so much footage our cameras are out of storage space. Can you believe it?"

Brooks and Smith stared at her.

"You don't believe me." Claire motioned them into the van. "Come see."

One side of the van was a long bench, where all three seated themselves. The other side was a wall of monitors. The Spook Seeker grabbed a remote and turned on a video her team had recently captured. The camera focused on a recently dug grave at the local cemetery. It lingered for a few moments. Just as Brooks and Smith were getting impatient, a translucent figure arose from the dirt.

"Did you just feel a chill?" asked an off-camera voice.

"It's getting really cold over here," said another.

The figure stood for a good ten seconds, revealing itself to be a Victorian woman in a tiny hat. She curtsied, then vanished.

Smith blew it off. "Wow, you're getting really good at CGI."

"What?" Claire's red coils went limp. "It's not—"

"We're gonna go do some real work," Smith said. He held the van door open for Brooks and escorted him outside.

"That looked... really real," Brooks said when they were out of earshot.

"It *was* real," Smith said. "Cold aside. Kinda weird to see an old-timey ghost pop out of a new grave, though..."

Brooks looked at him, anticipating something.

"There are ghosts," Smith said. "Happy?"

Brooks smirked. "Not as happy as I'll be when we're back in bed together."

"*Nothing happened*," Smith said.

"Cuddling isn't *nothing*," Brooks said.

"I did not cud—"

Brooks cut him off. "You know you talk in your sleep?"

"Yeah, I've heard that. What did I say?"

"Just gibberish," Brooks said.

"Not worth bringing up then, is it?" Smith asked.

"You did say my name," Brooks said.

"*And?* You were right there. Of course it would come up," Smith said.

"Not *Agent Brooks*. My first name," Brooks said.

"Never gonna happen," Smith said. "We're keeping it professional. Now let's find some ghosts."

They didn't find any ghosts. Not at the cemetery or anywhere else the *Spook Seekers* had sought spooks. All they encountered was another day of fruitless investigation, followed by another evening of greasy bar food. After an angry phone call from their boss, wondering why this investigation was taking "so goddamn long," it was time for another night at the Ramshackle Inn.

"Have you been to the front desk? They might have another vacancy now," Smith said.

Brooks mumbled a response while brushing his teeth.

"All my stuff's already here."

"Uh huh." Part of Smith wanted to argue. Another part loved having Brooks around. The professional and non-professional sides battled it out in his mind.

Brooks finished brushing, turned off the tap, and complained. "I can still taste the chilidog onion rings." He poured a glass of water and sipped. "I'm going to go get some ice."

"I don't care. Have fun?"

Smith's eyes lingered on Brooks's ass a little too long as he slid out the door.

"Fuck," he said to himself, realizing that his non-professional side was winning.

He's cute, but he's doomed.

Brooks returned with a bucket of ice. He opened the door, prepared to set it on the room's desk. Instead, he set it all over the floor. Smith knocked the bucket out of his hands and shoved him against the door, forcing it shut.

Brooks gasped. "What are you doing?"

The answer became apparent when Smith slid his tongue into Brooks's mouth, kissing him passionately. He'd been aching to do this ever since their kiss at the bar, and he probed the inside of his partner's mouth like he was lapping the cheese from a knot-cho.

Brooks savored things for a moment before pulling away. "I'm into it, *really*, but what are you doing? You keep saying you want to keep it professional..."

"Fuck professional," said Smith.

It was hard to argue with that. Brooks kissed back and shoved Smith toward the bed. Over the next few hours, the raucous pair broke no fewer than sixteen Reticent rules, as well as one corner of the bedframe.

Afterward, Smith decided to take a shower.

Brooks waited to do the same. He sat naked at the edge

of the bed, satisfied but discomfited. He'd let himself think with his dick. Again. There was no reason The Reticent would find out, but he worried about what would happen if they did. Fire him, just when things were starting to get interesting? Not good. He had no backup plans, after all. Then there was the small matter of Smith *really* not being an ideal love interest, what with the smoking and being an asshole. But like the knot-chos, he was oddly enticing—

THUNK. A loud sound in the bathroom jarred Brooks from his existential crisis, and he realized that Smith had been taking a long time. A weirdly long time. He stood and approached the bathroom.

"Are you okay in there?" Brooks tapped at the door.

An angry, muffled mumble was the only response.

"I'm coming in," Brooks announced.

When he opened the door, a cloud of steam greeted him. It took a moment to see through the fog. Brooks's eyes followed the line of the shower curtain and spotted the figure behind it. He shoved the curtain aside.

Smith was against the wall of the shower, his back to it, held in place by a forceful stream of water that hovered mid-air and pressed his shoulders to the wall. His head jerked back and hit the wall with another THUNK as the stream made its way into his mouth and nostrils.

"Ghost pond!" Brooks turned the spigot. When that had no effect on the magic water that was drowning Smith, he smacked at it with his hands, splashing water all over the place. "Stop it!"

For some reason, the water obeyed. It fell to the tub and ran down the drain.

Smith fell with it, and Brooks knelt down to check on him.

Smith doubled over the side of the tub, coughing. "It's not a ghost."

Brooks gestured at the faucet. "Did you not just see...?"

"It's not a ghost." Smith coughed some more. "It's a wishing well."

Brooks helped him up. "...What?"

Smith seated himself on the tub's rim, and Brooks took a seat next to him.

"Not an actual well," Smith said. "The water supply. When we first got here, I was hoping for a lead and stepped in mud. Boom. Old man in a straw hat. The quarry pond... when I stepped into it, I didn't want to get wet, so it moved out of the way. The workers wanted it dry. It was dry. Leewood Tankle wanted a place to drown, so he drowned. Whatshisname won the lottery. His scorned wife wanted him dead. That one loser with the anime posters wanted to get laid. The retired dude wanted the quarry to need him. The disappearing workers probably got whatever wish took them out of fucking Lititz, Pennsylvania."

Brooks turned red. "Oh no."

"I'm guessing you and your glass of tap water wanted me to fuck you," Smith said.

"Oh my God. Did I mind control you?" Brooks panicked. "Am I a rapist?"

Smith motioned for him to calm down. "*Relax*. You didn't make me do anything I didn't already want to do. But I'm also guessing... that whole production at the bar... you wanted those weirdos to accept you for the fruit you are?"

Brooks reacted to the half-insult with a glare. "*We just had sex.*"

Smith shrugged.

Brooks still wasn't completely sold on the explanation. "If it's a wishing well, why did it try to drown you in the shower?"

"You really wanna go down that road?" Smith asked.

"No..." Brooks smacked him on the shoulder. "*No.*"

"Can we move on? It's not that weird to wish you were dead sometimes," Smith said.

"I... It... Yes. It is."

Smith changed the subject. "We've got a bigger problem. If someone—say, a certain TV ghost hunter—wished for ghosts to exist..."

"Then ghosts exist." Brooks's eyes widened. "That would explain why the townies are seeing different kinds of ghosts. They're wishing them into existence."

"This could go wrong so many ways," Smith said. "I need you to promise me something."

"Anything," Brooks said, coming on just a bit too strong.

Smith squinted. "Don't wish for anything. Don't even think about what you'd wish for if you wished for something."

"I'm not going to—"

Smith cut him off. "*Yes, you are.* You're gonna think about wishing your family back to life—"

"Well, what's wrong with that?"

"This shit always goes wrong is what. Mind-rape is just the tip of the iceberg," Smith said.

Brooks freaked. "You said you wanted to—"

"*I did.* I didn't mean you," Smith said.

Brooks crossed his arms. "How could someone *being alive* go bad?"

Smith raised his fingers one-by-one to count the ways. "They could come back zombies. Vampires. Wraiths. Your sister could grow up to be the next Hitler."

"My sister's not Hitler."

"Not now. She's dead," Smith said. "We need to disenchant this town's water before these people realize what they have here."

"How do we do that?" Brooks asked.

"I have no fucking clue," Smith said.

Brooks made a suggestion. "Research sleepover?"

"Depends on what you mean by research," Smith said.

"I mean *research*," Brooks said. "If people's lives are in danger, I can keep it in my pants."

"You're not wearing pants," Smith noted.

Brooks grabbed a towel and covered himself.

Two showers and four hours of grueling research later, both men's eyes hurt from staring at laptop screens. Myths about wishing wells varied from culture to culture, but generally they were seen as forces of good. One thing was consistent: In order to receive something from a wishing well, a person had to give something up, whether it was a simple coin or something more valuable, like a Macbook Pro or an eyeball.

Brooks kept coming back to this point. "What's the price?"

"I don't know," Smith said, "but Lititz wasn't always a wishing well, or we'd have been sent here a long time ago."

"*Or*, someone from The Reticent *was* sent here at some point, and a local wished they'd go away and forget about it," Brooks said. "We can't rely on history being accurate."

Smith groaned. "So we're relying on thousand-year-old lore, like that's better."

"*I know*," Brooks said. "I can't really wrap my head around magic either. You know, vampires and werewolves and wraiths... they're just previously undiscovered species. I get it. Ghosts... don't really conflict with my views on the afterlife. Sitting here reading the story of Mímir and the Well of Wisdom like it has any basis in reality, though..."

Smith gave him a look, but didn't say anything.

"What?" Brooks asked.

"I don't wanna be a dick..."

Brooks raised his brow. "That's new. Just say it."

"It's no stupider than what you believe," Smith said, with a pointed glance at the cross dangling from his partner's neck.

Brooks sighed and shut his laptop.

"You asked for it," Smith said, doing the same.

Brooks turned to face Smith. "I know, but... how do you reconcile believing in *nothing* with, like... performing an exorcism? I mean, *it works*. Something about it works."

"How do *you* reconcile believing in heaven and hell?"

Brooks shifted a little. "Well, I don't agree with the Church's teachings on everyth—"

"I'm not talking about you being light in the loafers." Smith ignored the glare he received in response. "I mean... there *cannot* be a heaven. Not for you."

"Because...?"

"A little light sinning aside, there has to be *someone* you care about who'd be condemned to hell. And you couldn't possibly be content in heaven knowing that."

"That's not how it's supposed to work," Brooks explained. "I'd be at peace. I'd be beyond any Earthly concerns like that."

"Then you wouldn't be you. So *you* couldn't be in heaven," Smith said. "Like I said."

Brooks roped him back to the original question. "What's your explanation for exorcisms?"

Smith shook his head. "Fuck if I know. There's supposed to be infinite universes, right?"

"So they say."

"Then there's a universe where any time I say you have a nice ass you turn into a fucking squid." Smith wriggled his fingers in a gesture reminiscent of jazz hands. "Infinity!" He lowered his hands. "No reason demons can't be from a dimension where whatever phrase is enough to send them back."

"What are ghosts?" Brooks asked.

"One form of energy converted into another?" Smith wondered. "Again, fuck if I know."

Brooks became visibly frustrated and huffed a little.

For reasons that weren't clear to him, Smith felt compelled to lessen his partner's frustration. "Look. It's not that I believe in *nothing*. I'd have to be stupid to think there's nothing more powerful than us. Maybe there are Norse gods, I don't know. I just don't think it matters. For one, we'll never know until we're dead. And for another... what good are magical forces of... good? What'd they ever do for me? What'd they ever do for you? For all I know, this is all just a poorly written simulation where the rules are constantly changing. So I just take it for what it is. Wishing wells exist?" He shrugged his hands. "Sure. Might as well."

"Might as *well*?" Brooks groaned.

"Yeah, I'm proud of that one. Also, I'm not drunk enough for this shit. We slept together one time, now you wanna talk philosophy."

Brooks looked into his eyes. "How many times do we need to sleep together before you think this is appropriate?"

Smith let out a short laugh. "*Wishing wells*. Forces of *good* that for some reason also try to help people kill themselves..."

"Yeah..." His partner's attempt at getting him to focus had only brought something else to the forefront of Brooks's mind. "You don't really want to die, do you?"

Smith—unsure of his own thoughts on the matter—

stared for a moment before answering. "No. I'm not fond of being alive, but no. It's just my brain being a shitbag."

"Right," Brooks said. "And the sex thing... it was just a passing thought. *I'd love to fuck him.* It doesn't sit right with the lore that says it's usually a deep, intentional desire... and again, we haven't paid *any* price to have our wishes granted."

Smith shook his head. "I've got nothing. I say we get up bright and early and start checking the reservoir, the water tower, the treatment plant..."

"No sense going while it's dark and we can't see anything..."

"Exactly," Smith said.

"So... there's not really anything we can do tonight..." Brooks leaned forward.

Against his better judgment, Smith smirked. "You wanna earn another conversation about philosophy?"

"Oh, but that would be unprofessional, *Agent Smith.*"

"Bite me, Arturo."

The next morning, two very tired detectives started checking the water supply. First, the reservoir, since it was closest. There was nothing weird about it, at least for as much as Brooks and Smith knew about reservoirs.

Their next stop was the water tower. There was nothing weird about it either, at least for as much as Brooks and Smith knew about water towers.

Their final stop was the water treatment plant.

An employee of thirty-seven years named Larry Carmichael took the lead on giving Brooks and Smith a tour of the place. He was a scruffy, blue-collar sort of guy with a thick mustache and a navy-blue utility jumpsuit. Despite his decades of service, he walked with a proud enthusiasm as he escorted the detectives around the plant and explained every boring detail.

Larry showed them the pump station, which was of little interest, except to Smith, who made a few lewd comments about pumping. They moved on to the bar screens, the grit and sludge removal tanks, the sedimentation tank, the aeration tank... basically just a bunch of huge tanks of water in various states of cleanliness. The last among them was the disinfection and final treatment tank, which was the last stop before the water went back into the drinking supply.

There was something interesting about that one. Dead center in the circular tank was something flat and golden—somewhere between the size of a saucer and a dessert plate.

"What's that?" Brooks asked, pointing to it.

"Not sure," Larry said.

Smith eyed Brooks, then Larry. "Not sure? You said this is the last stop before the water goes back into the supply."

"Oh, it's safe," Larry said. "It's solid gold, and gold has fantastic antibacterial properties. I'm just not sure how it got there."

"When did it show up?" asked Brooks.

"Maybe a month or two back," Larry said. "We tried removing it but the darn thing is stuck. Shut the whole place down and everything to analyze it, but couldn't get it out."

"Stuck how?" Smith asked.

Larry fetched a large skimming net and demonstrated by inserting it into the pool and sliding it across the bottom. The golden disc didn't budge.

"Can I try?" Smith asked.

"Be my guest." Larry handed him the net.

Smith positioned the net on the side of the disc closest

to him and gave it a hearty push. He nearly fell into the pool as the net got stuck on the coin, then jumped over it suddenly and with force.

"Shit." Smith turned to Brooks. "You wanna try?"

"What's the point? I know you're strong enough to do it." Brooks smiled.

Smith shook his head.

Matters got worse than the lame flirting.

"Um..." Brooks noticed that he could see his breath. "You feel that?"

Smith shivered a little. "Yeah."

A fog descended on the men. The area around the pond became freezing cold. From the water tank arose a pair of perfect, wispy Victorian ghosts. One man in a fancy suit and hat, and one woman in a thick, layered gown. Their elbows were entwined, as if they were a couple going for a friendly stroll.

"Stay out of our poooond," said the man, stretching the word pond. It was more ghastly that way.

"Stay ouuttttt," repeated the female ghost.

"Uh huh," Smith said with no emotion. He turned to Brooks. "You wanna go get your kit from your trunk?"

"Sure. What are you gonna—"

Smith answered him by jumping—fully clothed—into the icy water. Larry would have looked on in dismay, but the ghost matter was a little more pressing than water sanitation.

Brooks hurried off to the parking lot to retrieve ghost-banishing supplies.

As Smith treaded water, he looked to Larry. "This safe to drink?"

"Sure is," Larry said. "Safer than most any water anywhere. Why—"

Smith didn't care to hear more. He dropped underwater

and took a large gulp on his way back to the surface.

The Victorian woman clutched her translucent necklace in fright. "He's going to wish us away!"

Her ghost lover wasn't having any of that. He knelt down on the surface of the water and pushed Smith back down below.

That was bad. Ghosts weren't supposed to be able to do that. Then again, these ghosts could do whatever the people who wished them into existence thought they could do.

Fuck, Smith thought, drowning.

He let himself sink to the bottom of the pool, knelt down, and used all the force his legs could generate to launch himself back above the surface, where he gasped for air.

The ghost shoved him back under.

I wish there were no ghosts. I wish there were no ghosts.

And for good measure: *He's cute, but he's doomed.*

Smith repeated his routine, and launched himself toward the surface again—just as the resistance from the ghost stopped as it vanished into thin air. His mouth gaped open just in time to catch a mouthful of almonds, tossed his way by Brooks.

Smith coughed and sputtered and spat nuts into the pool. "*What are you doing?*"

"Almonds are on the list of substances that ward off ghosts," Brooks explained.

"They're also on my list of allergies, so I'm gonna die now." The last few words came out slurred, an effect of the allergic reaction caused by inadvertently swallowing nut fragments.

Brooks pulled him out of the tank and onto the walkway. "You are not."

While Smith gagged and gasped for air, Brooks opened

his briefcase, pulled out an EpiPen, and stabbed it through Smith's pants into his thigh.

"Why'd you bring that?" Smith asked.

"Why didn't you? It's part of the required toolkit *and you have an allergy*."

Smith shrugged.

Larry was still fiddling with the net. "This coin ain't budging."

"It's definitely the thing enchanting this water supply," Brooks said.

"Yeah, you think?" Smith said. "So how do we disenchant it?"

Brooks looked like a glowing lightbulb was about to appear over his head. "Wishing wells are forces of good, forces of purity... it's in the pure side of the plant, where the water is as clean as it's ever going to be... before it starts hitting lead pipes and quarry ponds. The effect gets diluted down the line, to the point where it doesn't always work. Every house has city water, not everyone's wishes are coming true..."

"Okay...?" Smith didn't follow.

"We have to make the water impure. Get that coin into the poop tanks or something..."

Smith followed. He stood on the edge of the catwalk and unzipped his fly.

"Or... we could pee in the wishing well..." Brooks reluctantly unzipped his own fly as Larry looked on in confusion and disgust. "Just keep trying to get the coin, Larry."

Like true ghost busters, Brooks and Smith didn't cross their streams. As they thinned to a trickle, Larry's net was finally able to scoop up the coin.

"Got it!" Larry said, fishing it out. "I reckon you two will be wanting this?"

"Yeah, I guess..." Brooks grabbed the pee-tainted coin

and watched it corrode in his hand.

"Make a wish," Smith said.

"You told me not to," Brooks said.

"Not something big. Just something to see if the damn coin is still working," Smith said.

Brooks thought about a wish. After a few moments of nothing happening, he made a declaration. "It doesn't work."

"Good," Smith said.

Brooks eyed the tank with a frown. "What about the water?"

Smith reached down, scooped up a handful of piss water, and drank it. After a few seconds of his wish not coming true, he spat it back out.

"Gross," Brooks said.

"It's disenchanted," Smith said.

With the pondtergeists defeated and the wishing well disenchanted, the detectives made their way back to their Pontiac Azteks. Smith opened his driver's side door and tossed his briefcase across the vehicle. As he was about to get in, he heard Brooks call out a question.

"What did you wish for?"

Smith turned to look at him. "A bigger dick."

Brooks scoffed. "*Why?*"

"What'd *you* wish for?" Smith asked.

"That's private," Brooks said.

"Uh huh." Smith's face took on a knowing look. "I looked it up. There was no cheese convention."

Brooks smiled. "No, there wasn't. See you around, Eddie."

"Edward," Smith corrected.

"I'm not calling you that," Brooks said. "I don't like it."

"It's not *your* name," Smith noted. "How would you like it if I called you Turo?"

"That's a nickname for my name, so... fine?"

"Art, then," Smith said.

"Also fine."

"Arty."

"Whatever you want," Brooks said.

"Brooksy," said Smith.

Brooks frowned.

"Aha." Smith offered a sarcastic wave as he seated himself. "Later, *Brooksy*."

Brooks opened his car door and looked back with a smirk. "It's not going to bother me as much as it bothers you, *Eddie*."

Smith's Aztek pulled away, tapped a guide rail, then backed up and pulled away again.

When he was alone, Brooks twisted the cap off a bottle of water he'd saved.

One request couldn't hurt.

TEAM-BUILDING EXERCISE

IVE BEEN HOLDING MY PEN OVER THIS PIECE OF PAPER FOR FIVE FUCKING MINUTES. AND NOW IM WRITING THIS SO MAYBE THE INSTRUCTOR WILL STOP STARING AT ME EXPECTING ME TO START WRITING SOMETHING. WORDS WORDS WORDS. WHAT KIND OF HOKEY CORPORATE BULLSHIT IS THIS ANYWAY? TEAM BUILDING EXERCISE. SURE. ~~EXPRESS YOURSELF IN FREE FORM WRITING~~ IF I WANTED TO DO THIS KIND OF STUPID SHIT I WOULD HAVE FINISHED HIGH SCHOOL. OKAY SO— ——THAT WAS LIKE HALF A MINUTE??? WERE SUPPOSED TO GO FOR FIFTEEN??? FUCK.

THOSE DONT MEAN ANYTHING. IM DRAWING DICKS BECAUSE THAT'S WHAT YOU DO WHEN YOURE FORCED TO WRITE FOR NO REASON. EITHER THAT OR THAT WEIRD S THING. HOW DID THAT GO?

THATS IT. FIVE MORE MINUTES? FIVE MORE MINUTES———— I THINK THE GENVA CONVENTION SHOULD BAN THIS KIND OF TORTURE. WRITE. WRITE. WRITE. WRITE ABOUT WHAT??? OH. BROOKSY IS ON HIS 4TH SHEET OF PAPER. OF COURSE HE IS. OVERACHIEVING POS. HES HOT. REALLY HOT. REALLY REALLY HOT. I COULD JUST KEEP WRITING REALLYS AND THIS WILL ALL BE OVER REALLY REALLY REALLY REALLY FAST. REALLY. REALLY. REALLY. ITS STARTING TO LOOK LIKE ITS NOT REALLY A WORD————

FUCK IT. HES HOT. HES FUN. HE JUST CAUGHT ME LOOKING AT HIM. IT WAS KIND OF HOT. HES TOO GOOD FOR ME. HE WILL ~~BREAK MY HEART~~ TOO GAY. NEED TO KEEP THIS CASUAL. HOT. REALLY REALLY REALLY REALLY REALLY

"Okay, now go ahead and give the paper back to the person who wrote it."

Brooks shook his head and glanced at the scribbles one last time before handing the sheet back to Smith.

LONELY SPIRITS

Brooks stared into the mirror beside his desk and corrected a misbehaving strand of hair. He made eye contact with himself and began pouring his heart out.

"Eddie... I appreciate what we have here. I really do. But the thing is—"

The doorknob rattled, and Smith walked into their office, balancing two to-go coffees between his hand and chin.

He offered Brooks one of them. "Were you just talking to yourself?"

"Yeah..." Brooks admitted, taking the cup.

"'Kay." Smith shrugged. "We've got a new case. MacGuffin's in Jersey City."

Brooks responded with a puzzled face. "Is that a word?"

Smith flopped into his office chair. It complained with a CREAK as he took a sip of coffee. "It's a dive bar. Glasses have been shattering themselves, speaker system's blown out three times, people keep spotting a specter in the men's room..."

"Has anyone died in the bar?" Brooks asked.

Smith smiled. "Nope."

"Ohh," Brooks said. "I'm into you. It. I'm into it."

"That was the worst recovery I've ever seen," Smith said.

"Guess you haven't been paying attention to the economy," said Brooks.

"Goes without saying." Smith rolled his chair closer. "What's up, Taxi Driver?"

"Ugh... I was trying to come up with a whole speech." Brooks exhaled. "The thing is... I'm sort of... falling for you."

Smith looked at him like he was stupid, and laughed in disbelief. "*Why?*"

Brooks blinked a few times. "First of all, that's a weird way to react..."

"I'm a detective. I ask questions," Smith said.

"Well... you're fun, and funny, and really good in bed."

Smith objected. "No one has ever called me *fun.*"

"I just did. I have fun when I'm with you. And... you're kind of sweet."

Smith stopped sipping his coffee to spray it across the room. "*How?*"

"You're always bringing me coffee or holding the door for me or—"

"That's not sweet. Take it back," Smith said.

"It *is* sweet," Brooks said.

"No. No. Nope." Smith shook his head. "You know what this is. Coworkers with benefits. Any time you wanna fuck, I'm game. You wanna share googly eyes over an ice cream sundae? Hard pass."

"You've dated people before, right? However short term—"

"Yeah. Never ends well," Smith said.

Brooks crossed his arms. "So, you're not opposed in principle. Just to me."

Smith muttered "goddamn it" under his breath before elaborating. "Listen. You're great, and you're gorgeous, and... if I wanted to date anyone, it'd be you. But I don't."

"Because you don't like getting hurt," Brooks said.

Smith glowered. "*I'm* not the one getting hurt in these

scenarios, chief."

"You don't want to date me because *I'll* get hurt then. Is that right?" Brooks smirked. "Kinda betraying your don't-give-a-damn attitude there."

"I can't win with you, can I?" Smith asked.

Brooks shook his head.

Smith spoke drolly. "This is sexual harassment in the workplace. I feel harassed."

"I bet." Brooks eyed him up and down. "Give me one *good* reason, and I'll drop it."

"Because. I. Said. So."

Philosophically, it was a good enough reason. But it wasn't a good enough reason for Brooks, who didn't drop the issue the entire train ride over to Jersey City. Eventually, Smith resorted to plugging his ears and saying "I can't hear you." It was very mature.

Brooks dropped it—finally—when they arrived at their assignment.

MacGuffin's was a prototypical dive bar. It occupied the ground floor of a three-story brick building built in 1892. Elaborate metal ceiling tiles hadn't been dusted in a decade. Crowding the bar were stools with punctured leather cushions held on by little rivets. TVs were tuned to every New Jersey and New York sport in existence, including Jersey Shore Roller Derby, the non-Springsteen pride of Asbury Park. A pool table in the corner had been ruined by the moisture rings of thousands of beers. There were dining tables for anyone who came for the food. No one ever did, and half the tables still had chairs resting upside down atop them from the last time the dining area had been cleaned—sometime during the Clinton Administration, probably.

Brooks and Smith made their way to the bar. They were tall enough to get the bartender's attention ahead of several short people who'd been waiting for a while. The height-challenged individuals scowled as the detectives brushed by them.

The bartender was a bartender in the classic sense. An elderly man with mutton chops, a vest, and a bowtie. Brooks and Smith exchanged confused glances, having expected something a bit more New Jersey.

"What can I get for youse guys?" the bartender asked. "Jäger-bombs?"

"There it is," Brooks muttered under his breath.

"We're here about your alleged ghost," Smith said.

He and Brooks flashed vaguely authoritative badges, which contained little more than a bunch of lorem ipsum text. No one ever challenged them because no one likes reading.

"Youse picked the right night," the bartender said. "Trivia starts in an hour. Ghosty boy tends to pop up 'round eight or nine. You want somethin' to eat 'til then, I can get youse some fried mutz balls or rippers."

"No thanks," Brooks said.

"You said he shows up during trivia night," Smith said. "Anyone ever died during that?"

The bartender shook his head. "Not that I've ever seen."

"How long have you been working here?" Brooks asked.

"Forty-five years next month."

"But the haunting is new?" Brooks asked.

"Oh, yeah," the bartender said. "Nothin' for forty-four years and eight months. Then BOO. We got a spook. I'm gettin' real tired of pickin' up broken glass, I'll tell you that."

"Have any new employees started lately?" Smith asked.

"Nah, it's just me an' Lucy in the kitchen, like always."

"Either of you lose anyone close to you recently?" Smith asked.

The bartender shook his head. "Nope. I'd know since me an' Luce have been schtuppin' for twenty years."

"You mind if we check out the bathroom?" Smith asked.

"Knock yourselves out," the bartender said.

Brooks and Smith left the bar. The bartender ignored the 5'4" patron who'd been standing next to them and went to serve someone seated at the other end of the bar.

The restroom looked like a dive bar restroom. Where they weren't covered in graffiti or stickers, the walls were green, as were the tiles on the floor—though those were supposed to be white. There were two urinals and two stalls, against opposite walls. Next to the urinals was a lone, sad pedestal sink with a pristine bottle of soap sitting unused next to the tap. Above it, a vandalized and cracked mirror. Next to it, a broken paper towel dispenser that didn't detect motion as promised.

Smith fiddled with the side of the dispenser until a wrinkled clump of paper towel emerged. He ripped it from the dispenser and grabbed a permanent marker from an inner jacket pocket. He scribbled 'CLOSED FOR CLEANING' on the sheet, wedged it into the gap between the door and frame, and closed the door to secure it.

"Here, ghost ghost ghost," Smith said, like he was calling a dog.

Nothing happened.

Brooks opened each stall door and found nothing but stank.

"This is a weird one," he said. "Ghosts are usually bound to a place, right?"

"Yep," Smith said.

Brooks continued. "But no one died here—"

Smith corrected himself. "Well—"

"Well, what?" Brooks asked.

"Sometimes they're bound to an object. That's why I

asked about new employees, in case some kitchen rat brought it in on a bracelet or something."

"A customer could have left something behind," Brooks suggested.

"Could have, but you'd think whatever it was, they'd have come back to claim it." Ghosts generally haunted items with meaning, after all.

"People keep seeing him in here," Brooks said, pondering the men's room.

"People *think* they're seeing something in here," Smith corrected.

Brooks had an idea, and reopened one of the stalls. He lifted the tank lid to see if anything had been dropped inside the back of the toilet.

Smith caught on and checked the toilet in the other stall.

"Nice thought," Smith said. "Nothing here, though."

"Nothing here either." Brooks sighed.

"Haunted urinal cake?" Smith suggested.

"Maybe." Brooks grabbed the cake from the only urinal that had one, tossed it in the sink, and started running the water, as hot as it would run. He nearly boiled his hands off cleaning urinal cake crumbs from them.

Smith tisk-tisked and pretended to chastise him. "You know, there's a drought in California."

Brooks tilted his head, unamused.

Smith grinned. "Anyway. We've got almost an hour 'til this ghost shows up for trivia. I can think of a few ways to pass the time..."

Brooks rebuffed him. "No. We're not done talking about what this is."

"I am," Smith said.

Brooks crossed his arms.

"What do you want me to say?" Smith offered a pretend sniffle and made his voice soft and dramatic as he looked into his partner's eyes. "You've changed me, Brooksy. I never wanted to date anyone until I met you. Now I can't imagine life without you." His voice returned to normal as he scoffed. "Please."

Brooks didn't say a word. He marched across the room into a stall and latched it shut.

"Oh, for fuck's sa—" Smith stopped himself when he heard soft sobbing. "Sorry. I didn't think it was that serious you were gonna cry about it..."

"That's not me, asshole." Brooks emerged from his stall and tucked his phone into his pocket. "I was rage-texting my cousin Jenn—"

Smith was briefly taken aback. "You told your cousin about me?"

Brooks hushed him.

The pair stood, eyeing the now-latched door of the next stall over. From within came more sniffling.

Brooks peeked under the door. "There's no one in there."

Smith kicked the door open, breaking the latch and revealing that there was someone. Sort of.

A ghost sat on the back of the toilet, its feet on the bowl and its arms wrapped around its legs. It was a presumably male figure, somewhat transparent. Its visibility flickered from invisible to faint to lifelike, over and over, in no particular order. The spirit's face was hidden as it sobbed into its knees, but the attire seemed to show it hadn't been dead long. The ghost was the pinnacle of early-2000s fashion, with a trucker hat, a patchwork denim jacket, and a pair of checkered Vans.

The ghost didn't acknowledge the men. It just kept sobbing into its legs.

"Hello?" Brooks asked.

Nothing.

Smith was brasher, and mimicked the bartender. "Hey! Ghosty boy!"

The ghost looked up, despondent—a youthful face in its early twenties, with big sad eyes. In a bit of misfortune, this young man had died while sporting a soul patch. But that just meant he'd had bad taste. His current form was a far cry from an evil specter smashing glasses and terrorizing patrons.

"Are you okay?" Brooks asked.

The ghost shook its head no.

"What's your name?" Brooks asked.

"Tyler," said the ghost.

Brooks knelt to meet Tyler at eye level. "What's going on, Tyler?"

"My best friend is dead," Tyler sobbed.

"*You're* dead," Smith said.

"Really dead," Tyler explained. "My bro Ashton and me used to come here every Wednesday for trivia night, and then he stopped showing up. I found out someone *exorcised him*."

"Was he possessing someone?" Smith asked.

The ghost was confused. "No?"

"Not an exorcism, then," said Smith.

"I don't care what you call it," Tyler said. "He was around, then he got hit with a bunch of sage and now he's gone." He broke into uncontrolled sobs.

"How'd you find out this happened?" Brooks asked.

"I went back to the frat house and the new pledges were *laughing* about it."

Brooks and Smith shared a look. Ghosts weren't supposed to travel.

"Where and how did you die?" Brooks asked.

Tyler told the story of his death. "Ashton and me were at the house one night, and we heard about something called boofing."

"What's that?" Brooks asked.

Smith knew. "Butt chugging. What'd you shoot up there that it killed you?"

"Absinthe. Like... a lot."

Smith shook his head. "Tyler, man..."

"I know, bro. We were stupid. Anyway, once we started ghosting around, we realized we could be anywhere there's alcohol."

Smith chuckled. "So you were spirit spirits."

Brooks frowned at the joke.

Tyler didn't get the joke because Tyler was an idiot. "We mostly hung around the frat house watching them like it was reality TV or something. But we liked hanging out in bars too, y'know. We were soul mates, but like... no homo. Wednesdays were trivia night. 'Til they killed him." He broke into tears again.

"So you're haunting this place because your best friend died," Brooks said.

"I didn't mean to haunt anything," Tyler said. "I'm just, like... it's real lonely now. I try to grab a drink with people but they either can't see me or they do see me and scream and then I shatter a glass. I've met a few other ghosts at some bars, but they're all boomers or whatever. None of them wanna be bros. Some dude from 18-whatever hit me with a coal shovel."

Brooks stood and conferred with his partner. "He's just grieving."

"By the book, we should still get rid of him," Smith said.

"You don't work by the book," Brooks noted.

"No. I don't," Smith said. "I'm with you. No reason to kill this kid again."

Tyler stood up and stared at them. "You can un-ghost me?"

"Umm..." Brooks didn't know how to answer that.

"No," Smith said. "You're dead. You're always gonna be dead. The only thing we can do is force your spirit to move on to... whatever."

Brooks added, "It might be heaven. It might be hell."

"It might be *nothing*," Smith said. "Whatever it is, it's beyond our pay grade."

"That's where Ashton went?" Tyler asked.

"I guess," Smith said.

Tyler stood with full posture, for once. "Exorcise me, bros."

"It's not an exorc—" Smith started, before he was cut off.

"Are you sure?" Brooks asked. "You don't need some time to think about this? You're talking about forever."

Tyler shook his head. "Nah. I'm good."

"Okay..." Brooks didn't feel great about it as he removed some sage from his pocket to begin the banishing ritual.

Tyler reassured him. "It's chill. When you know, you know. You know?"

Brooks glanced at Smith.

Smith noticed and looked away.

Brooks lit the sage and waved it around Tyler. The ghost coughed a little.

Smith recited some Latin he'd memorized over the years. "*Abjicimus te, molestus spiritus, omnem spiritum potentiae, omnem incursum hostis invisibilis, omnem legionem, omnem mortis partem—*" Before he'd even finished, Tyler vanished—his spirit eager to move on. Smith saw him off. "Good luck, kid."

Brooks went misty-eyed.

"You okay?" Smith asked.

"Yeah." Brooks tossed the singed sage bundle into the toilet and flushed. "It's just kind of sweet."

"You and I have *very* different definitions of sweet," said Smith.

"I know we do," Brooks said, "but they had a bond so strong that he was happy to *die* for the smallest chance of seeing his best friend again. It's sad, but it's kind of sweet."

Smith took a deep breath. "Listen... about this thing... us..."

"It's fine," Brooks said. "You don't have to lie to me because I'm ghost sad—"

"You want to do this again sometime?" Smith asked.

"What? Euthanize a ghost?" Brooks asked.

Smith stared at him. "I mean... go out to a bar or something."

"Are you serious?" Brooks asked.

"I am," Smith said.

Brooks beamed. "Trivia night starts in twenty minutes."

Smith's stomach sank as he answered. "It's a date."

SLEEP TIGHT

TAP TAP turned into TAP TAP TAP, which turned into TAPTAPTAPTAPTAP. Brooks stood at the door to Smith's apartment, tapping away. Their dates had become a regular occurrence, and Smith not answering the door was irregular. Brooks pulled out his cell phone and gave his partner's number a call.

From the other side of the door, Smith's ringtone blared. A nu metal cover of "Unchained Melody" by the Cleveland-based band Trashmouth.

Brooks's stomach sank. First, because the song was terrible. Then because Smith was home. He was right there, just a few feet away, and he wasn't answering the door or his phone. Something was wrong, and in their line of work that something was usually death.

The lock on the door was a pin pad. Four digits.

Brooks tried Smith's birthday. 1204. Nope. His birth year. 1976. Not it. He sighed and tried 6969. That wasn't it either. Nor were 0000, 1111, or 1234, which account for twenty-percent of four-digit passwords in the world.* Brooks tried 2001, for the space odyssey. He tried 7777, but had no luck there.

No luck...

Brooks thought like a contrarian. The opposite of good luck. 1313.

---

* This is a fact. Try it sometime!

The lock beeped, and Brooks pressed into the room. "Eddie?"

His eyes were drawn downward.

Smith's body lay sprawled in the middle of the floor, in an awkward pose somewhere between being face-down and being on his side.

Brooks dropped to his knees and checked Smith's neck for a pulse. It was palpable.

The Reticent forced its agents to take some basic medical training, but they weren't doctors. Brooks dialed 911, put the phone on speaker, and tossed it on the floor next to him so he could get an ambulance on its way ASAP.

While he gave an emergency dispatcher the address and what little information he knew, Brooks rolled Smith onto his back. He was breathing and not bleeding from anywhere. A good start. No surprise incontinence. Brooks snapped his fingers in front of Smith's face a few times, hoping for a reaction. Nothing. He opened Smith's eyelids because he'd seen people on TV do that, but he didn't know what he was looking for. The eyes looked the same as ever. The pupils might have been smaller, but Brooks wasn't sure. In any case, they didn't respond. He rolled Smith back onto his side, into what loosely counted as a recovery position. Then he waited, in agony. Sure, last night was great, but if it was the last night they ever had together... that would be some bullshit.

It was only seven minutes from the time he dialed to when two paramedics came through the door. They asked questions as they loaded Smith onto a stretcher.

"How long has he been like this?"

"I, uh... I don't know. I called as soon as I found him," Brooks said.

"Any drug use?"

Brooks shook his head. "I don't think so... I mean, he's

done some stuff in the past, but..."

"Are you family?"

"No. We're, uh... coworkers," Brooks said.

"Okay. We're going to Presby, if you know anyone to contact."

"Okay..." Brooks stood still, gazing at the doorway long after they were gone.

The sudden sound of the icemaker in Smith's fridge snapped him to.

Treat it like a case. What knocks people out cold? Not ghosts. A vampire could, but then it probably would have bitten him. No wounds. Could have pissed off a witch, but we haven't seen any of those lately. Poison? Poison seems plausible...

Brooks started poking around the kitchen, invading Smith's privacy.

There's nothing to eat or drink here. Not poison. Unless...

Something the paramedic had said gave him an idea. Brooks went into the bathroom and opened the medicine cabinet. He let out a gasp.

There were some over-the-counter allergy meds and co-deine-infused cough syrup, and an herbal supplement la-beled entirely in Chinese, with a tasteful watercolor depic-tion of an eggplant. Brooks could imagine what that was supposed to do. Everything else was in orange prescrip-tion bottles, and there was a lot of 'everything else.'

Brooks started rotating and reading vials. Only three had ever been prescribed to Smith. Those were a full bottle of Paxil, a half-full bottle of Ambien, and a handful of expired Percocets left over from some dental surgery or another. The remaining prescriptions—Vicodin, Adderall, Xanax, Ativan, and Valium—had strangers' names on them. One had no label at all and was filled with colorful tablets im-pressed with the images of smiley faces and butterflies. Ec-stasy, based on what Brooks knew from college. His face warmed as he muttered to himself.

"You goddamned idiot..."

Sometime later, Brooks stormed into a hospital room, furious.

"*What the fuck, Eddie*?"

Smith looked up from a copy of *Pretend You Like Sports* magazine. "Hi. Nice to see you too."

Brooks approached the bed and loomed over his partner. "Seriously. *What the fuck*?"

"Okay..." Smith sat up straight and scratched at an IV on his arm. "I'm hospitalized and you're swearing like you're me. What'd I do?"

"I don't know. I'm guessing some combo of all the shit in your medicine cabinet. *You tell me*."

Smith's face scrunched. "I didn't take anything."

"Sure." Brooks made a short, sarcastic nod as he said it.

"*I didn't*." Smith reconsidered that. "Well... I took a Chinese boner pill, but I do that every time you come over."

"I don't believe you," Brooks said.

Smith laughed. "You should."

"What *else* did you take?"

"Nothing," Smith said. "Why's that so hard to believe?"

"Because addicts lie?"

"Well, yeah. But I'm not," said Smith.

"Not an addict or not lying?"

Smith stared into his eyes with more than a little annoyance. "I'm not lying. Doctors didn't find shit. No evidence of heart attack or stroke. No brain trauma. Piss test was clean."

Brooks seated himself on the edge of the hospital bed. "Then what happened?"

"I don't know. I was pacing back and forth, trying to figure out if I forgot anything. You know, deodorant check... do I need a mint... then everything goes blue."

Brooks stared at him like he was stupid. "*Blue?*"

"Yeah. Eiffel 65 blue. Blue Man Group blue. Like the whole world had a filter on it. Next thing I know, I'm here," Smith said.

"If you're trying to convince me you weren't high, it's not working," Brooks said.

"How do we feel about alien abductions?" Smith wondered.

Brooks deadpanned. "Not great, Mulder."

Smith scoffed. "Dead sister. Weirdly enthusiastic. If anyone here's Mulder, it's you."

"Um, no. I'm Catholic and skeptical of your bullshit. I'm Scully."

"Yeah, you are the hot one..." Smith shook his head to refocus, and crossed his arms. "Believe me or don't. I get to leave in four hours. I'm gonna go home and start researching blue roofie monsters."

"Okay..."

"Okay?" Smith's eyes shifted back and forth. "Sure you don't wanna yell some more?"

"I don't know if I believe you, but I'm going with you, and I'm staying over," Brooks said.

He didn't, he did, and he did. In that order.

Brooks brought an overnight bag for the occasion, loaded with books from The Reticent's library of paranormal texts that hadn't yet been scanned into Reti-net. Everything remotely related to sleep. He set the heavy bag on the floor and stretched his sore arms.

"I swear, if I carried all this and it turns out to be Ambien—"

Smith's voice became angry. "I told you I didn't take

anything."

"Then throw it all out," Brooks said.

"*No.*"

"Why not? Could it be... because you've been using them?"

"Because *fuck off* is why. Whatever this is—" Smith pointed a finger at his partner, then back at himself. "—we've been doing it for like a month and a half. You don't get to make demands. If you don't trust me, there's the door." He pointed. It was still open.

Brooks's voice dripped with sarcasm. "Oh, I can't imagine why all your relationships have failed."

Smith pointed again. "Door."

"No," Brooks said, defiant.

"You're so annoying," Smith said.

"And you're afraid to be vulnerable," Brooks said.

"Okay, Dr. Phil," Smith said.

Brooks threw up a hand. "*See?*"

Smith flopped onto his recliner. "Tell me more, oh wise man who's known me for a few months."

Brooks unironically thought back to all the episodes of *Dr. Phil* he'd watched. He sat on the coffee table and observed his partner. "You push people away so they can't leave you. That way it was your call, not theirs. I've had a read on that since day one. Probably comes from all the foster families."

Smith snapped back. "Then *why are you here,* if you know I'm a worthless piece of shit?"

"That's not what I said. At all." Brooks eyed him with concern. "And you're doing it again. I'm here because I think you're great. I love spending time with you, and I'm worried about you... I..."

Brooks swayed a little.

Smith squinted, waiting for the end of that sentence.

"You *what?*"

"I... um..." Brooks braced himself on the table as Smith's face became a blue haze.

He awoke on the floor, with Smith behind him, holding him in a seated position.

Brooks leaned forward. "What just happened?"

"You were speeching and you passed out. Bonked your head on the table."

Brooks felt at a sore spot on his forehead, then looked at his hand. There was blood. "How long was I out?"

"About two minutes," Smith said.

Brooks pulled himself forward and turned to face his partner.

"I believe you," he declared.

"About...?"

"Everything was blue. Next thing I know, I'm on the floor," Brooks said.

"Glad we're on the same page," Smith said, "but you lost two minutes. I lost hours."

"Yeah. That part is weird," Brooks said.

"The whole thing is weird." Smith stood and headed toward the bathroom. "I'm gonna grab the first aid kit."

"I'll come with you." Brooks rose from the ground.

Smith snorted. "Yeah. You believe me. That's why I need a chaperone."

"*In case one of us passes out again,*" Brooks said.

There was no furniture in Smith's living room other than the recliner and coffee table, so when Brooks had patched himself up, the detectives changed into sleepwear and settled in on Smith's bed—more accurately, a mattress on the floor—with laptops and a pile of books.

Brooks looked up from one. "You think it could be an incubus or succubus?"

"I think if it was, we'd have woken up with boners,"

Smith said.

"If it were a succubus, *I* wouldn't have, but... fair point," Brooks said.

"Maybe the Sandman is real," Smith suggested.

That gave Brooks an idea. "What did you dream about while you were out?"

"I don't remember anything."

"Me neither," Brooks said. "That's weird..."

"Is it?" Smith shot him a skeptical look. "You were out for *two minutes.*"

"No, I mean it's weird for you. You're always waking up sweating and flailing. I assumed your dreams were pretty memorable."

Smith glowered. "*Generally.*"

"Do you have any dreamcatchers in your apartment?" Brooks asked.

"Yeah, right next to my bongos and incense. No, I don't have any fucking dreamcatchers."

"Don't scoff. We have nothing to narrow it down. This is going to take forever."

It wasn't forever, but it felt like it. An hour later, Smith was fast asleep with a book about dreamcatchers on his chest. Brooks was slumped forward, drooling onto a copy of *Meiji Period Folklore.*

Brooks awoke first, and wiped his mouth on his sleeve. He shoved a few books aside so he could scoot next to his partner. "Eddie. Wake up."

His plea worked as well as it had before, which is to say... it didn't. Brooks waited almost an hour for Smith to rouse.

Smith awoke with a confused look. "Did you fall asleep too?"

"Yeah... at least this time it was on a bed."

"You see anything?" Smith asked.

"No...? Did you?"

"I dreamed about an anteater," Smith said. "I think. I've never seen an anteater in my life."

"An anteater..." Brooks had a revelation. "Was it blue?"

"Yeah." Smith wasn't sure where he was going with this.

"I saw something like that..." Brooks returned to his *Meiji Period Folklore* and flipped to a specific page. "Did it look like this?"

Smith leaned over to see a drawing of the world's angriest blue anteater, with a set of sharp tusks at the sides of its snout. "Yeah. What's that?"

"It's a baku. They're said to eat nightmares," Brooks said.

"And I'm an all-you-can-eat buffet," Smith said. "So what's the catch? How's it kill me?"

Brooks shook his head. "There isn't any. It doesn't. By all accounts, baku are beneficial to humans. But... they're supposed to come while you're asleep, not *make* you fall asleep..."

"What's that symbol?" Smith pointed at the book.

獏

"I don't know," Brooks said. "I only speak English and Spanish."

"I've seen it before. Maybe on a manga cover?"

"On a..." Brooks realized how big a nerd he'd been fucking. "Wait. No."

"No?" Smith wondered.

Brooks hopped off the bed and headed for the bathroom. He swung open the medicine cabinet and grabbed the bottle of eggplant pills.

Smith, who'd followed close behind, cleared his throat. "Is that what we're doing now?"

Brooks shoved the bottle at him. "Look."

There it was, right across the tasteful eggplant:

獏

"Same symbol," Smith said.

"Yeah." Brooks took the bottle back and snapped a few pictures of it with his phone. He texted them to The Reticent's Translation department.

Smith snarled. "You've been dead set on blaming me all day. For all we know, it's a symbol for the word 'the.'"

A response came:

Baku Food
Take 1 per day to summon baku
Eats bad dreams
Eggplant Flavor
Caution: Taking more than 1 may cause drowsiness.

Brooks showed Smith his phone.

"Goddamn it," Smith said.

"How many did you take?" Brooks asked.

Smith threw his hands up. "In my defense, I couldn't read it..."

"How many?" Brooks demanded.

"Four," Smith admitted.

"Jesus Christ, Eddie."

Smith crossed his arms in a huff. "*Sorry I wanted to fuck you good.*"

Brooks ignored him and kept fiddling with the bottle. "There's one thing I don't get."

"What?" Smith asked.

"I got the blue knockout experience, but I didn't take any..."

"No, but I can think of how some might have gotten in your system." Smith smirked.

Brooks cringed. "*Gross.*"

"Not what you said at the time."

"Well, that would explain why I was barely knocked out and you were gone for hours."

"Different dosage," Smith said.

"Ugh," Brooks said. "I knew you had skeletons in your closet, but I didn't think they'd end up roofying me."

Feeling like he owed Brooks after causing so much research and despair, Smith sighed. "You wanna know what's in my closet?"

Brooks blinked. "It's a figure of speech..."

"I know," Smith said, "but let me show you something."

Brooks shot him a suspicious look.

"It's not my dick," Smith assured him.

Smith escorted Brooks back to the bedroom and yanked at his closet door. After a few pulls, the stiff door lurched open and there was a CLANK as contents somewhere inside the closet shifted.

There were no skeletons, but the tiny space was stuffed to the brim. The only three suits Smith owned hung askew, their bottoms contorted by the dozens of boxes beneath them. The bottom half of the closet was nothing but boxes, in sizes ranging from microwave box to shoe box. Hanging next to the suits were plastic grocery bags, their contents distorting the bags' shapes into all sorts of odd curves and angles. At the top of the closet, on a wire shelf, were some unboxed items. A pair of ice skates. An old lamp. A 1992 high school yearbook. Controllers from all three generations of PlayStations.

"You're a hoarder?" Brooks asked.

"I'm not a hoarder." Smith seated himself on the edge of the bed. "Go ahead and look through anything you want. I'm an open book."

Brooks poked around in some of the hanging bags. There were miscellaneous cables, dozens of BIC lighters, bobby pins, safety pins, duct tape, plastic Tupperware containers...

"It still looks like you're a hoarder." Brooks gave up and sat next to Smith. "I don't get it."

"You know how hobos push around all their useless shit?" Smith explained. "When you've been poor... I mean... really poor... not knowing if you're gonna eat poor... you learn not to throw anything away. Cause you might not ever get it again." Smith kept his eyes on the floor as he continued. "I'm not using all that shit in my medicine cabinet. I'm just not throwing anything away."

"You're not using *all of it?*" Brooks wondered, rightly suspicious.

"Not that it's any of your business, *at all*, but... I haven't taken uppers in years. I'm supposed to be taking the Paxil, but I'm not 'cause it sucks. I'm supposed to be taking the Ambien, but I'm not 'cause it sucks even worse. But... I'll cop to poppin' benzos when the situation calls for it."

"The situation?"

"I don't sleep great, in case you hadn't noticed," Smith said. "Reticent docs won't give me anything else, so I make do."

"You know that stuff probably makes you feel worse," Brooks said.

"A man's gotta sleep."

"Okay," Brooks said. A look of determination came over his face. "Get under the covers."

"I'm not tired," Smith said.

"I didn't ask," Brooks said.

While Smith obliged, Brooks walked over to the light switch and flipped it. He stepped around to the other side of the mattress, sat next to where Smith lay, and pulled out his cell phone.

"What are you doing?" Smith asked.

"Roll over and relax."

With Smith facing away from the glow of the cell phone, Brooks began reading from Wikipedia. "The traditional Japanese nightmare-devouring baku originates in Chinese folklore about the mo (Giant panda) and was familiar in Japan as early as the Muromachi period. Hori Tadao has described the dream-eating abilities attributed to the traditional baku and relates them to other preventatives against nightmare, such as amulets. Kaii-Yōkai Denshō Database, citing a 1957 paper, and Mizuki also describe the dream-devouring capacities of the traditional baku—"

A soft snoring sound let Brooks know he could stop.

CHANGELINGS

Rehoboth Beach, Delaware is a premier East Coast destination for members of the LGBTQ community. Its shores were surprisingly lightly populated on a late-July day, as Brooks and Smith patrolled the boardwalk looking for any sign of changelings.

In their natural state, changelings were pale, noseless creatures about four feet tall. As their name suggests, they could change their appearance to take the form of any person. Something about compressing, expanding, and recomposing the molecules that comprised their bodies. There was no way to tell, at any given time, who might be a changeling. The only tells were either witnessing them shift or catching them in the act of harvesting human kidneys.

One could also look for their nest. Changelings lived in groups of three or more, near sources of salt water, which they drank to stay alive. They also did their kidney harvesting in it. And their breeding. Everything, really. Typically, changelings lived under piers or in grottos. On occasion, they could be found sipping piña coladas under a palapa in the Caribbean.

Several corpses had washed up on Rehoboth Beach, each missing their kidneys. Under interrogation from the police, one beachgoer claimed to have spotted something under the boardwalk. The investigation went nowhere. That led The Reticent to send Brooks and Smith to the gay destination, in what Brooks considered to be an act of homophobia.

Changelings weren't the only thing that had been spotted. As the detectives walked, Smith in particular was on the receiving end of some lecherous glances.

He griped. "What are they looking at?"

"*You*," Brooks said.

Smith let out a doubtful laugh.

"Why is that so hard to believe?" Brooks asked.

"Because you're standing right there," Smith said. "Are they racist or blind?" He noticed yet another man eyeing his shorts and defensively grabbed Brooks's hand.

Brooks chuckled at his partner's annoyance.

Smith harrumphed. Of all places, he figured they would have blended in here. "I don't like being noticed. You start getting noticed, next thing you're changeling chow."

"Good thing there aren't any changelings here then," said Brooks. They'd scoured the beach and found precisely zero evidence of any nests.

"No changelings yet—" Smith swatted at his head "—but if I see one more goddamn bee—"

"Bees are good," Brooks said.

"The fuck they are."

"You need bees to pollinate crops. No bees, no food." Brooks refocused. "But without a nest, how are we supposed to find the monsters eating people's kidneys?"

"The old-fashioned way. Interrogating yokels 'til they rat out the weirdos," Smith said.

"You have such a way with words," Brooks said.

"You mean I'm—"

"*No.*"

"—a wordsmith."

Brooks groaned. "Where do you want to go next?"

Smith grinned. He knew just where to find some yokels.

ₑ

Smith stared at the menu board, flummoxed. He and Brooks were seated at a bar lit by dangling Edison bulbs. Behind the bartender was a similarly lit sign that read 'EAT' and a chalkboard listing fifteen different beer options. Salty Knob brew pub was the hottest place in town to grab a drink, but Smith couldn't find anything resembling a drink on the menu.

"Where's the beer?" he asked.

"They're all beer," Brooks said.

Among the beers were 69-Minute IPA, Legalize Witbier, Slam Bam Dunkel Ma'am, Saison d'Etre, Kölsch Money Millionaires, Aft Stern Starboard Porter, Dream a Little Cream Ale Me, Three Bitter Exes, and Casper the Friendly Gose.*

Not knowing what any of it meant, Smith ordered the 69-Minute IPA.

Knowing exactly what all of it meant, Brooks ordered gin.

The bartender was too busy slinging drinks to entertain their questions about murder, but the patron seated next to Brooks was several dunkels deep and very willing to talk.

"They ruined my business," he lamented, slurring.

"Who did?" Brooks asked.

"The kidney snatchers. I own an inn a few blocks over. One of the corpses turned up in the bathtub of my best room. Now no one wants to book."

"In the bathtub?" Brooks wondered. The report only

---

* At the time of writing, none of these were actual craft beers. They probably all are now.

noted bodies found on the beach.

The innkeeper nodded. "Yeah. The bathtub."

"Was it full or empty?" Brooks asked.

"Full," the innkeeper said through a hiccup. "It was a bloated mess."

The bartender returned with an IPA and a gin.

Smith took a sip of his beer and spat it back into the glass. His face wrinkled with disgust. "It's like drinking a gingerbread man's cum."

Brooks ignored that. "When have you ever known a changeling to leave a body in a bathtub?"

"Never," Smith said. "Unless your crappy inn has salt water running through its pipes."

Confused and slightly offended, the innkeeper shook his head. "It's city water."

"You mind if we come by and take a look at the room?" Brooks asked.

"Be my guest," said the innkeeper. "*Please.*"

The murder room seemed perfectly normal. Each room at the Sea Dew Inn was themed after a color. This one—the Purple Room—lived up to its name. The walls were lilac, while the curtains and bedspread were a darker eggplant. Everything in between—from the lamps to the bedposts to the accent rug—was gold. Very regal. Very tacky.

Something other than the interior design didn't sit right with Brooks.

"Did we have to rent the murder room?" he asked.

Smith shrugged. "The man needs money."

As they discussed the matter, they made their way into the bathroom.

"Sure, but we could have rented *any other room*," Brooks

said, inspecting the golden tub.

"Where's the fun in that?" Smith paused. "What, you afraid of ghosts now?"

"No. It's just... gauche."

Smith turned on the tap and ran a finger under it. He brought the finger to his mouth and came to a conclusion. "Tap water. Not salt."

"We're a few blocks from the beach," Brooks said. "That would be a lot of salt water to tote."

Smith swatted at his head, distracted. "Maybe it's not the murder. Maybe no one wants to book *because of the bees.*" One had somehow made its way into the room. As the swatting continued, it buzzed away in irritation.

Brooks focused on the case. "I don't think there are changelings here. There's no reason they'd come this far and kill someone in a hotel room when they could do it on the beach and let the tide carry the bodies away."

"What are you thinking?" Smith wondered. "Organ trafficking?"

"Maybe... but in that case, you usually don't find the bodies."

"Sloppy work," Smith said.

The room phone rang, and Smith was the first to reach it. On the other end, the drunk innkeeper mumbled something about "another ova shore stillive gibba hobidal."

Smith spoke fluent drunk. He hung up and explained. "Another body turned up. Alive. We need to check the hospital." He swatted at the air. "*And an exterminator.*"

In front of the hospital, there were dozens of bees. Here, at least, it made sense. The hospital had a large, tasteful flowerbed that made illness and death more aesthetically pleasing.

The detectives made their way inside and faked their way into the room where an unfortunate young woman was hooked up to dialysis.

An irritated nurse was changing out some tubing and didn't want them there.

"Come back later," she said.

They quickly flashed some fake badges, and Smith spoke before she could read them. "We need to speak with the patient about an ongoing criminal investigation."

"Good luck with that," the nurse said. "Even when she's awake, the patient is out of her mind."

Brooks raised an eyebrow. "Out of her mind how?"

"She won't stop rambling about being abducted by aliens. Little grey men. She said they were still in the room with her when I was the only one here."

"Where did they find her?" Smith asked.

"The aliens?" the nurse asked.

Smith clarified, "Whoever reported the body."

"You're detectives, aren't you?" the nurse asked. "Shouldn't you know?"

"We're corroborating stories," Brooks lied.

"Some hotel near the beach. The Sea-Doo Inn, I think?"

The innkeeper hadn't mentioned that this woman was also found at his hotel.

The detectives shared a concerned glance.

Soon, they were hovering over the front desk at the Sea Dew Inn, intimidating its drunk owner.

"Who rented the room?" Smith demanded. He leaned over the counter with a ready-to-fight attitude.

"You twoda only ones who... renta adything..."

"At least two people have had their kidneys removed *right under your nose*, and you have no idea who might be doing it? In an empty hotel?" Brooks shook his head. "I find that hard to believe."

Smith squinted at something behind the desk. An unlabeled jug of murky brown liquid. "What's that?" He stretched forward, grabbed it and uncapped it. He immediately regretted that.

A potent smell assaulted the air, akin to the smell of earthworms lying on the sidewalk after a heavy rain. Mixed with diesel.

"Oh my God," Brooks said, choking a little.

"Hey," the innkeeper complained. "Dasma ayahuasca."

"Can you translate?" Brooks asked.

"Ayahuasca. He's not drunk. Dude's tripping balls," Smith said.

"You think he's attacking people?" Brooks asked.

"No..." Smith held the jug in the innkeeper's line of sight. "Where'd you get this?"

"Guests a cupla weeksago," the innkeeper said.

"We need to see their records," Brooks said.

The innkeeper motioned at a file cabinet. Then he became hyperfocused on a bee, got dizzy, and passed out.

Carrying stacks of non-digitized records, Brooks and Smith made their way back to the Purple Room for a night of heavy research.

They were spared by a scream coming from down the hallway. It only came once.

Smith turned to Brooks. "No other guests, huh?"

They dropped the files and hurried into the Green Room.

The room was dark, but a beam of light came from the cracked bathroom door. Smith swatted another bee away and pushed the door open. The detectives marched into the bathroom. There, they found a young vacationer lying in a bathtub full of bloody ice water. Very dead. Looming above were two heavyset mobsters, one tucking two kidneys into an organ transport box.

"Ugh, it's just the mob," Brooks said.

Because it was the mob, one of the men pulled a gun and aimed it squarely at Smith.

Brooks tackled his partner to the ground, taking a bullet to his right arm in the process.

Smith freaked, for various reasons. One was that a swarm of bees buzzed past his head, toward the organ trafficking mobsters. Hundreds of them, and they'd seemingly come from nowhere.

"*What the fuck?*" Smith said.

The bees moved with intention toward the criminals, and began stinging.

"*What the fuck?*" Smith repeated.

Brooks and Smith looked on from the floor as the gangsters flailed their arms around, batting some bees away and being stung by others. Their skin began to bubble and puff, inflamed by thousands of stings. At almost the same time, they collapsed to the ground, gasping and grasping at their necks as they tried to breathe through swollen throats.

They failed, and each mobster shut his eyes for the last time.

The bees happily buzzed away, flying over the detectives and out the door.

Smith sat on the floor, looking like he'd seen a ghost rather than a swarm of bees stinging people to death. "*What the fuck?*"

"You okay?" Brooks leaned closer.

Smith leaned back, away from him. "Don't ever do that again."

"Do what?" Brooks glanced down at his arm and took an annoyed tone. "Yes. *I'm fine.* Thanks for asking."

Smith stared at the shallow, bleeding divot across Brooks's bicep. "That."

Brooks eyed his own wound. "That's nothing. It's barely grazed. You want me to let you get shot next time?"

"Yes," Smith said, completely in earnest.

Brooks chuckled at the absurdity of that. "No."

"I'm serious. Don't—Ughhh—"

Two bees buzzed around in front of Smith's face. He swatted at them, and the bees moved to hover over the Green Room's green bed.

Both men watched in confusion as the bees came together and merged into one larger bee. That bee expanded, first to a fuzzy flying lump the size of a softball. The lump fell to the bed, and grew again. The wings and hairs became absorbed into a growing, pulsating mass of grey flesh.

The detectives stood and readied their guns as the mass continued to grow. For a moment, it looked like a changeling—or an alien, if you were a hallucinating victim of kidney theft—but it continued growing until it was the size of an adult man. Twisting and warping, the skin began emitting human hair and cotton cloth. Soon, their drunken innkeeper sat on the edge of the bed, looking down the barrels of two guns.

"Please don't kill me," he said.

"We may or may not," Brooks said. "But you can tell us what's going on."

"I'm not the innkeeper," the changeling explained, in an almost exact impersonation of the innkeeper's voice.

"He's high on ayahuasca right now. I just thought this would be a friendlier face..."

"We know what you are," Smith said.

"A changeling," Brooks said.

"Yes, but we're not what you think," said the changeling. "There are dozens of us here in town. We get our kidneys from the local butcher. Cows only. We haven't had any problems in a hundred years. A few weeks ago, organ traders roll into town. Somehow they knew about our kind. They drugged anyone who saw what they were doing and made them think aliens or—that we were doing it. I've been following you since you got here, hoping you'd track them down."

"Could have just come to us to begin with," Brooks said.

"As if you wouldn't have immediately shot a changeling?"

"Fair," said Brooks.

"Why bees, though?" Smith asked.

"The world is running out of bees," the changeling said. "They're essential pollinators. My family and I are trying to do our part to help."

"*I told you*," Brooks said.

Smith lowered his gun and spoke to the changeling. "We're supposed to murder you, but uh... I guess we owe you one?"

"Tell whoever you work for it was the mob," the changeling said.

"It *was* the mob," Brooks said.

"Don't mention us at all."

Smith shrugged. "Works for me, as long as you all don't start ripping out kidneys."

"We won't," the changeling assured him.

He condensed back into a bee, split into half a dozen bees, and flew away.

Smith seated himself on the side of the bed. "Don't ever do that again."

Brooks stared at Smith and shook his head, in total disbelief that he was being chastised for saving a life. "You take care of me. I take care of you. That's how this works."

Smith didn't reply. His eyes were still fixed on his partner's arm.

THE ELVES ARE COMMUNISTS

Most believe that Times Square is named such because it once housed the home office of *The New York Times*. In fact, the name actually comes from the area's ability to multiply any visitor's misery, several times over. Excepting tourists, anyone who can avoid that part of Midtown Manhattan does.

Brooks and Smith couldn't avoid it, thanks to an assignment. They pushed past crowds of people standing in the middle of the sidewalk staring at billboards. They pushed past more crowds, waiting in blocks-long lines for discount Broadway tickets. They pushed past even more crowds gathering to pay hard-earned money to take pictures with a cowboy in underpants and a coked-out Elmo.

Outside a building obscured by scaffolding and sheets of plywood, they reached their destination: the former home of Skittles Planet and future home of Toy Depot. An even crowdier crowd gathered around the construction site. In dozens of hands were dozens of picket signs, reading 'Local 37 on Strike,' 'Don't Be a Scab' and 'This Is a Picket Line.' They got right to the point. At the center of the mob was a giant, inflatable rat wearing an inflatable yellow hard hat. That was a little more subtle.

At the front of the crowd, a thin line of barricade tape prevented the protestors from making their way under the scaffolding. Brooks and Smith made it to the tape, where they witnessed the arrival of the crowd's enemies: scab laborers. Dozens of them—the same number that there were picketers—ducked their hard-hatted heads and avoided eye contact as they made their way into the building, toolboxes and lunch pails in hand.

Brooks, caught up in the moment, cleared his throat and launched a loogie at one of the scabs.

Smith pulled him back. "Dial it down, Cesar Chavez."

Brooks narrowed his eyes. "Is that because I'm Mexican, or do you not know any other labor leaders?"

"Yes," Smith answered ambiguously. "Are we undercover or not?"

"We are. I just... really hate scab labor."

"Yeah, so does someone else judging from the case," Smith said.

Yes, there was a case. Every day for two weeks running, Toy Depot had brought in a crew of non-union workers to put together their new flagship store in Times Square. Every day for two weeks running, those workers disappeared. Somehow, it was better business for the company to bring in an endless stream of underpaid laborers than to provide fair, union wages. The detectives were there to join the crew, figure out what was going on, and hopefully not disappear themselves.

"I don't get the big deal," Smith said.

"*About underpaid labor?*" Brooks knew his partner could be cold, but surely he wasn't that monstrous.

"*Easy,*" Smith pleaded. "Of course it's bad. It's just... who cares?"

"*Who cares?* You—"

Smith defensively raised his hands. "*Hear me out.* You hire the union guys, everything goes according to plan... now we've got a big-ass Toy Depot selling plastic shit made by kids in the third world. *Wow.* Only ninety percent of the workers involved in this operation got ratfucked instead of one hundred percent. It's exploitation all the way down. It's not worse just because it's happening here."

"That's a reason to care about it happening *everywhere*," Brooks said. "It's not a reason to not care about it happening *anywhere*. You fix what you can then try to fix the rest."

Smith shrugged. "There's always someone at the bottom. Improve the slave kids' lives, it's probably because we're enslaving robots. Then the robots enslave us, babe."

Brooks huffed. "Well, at least you agree it's *bad*."

They slipped under the tape and followed the workers into the site.

Inside, the building was pleasantly empty. The floor had been stripped to cement, and all Skittles Planet fixtures—the whole Skittle Solar System—had been removed. New interior walls were being framed to divide the store into various toy-themed areas. Accordingly, drilling sounds and hammering echoed through the area.

Not long after the detectives made it through the door, a very large man in a flannel shirt pushed his hands forward to stop them from proceeding any further. "Can I help you fellas?"

"We're here to apply for work," Smith said.

The foreman eyed their suits and scoffed. "Yeah, sure."

Brooks deployed his greatest asset in disguising as exploitable labor. He turned to Smith with faux confusion. "*Que dijo?*"

"*Uh... no trabajo*," Smith said, hoping that was correct.

Suddenly, the foreman perked up. "When can you start?"

Smith didn't know enough Spanish to pretend he was translating that for his partner. He mumbled something incoherent that loosely translated as "pawn my parrot."

Brooks pretended it made sense. "*Ahora.*"

"We can start now," Smith said.

☜

They weren't asked to fill out any paperwork. Payment would be made in cash, at the end of the day—should they make it to the end of the day. That was the rub. If the workers disappeared, they didn't have to be paid at all. The detectives removed their coats and collected yellow safety vests and helmets from a wire bin that would someday hold giant bouncy balls.

"You know how to install insulation?" the foreman asked.

"Yeah," Smith lied. He mumbled something about "insulación" to Brooks. Not a real word.

The foreman pointed to an area of wall that was framed and ready. Next to it were rolls of insulation, pink and piled high. They may or may not have contained asbestos. Brooks and Smith made their way across the room toward the pile.

One worker was already there, shoving insulation between the boards with gloved hands.

"Don't touch that," he said to Smith. Then, to Brooks, "*No toques.*"

"I speak English," Brooks said.

"You two've never done this before," the worker said.

Brooks and Smith eyed each other. Guilty.

"I ain't a snitch." He pulled the glove off his right hand to shake theirs. "Name's Jackie."

"Not a snitch, but not afraid to be a scab," Brooks said snidely.

"I know, right?" Jackie shook his head. "I used to be in the 37, but I couldn't hold out no more. I got a kid in speech therapy, y'know?"

"Do you know strikebreakers have been disappearing?"

Smith asked.

"Yeah, I've heard," Jackie said. "Every day. I got a yellow belt in karate. I'm takin' my chances."

"Isn't that the lowest belt?" Smith wondered.

Jackie shrugged. "What're you two doin' here anyway?"

"We're investigating what's going on," Brooks said.

"You cops?" Jackie asked.

"Not exactly," Brooks said.

"Private investigators," Smith said.

"Well, you wanna find anything out, you gotta talk to the foreman. It's everyone else's first day."

"Yeah, he's not exactly forthcoming," Brooks said.

Jackie popped open a toolbox. "I got spare gloves in here, if you wanna slip 'em on and keep spyin'. Wouldn't hate seein' this place back in the 37's hands."

The detectives accepted the offer, donned the gloves, and followed Jackie's lead.

Three hours later, it was time for lunch. Brooks and Smith hadn't brought anything, so they grabbed some stale potato chips and snack cakes from the on-site vending machine. They settled in on the cement floor, amongst the workers.

Their nosiness got them nowhere. No one had seen anything weird. No one had heard anything weird. No one had even smelled, touched, tasted, or sixth-sensed anything weird. As far as anyone could tell, it was a normal construction site, or *sitio de construcción*. Brooks and Smith had no choice but to wait out the paranormal, assuming there was any.

"You got ten more minutes," said the foreman, on his way out the door for a warm lunch. "*Diez minutos.*" He added, "Nobody disappear."

"You think it's him?" Brooks asked.

"Could be," said Smith. "I'm not exactly getting mage energy from the guy, though."

Soon after the foreman disappeared out the door, it became difficult to breathe.

Smith's cigarette-damaged lungs noticed first. He leaned forward and gasped for air.

Brooks put a worried hand on his shoulder. "Are you okay—" Then his own lungs caught on and he started coughing.

Smith coughed harder, unable to answer with a "no." He tried to stand, but found himself woozy amidst his coughing fit, and dropped back to the cold, hard floor.

A thick green fog filled the air—the impediment to breathing revealing itself. It came from nowhere. Not from a doorway. Not from a vent. It simply spread from mid-air in the middle of the room.

All around, workers doubled over, coughing and wheezing. No one could see anything, as the green became thicker and thicker. One by one, they passed out.

Brooks came to with his head resting on his groggy partner's lap. He heard chirping, and felt a breeze against his forehead. He sat up, in a forest clearing.

"*What happened?*" Brooks asked.

"Welcome back," Smith said.

"Where are we?" Brooks asked.

"Dunno." Smith hazarded a nerdy guess. "Mirkwood?"

It looked like a setting straight out of a fantasy novel. Around the emerald, grassy clearing stood enormous trees, at least a thousand years old. Instead of green fumes, a fine, sparkling mist filled the air. Somewhere in the distance was a waterfall. Its sound provided relaxing background noise.

All of the gassed workers had made it to the clearing. They exchanged looks of panic, fear, and confusion. Those gave way to looks of awe, as the moss beneath them began glowing in circular patterns that expanded and contracted like a frog's vocal sac. The forest itself seemed to sing in concert with the glow. Faint aaahs, presumably from wood nymphs.

"Well, ain't this somethin'," Jackie said.

"Oh, it's *something*," Brooks said. He patted at his leg, searching for his backup gun. It was gone. "Crap."

Smith's was gone as well.

"Do you have any idea what happened?" Brooks asked.

Smith shook his head. "No, but we're about to find out..."

The sudden, clopping sound of inbound horses drowned out the waterfall.

They were beautiful. A trio of pointy-eared white horses emerged from the woods. From their forehands spiraled dainty little horns. Unicorns. Their coats shimmered and glowed, like they were literally anything in a JJ Abrams movie.

On the unicorns' backs were ethereal creatures, equal in beauty. Thin humanoids with pointed ears, who sparkled. Each had salon-quality black hair that reached their waist, even when braided.

"I know this one," Brooks said.

Smith nodded. "Elves."

"Yeah, but not like you're thinking." Brooks speculated. "Huldufólk. Icelandic elves. They're supposed to live in a parallel world that's here, but not here, usually making themselves invisible."

"*Why* do you know that?" Smith asked.

"I took the Norse Mythology class for my continuing education," Brooks said.

"They evil?" Smith asked.

"I don't know. They're not supposed to exist." Huldufólk had been in the chapter of his textbook titled 'Nonsense.'

They were real, though, and at least one of them recognized the detectives.

"Hello there again," said an elf, from atop its unicorn.

Smith looked around for who it could have been taking to. "Me?"

"Yes, Edward."

"You've met?" Brooks wondered.

"No?" Smith said.

"It's nice to see you too, Arturo," said the elf.

"*You've* met?" Smith asked.

Brooks shook his head. "No. I think I'd remember meeting an elf."

A different elf dismounted its unicorn and spoke to the laborers. "My name is Trjáálfur."

Next to Trjáálfur, the third elf translated to Spanish. "*Me llamo Trjáálfur.*" The elf continued doing that after each sentence Trjáálfur spoke. This text will not, because that is tedious.

"These are my companions, Fallegur and Heittálfur," Trjáálfur continued. "We know the world of man has been difficult for all of you. We come to you today to offer you something better. Our homes of a thousand years were recently destroyed by allfire, and we need help rebuildi—"

While Fallegur translated that to Spanish, Smith began cackling. "The elves wanna exploit cheap labor."

Brooks frowned.

Smith pointed at him. "I fucking *told you*. Blood all the way down. Even in the parallel elf world!"

Trjáálfur disputed that. "While it's true we cannot offer payment in the form of money, we offer a society where all are equal. You'll perform labor beside us, live among us, and in turn become one of us. All elves prosper from the work of all elves."

Smith scoffed. "Oh, the elves are communists."

"It doesn't sound bad," Brooks admitted. "From each according to his ability to each according to his needs... everyone receiving the fruits of their labor..."

"No one's gonna go for this." Smith motioned at some immigrants. "These guys didn't flee their shithole countries to be elf slaves—"

Brooks's mouth gaped. "*Shithole countries?*"

But Smith was very wrong. The prospect of living thousands of years in a forest paradise with hot, sparkling elves was irresistible. One by one, workers stepped toward the elves, seeking futures with more prosperity and fewer sad, cold lunches. They could work out the other details—like how to bring their families along via chain migration—later on.

When everyone was ready to go, Fallegur addressed the detectives. "Are you two coming?"

"Um..." Brooks thought about it. "Eddie?"

Smith shook his head. "You do you, but I'm not joining Habitat for Elfmanity."

"We have a job to do in our world," Brooks said, to the elves.

The unicorns turned around and headed into the forest, followed by a pack of construction workers.

"Bye!" Jackie said. "Nice meetin' ya!"

"See you soon," said Fallegur. "Unless the 37 get their jobs back." The elf winked.

The next thing they knew, the detectives sat alone in the sparkly clearing.

"Maybe we should have gone with them," Brooks said. "Live forever in a magical world with unicorns, or—"

"—or struggle to pay rent and probably get murdered by a monster some day?" Smith finished, with a realistic outlook for their futures.

Brooks nodded.

"Nah," Smith said. "I'd find a way to get kicked out. But while we're here in the fairytale forest—" Smith reached for his partner's hand. "—I wouldn't mind getting some fairy tail."

Brooks pulled his hand away. "You're getting really comfortable slinging slurs."

Smith grinned. "Well, Brooksy. It's what I'm good at. Like you said, from each according to his ability to..."

Brooks and Smith awoke in Smith's bed. On their phones were emails containing their next assignment. Apparently, scab laborers were going missing in Times Square...

HUDDLED ASSES

August 16, 2009

    Eddie and I got sent to Liberty Island because a bunch of tourists claim they saw the statue's arm move. Of course, you can't just go to Liberty Island whenever you feel like (how does The Reticent not have boats???), so we had to take the last ferry of the day there and hide until everyone but one security guard was gone. That meant ~~chilling~~ hiding in the walk-in cooler for the café, and that meant Eddie stealing and eating a ton of the statue-shaped cheese slices they put on their burgers.

    After dark, we went outside to see the statue. Almost

immediately, Eddie started freaking out, saying the statue was flipping him off. I didn't see that. It wasn't moving at all. So at this point, I'm assuming he's either on drugs or he's been poisoned, and the only thing he's had that I haven't is the cheese from the Liberty Café. The tourists who saw the statue move probably also had the cheese, right? Delusions from food-poisoning. Case closed.

Not so fast. Since he's been poisoned from eating crap food before and he's done every drug known to man, Eddie decides it's not food poisoning. If the statue isn't moving (thankfully he trusts me that it isn't), he says it's hallucinogens because the statue looks "extra green" and because he feels itchy. I wondered if the cheese could have been tainted by mistake.

Eddie doubted it was an accident because, according to him,

no one shares good drugs. Honestly, an accident seemed more

likely to me. Why spike crappy cheese slices with

hallucinogens? What purpose could that serve? But then again,

how would someone accidentally get drugs into cheese?

We went back to the cooler, and the labels on the boxes told

us the cheese came from Pitchfork Pastures in Connecticut.

The name made me wonder if it might be something Satanic,

but again... Why? There'd been no ill effects other than the

statue delusions. Eddie was about to eat another slice for

"research purposes" but I stopped him. He then offered me a

cheese slice. I declined. We ended up passing the rest of the night outside behind some bushes. I'm pretty sure the security guard should be fired because we weren't quiet at all. We spent a long time talking about anything and everything.

Almost everything. I <u>almost</u> got him to talk about Indiana. Someday. I don't know why I'm so patient with him. If anyone else straight up refused to talk about their past, I'd be over it. Eddie, if I'm dead and you're going through my journals: I'm madly in love with you. That's the reason. I just haven't told you because I'm 100% sure you'd freak out.

August 17, 2009

We left on the first ferry, got cleaned up, and took an Aztek to Connecticut. From the start, the people working there were shady as hell. We've been to farms before, and they're usually full of serious hard workers. The people at Pitchfork Pastures were way too relaxed, and way too into cows. Half of them were wearing tie dye. They claimed to have the happiest dairy cows in New England. It was a point of pride, and they were quick to show us their "prize cow" Bessie, who they said could do tricks.

Bessie did a ~~fucking backflip~~.

That shouldn't be physically possible for a cow, so we poked around the farm until we found an unmarked barn with a bunch of locks on the door. We picked those in a snap, and when we got inside we found a bunch of cows that looked like they were asleep. Upon closer inspection, they were in a daze, their heads swaying and their pupils dilated.

Despite my protests, Eddie licked a piece of straw from one of the troughs. Gross. Apparently it didn't taste like anything, but pretty soon he was complaining he was itchy and saying the straw was moving (it wasn't). The cows were tripping on LSD. "The happiest dairy cows in New England" indeed. Eddie called it "Project M-Cow Ultra" and I struggled not to laugh. How can someone be drugged with farm-grade LSD and still come up with the worst puns in the world? And why am I absolutely obsessed with this person?

Apparently Pitchfork Pastures normally filters the LSD out of the milk used for making cheese, but there'd been some sort of mechanical failure. When we confronted them, they <u>thanked us</u> for bringing it to their attention and promised to implement better quality control procedures in the future. What does the FDA even do, if we're the ones who had to catch this? How is this real life? Five years ago, I was in college, and now I'm vetting dairy farms and in love with an insane person.

Life is weird.

FAMILY ISN'T JUST BLOOD (THERE'S ALSO VISCERA)

Smith was almost never the first one to get to work in the morning—the rare exception only occurring when he hadn't left work the night before. So when he arrived at the office he shared with Brooks, holding two coffees, and there was no one to receive the extra cup, he knew something was wrong.

While he sat and debated how long to wait to text his partner before it would seem desperate and pathetic, Brooks spared him the indignity by sulking into the room, pale and sullen.

Smith eyed him up. "Sleep in?"

"I just got off the phone with my aunt..."

"Tamale aunt?" Smith asked, concerned he would never again receive leftovers.

"Not Tía Sofía," Brooks clarified. "Other side of the family. Aunt Barb. She wants me to come over for dinner."

"That's bad?" Smith wondered.

Brooks seated himself. "Barb's family is a trainwreck. All four of her kids have been to jail. One's still in. None of them ever hold a job for more than a few months, and half of them have kids of their own they don't support. I'm sure at least one person there is going to ask me for money."

"So say no," Smith said, offering the extra coffee.

Brooks thanked him with a silent nod. "I already said yes. I'm going to be dreading it all day."

"*Why?*"

Brooks stared at him with skeptical eyes. "Why did I say 'yes' to dinner with the only Brookses other than me who are still alive?"

"Ah, that old chestnut." Smith turned to look at his in-box. "Well, you can distract yourself with a centaur if—"

"Come with me."

Smith rolled his chair back around. "Excuse me?"

"To dinner," Brooks said.

"I got that. I just didn't think we were at 'meet the family' yet."

"I couldn't care less if you meet any of my relatives," Brooks said. "I need you to be my escape hatch. I can't say no to these people because... I don't know... guilt?"

Smith followed. "But I can say 'let's get the fuck out of here' whenever I want."

"Exactly. Just be yourself and we'll be out in no time."

"Yeah, okay," said Smith.

Brooks's eyes lit up. "*Okay?*"

"I'll rescue you, princess."

The workday was uneventful—unless doing a deep dive into centaur lore could be considered an event. At 5:00 on the dot, the detectives parted ways to get changed because, in Brooks's words, "they'll make fun of you if you wear a suit." At 7:30, Brooks and Smith reconvened outside a sex shop in Bayonne, New Jersey. The Brookses lived upstairs.

Smith was wearing the same suit he wore to work, minus the jacket.

Brooks shook his head. "I told you—"

Smith shrugged. "I looked. It was either this or sweat-pants."

"Could have gone with the sweatpants," Brooks said. He himself was wearing jeans and a grey sweater. "So what did you do for the last two and a half hours?"

"Went to a bar and drank enough to put up with whatever this is going to be."

Brooks considered that for a moment. "Thank you for doing this."

"Just a quick debrief... am I your coworker or your boyfriend?"

"Up to you. They know I'm gay," Brooks said.

"They good with it?" Smith asked.

Brooks waved his hand in a so-so gesture. "Five out of ten."

Smith developed a mischievous grin. "Oh, I am *so* your boyfriend." He roped an arm around Brooks and escorted him into the building. "Let's get this shitshow started."

The apartment door flung open to reveal a tall, grey-haired woman in her mid-fifties. Barb.

"Arturo!" She threw her arms around him. He reciprocated mildly. When Barb was done, she pulled back and registered Smith's presence. "And who's this?"

"That's... um..."

"I'm Eddie," Smith said, extending a hand.

"We're dating," Brooks said, finally.

"Well that's... nice," Barb said, shaking Smith's hand. "You didn't have to dress up."

"I came here from work," Smith offered.

She seemed to accept that, and welcomed them both

inside.

"Have a seat," Barb said. "Can I get you something to drink? We've got soda, beer—"

"Beer," Smith said.

Brooks concurred. "Beer's fine."

While Barb went to retrieve their drinks, the pair nosed around in the living area. Six people lived in Barb's two-bedroom apartment: Barb herself, her three non-jailed adult children (Jonathan, Jason, and Jennifer), and Jennifer's twins, Emma and Emilia. It showed. Anything that wasn't covered with a plastic tarp like the couch was covered in a mess. There were toys everywhere, clothes everywhere, and shelves full of little tchotchkes everywhere. Virgin Marys, angel figurines, family photos, and so on—all caked with a layer of dust.

Brooks and Smith eyed the family photographs on a nearby shelf.

"So Barb is your... dad's sister?" Smith asked.

"Aunt by marriage," Brooks corrected, pointing at a photo of Barb with some generic-looking dude. "Her husband Nick was my dad's brother."

"Was?"

"He died a few years ago," Brooks said. "Cancer."

"Wow, the Brookses are doing about as well as the Kennedys." Smith eyed a recent photo of two young siblings. "How many twins are in your family?"

"Lots," Brooks said. "My sister and me. Barb's two oldest sons." He gestured at the photograph in question. "My cousin Jennifer's kids."

Smith shuddered. "What a nightmare."

"They're sweet kids," Brooks said.

Smith rolled his eyes. "I'm sure."

"It's not their fault their parents are... well..."

Barb re-emerged from the kitchen and handed the men

their drinks. All of them seated themselves on the squeaky plastic couch.

"So, how'd you two meet?" Barb asked.

"Work," said Smith.

"You're a chemist too?"

As far as the public knew, The Reticent was a publicly traded pharmaceutical company with a weird and annoyingly capitalized name. Brooks's cover story was that he worked in a lab developing drugs. Smith hadn't fleshed out his fake backstory, but he didn't know enough about chemistry to fake a career in science.

"I'm in sales," he lied.

"We met in the cafeteria," Brooks added.

"What are the odds?" Barb asked. "You people must have some sort of sixth sense for finding each other."

Smith couldn't help himself. "Actually, I was wearing a hat that said 'I heart cock.'"

Brooks was mortified.

"Oh. Well. That's... nice." Barb swiftly changed the subject. "Chili's ready... just waiting for the boys to get back. The kiddos are out with their mother so it will just be us, Jonathan, and Jason tonight."

"What are they up to these days?" Brooks asked.

"Still figuring things out," said Barb.

"They're twenty-seven," Brooks said.

"Hey, better to have them here than homeless or out there dealing drugs or something."

Soon after she said that, the door flew open and the men in question arrived. Jonathan and Jason were both in their late twenties, tall, blue-eyed, and brown-haired. Both wore jeans and hooded sweatshirts. The only difference between the identical twins was that Jonathan let his hair hang to his shoulders and Jason pulled his back in a ponytail. The pair wasted no time on pleasantries, but seated themselves immediately at the dinner table.

Barb found that a bit rude. She stood and stepped toward them. "Boys, we have guests tonight." Then she made her way into the kitchen.

"Yeah, we know," Jonathan said. "I'm sure Turo wants to start eating too."

"Do you need help, Barb?" Brooks asked.

"No, go on and have a seat. I'll bring the food out in a minute."

Brooks and Smith exchanged looks of misery, then ambled toward the table.

"Who's the blond?" Jason asked.

Brooks gestured as he and Smith seated themselves. "This is Eddie. We're dating."

Jason laughed a little. "Man, you're still gay?"

"Yeah, doubt that's changing at this point," Brooks said.

Jason looked directly into Smith's eyes. "Good luck, man."

Brooks squinted. "What's that supposed to mean?"

Jonathan laughed and spoke to Smith. "He's a little high maintenance."

"How am I..." Brooks didn't get to finish before his cousins started telling stories about him.

"Has to be the center of attention," Jason said.

"He turned Jen's graduation party into a whole thing," Jonathan said.

Brooks fumed. "You held the graduation party *in the park where my family was murdered.*"

"Our dad's dead too," Jason said.

"Yeah, we're not freaking out every time we see a cancer ward," Jonathan said.

Brooks pinched at the bridge of his nose and tried not to say something he'd regret.

"You okay?" Smith asked.

"Yeah. It's fine. I'm fine," Brooks lied.

It was a good time to drop it, as Barb set a bowl of chili in front of him. Then in front of Smith. Then her sons. And finally, a bowl for herself. Then Barb said grace.

"Bless us, Lord, for these, thy gifts, which we are about to receive from thy bounty. Through Christ, our Lord. Amen."

"Amen," said everyone but Smith, and they started eating.

"I have some news," Jason said.

Everyone turned to him except Smith, who stared at the bowl of chili in front of him. It looked very, very mediocre—like something that had come from a can. *God should learn to cook*, he thought.

Jason beamed. "I just came from Lana's house. She's pregnant."

"Congrats," said Jonathan.

"That's wonderful," said Barb. "I'll never say no to another grandbaby."

Brooks was still feeling prickly, so he poked. "Do you ever see your other kids?"

Jason stared at him. "Sometimes. They all live with their moms."

"Must be nice," Brooks said. "Being able to dodge responsibility like that."

"You're one to talk," Jason said.

"Boys," Barb warned.

Brooks sneered. "Oh, I wanna hear where this is going."

"You're gonna be the last person in your family tree because you care more about what revs your engine than you do about God and family," Jason said.

"There it is," Brooks said.

Smith just kept shoveling chili into his mouth. It wasn't the worst thing he'd ever eaten, but it was weirdly sweet.

At this point, he was convinced Barb's recipe was a few cans of Hormel with a jar of honey poured in.

Jason wasn't sweet. "Your dad's lucky he's not alive to see—"

"My dad wanted me to be happy," Brooks snapped.

Jonathan tried to calm his brother. "Not everyone has to be that devout, man. Chill out."

Jason looked directly at Smith. "You got any kids?"

Smith swallowed a gristly bit of meat. "God, I hope not."

"He's gay, man," Jonathan said.

Smith had two choices: either roll with that and let the conversation move on, or dispute it and create more drama. He shot Brooks a smirk and went with the latter. "Bi, actually."

Jason nearly choked on his chili. "Hold on."

"Oh, great," Brooks sighed.

"You mean you've had pussy and you—"

"Jason!" Barb scolded.

"Sorry. You mean you've been with women but you're choosing to be with my cousin here."

Smith nodded. "Yeah. That's what it means."

"That's nuts," Jason said.

"It's not nuts," Jonathan said.

"Don't you want to leave a legacy?" Jason asked.

"Oh, there's nothing about me worth passing down," Smith said.

Argument came from a place Smith didn't expect: right next to him. Brooks squinted at him and said, "What the hell, Eddie?"

Smith just shrugged.

"See?" Jason said. "Nuts. Turo's all messed up from watching his family die or whatever, and this guy's crazy from who knows what. If they were right in the head, they'd start families and—"

Brooks snapped. "Three kids by three different women isn't a family!"

"*Four* kids," Jason corrected. "Two of them were twins, which you'd know if you were ever around."

"If I were..." Brooks trailed off, flabbergasted.

"Aww shoot, I forgot the bread." Barb excused herself from the conflict.

Smith, who'd been mindlessly prodding chili with his spoon, noticed something out of place: a fingernail clipping. It didn't seem like a sinister clipping, just an unhygienic one, but nevertheless he stopped prodding and stared at his partner as Brooks continued his rant toward Jason.

"You haven't devoted your life to God or family," Brooks said. "You haven't devoted your life to *anything*. You do whatever you feel like and wrap it up in moralism so you can feel better than other people. Well, you're not. I guarantee I care more about Eddie than you've ever cared about anything."

Smith wasn't sure how much of a compliment that was, but it made him smile.

"If nothing else," Brooks said, "the work I do is my legacy. How many people have you saved?"

"I'm trying to save *you*, stupid," said Jason.

"What does that mean?" Brooks asked. "Save me from going to Hell?"

"Something like that," Jason said. He stared into Brooks's eyes with a look that said, "pay attention."

Brooks was too angry to notice.

Jonathan gestured at both of them. "Guys. Chill."

Barb returned with a shiny platter—one that only got dragged out for company—piled high with rolls. As they were taken one by one, more of the platter became visible.

Smith reached for one, hoping it wouldn't contain any nail clippings. Something shocked him. He looked from the tray to Barb, smiled as he took a roll, and turned to Brooks.

Smith leaned in toward his partner and whispered. "Don't react, but I just caught a glimpse of Barb's reflection on that platter." He brushed his lip against Brooks's ear. "She's a ghoul. Pretend I'm flirting with you."

Brooks turned to Smith and smiled, doing just that. He giggled. "*Later.*"

Jason groaned.

This was just what Brooks needed. If Smith was right—and he always was when it came to this sort of thing—then Aunt Barb was dead, and the creature that had eaten her had taken her place. On the bright side, if he murdered his aunt in front of his cousins, he'd probably never have to see them again. On the other hand, they'd probably try to send him to jail. Maybe Smith would do it, and Brooks could pretend his partner was just some escort he'd hired—

"So, Arturo," Barb said, dragging him out of his thoughts. "Have you ever considered donating your sperm?"

Brooks blinked a few times. "Why is everybody suddenly so concerned about where I come?" When no one answered that, he added, "No. I haven't. Unlike Jason over there, I have no interest in fathering kids unless I'm actually going to be a parent to them."

"So there's a chance you hire a surrogate later," Jonathan said.

"Not really," Brooks said. "No. I don't feel good about bringing anyone into a world where they could end up like my dad and sister. I might adopt some day..."

Smith choked on his dry roll.

"God," Jason said. "You couldn't give us anything at

all."

"Excuse me?" Brooks looked around the table, confused.

Barb sighed. "I was really hoping there'd be more little Brooks babies in the works."

"Well, sorry to break your heart," said Brooks.

Jonathan shook his head. "*Man*. She's gonna eat you now."

In almost-synchronized fashion, Brooks and Smith scooted their seats backward and stood. Ghouls weren't particularly hard to kill. In their native form, they were wispy and incapable of doing much but nibbling dead bodies. When they shifted into human form—the forms of those they'd already eaten—they could feast, but they also had human vulnerabilities.

"You're not surprised," Jason said, with a perplexed tone.

"She's a ghoul," Smith said. "Reflection gave it away."

"You see—" started Barb.

Brooks interjected. "You ate my dying uncle and got a taste for Brooks family flesh, then ate Barb and took her place so you'd have easy access to more delicious Brookses?"

"Well... yes, actually..."

Jonathan and Jason exchanged worried looks.

Brooks recited information almost emotionlessly. "Ghouls only need to feed once a year or so. Uncle Nick died three years ago. Then Barb. Who'd you eat next? Emma? Emilia?"

"I tried," Barb said. "The girls didn't taste very good."

Brooks stared at Jason. "Your kids."

"It's them or me," Jason said. "I'll keep 'em coming, I don't get eaten, and I get a place to stay without having to work."

Brooks turned to Jonathan. "And you?"

"I'm trying to make some sons," Jonathan said. "I think my sperm might be crooked."

"I don't even know where to start," Brooks said. "Eddie?"

In a swift series of movements, Smith reached into his coat, grabbed a pocket knife, flipped it open, and chucked it at Barb. It embedded itself in her neck, and he stepped around the table to retrieve it, causing both blood and green goop to gush from the wound when the knife was removed. Both sprayed all over the room—only the plastic-wrapped couch was protected.

Jonathan shrieked. "*What did you do?*"

"Killed the ghoul that ate your mom and your nieces," said Smith. "You're welcome."

"Now I'm gonna have to get a job!"

"Wow, that's horrible," Brooks said. "Way worse than *feeding your kids to a ghoul.*"

Brooks and Smith made their way toward the door.

Jonathan called after them. "Wait. How'd you know about ghou—"

"It doesn't matter," Brooks said. "Don't ever call me again."

The sticky detectives made their way outside and out of view of Brooks's shitbag cousins. There, under a glowing red 'XXX DVDs' sign, Brooks lost it.

"Fuck fuck fuck fuck. Fuck!" He kicked a sandwich board advertising half-priced ben wa balls. It hit the sidewalk with a clatter. "I'm cursed. I'm fucking cursed. Fuck." Brooks looked for something else to kick and saw nothing but his partner, so instead, he let out a fierce scream.

"*Fuuuuuuuuuuck!*"

"Do I need to call someone?" Smith asked with slight concern.

Brooks paced back and forth, dragging his feet on the cement. "All I ever wanted was a normal fucking life and a normal fucking family and a normal fucking job. And here I am, covered in ectoplasm from my dead ghoul aunt and... and... that's fucking normal for me now. I'm not even surprised. This is fucking life. This is my life!"

Smith thought about dropping an "I told you so," on account of him having explicitly told Brooks not to join The Reticent. But he thought better of it, and offered consolation. "Yeah. It is. You know you can quit The Reticent if you want. Won't stop you from running into the occasional ghoul, but—"

Brooks shook his head. "There's no going back. I'm just... processing that. I'm never going to have anything remotely normal..."

He did have something—something that remained unspoken between the detectives.

"For what it's worth," Smith said, "I think normal's overrated."

"You don't ever wish you had a family?"

"Hell no. I've got you."

WEST COAST SATELLITE OFFICE

The plane sat at the gate for what seemed like forever. It was ninety seconds, the amount of time it takes to connect a jetway. Brooks and Smith stood impatiently in the aisle, desperate to stretch after spending six hours cramped in seats that barely accommodated short people, let alone anyone over six feet tall. Smith was especially grumpy, having been stuck in a middle seat.

They rolled their carry-ons into the airport, where the smell of dank weed permeated the air.

Smith took an exaggerated whiff. "I hate California."

"You love drugs," Brooks noted.

"But I *hate* potheads. Ohh, it helps with glaucoma. Ohh, it helps with Parkinson's. Ohh, it helps with autism. Ohh, it helps with AIDS. Ohh, it fights MRSA. That must be why I'm on my fourth fucking antibiotic, shitting my brains out just to get rid of a rash." He scratched at his arm.

"You're in a mood," Brooks said, with no emphasis.

"Yeah. I'm in *California*."

Worse, Smith had no idea why he was in California. Neither of them did.

The Reticent held several offices, most of which rarely communicated. Corporate headquarters in Manhattan saw the majority of paranormal activity. There was a manufacturing facility/tax shelter in Delaware, a government liaison in D.C., a warehouse and distribution center in

Chicago, and a West Coast satellite office in La Jolla, California. When workers there weren't investigating the supernatural, their job was to print little 'This product contains substances known to the state of California to cause cancer' labels and apply them to everything The Reticent produced.

Brooks and Smith had been sent to visit that office. Top Secret, the memo said. For an organization whose entire existence and purpose were a secret, that meant something.

The pair collected their rental car and made their way toward La Jolla—an eleven-mile drive that took a little over an hour. There, they found the West Coast satellite office, tucked between two $25,000,000 homes that came in under a thousand square feet each.

Only street parking was available. That was fine, since their rental was a Smart Fortwo, a two-passenger microcar with annual sales in the dozens. Brooks navigated it into a tiny space, boldly going where no subcompact would dare.

The office was—essentially—a house. Two stories, featuring a stucco exterior with rounded corners, arched windows, and a red tile roof.

Brooks and Smith made their way through an arched entryway and an open front door to find themselves in an open-concept living area.

Smith put his hands on his hips and looked around. "*This* is the satellite office? It's a house."

"Steve Jobs started in a house," said a relaxed voice. It came from the couch, where two Reticent employees sat waiting to greet their New York colleagues.

They looked like professionals, for California. The voice came from a male agent wearing loose-fit skater pants and a white t-shirt. He had dreadlocks, despite being white. Next to him was a shorter, Filipina woman in pot leaf print leggings and a green crop top. She may have come to work stoned, judging from the airy look on her face.

The dreadlocked agent, whose lanyard badge identified him as Kai Neptune, stepped toward the new arrivals. "What are you dudes wearing?"

Brooks—always in a full suit and tie, as was his partner—looked at him with scorn. "What the handbook tells us to...?"

"Pssht." Neptune dismissed that with a wave. "We don't, like... do that here."

The woman giggled in agreement, from the couch. "Yeah, man. You gotta go cas." Her badge identified her as Evian Aquino, and by 'cas' she meant 'casual.'

"We'll give you a tour of the office, then you gotta go for new outfits," Neptune said. "You go out lookin' like that, everyone's gonna think you're narcs."

"We don't want a tour," Smith said. "We wanna know why we're here."

"Due time, man. Come on." Neptune stepped toward the kitchen area and motioned for them to follow.

Brooks and Smith exchanged an uncertain glance, then followed.

"This is our break space." Neptune stopped and shifted his eyes around like he'd forgotten something. "Oh. Damn. I didn't introduce myself. I'm Agent Neptune."

"Got that from the badge, chief." Smith gestured at himself, then his partner. "Agent Smith. That's Agent Brooks."

Aquino giggled as she lumbered over to introduce herself. "Agent Aquino."

Neptune pointed at different parts of the room. "If you're thirsty, there's a cooler over there. Um. We have free granola bars and fruit leather in the basket on the counter."

Smith stepped over to the water cooler, poured himself a paper cup, and chugged it without looking. That was a mistake. It left his mouth faster than it had gone in, as he sprayed yellowish liquid across the room.

"It's fizzy toilet water," he coughed.

"Chill out, man. It's kombucha," Aquino said.

"Brooksy...?" Smith pleaded with his partner to get him out of here.

Brooks spoke to the Californians with an air of authority. "Listen. We don't need the rest of the tour. We need to know why we're here. I'm going to guess lives are at stake since they flew us all the way out here from New York."

"'Kay." Neptune seemed disappointed. "I'll be right back with the case stuff."

Aquino giggled and followed him down a hallway.

When they were out of earshot, Brooks turned to Smith and crossed his arms. "*Brooksy*?" he wondered in disbelief.

"It's fine. They're *cas*," Smith said.

"Why don't you just tell them we're together?" Brooks snapped.

"I can if you want. They're probably too high to remember."

Before Brooks could respond, Neptune and Aquino interrupted, rolling a whiteboard into the room. Very little effort had been put into it. On the whiteboard were two crooked columns, unlabeled. In the left column were names. In the right, locations.

Angela Tortuga	La Jolla Shores
Gary Sinise	La Jolla Shores
Carmen Garcia	La Jolla Shores
Alton Svenya	La Jolla Shores
Lixue Zhao	La Jolla Shores

"So, um... all our other agents have gone missing," Neptune said.

"*All of them*?" Brooks wondered.

"You only had seven total?" Smith asked.

"It's a tightknit community," Aquino said, giggling.

"They all went missing at the beach?" Brooks asked.

Neptune nodded. "Affirmative."

"Has anyone else gone missing?" Smith asked.

"Couple surfers," Aquino said.

"They go missing at the beach too?" Smith asked.

"Yeah, man," Neptune said.

"Has anything else strange happened?" Brooks asked.

"Yeah." A single tear fell down Neptune's cheek. "Someone took our SCOBY."

"Your what?" Smith asked.

Brooks explained. "Their kombucha culture."

Neptune nodded. "What's in that cooler is all we have left."

"What a shame," Smith said, his mouth still burning with the taste of ginger and nail polish remover.

"We need to go down to the beach," Brooks said.

"See why you gotta get new outfits now?" Neptune asked. "It's time to blend, boys."

Brooks and Smith shared frowns.

Neptune thought on it. "There's a couple beach shops down the road. Maybe ten minutes walking."

For the New Yorkers, it was a two-minute walk. Brooks and Smith each entered a different shop, ready to surprise the other.

Smith was done first, and he waited on the sidewalk, carrying his previous clothes in a reusable tote he'd been coerced into buying.

Brooks emerged—also carrying a tote—in white shorts

that rested just above the knee, white sneakers, and a pink linen shirt with its sleeves rolled to the elbows.

Smith stared at him, in horror. "You look like a fa—"

Brooks cut him off. "*Hard line*, Eddie. Besides, you're one to talk about outfits."

He was referring to Smith's new ensemble, which consisted of baggy jeans, black Converse sneakers, and an oversized grey and blue striped baja jacket.

"You look like you're going to ask me for money," Brooks said. "Or drugs."

"I might, if we have to keep hanging out with these two—"

Aquino and Neptune rejoined them, holding avocado smoothies.

"You don't look like cops now," Aquino said. She reached up to give Smith a high five, and was rebuffed. She shrugged it off.

"Now you're ready to save some people," Neptune said.

Smith sneered. "Californians aren't people."

Neptune and Aquino were unbothered, as usual.

The group headed for the shore.

In four blocks, they passed five homeless camps.

"I will say the hobos are nicer than ours," Smith said. "Shit. Shoe's untied." He motioned for the others to go on without him, while he discreetly slipped some cash through a particularly charming tent door.

When the group got to the beach, it was late in the afternoon. The mid-day crowds had thinned, which meant it was tolerably crowded rather than jam-packed. Where the sand of the beach met the cement of the pavement, a woman and three young girls sat behind a folding table. They were Laguna Lasses, selling the California equivalent of Girl Scout cookies.

One sweet child jutted a box made from recycled

material toward the agents. "You wanna buy some sugar-free brownies?"

"They're made with Stevia!" another added.

"For sure," Neptune said. "We gotta hit the surf first, though."

"Maybe later," Brooks said.

"Have you seen anyone get murdered?" Smith blurted.

The adult behind the table looked at him with horror in her eyes. "No...?"

"Come on." Brooks pulled Smith away toward the sand. "We can find someone to interview who isn't surrounded by kids."

Neptune and Aquino followed at a leisurely pace.

Brooks scanned the beach for someone who'd have been there often. He spotted an oversized canopy with a pair of feather flags waving in the sand around it. One read 'SURF' and the other 'LESSONS.'

The group made their way to the makeshift surf school.

"Sup, Ryan," Neptune said.

The surf instructor—the one he knew by name—was as tanned as a white human could be without being burnt. She had sun-bleached hair that cascaded down the length of her back. It lay in stark contrast to the black wetsuit beneath.

"You bring your friends for lessons?" Ryan asked, hopeful.

Smith eyed her form-fitting wetsuit like the lecher he was. "Yes."

"No," Brooks said. "We're here to talk to you about the recent deaths."

"Oh. Bummer," Ryan said.

"Did you know the surfers who went missing?" Brooks asked.

"Some of 'em," Ryan said.

"Were they amateurs?" Smith asked.

"Some of 'em," Ryan said. "It's been a mix of people. Some amateurs, some pros. RIP, Gordy." She kissed her fist, then directed it toward the ocean.

"What makes you say he's dead?" Brooks wondered. "They've only gone missing..."

Ryan showed them her wrist. On it, a thick hemp bracelet dangled loosely. "I found his bracelet. He wore it snug, man."

Smith pointed at it. "What's that?"

A small yellowish bit of goop—maybe half an inch in diameter—was stuck to the bracelet.

"Seaweed, probably," Ryan said.

"Did everyone go missing in the same area?" Brooks asked.

"For sure," Ryan said. She pointed out two locations. "Between that buoy and that one."

In the area she noted, there were dozens of swimmers.

"Jesus Christ," Smith sighed.

"Yeah. Let's get a lesson," Brooks said.

Smith stared at him. "Seriously?"

"Everyone went missing there. Let's see if we do too."

"I'm good," Aquino said, bowing out.

"Yeah, like... we're the only ones left in our office," Neptune said. "You dudes go."

Ryan handed Brooks and Smith a pair of wetsuits. After a few uncomfortable minutes in a pair of porta potties, they emerged from yet another clothing change in skin-tight attire.

"Another reason to hate it here," Smith griped. He turned to show Brooks his partially zipped back and sucked in his stomach. "Help?"

"I've got you." Brooks grabbed the zipper and gave it a yank.

Smith exhaled and resumed his terrible posture.

The detectives set their tote bags—now overflowing with clothing—under the surf tent.

Ryan directed them to their surfboards, and picked up her own. The three trudged through the sand toward the surf.

They'd taken only a few steps into the Pacific when a nearby swimmer emitted an "eeww" that turned into an "aggggh" that turned into a high-pitched scream. It was drowned out when the swimmer sank beneath the water.

Brooks and Smith abandoned their surfboards and fought against the current toward where the swimmer disappeared.

Smith was in front, and something stuck to his hand. A small piece of gooey crud. He came to a stop, brushed it off, and spread his arms wide to stop Brooks from proceeding any farther. "Nope. We gotta go."

Brooks drifted to a halt. "Why?"

Ahead of Smith was a huge shadow beneath the water. "Whatever it is, it's big." He backed into his partner.

Brooks, accordingly, took a step back. He shouted a lie for everyone's benefit. "Shark!"

Every swimmer, surfer, and floater began making their way toward the sand. That included Brooks and Smith.

People screamed. Crowds panicked. Sand castles were toppled in the commotion. A few stoned citizens sat cross-legged on the beach, unbothered.

As the detectives trudged toward the beach as quickly as the water would allow, the gooey mystery monster caught Smith's left leg. What began as a small glob between his toes stretched and spread and wrapped itself around the fine-haired appendage, up to his thigh. With a tug, it trawled him along the shallow water like he was a clam net.

Brooks turned at the splashing sounds. As his partner's

head bobbed in and out of the water, the sound of gasping breaths filled the air. Brooks had nearly reached his abandoned surfboard. He moved toward it, grabbed the thing, and skidded it across the surface toward Smith.

Surfboards prefer to float, but Smith took the board and used every bit of his strength to force it underwater, between the bottom of his foot and the goop. He pressed at it with his arms and kicked with his free leg. It worked. The tendril was severed. He freed himself and made his way closer to the beach.

Brooks grabbed his hand and pulled him onto the sand. "Are you oka—aggh."

Smith looked down at his leg to see what Brooks had seen. A bubbling blob of yellowish goo bubbled and bobbed around his ankle. He scraped his leg through the sand, until the blob was off of him and sat lumpy, covered in sand. A bubble burst at the top of it, sending a tiny spurt of sand into the air.

In the water, a similar, larger blob surfaced. It was as tall as the New Yorkers, and at least as angry. It slowly lurched onto the sand, looking to recover its missing piece.

"What is that thing?" Brooks asked.

"Fuck if I know," Smith said.

Neptune and Aquino approached, not nearly as panicked as they should have been.

"That's our SCOBY," Aquino said.

Brooks looked at her in disbelief. "*What?*"

Neptune nodded. "Yeah. I'd recognize it anywhere."

"Well, what happened to it?" Brooks asked.

"I don't know, man, but we should try and talk it out," Neptune said.

Aquino nodded. "Yeah."

The SCOBY loomed large, an SUV-sized blob the texture of cranberry sauce and the color of wax beans. Within its semitransparent form, patches of black and dark red were all that remained of the humans and sea creatures it had consumed. Neptune and Aquino approached the killer SCOBY, unaware that was exactly what the other agents at the West Coast Satellite Office had done.

"We've missed you," Aquino said.

"Yeah, SCOBY. Come home," Neptune said.

The SCOBY was a culture and was thus unmoved by the speech. The blob of goop stretched forward and absorbed both Neptune and Aquino, effectively shuttering the West Coast Satellite Office. Their casual outfits were briefly visible through the creature's translucence but quickly dissolved, along with the rest of their bodies. They left behind small red and black patches.

Brooks and Smith ran back to the surf canopy to look through their things. It wasn't clear what guns would do against a giant probiotic glob, but they grabbed them. In his jacket, Smith found something else that might be useful. He shook a pill bottle.

"You said it's bacteria?" Smith asked.

"And yeast..." Brooks noted the bottle of antibiotics. "Worth a shot."

Smith popped the cap and dumped the contents of the bottle into his hand. He scurried across the sand and chucked the handful of pills at the SCOBY.

The spot where they struck the creature turned white, for a brief moment. Then the pills were absorbed like everything else. The SCOBY had spent enough time in the drug-filled ocean that it had become antibiotic resistant.

Smith fired a few fruitless bullets at the monster. Nothing happened. He ran back to the canopy.

"You got any cash?" Smith asked. "I have another idea."

Brooks squinted. "What happened to your money?"

"Cigarettes," Smith lied.

Brooks pulled a twenty-dollar bill from his wallet and handed it over. "What's the pl—"

Smith didn't take time to explain. He ran across the sand to the brownie booth, where one nervous young girl stood guarding the snacks.

"Where'd your adult go?" Smith asked.

"She took Amy and Ava home." The girl beamed with pride. "She left me in charge."

Smith didn't have the heart to tell the child that being left behind wasn't exactly an honor. "How many brownies can I get for twenty bucks?"

"Um..." The girl did the math in her head. "Four."

That wouldn't do. Smith handed over the bill. "I'm gonna take all of them. I'll pay you the rest later."

"Okay!" the girl said.

"And for fuck's sake, go hide indoors somewhere," Smith said.

"Okay!"

Smith grabbed the large crate holding all of the brownie boxes and ran back to the beach.

There, Brooks was busy freeing a random beachgoer from a goo tendril using the pointy end of a beach umbrella.

Smith rushed past him. He set the crate on the ground and began feeding the SCOBY, one box of brownies at a time, in rapid succession.

With each box, the SCOBY shrank a little. It went from a Hummer to a crossover SUV to a Smart Fortwo. After two dozen brownies, it was the size of a Pomeranian.

Smith opened one of the few boxes remaining and tossed a few loose brownies at it.

The SCOBY shriveled into a dried-out disc, no bigger than a CD. Dead.

Brooks ran over to Smith. "What did you do?"

"Yeast eats sugar," Smith said.

"So you gave it *brownies*?" Brooks was horrified.

"*Stevia* brownies," Smith corrected. "I figured if I can't stand that shit, neither could it."

There was only a teaspoon or so of sugar in each of the humans the SCOBY had consumed. It was already borderline starving when Smith gave it something completely inedible.

"That's... weirdly smart," Brooks said.

"I know, I'm normally a dumbass—"

"Shut up. It was a compliment."

The pair made their way back to the porta potties, peeled off their wetsuits, and changed back into their dry West Coast attire to wrap things up. While Brooks walked around asking survivors whether they were okay, Smith hung around the surf canopy and lit a cigarette. In his baja jacket, he looked like a perfect caricature of West Coast laxity.

It took thirty minutes for Brooks to rejoin him. By then, there were half a dozen butts scattered around the sand.

"Neptune and Aquino are the only ones who died," Brooks said.

"RIP." Smith sarcastically kissed his fist and raised it toward the sea.

Brooks continued. "A few people got scraped up trying to escape, but nothing too serious. Everyone seems fine, and I think they're buying the 'filming a movie' excuse..."

"Huzzah," Smith said, as dryly as possible.

"You don't feel good about helping people?" Brooks asked.

"*Californians aren't people.*"

Brooks looked at him, his eyes demanding better.

Smith shrugged. "I don't feel *bad* about it."

"Sit with me. I want to talk to you about something."

"Uh oh," Smith said. "You're either lecturing me or dumping me."

"I'm really not." Brooks dropped to the sand.

Smith's knees creaked as he did the same.

Brooks spoke from the heart. "I haven't been on this coast in years. I don't know if I'll ever see it again, so I'm going to watch the sunset. You should too."

Smith laughed in disbelief. "*Why?*"

"Because... we don't see very many nice things," Brooks said. "It's nice to remember the world isn't all corpses and monsters and ghosts."

"It's the sun. I've seen it. It looks like the sun. Bright. Hot."

Brooks took a deep breath. "Do you care about *anything?*"

Smith tilted his head. "You wanna load that question a little more?"

"You've got the dead-inside thing going, and that's fine. It's funny and all... I just..." Brooks couldn't quite find the words he was looking for.

Smith finished for him. "I'm not dead inside. I have a *very* vibrant imagination. I just find it hard to care about some randos who've been attacked by whatever."

"You care about me," Brooks said, with the slightest hint of questioning.

Smith offered a soft snort. "Yeah. I do."

"I was one of those randos," Brooks said.

"Yeah. You were." Smith looked toward the brownie booth, where the Laguna Lasses were reuniting. His reaction was a complicated mix of relief, concern, and anger toward their chaperone.

Brooks observed his face. "You do care about them."

Smith's eyes were damp, and when he let himself blink a single tear flowed down the side of his nose. "Shit. You got me."

It was the first time Brooks saw Smith's tears.

"All of them...?" Brooks wondered.

Smith nodded and groaned. "Even the fucking Californians."

"I *knew* I saw you give your money away."

"Yeah..." Smith swallowed. "I, uh... I know what it feels like to get a shit hand, but... nobody helped me."

"I would have," Brooks offered.

"Yeah. You would have." Smith laughed bitterly and pressed another cigarette butt into the sand.

"Is there anything you need help with now?" Brooks asked.

Somewhere deep inside Smith was a desire to tell his partner everything that ate away at him and let someone help him for a change. He pushed that desire back down where it belonged—in a nice little repression zone of his brain, right next to the lyrics to "Candle in the Wind"—and turned on some false charm instead.

"I need help making the most of that sunset," he said with a smile.

With no West Coast Reticent agents alive to witness it, the pair kissed beneath the glow of a cloudless orange sunset. The only sounds other than the smacking of their lips were the crashing of waves and the occasional cough from the nearest homeless camp.

As they pulled apart, Smith's single tear morphed into a steady stream.

Brooks panicked. "Oh my God. What's wrong?"

"Nothing." Smith pulled the baja jacket up to his face and wiped the tears away, leaving some red scratch marks on his skin in the process. "Ow."

"You've never cried in front of me," Brooks said. "Are you dying?"

"Only of embarrassment," Smith said. He knew what he was about to say was weird and off-putting. "Uh... I don't know from love, but... I think I'm in love with you."

"*What?*" Brooks snorted. "You've seen actual massacres and *this* is what makes you cry?"

"What can I say, babe? I'm fucked up." Smith looked into Brooks's eyes, which seemed a little hazy through the tears. Since he was already embarrassing himself, he went all in. "I love you. Your brains. Your looks. Your long-winded speeches. That little scrunch your eyebrows do when I say something shitty. All of it."

"You know what's fucked up?" Brooks asked.

"What?"

"I love you too," Brooks said.

Smith threw his head back and chuckled at the sky.

LOVE COUPONS

Agent Hammerfield was always selling something. Active PTA parents were like that. In August, it was candy bars to fund the school band. In September, discounted pizza cards to decorate for homecoming. In October, pumpkin carving kits to help upgrade the cafeteria. In November, gourmet popcorn for theater club. In December, a basket raffle to purchase new gym equipment. In January, heirloom flower bulbs to get the teachers their first raise in three years. And in February, love coupons to raise money for the school's STD clinic. Guilt-inducing emails addressed to the entire Reticent staff—and the dozens of REPLY ALL responses cheering the effort—convinced nearly everyone to buy.

On a Friday evening, Brooks and Smith sat at Brooks's tiny kitchen table, staring each other down. Before them were two coupon booklets—identical in appearance but with randomized coupons—each purchased and given to the other with love.

Brooks laid a coupon on the table.

Night on the Town

Smith held his open booklet in front of him and flipped through slowly, deliberately. He eyed each coupon like it was a playing card in a particularly high-stakes round of poker. In the end, he found what he needed, and set a coupon on the table.

Nice Quiet Evening In

Brooks's face scrunched in dismay. He shook it off and aimed his hopes at the next day. He had just the coupon...

Weekend Getaway

Smith rifled through his booklet again—this time knowing what he wanted and where in the book it was located—and softly set a coupon down on the table with a smile.

Sleep In

Visibly frustrated, Brooks set his next coupon down with force.

Take a Road Trip Together

Smith issued a response.

Spend a Whole Day in Bed

Brooks huffed. "I never should have convinced you to buy these."

He flipped through, and found a smaller request. Surely his partner wouldn't have a problem with—

Picnic in the Park

Smith developed a mischievous grin before displaying his next coupon.

One Veto on Anything

Brooks aimed further into the future. There couldn't possibly be a counter to—

Plan a Vacation

Smith stared at the coupon and bit his lip. He appeared to have been beaten.

Appearances were deceiving. He played his card.

Stay-cation

Brooks threw his coupon booklet down on the table. "I quit."

"Don't quit now," Smith said. "We're having fun."

"Is that what you think we're doing?" Brooks asked, before going on a rant. "I'm *sorry* I want to spend time with you, okay? I'm *sorry* I want to do things before I get turned into a vampire or get murdered by pirate ghosts or whatever eventually happens to everyone who works for The Reticent. *I'm so sorry.*"

"You done?" Smith asked, amused by the tirade.

"*Yes,*" Brooks huffed. "*I'm done.*"

"Just pick one more..." Smith said.

"*No.*"

Smith shot him two wide eyes. "Please?"

"So you can cancel it out for the tenth time? *No.*"

"Come on. Please."

"*Fine.*"

Brooks rage-flipped through the pages and set down the most sarcastic coupon he could find.

Surprise Me

Smith chuckled and set down his pièce de résistance.

You Win an Argument

GLASS HOUSES

Brooks was alone in his apartment when the doorbell rang. He didn't expect any visitors on a Saturday afternoon, except for Smith, who had a key of his own. Curious, Brooks crossed the living room and looked out the peephole.

Everyone knows the five standard human senses: touch, sight, smell, taste, and sound. There is, however, a sixth sense—one that knows when someone is trying to sell something. That sense activated in Brooks as he observed a young woman in an NYU sweatshirt wearing a large backpack shuffling in place on the other side of his door.

He was torn. On one hand, she could be some sort of missionary and it would take forever to get her to leave. On the other hand, she could be selling food. Smith was an hour late, and Brooks was starving. He decided to chance it, and opened the door.

The woman barely looked up, and spoke her memorized lines with little flair. "Hi. My name is Zola. I'm going door to door telling everyone about this incredible product called Metaboluxe…"

"Not interested. Sorry." Brooks reached out to close the door.

"Are you or anyone you know suffering from insomnia, lethargy, depression, fatigue, thinning hair, brittle nails, or dry skin?" Zola asked.

He looked her in the unenthusiastic eyes. "Yeah, and that's what doctors are for. Bye."

Brooks was ready to shut the door when Smith arrived.

Smith brushed past the Metaboluxe saleswoman on his way through, then slammed the door behind himself.

"Who was that?" he asked.

"Some multilevel marketing scam," Brooks said. "You got the tickets?"

"No, I got mugged." Smith pulled two concert tickets from his jacket.

They were for Tortuga and the Angry Heart, the only band Brooks and Smith had ever agreed on. Tickets had sold out months in advance, but Smith found someone on Craigslist willing to trade for his collection of vintage *Sailor Moon* trading cards.

Brooks pumped his fists. "Thank you."

"Now we just gotta find a way to pass the next four hours," Smith said.

"I can think of a few—" Brooks coughed a little.

Smith took a step back. "You sick?"

"No. My throat's dry," Brooks said.

"Well, it ruined whatever you were trying to do there with the flirting," Smith said.

"Wasn't flirting. I was going to suggest a few places to eat—" This time, Brooks felt the coughs coming and aimed for his elbow.

"Tell me you're not getting sick four hours from Tortuga time," Smith said.

"I'm not. I'm fine," Brooks said. "Just thirsty... and hungry."

"I get the point," Smith said.

Brooks lumbered over to his couch and took a seat. "You want to just order in?"

Smith groaned. "You're getting sick four hours from Tortuga time."

"*I'm not*," Brooks insisted.

Smith went to the kitchen and returned with a glass of water. "Here."

Brooks took one sad little sip and coughed some more.

Smith shook his head. "Babe."

"I'm not getting sick. I *refuse* to be getting sick," Brooks said. "Pizza?"

"Pizza's fine," Smith said.

By the time the pizza arrived, Brooks couldn't eat any. Still, he insisted he was in good enough shape for Tortuga and the Angry Heart—that if it was anything, it was a light cold. He removed himself from the couch and struggled toward the door.

"I don't think you should go anywhere," Smith said.

Brooks responded with a hoarse voice. "It's fine. I—"

He fainted, the lack of food and water sending him straight to the floor.

Smith helped his delirious, sick partner to bed and tucked him in. He seated himself on the edge of the bed.

"I'm so sorry," Brooks said.

Smith brushed that off. "Don't be."

"You should go," Brooks said. "You gave up your *Sailor Moon* cards for those tickets."

"I'm thirty-four. I don't need *Sailor Moon* trading cards. There'll be another show."

"Well, you should go home so you don't catch whatever I have," Brooks said.

"*Like hell.* I get a whole week of sick leave, I'm gonna use it." Smith brushed a hand across Brooks's cheek. "I'll take care of you 'til I get the plague. Then you'll be over it and you can take care of me. I take care of you, you take care of me, right?"

"That's the deal..." Brooks coughed.

"You need anything?"

Brooks shook his head. "I don't think so..."

"Soup? Ice cream? Blowjob?" Smith said. "Name it."

"Just sleep," Brooks said.

"You got it." Smith kissed him on the forehead. "I'm gonna polish off that pizza and watch bad movies. Let me know if I'm too loud, or if you change your mind about the blowjob."

Brooks chuckled. "I will."

While Tortuga and the Angry Heart were rocking out on the other side of town, Brooks was rocking in his bed. It was too hot, then too cold. He rolled to shake his blankets off, then to pull them back over his body. Back off, back on. Over and over. Eventually, the motion made him sick. He put a hand over his mouth and slid off the bed in a pathetic attempt to make it to the bathroom. He doubled over and puked all over the floor—thanking both God and his landlord that it wasn't carpeted.

Smith heard the thump of his partner falling out of bed and rushed in to investigate. He walked in on Brooks spraying his floor with a second round of greenish-yellow fluid.

Brooks finished and leaned back against the bed.

"Christ, what do you even have in you to puke?" Smith asked.

"I think I have swine flu or something," Brooks groaned.

Smith helped Brooks back into bed and pondered. "Is that still a thing?"

"Eddie... this is bad," Brooks said.

"You need to go to a hospital?" Smith asked.

"No." Brooks coughed. "But could you just... stay here?"

"Yeah. Lemme see if I can't do that trick of yours and read you to sleep..." Smith got up and poked around Brooks's bookshelf, looking for something boring. *To Kill a Mockingbird* seemed like it would do the trick, so he grabbed it and settled in next to his shivering partner.

"You know my favorite book?" Brooks wondered.

"Of course," Smith lied.

Brooks made a slight smile.

Smith started reading. "When he was nearly thirteen, my brother Jem got his arm badly broken at the elbow..."

A few chapters later, Brooks was asleep.

A few chapters after that—as Smith continued silently reading to himself, not getting the big to-do about the book—Brooks started gasping for air. First, slight gasps. Then deep, raspy gasps that made his face turn red.

"Nope." Smith poked Brooks's shoulder to wake him. "Come on. You're going to a hospital."

Brooks coughed and squirmed. "Nooo... they'll just... send me back here..."

"Maybe. *You're still going*," Smith said.

"Can't... make me... bigger than you..."

"You're *taller* than me, not bigger. And I can call an ambulance. That'll be two thousand dollars."

"It's a flu, Eddie. *Please*."

Somehow, Smith let himself be convinced. While Brooks lay tucked in bed, running the symptom gamut from coughing to shaking with chills to throwing off his covers due to heat, Smith sat next to him, browsing WebMD on his phone.

"Chills. Hot. Coughing. Wheezing. Vomiting." Smith kept tapping. "Poor appetite. Looking a little pale... I miss anything?"

Brooks shivered and mumbled "no."

The results came in. "It says you have either pneumonia, Scarlet Fever, or... septicemia. I don't know what that is."

"Sepsis," Brooks said. "Look it up."

Smith did. "Gross."

"I don't... think it's that," Brooks said, hoping he wasn't on his way to total organ failure.

To Smith, it seemed like he might be. It was a confusing turn of events, considering he'd already seen the exact moment when Brooks would die in Willowbrook Park, and this wasn't it.

"Babe, you're turning blue," Smith said.

"Am not," Brooks said, burying himself deeper into his pillow.

"We're going to the hospital," Smith said.

"No," Brooks said.

Smith grabbed an arm and tried to pull his partner off the bed, but the arm was immovable. Smith tried another arm. Same thing. Whether he tugged an arm, a leg, or torso, it was as though Brooks was bolted to the bed.

"Stop fighting me," Smith said.

"I'm not—" Brooks stared at his arm, where Smith was once again tugging.

A thin, flaky white sheath of dead skin had been rolled halfway down his forearm.

Smith jumped back and grimaced. "Are you *molting*?"

"Maybe..." Brooks gagged a little. Then a lot.

His body was too heavy to lean forward as he retched, so he coughed straight up into the air. Brooks emitted a HUGGGHK sound as something emerged from deep within his throat. A small, round object flew from his mouth and landed on the bed with a THUNK.

Smith reached across his heavy partner and picked it up.

Brooks tried to speak through coughs. "Don't... touch... strange... orbs."

Too late. In his hand, Smith held a perfectly round stone, about two inches in diameter. It was a deep brown—almost black—and shone as though it had been polished.

"Okay, this isn't a WebMD situation," Smith said.

He called The Reticent and reported everything Brooks had experienced. Both detectives were directed to remain quarantined in Brooks's apartment while professional researchers did their jobs. The Reticent offered no additional advice, but said they may or may not send someone to retrieve the orb, depending on the results of their research.

When Smith got off the phone, Brooks looked at him with sad eyes.

"I'm dying, aren't I?" Brooks asked.

"No," Smith said, taking a seat next to him.

"I'm turning into a snake," Brooks said.

Smith shook his head. "No."

"What's happening?" Brooks asked.

"I don't know," Smith said.

During the lull in conversation, Smith could hear Brooks's breathing. It was more ragged than before, like the air inside him was being forced through a fifty-year-old HVAC system. He texted the one coworker he knew he could trust:

> I think brooks is dying
> some weird snake virus
> if you want to break quarenteen and help were at
> 904 pacific st apt 201

Smith tossed his phone to the side and settled in close to Brooks.

Brooks turned his head away. "You're gonna catch it..."

"I don't care," Smith said, pulling his head back.

Brooks's eyes were yellowing with jaundice, washing out his irises' normal warm brown color. It hurt Smith to look into them and lie, but that's what he did. "It's nothing. You're gonna be fine, and if I catch it I'm gonna be fine too."

"Eddie—" Brooks fainted again before he could finish a sentence.

Smith panic-checked Brooks's pulse. His wrist was so stiff it was impossible to tell whether it was still there or not. Same with the side of his neck. He leaned in close to his partner's face and felt the faintest breath. Brooks was still hanging onto life, which fit the narrative Smith had told himself about Willowbrook Park. But maybe he hadn't seen what he thought he had. Maybe there'd never been a Code Fourteen. Maybe there'd been a ghost or a shapeshifter or—It sure as shit seemed like Brooks was about to die, right here and now. Smith wasn't ready.

The doorbell rang, forcing him to focus. When he answered the door, Burroughs entered, wearing goggles, gloves, and a facemask.

"Is all that necessary?" Smith asked.

Burroughs set a duffel bag on the floor and stared at him through her goggles. "Yes. I'm not going to be an idiot just because you are." She looked around the unfamiliar apartment and gestured broadly toward a corner. "Bedroom over there?"

Smith nodded.

"What were you doing here on a Saturday anyway?" Burroughs asked.

"I had tickets to Tortuga and the Angry Heart," Smith said. "No one else wanted to go."

"Probably because they're awful," Burroughs said.

"Yeah, well." Smith was too stressed for a comeback.

Burroughs entered the bedroom, where Brooks was fluttering in and out of consciousness. She tried to move his arm and found that she couldn't. It was too heavy, as reported.

"Did you eat anything unusual?" she asked.

"Didn't... eat anything..." Brooks said.

"Has anyone threatened you recently?" she asked.

"No..."

"Have you gone anywhere that you don't normally?" she asked.

Brooks was out again, and couldn't answer.

Burroughs was asking good questions. Ones Smith should have asked, if he hadn't been preoccupied fluffing pillows and reading out loud. He shouldn't have blamed himself for not knowing how serious things were from the jump, but he did.

"I brought everything I have on mystical diseases," Burroughs said. "I assume you already did a search on Reti-net?"

Smith hadn't. "Uh... not yet."

Burroughs shook her head. "*Seriously?* Well, start now."

Smith looked at the bed, hesitant to leave Brooks lying there alone. "Uh... shouldn't someone keep an eye on him in case some weird new thing happens?"

"We don't need to check constantly," Burroughs said. "Whatever it is, the less we expose ourselves, the less chance we have of catching it."

"Yeah..." Smith followed Burroughs into the living room, where they hit the books and Reti-net.

He couldn't keep his focus. Every few minutes, Smith had a new excuse to go check on Brooks. First, he'd left his phone behind. Had to have that in case The Reticent called with a cure. Then he'd left his coat behind, and it was cold in the apartment. Then he thought he heard something, when the room was completely silent.

He returned from that trip to an irritated Burroughs.

"I know reading isn't one of your strong suits, Eddie, but you could at least pretend to be working on this since, y'know... it might kill him... or you."

Smith mumbled under his breath. "If this kills him, it better kill me."

"What?" Burroughs asked.

"*Nothing.* I think I heard something again." Smith went back into the bedroom.

"*Goddamn it.*" Burroughs slammed an ancient tome in frustration, and followed him.

There, she found Smith knelt next to the bed, holding his partner's stiff hand and looking into his eyes. He was whispering something to an unresponsive Brooks.

"What are you doing?" Burroughs asked.

Smith turned, his face completely drained of color except for redness in his eyes.

A realization hit Burroughs. "Oh my God."

"I want to help, but I can't leave him."

"How long have—"

"2008," Smith said.

"*Three years?*" Burroughs's mask stifled her gasp. "I'm sorry."

Smith's voice wavered. "Yeah..."

Burroughs offered a sympathetic nod. "Stay here and let me know if anything changes. I'll see what I can find."

Smith stayed, talking to Brooks and hating himself for not doing the research instead.

The next time Brooks came to, it was with wide, frightened eyes.

"I'm dying," he said into the air.

Smith didn't reply.

"If I weren't... dying..." Brooks coughed. "...you'd make jokes." He coughed harder and trailed off into short gasps.

Smith looked at him with all the love in his heart. "What, uh... what part of a hospital has the least privacy?"

Brooks stared at him.

"The ICU," Smith said.

Brooks responded with a pained smile.

Smith tried again. "Why couldn't the brain go skydiving?"

Brooks stared again.

"It lost its nerve..." Smith barely finished the joke. He quickly wiped his eye. "Sorry."

That told Brooks everything he needed to know.

"I don't think I'm ready to go..." he said.

"I know I'm not. Can I do anything for you?"

"Hold me?"

"Gonna be tough with you being a lead weight and all, but I'll try." Smith laid on his side next to Brooks and draped one arm over his chest. He gently stroked his hand up and down Brooks's side.

"Thanks..." Brooks coughed.

As his arm brushed back and forth, Smith felt something. "What the fuck?" He leaned over his partner's body and pressed both hands into his abdomen, hard.

"Ow..." Brooks complained.

The skin didn't give at all. It felt like there was cement underneath. Smith prodded around. Some areas felt fleshy and normal. Others were like brick. He jumped out of bed and ran to the living room.

"Snake lady," Smith said, in a frenzy.

"Fuck you. I'm trying to help," said Burroughs.

"*Not you.*" Smith rolled a hand at her, like he wanted her to finish a statement for him. "What's the name of the snake lady? The one that turns people to stone?"

"Medusa?"

Smith jumped a little. "Yes! I gave Brooksy a poke, and it feels like his organs are turning into stone. Not all at once, just—"

"*Brooksy?*" Burroughs squinted.

"Shut up, Erin. He's dying," Smith said.

Burroughs scooted a few books around, and grabbed one. "This book covers petrifaction. You're saying he's turning to stone from the inside out?"

"Yeah. Probably."

Burroughs thought about it. "That actually tracks... peeling skin can be a sign of kidney failure. Yellow eyes are a sign of liver failure. Turning blue and being unable to breath—"

"Lungs," Smith said.

"Right," Burroughs said.

"What's the cure for a Medusa?" Smith asked.

Burroughs sighed. "The generic term is *gorgon*, but I think Agent Brooks would have mentioned meeting a snake person."

"You ever run into one?" Smith asked.

"No, they're extremely rare," Burroughs said. "Have you?"

"No. *That's my point*. When has anything *ever* been exactly like the lore says? Maybe they can hide their snake bits," Smith said.

"Okay, well..." She flipped to the Gorgon section of her Petrifaction text. "From what I recall... yeah. Blood taken from the right side of a gorgon can heal a person. Blood taken from their left side is poison."

"Our right or their right?" Smith asked, poking his head back into the bedroom.

"Their right," Burroughs said. "I think..."

Smith stepped into the bedroom and gave Brooks a quick kiss on the forehead.

"Snake lady. We're gonna get you some gorgon blood and you'll be right as rain," he said.

Brooks looked at him with a mixture of confusion and imminent death.

"Just hang in there," Smith said. "Please."

"Trying..." Brooks coughed.

Smith hurried back into the living room. "We find a gorgon, steal its blood, and what? Inject it into his veins? Feed it to him?"

"You're getting way too excited. Finding a gorgon is a big ask," Burroughs said.

DING DONG.

The doorbell rang, and Smith headed for the door.

"You are *in quarantine*," Burroughs said.

"Gorgons aren't contagious. It's probably agents coming for that orb. Maybe I'll get lucky and it'll be someone who blows my brains out." Smith opened the door.

The voice that greeted him wasn't much cheerier than his own. "Hi. My name is Zola. I'm going door-to-door telling everyone about this incredible product called Metaboluxe..."

"Jesus Christ," Smith complained. "You've already been here."

Zola droned on. "Are you or anyone you know suffering from insomnia, lethargy, depression, fatigue, thinning hair, brittle nails, or dry skin?"

"Take your snake oil somewhere el—"

Smith realized what he'd just said. He grabbed the young woman by her backpack straps and pulled her into the apartment.

She flailed away from him and reached for her danger whistle. "*What are you doing?*" She blew into the whistle—BRRRRRRRT BRRRRRRRT—until Smith violently yanked it from her neck.

"You came here earlier, and my partner started getting sick," he said.

"I apologize for him," Burroughs said from the couch. "*Eddie.*"

Zola's eyes widened when she noticed the woman in

PPE. "Why are you dressed like that?"

"Shut up. I wanna know what you did to him," Smith said.

Burroughs stood and confronted him. "Calm down. Does she look like a damn Medusa to you?"

"Gorgon," Smith corrected.

Zola looked from Burroughs to Smith and back, frightened but compelled to say something at the chance of making money. "If you have a sick friend, Metaboluxe might help..."

"What the fuck is Metaboluxe?" Smith asked.

"I'm glad you asked!" Zola said. "Metaboluxe is a proprietary blend of B vitamins, L-Theanine, green tea extract, guarana, hemp, ephedra, and gorgon blood."

Smith and Burroughs both stared at her.

"And *what*?" Smith asked.

Zola couldn't remember what came last, so she repeated her script. "B vitamins, L-Theanine, green tea extract, guarana, hemp, ephedra, and gorgon blood."

Smith seethed. "And you're telling me you're not a gorgon?"

"I don't know what that is," Zola said. "But all of our ingredients are all-natural."

"I'll take one," Smith said.

"Well, it's a subscription plan. You'll receive a delivery every four weeks..."

While she listened to the pitch, Burroughs unzipped the young woman's backpack and rifled through it. She pulled out a large, brown bottle of Metaboluxe, and gave it a shake.

"What's the dose?" she asked.

Zola launched into another script. "Just three pills a day, and you'll feel better than you have your entire life."

Burroughs tossed Smith the bottle, and he hurried into

the bedroom. Burroughs escorted the saleswoman in after him.

Brooks was in worse shape than ever. The skin of his arms had begun petrifying. Tan, blue, and stone grey mixed together in splotches, giving his skin the appearance of some gemstone for sale in a tacky gift shop.

Smith approached and showed him the bottle. "Open up, babe. Time for your snake oil."

Brooks expressed his disbelief, even through a series of coughs. "*Metaboluxe?*"

"I know." Smith popped a large, herb-smelling pill in his partner's mouth, then put a glass of water to his lips.

Brooks choked a little, but managed to get it down.

"...tastes like a music festival..."

That he had the energy to complain was a sure sign the pills were what they advertised. The next sign was that Brooks's eyes began returning to their normal shade.

"Two to go," Smith said.

Brooks looked at him with eyes that said "smother me instead."

Smith didn't smother him. Instead, he gently helped Brooks swallow another pill.

With the second, Brooks's skin was restored to its normal color. He raised an arm from the bed, ever so slightly. With confirmation that it worked, he hoisted himself into a seated position. Then groaned because his internal organs were still incredibly heavy.

By the time he downed the third pill, Brooks was able to chug the entire glass of water with it. Smith hurried away and brought him back another. He downed that one too.

"Are you going to pay me, or can I go?" Zola asked.

"We're not paying you, and you're staying," Burroughs said. "Come with me."

Sensing that the men might need a few moments, she

took Zola to the couch.

Smith sat on the edge of the bed, next to Brooks.

"I smell like death," Brooks said.

"Yeah. You do," Smith said.

Brooks glanced around his bedroom. "Did you just... cover my puke in paper towels?"

"Yeah. I did," Smith said.

Brooks looked deep into his eyes. "Thank you."

"For being lazy with the cleanup?"

"For staying with me."

Smith's face scrunched. "Didn't have any other option. Quarantine."

"I'm sure you wanted to go join the research, but I asked you to stay and you stayed—"

"I didn't," Smith said. "Not because you asked me to, anyway."

Brooks stared at him and blinked a few times.

Smith explained. "The thing is... when I realized you were dying... I couldn't read a paragraph about Medusa without coming back in here to check on you. I've never... I've always been good in a crisis... I don't know what I'm trying to say here..."

"It's been a long day," Brooks said.

Smith continued thinking out loud. "If I die, that's fine. If we die together, that's fine. But I don't wanna live without you." He scoffed. "I hate this."

Brooks squinted at him. "What? Being in love?"

"It fucking blows," Smith said.

"Well, I'll try my best not to die without you," Brooks said dryly.

Smith snorted. *"Thanks."*

"Am I too gross to kiss?" Brooks asked.

"You really are," Smith said.

He leaned in and kissed him anyway.

❧

Brooks emerged from his bathroom—smelling less like death and more like body wash—to find Zola propositioning Burroughs. Smith, meanwhile, sat in a corner drinking bourbon directly from a bottle.

"Why would I want to join an MLM?" Burroughs asked.

Zola gave another of her prewritten spiels. "Metaboluxe empowers women to become small business owners. Be your own boss and earn monthly revenue streams of up to twenty thousand dollars. You'll receive real margins from every subscription to Metaboluxe sold, as well as bonuses calculated from business growth, and incentives for reaching key milestones."

"Do you have an original sentence anywhere in your brain?" Burroughs asked.

Brooks eyed the scene. "Um... what's going on?"

Smith took another swig of bourbon. "She's been trying to get info out of little miss snake oil for half an hour."

"Not working?" Brooks asked.

"I've heard the same pitch a dozen different ways," Burroughs said. "I'm sure I'll crack her any minute."

Brooks eyed bottles of Metaboluxe and brochures piled on the coffee table. "You looked through all of—"

Burroughs nodded. "Yeah. It says the same stuff she says, but in print."

Smith coughed a little, popped a Metaboluxe, and chased it with bourbon.

Brooks sat next to him. "You caught it too?"

"Maybe. Doesn't really matter since we have the cure," Smith said.

"Sure, but that girl is the only one we've both interacted with in the last twenty-four hours," Brooks said. "She's our suspect."

"She's not a gorgon," Burroughs said with confidence. "Just an idiot."

Zola droned on. "This is an opportunity to get in on the ground floor of a business that's growing every day. It's going to happen with or without you. Why work in an office, when you could work from anywhere, during the flexible hours you choose? Metaboluxe fits every lifestyle."

"How do you know?" Brooks asked.

"Glad you asked," Burroughs said. "Blood from the right side of a gorgon heals just about anything, like you found out this evening. Blood from the left side of a gorgon kills just about anything." She gestured at the tiny plastic bandage on Zola's left hand. "I took a sample and dumped it on your succulent over there."

Brooks inspected his plant, which was covered in blood but still very much alive.

"Gross," he said.

"Yep," Burroughs said, then casually changed subjects. "So, how'd you two become an item?"

"Um..." Brooks wasn't sure how to respond.

"Couldn't keep it a secret," Smith said.

"I dunno," Brooks said. "We started working together and something just... clicked."

Burroughs eyed Smith. "You know he's an asshole, right?"

"*Fuck you, Erin*," Smith said.

She cackled.

"I know. That's one of the things I like about him," Brooks said.

"*Hey*," Smith objected.

Brooks grinned. "Besides, my last boyfriend was from New Jersey, so anything's an improvement."

His statement activated something in Zola, who made

another pitch. "Metaboluxe is made right here in the USA, in our factory in Manville, New Jersey."

"That's something," Smith said.

Burroughs tapped at her laptop's keyboard. "There's no address online for Metaboluxe in Manville, New Jersey."

Smith took another swig of bourbon. "Not something."

"Manville only has ten thousand people, though," Burroughs said. "We should be able to find it."

"Then what?" Brooks asked.

"Then we figure out how this lady turned your insides into rocks without being a gorgon," Burroughs said.

"Right, but if there's actually one there, we're just going to end up statues," Brooks said.

"Wouldn't be the first time I was rock hard," Smith slurred.

"Eddie, stop drinking." Brooks turned to Zola. "Who founded Metaboluxe?"

Burroughs sighed. "Already asked that one. She wouldn't answer—"

"Medusa Myers," Zola said.

"Not at all suspicious," Brooks said.

"Medusa Myers was born in—" Zola's droning pitch suddenly took a deep, hissing tone. Her eyes went solid white. Her mouth hung agape as a monstrous voice that wasn't hers emerged from within her throat. "If you keep asking questions, I'll make sure you all die."

"Medusa Myers?" Burroughs wondered. "Are you... talking through your minion?"

"She's not a minion. She's a fully empowered salesperson," the voice said.

"Empowered to kill people?" Smith asked.

"I haven't killed anyone. My salespeople return to every house. Everyone I poison buys Metaboluxe and lives a long, healthy life. Let's keep it that way, shall we?" Zola's eyes returned to their normal, depressed state. "—So would you like an annual subscription or not?"

Brooks, Smith, and Burroughs each surrendered a credit card and signed up. The detectives told themselves they'd cancel their credit cards and end the subscriptions, but somehow they never remembered to do so.

Ladies!

IF YOU WANT A JOB WITH:

- Super flexible schedule
- Can pay BIG money $$$
- Always empowering
- Many great perks (did someone say free leggings???)

Metaboluxe is LOOKING
for BOSS BABES LIKE YOU

Perfect For:

- Misses, Mrs., and Mxes
- Old ladies with cats
- RNs looking for xtra cash
- Oscar-winner Gwyneth Paltrow
- New Moms
- Sidehustle

Become a Metaboluxe Consultant TODAY!

NECROMANCER

When families bury the bodies of their loved ones, it's generally with the understanding that graves are a place for eternal rest. According to a recent Monmouth University poll, only 21% of bereaved Americans would choose burial over cremation if they knew the body would be revived as a soulless husk.

Unfortunately, there was no way of knowing which corpses would rise in advance. Fortunately, The Reticent had developed technology to test whether graves had been abandoned by their occupants. It was essentially a metal detector, but for bones. Every cemetery in New York City had to be checked once a month. It was one of the worst duties an agent could receive, generally reserved for those who'd managed to piss off their superiors.

Thus, Brooks and Smith strolled through Cypress Hills Cemetery, Queens, carrying handheld corpse scanners that looked like old-fashioned label makers. As the cemetery housed corpses numbering in the hundred thousands, the agents had their work cut out for them.

They casually strolled down alternating rows, briefly holding a scanner above each grave until it made a friendly chime and the screen read 'STILL DEAD.'

"When we're done, you wanna hit the Ren Fest?" Brooks asked.

There was a renaissance festival in Forest Park, adjacent to the cemetery. The detectives could occasionally hear a "hurrah!" or some joust-induced gasps through the trees, and the wind occasionally blew a waft of funnel cake grease.

"Oversized drumsticks?" Smith beamed. "Fuck yes. Can we make fun of the doofs pretending they know how to use medieval weapons?"

"Of course. And the shitty arts and crafts."

Smith grinned. "I love you so much."

BEEP BEEP BEEP.

Brooks's scanner read 'CORPSE MISSING' over the crumbling grave of Leonard Cronk, 1879 - 1924. Smith recognized the beeps and moved to join his partner.

"Crap," Brooks said. "Now we have to go get the shovels..."

BEEP BEEP BEEP.

As he passed a different grave, Smith's scanner went off. Another missing corpse.

"*Great*," Smith said, more annoyed he might miss out on the giant drumsticks than he was worried. Most of the time, when a corpse went missing, it had either been stolen for use in some magic ritual, stolen for use in some perverse manner, or it had become a zombie. Those were slow, stupid, and easy to kill. No big deal.

Human bodies sometimes process danger before their brains do. Something deep inside Brooks told him it was, in fact, a big deal. A chill hit his neck and moved to his arms, where every hair stood up straight. He stepped one grave to the left, over Leonard's wife, Hattie Cronk, who had—unsettlingly—lived from 1911 to 2011.

BEEP BEEP BEEP.

"Eddie..." Brooks froze in place.

"This isn't great," Smith said, triggering another BEEP BEEP BEEP of his own.

Then another.

Then another.

Smith reached for his sidearm. "Hopefully just some corpsefucker collecting—"

A gargling, hissing sound came from nearby, and Brooks turned and spotted what his brain already knew was there. A wraith.

In the pantheon of Reticent monsters, wraiths were one of the rarest and most dreaded. Like vampires, wraiths possessed haunting yellow eyes and sharp fangs. Unlike vampires, they had a whole mouth full of them instead of two incisors. They also weren't sexually exciting. Like zombies, wraiths were resurrected corpses that consumed human flesh. Unlike zombies, they moved swiftly, like natural predators. Wraiths were the worst of both worlds.

This one—with its translucent, decaying flesh draping loosely from its bones—had its eyes fixed on its next meal.

Brooks knew what to do. He'd had all the training. But he couldn't do it. The brain that had been considerate enough to alert him to danger was now rude enough to bring back memories of Willowbrook Park. Forcefully. He stood dumbstruck, staring as the creature bounded toward him, eyes glowing, still hissing.

Smith saw the look on his partner's face and knew he had to deal with the monster himself. It was easy enough, in theory. Just like zombies. Destroy the brain. He fired off a shot that whizzed past the wraith and took a chip out of an old mausoleum.

"Shit," he said.

The wraith reached Brooks, claws first, and tackled him to the ground. It wasted no time digging its fangs into his shoulder. Fortunately, Brooks had dressed for the weather and the creature's first bite was mostly coat. It gargled and hissed and spat out bits of wool. To Brooks, the wet chunks that hit his cheek weren't pieces of his coat, but violent memories. Blood, guts, screams of agony.

Smith stepped closer and shot the wraith through the side of its head. He reached a hand down toward Brooks. "You okay?"

"Uh huh…" Brooks glanced at the tattered wool at his shoulder, and quickly brushed a few bits from his face. He took Smith's hand and allowed himself to be brought to his feet.

Smith eyed his partner's pallid face with concern. "Is that the first wraith you've seen since—"

"Uh huh…" Brooks looked down at his dirty hands. They were shaking.

"Go home," Smith directed. "I'll get someone else in here and say you were sick."

Brooks's eyes looked past his hands and refocused. He took a step back. "It's too late."

From the direction of the Ren Fest came screams. Dozens of wraiths like the one Smith had just murdered rushed across the cemetery. They ignored the detectives and bounded toward the park. Some had already arrived, clearly.

Brooks dropped back to the ground and leaned against a headstone. His breaths came shallow and rapid. "*Dios te salve, Reina y Madre de misericordia, vida, dulzura y esperanza nuestra—*"

Smith dialed the Reticent dispatch number and summed things up. "At least a dozen wraiths in Forest Park. Send everyone you can." He hung up, knelt down, and knocked Brooks out of prayer. "Babe."

Brooks trembled. "I can't…"

"I know, but I kinda have to." Smith reached down, unholstered Brooks's gun, and put it in his hand. "They probably won't come back this way since there's a big fat feast over there, but if they do… shoot 'em in the head. Please.

I believe in you."

"Don't go alone..."

"I can take care of myself." Smith corrected that. "Sort of. My aim's good." Another correction. "It's *decent*. Don't worry." He planted a quick kiss on Brooks's lips. "Love you. Don't die."

"Love you too..."

Brooks watched Smith leave with a sense of impending doom. He wanted to get up. He wanted to go with his partner and help. He wanted to do his job.

His brain said, "Absolutely not. How about you remember the worst day of your life instead."

Before he had a traumatic backstory, Arturo Brooks had a family. In the late summer of 2004, he, his father Norman, and his sister Tasha came together to celebrate. Tasha had snagged an internship, and Arturo was a semester away from graduating with his Bachelor's. After his sister, he'd be the second person in Brooks family history to do so.

A free concert in Willowbrook Park, Staten Island. Some mediocre folk band that no one had ever heard of. But the band wasn't the point. Celebration was, and it was a point Arturo would never reach if he didn't hustle. Already an hour late, he scurried across the lawn with a sixer of beer in hand. He maneuvered around strollers and people getting their faces painted to find his family on a blue and white striped picnic blanket.

Tasha looked up at her brother. "Thank God. You brought beer."

Norman feigned offense. "Is it that difficult to spend some time with your old man?"

"I'm teasing," Tasha said.

Willowbrook Park had seen better days. More empty bottles than paddle boats floated in its lake. More trash than picnic blankets spread across the lawn. The park's chipped carousel stood next to not one but three dumpsters, all overflowing. Arturo—having finally caught his breath—looked around.

"We couldn't find any place better than *this*?" he wondered.

"Don't knock free," Norman said. "Plus, a park doesn't care if you're *late*."

"Sorry." Arturo handed his sister the beer, then flopped onto the blanket. "Catch me up."

"I was just telling dad about the internship. Nothing you haven't already heard," Tasha said.

Norman looked at his son with a serious face. "You should think about applying for some."

Arturo glowered. "I haven't even been here a minute, and you're comparing us..."

"Not comparing," Norman said.

Tasha interjected. "It's easy to get one. I did it, and you're way smarter than I am."

"If I were smarter than you, I wouldn't have taken that gap year and I'd already be done," Arturo said.

"Yeah, but then you wouldn't have—"

He nudged her into silence.

Tasha rolled her eyes. "Whatever. Like I said, it's easy. Unless you plan on getting a PhD and teaching, an internship is your best bet."

"I'm just... focused on passing this semester..." Arturo looked away.

He and Tasha were twins. That meant two things. One: They looked like the gender-swapped versions of each other—tall, thin twenty-somethings with the same deep brown eyes and dark brown hair. Two: They had that weird twin bond that let them know when something was wrong with their other half. Something in the way Arturo averted his eyes tipped off Tasha.

Because they were siblings, she egged him on instead of offering sympathy. "How do you pick a major like *chemistry* and not have a plan? It's not like the world's full of job openings for chemists."

"I'll figure something out," Arturo mumbled.

Norman chimed in. "Worse comes to worst, you can pick up a few of my shifts."

"I am *not* driving a cab."

Norman's tone and demeanor hardened. "I guess you can always go back to working at Subway."

"Not doing that either," Arturo said.

Tasha had an idea. "What if—"

Arturo cut her off. "Oh my God. I will *figure it out*. I have forever."

"You don't know that for sure," Norman said. "Your mother—"

"I don't plan on *giving birth* any time soon either," Arturo said.

Tasha poked her brother's shoulder. "What's got you so pissy?"

"Ow. *Nothing*," Arturo said.

She poked harder.

"Ow!"

Arturo poked her back, hardest.

Tasha groaned. "Lino broke up with you, didn't he?"

Norman's face was always paler than his children's, but it went even paler. While he accepted his son, it was the early 2000s and he had no desire to hear about any of his boyfriends. Ever.

Arturo spared him the agony. "None of your business."

For good measure, he poked his sister again.

"Yow!" Tasha yelped.

Norman pinched the bridge of his nose. "You're not twelve anymore, kids."

The twins glared at each other, each holding an index finger high as a threat.

Norman grabbed a bottle of beer. "Let's make a toast."

Arturo and Tasha raised their bottles.

The screaming at the Ren Fest intensified.

From his graveside vantage point, Brooks couldn't see why. All he saw was the occasional escapee, sprinting through the cemetery covered in blood, sweat, and/or tears.

One survivor slowed for a second to check whether Brooks was dead. The moment he blinked, the survivor kept moving. No reason to stay and wait to die with some random person in distress—especially not one trembling and pointing a gun.

Brooks dedicated his last ounce of energy toward keeping that gun ready. It's what Smith told him to do. It's what he had to do.

Every other ounce of energy was busy retraumatizing him.

There was nothing in his line of sight but grass and headstones, but he could see the wraiths clear as day. His mind had never forgotten them. How could it? He'd watched the damn things tear Tasha from him, leaving him holding nothing but his sister's disembodied hand. He'd felt his father's warm blood splash across his face. He felt it still. He could hear their visceral screams, clear as the day they happened.

☙

Back then, Agent Smith had offered Arturo a hand. He pulled the young man from a bloody patch of concrete to a standing position.

"What's your name?" Smith asked.

"I... uh..." Arturo didn't have an answer. He was too focused on his family's remains, spread across the sidewalk next to a fallen wraith in a distressingly cheery pineapple print dress.

"Don't look." Smith grabbed the young man by the shoulder and pulled him into focus.

"A... Arturo Brooks."

"Okay, Arturo. I'm Edward Smith."

Arturo's eyes drifted back to the ground. He'd never thought about what the inside of an eyeball looked like before. He gagged a little.

"Don't look. Just talk," Smith said.

"What... what were those?" Arturo asked.

Smith put no energy into selling the company line. "Bath salts. People do too much of 'em, they turn into cannibals."

"Don't lie to me," Arturo said.

"Wraiths. Like a zombie meets a ghost," Smith said.

"*Wraiths*," Arturo repeated, in disbelief.

"Yeah. Dead things. Don't like being decapitated," Smith said.

"Wh... what else is real?" Arturo asked.

"Be a lot easier to list what isn't." Smith began counting on his fingers. "Aliens. Dragons. Unconditional love..."

☙

In 2011, there was still no evidence of aliens or dragons, but the last one... Smith had been wrong about that. In the distance, sounds of gunfire came from what was probably Smith's gun.

Brooks pictured Smith as he was when they met, and as he was now. He'd aged a bit—more than most people, really—but as the lines of his face had hardened, his demeanor had softened. Brooks loved him, with every ounce of his being. He imagined the man he loved dying like his father and sister had. Bloodily. Painfully. Smith could take care of himself. He'd done it his entire life. But it would only take one lucky wraith, and there were dozens—

With that thought, fear became a moving force, rather than a paralyzing one.

Brooks stood and steadied himself. He took a series of deep breaths.

You can do this. You have to do this.

His feet moved toward Forest Park.

At first, they were slow. Then steady. Then he was sprinting.

Sirens blared. Multiple guns fired. NYPD had made it to the scene. They could take care of most of it, assuming they knew how to aim at something other than unarmed civilians.

Brooks just had to do one thing: find Smith. He moved in the opposite direction of the crowds—what little of them was left.

Just like it had been in Willowbrook Park, the ground was littered with remains. Wraiths would eat just about any part of a human being, but they preferred muscle. Real, human meat. They mostly left organs and bones behind. Brooks scanned the gore as briefly as he could—his mind mixing memories with the present. Amongst all the medieval tunics, gowns, teeth, and intestines, he saw nothing of his partner's. That was good.

Something was off about the wraiths, though.

From a distance, Brooks saw some of them gathering.

Wraiths didn't gather. They weren't human enough to understand the concept of group work. But there they were, standing in a circle. Something else about them was different too. Each monster had a faint red aura.

Brooks—against all common sense—approached the circle. He knew that's what Smith would have done, so he followed, his heart racing. Could they see him? Did they even need to see him to know he was there? Why were they glowing?

"Excellent work, darlings," said a nasal voice in the center of the circle.

Brooks raised his gun and shot two of the wraiths in the back of the head. They dropped to the ground, leaving an opening in the formation. The other wraiths didn't turn to face him. The other wraiths didn't react, at all. He shot a third. Again, the other wraiths failed to react.

"Would you stop that?" asked the same nasal voice.

Brooks approached, his weapon shaking in his hands. He was about to step where seven monsters could close in on him and tear him to pieces. He took a deep breath and stepped over the fallen wraiths. The others stared vacantly toward the center of the circle, at a skinny human in a red cloak, his face obscured by its shadows.

Some nerd, as Smith would have called him. If Smith had been there. That he wasn't there... it didn't bode well.

From up close, Brooks could see bullet holes in the wraiths' heads. They shouldn't have been mobile with their rotted brains turned to mush. One of them didn't even have a head. All wraiths were dead, but these were *dead* dead. They were also... busty. Brooks puzzled the situation out.

"You're a necromancer," he said.

"Mmhmm. New York's best," said the necromancer, who then introduced himself. "Lance Harper."

Necromancy was the easiest form of magic to learn, and the people who tended to learn it were unbearable. They thought highly of themselves, but anyone capable of basic spellwork or telekinesis looked down on them like they were incels. Most of them were, and they favored resurrecting large-breasted women for ogling. Thus the well-endowed monsters that surrounded this one.

Brooks eyed one wraith's outfit: a tattered pineapple dress. Distressingly cheery. "These are the same wraiths from Willowbrook Park..."

"Some of 'em. Yeah."

"Why?" Brooks asked.

"Just showing Blaze I can do better."

Brooks stared at him. "*Who?*"

"Blaze Arnold? The dickhead who runs the Astoria Guild? If you know about Willowbrook Park, you should know he did it. Dude hasn't stopped poppin' off on his vlog ever since." The necromancer laughed and spoke to the sky, as if Blaze could hear him. "Fuck you, Blaze. I raised every last one of your stupid wraiths *and* made more, with bigger tits. Gtfo."

"I was *at Willowbrook Park*. Blaze had nothing to do with it," said Brooks.

"Well, he's been taking credit for it. Now that little bitch can't say shit."

"This isn't some shitty video game," Brooks said. "You're *murdering people*."

The necromancer shrugged. "Ren Fest had it coming after they banned me for life."

Brooks didn't care to know what the Ren Fest had banned him for. He raised his gun and pointed it at the necromancer's head. "I'm guessing if I kill you, they all drop dead. For good."

"Yeah, buuuuut..."

"*What?*" Brooks snapped.

The necromancer waved his hand and murmured something in Latin. Two of the busty wraiths floated—in mid-air—away from each other. They parted to make way for a new corpse to float into the circle.

"I think this one's yours," the necromancer said, guiding a body in like he was landing a plane. It lay flat on its back, in the air. Male. Thirty-something. Bloody.

As he registered the situation, Brooks didn't lower his gun. His nightmare was real. He didn't need to stare at it. He knew the body by its dirty blond hair. There would be plenty of time for despair, but for the moment Brooks felt nothing but rage.

"Can you shoot me faster than I can have them murder you?" the necromancer wondered.

Brooks pressed his finger closer to the trigger. "Let's find out."

"Let's not." The nerdy necromancer bargained. "If you kill me, he stays dead. It's only been a few minutes. I can bring him back if you let me go."

"Yeah. *Right.*"

"I mean it. No big deal. 'Tis but a scratch. Simple revive spell. He'll be human, even."

"Human?" Brooks tilted his head.

"Yeah. All you have to do is let me go," the necromancer said.

Reticent training said never to make deals with monsters.

Brooks had slept through that training.

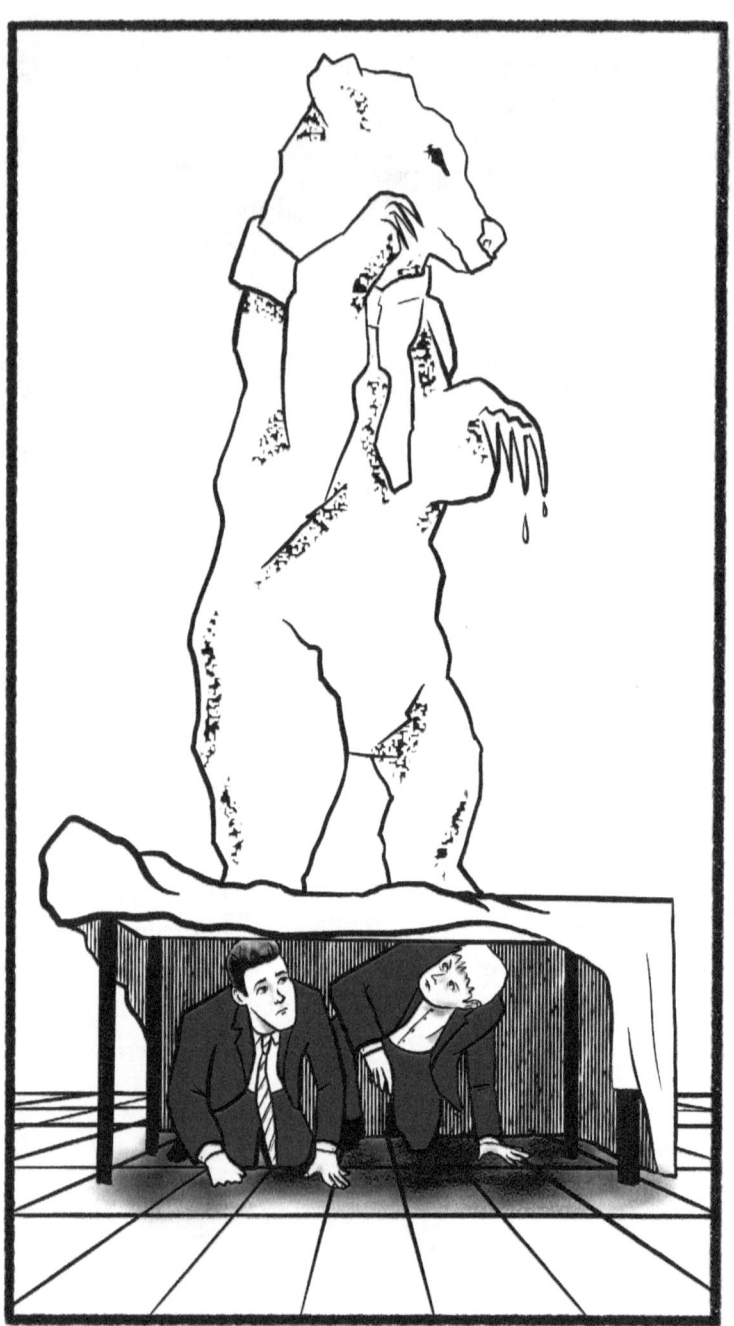

HOLIDAY PARTY

In four years of dating and being work partners, Brooks and Smith still hadn't lost their spark. Something about being in constant danger kept the thrill alive. Covered in ectoplasm—courtesy of a very annoying ghoul—they rode the elevator down to their office. Before they could leave for the night, they had to file some form for the bureaucracy.

"You staying at my place?" Brooks asked.

Smith had a question of his own. "You really wanna drag all this filth into your apartment?"

"No, but I have a bigger shower. We could get cleaned up together." Brooks smiled.

Smith grinned, then pointed at the corner of his partner's mouth. "Speaking of, you've got a little something on—"

Brooks wiped at his face. "Did I get it?"

"Nope." Smith motioned again.

"*Now?*" Brooks asked.

Smith shook his head and took a step closer. He brushed his thumb across Brooks's mouth, sending a teensy bit of ectoplasm to the floor. He took another step closer, and their lips locked. Soon they were making out in the elevator.

The elevator opened too soon.

Brooks reacted in an instant. He shoved Smith against the wall, hard, and raised his voice. "Don't tell me how to conduct an investigation."

Smith caught on to the faux fight scheme—they'd done this a time or two. He shoved Brooks across the elevator. "Stop fucking up and I won't have to."

In the doorway, a concerned intern in a Santa hat stared at them. She sheepishly took a step back, away from the door. "I'll catch the next one."

"Close call," Smith said, after the door shut.

They continued macking.

The horny detectives scurried into their office. Smith waited impatiently while Brooks hurried through the digital paperwork, making way more spelling and grammatical errors than normal. He didn't care. He smashed the Send button and logged out.

He stood to leave. "Let's go—"

Smith was already standing, and blocked his path. "*Or*, you could toss me around some more right here—"

"We really shouldn't," Brooks said.

"No, we shouldn't." Smith stepped closer.

They shouldn't have, given Reticent policy on intraoffice dating (and that they were covered in ectoplasm), but they did.

In their haste, the detectives hadn't closed their door all the way.

Smith was working some magic with his mouth when a voice in the doorway made him relinquish Brooks's dick.

"*Oh my God*," the voice said.

Brooks scrambled to pull up his pants.

Smith turned and let out a relieved, "*Jesus Christ, Erin*."

His former partner—Erin Burroughs—stood at the entry to their office, mouth agape.

"*Jesus Christ yourself, Eddie.*"

Brooks stood, realized his fly was still undone, and remedied it.

"Don't tell anyone," he said, pleading.

"Why would I tell anyone?" Burroughs wondered. "But if you don't want anyone to know you're banging in your office, you might remember to *close your door.*"

"What do you want?" Smith asked.

"I saw your light on. I was gonna ask if you're going to the holiday party," she said.

"No," Smith said.

"Why not? You love free drinks." Burroughs turned to Brooks. "You love... mingling? Probably?" She didn't really know him that well.

Smith saw right through her feigned interest. "Corporate's making you go and you're worried you won't have anyone to talk to."

"Bingo," Burroughs said.

"Still no," Smith said.

"Come on. *Please.*" Burroughs plastered her face with the fakest of smiles.

"Don't look at me," Smith said, glancing at Brooks. "Where Brooksy goes, I go. He's the one with the problem."

Brooks sighed. "I don't like the holiday party."

"Why?" Burroughs asked.

"Because I have to pretend Eddie and I are just coworkers while everyone else is drunk making out with their spouses under the mistletoe. I'd love a holiday party if we could just be... normal. It's bad enough we can't move in together."

Burroughs squinted. "Sure you can."

"The Reticent has all of our addresses on file," Brooks noted.

"Yeah, but—"

Smith made a cut-it-out gesture, but Burroughs continued.

"—you just make up a fake apartment number for one of you. Like, say you live in 201." She pointed at Brooks. "You live in 201A." She pointed at Smith. "You live in 201B. Paste a couple letters on your mail slot and the postal service won't know the difference. Plausible deniability. You work together enough, it's not surprising you'd let him know about a vacancy next door."

"That's brilliant," Brooks said.

"It's not my idea. Plenty of agents have done it," Burroughs said. "I'm surprised Eddie hasn't mentioned it..."

"Plenty of agents *who wanted to get caught* have done it," Smith said, convincing no one that he actually cared about that.

Brooks rolled his eyes. "You can just say you don't want to."

Burroughs tried to recapture control of the conversation. "So, holiday party—"

"I like having my own space," Smith said. "I'm already with you like twenty hours a day. What's the difference?"

"Exactly. *What's the difference?*" Brooks said.

Burroughs buried her head in her hands.

"The difference is, I'm gonna go back to my place, get cleaned up, and go to the holiday party," Smith said. "In the time it takes you to even get to your apartment."

"I never said you had to move in *with me*," Brooks said.

"It's implied," Smith said.

"I'm gonna..." Burroughs inched backward toward the door. "Bye."

Brooks stared at his partner, full of determination. "I'll make it home, get showered, and be at the holiday party before you."

"Bullshit," Smith said. "Chelsea versus Prospect Heights."

Brooks maintained his stare. They both lived about twenty-five minutes from Reticent HQ.

"Fine," Smith said. "You're on."

The detectives ran for the door, blasting right past Burroughs.

A little over an hour later, they returned to Reticent HQ at the exact same time. Each man spotted the other coming down the sidewalk.

"How is that even possible?" Brooks wondered as they met.

Smith shrugged and eyed his ectoplasm-free date. "You look good."

"So do you," Brooks said.

They looked the same as ever, since they always wore suits. But this time Brooks had replaced his standard black tie with a red and green striped one. Smith had removed his entirely.

Adjacent to Reticent HQ was a Reticent-owned conference center. Most of the year, it hosted benign corporate events and budget weddings. Come December, it was decked with multicolored string lights, gold tinsel, and festive trees, so that the clueless spouses of Reticent agents could believe their significant others worked for a normal pharmaceutical company that just happened to have a weird name.

Brooks and Smith entered the conference center, which smelled like the 1960s. Incidentally, it was built in the 1960s and sat musty with decades' worth of cigarette and cigar smoke. The decor, at least, was modern. Tasteful tile and recessed lighting ruled the day. There wasn't a lobby to speak of, just a hallway stretching left and a hallway stretching right. A letterboard on a metal tripod outlined the evening's events and pointed them in the right direction.

The Annual Reticent Non-Denominational Holiday Party was in the Paisley Room, a ballroom that could hold up to a thousand (standing room only). A check-in booth outside the door was staffed by one red-headed man with a laptop and a caged parakeet. As always when The Reticent was involved, appearances were deceiving. The bird was actually a Dror, a creature capable of detecting lies. Reticent HQ employed many of the creatures as a security measure, and it had enough illusion magic experts to obscure the creatures' purple, blistery forms.

"Are you here for the Non-Denominational Holiday Party?" the man asked.

"Yes," said Brooks and Smith.

The Dror detected no lies. If it had, it would have vomited all over its cage.

"Do you have any weapons on you?" the man asked.

"No," said Brooks and Smith.

The Dror kept its dinner down.

"Names?" the man asked.

"Arturo Brooks," said Brooks.

The man tapped at his keyboard to check Brooks in.

"Edward Smith," said Smith.

Tap. Taptap. Tap.

"Which one?" the man asked.

Smith sighed. "Middle initial L. Born 12/4/76."

"Gotcha," said the man. "Any guests for either of you?"

Brooks and Smith glanced at each other. "No."

The man grabbed a roll of blue tickets and ripped six off—three for each detective.

"These are your drink tickets," the man said.

Brooks and Smith stepped through the doorway.

Smith immediately griped. "*Three*? I'm supposed to put up with these people all night on three glasses of wine?"

"Actually—" Brooks pointed at the bar to their left. "They're not even full glasses."

The bar was the busiest part of the large ballroom. A crowd of Reticent employees and their significant others swarmed as two bartenders in burgundy vests hastily tapped into boxed wine. On the corner of the bar were the "glasses." A few stacks of six-ounce clear plastic cups.

A hand-scribbled posterboard sign in front of the bar read:

Do not give away unused drink tickets

Smith griped. "You were right. This is already a nightmare."

Aside from the backed-up bar, the ballroom contained a few dozen cocktail tables—each with a red or green tablecloth—and a non-alcoholic drink table, around which no one stood. There was a DJ in a far corner near the emergency exit, but no one danced to the family-friendly pop songs he cranked out. Instead, Reticent employees and their spouses awkwardly mingled, discussing their fake jobs and their real holiday plans. The room's centerpiece was a gigantic ice sculpture of a bear wearing a scarf. On its hind legs, it stood at least ten feet tall, brandishing a menacing set of paws. After fighting their way to the bar, Brooks and Smith—drinks in hand—parked themselves next to the table on which the beast rested.

Smith glanced up at the bear's icy claws, which were beginning to drip water in the heat of the agent-filled room. "That's festive." He raised his cup to take a sip, but was interrupted as Burroughs approached in a little black dress.

"Thank God you're here," she said.

Three female agents followed her over: Agents Foster, Cook, and Smirnova. All were thirty-somethings in little black dresses, and all reached into their clutches to retrieve twenty dollars. One by one, they handed Burroughs the money.

"What the fuck?" Smith wondered.

"They bet I couldn't get you to come," Burroughs said.

"Looks like somebody still has feelings for you," Smirnova teased.

"No," Smith and Burroughs said at once.

"Never did," Burroughs added.

Smith scowled at her.

Cook and Foster cackled while Burroughs flipped through the cash.

"Thanks, though," Burroughs said to Smith, blowing him a sarcastic kiss.

After a moment, she and her friends left. Smith once again raised the plastic cup to his mouth.

Brooks shuffled in place. "You don't think she actually—"

"*No*," Smith said, pausing his sip again.

"And you don't miss—"

"*No*." Smith stared. "Are you serious right now?"

Brooks sighed. "No... not really. No—"

Smith waited impatiently for his partner to figure out what he was trying to say.

"—I'm *really* not. It's just an intrusive thought."

"That I'm gonna get sick of dick?" Smith wondered.

Brooks nodded. "But no one ever gave a blowjob like you do because they hated it."

Brooks grinned, and Smith laughed.

A blinding flash hit them both.

"Aha!" Burroughs's voice followed the flash. "I got you smiling."

Brooks turned to her, confused. "What?"

"He never smiles for photos. I got one." Burroughs showed her phone to her companions. "Pay up, bitches."

Agents Foster, Cook, and Smirnova reached into their clutches once more, and pulled out more twenty-dollar bills.

Smith complained. "Everyone's making money off my body but me. I feel like a common whore."

"Speaking of..." Brooks eyed a piece of mistletoe hanging on one side of the ballroom. Underneath, three light-weight-drunken couples were macking on each other.

"*Rawr*," Smith teased. "Tell you what. We'll get one for your place—"

"How about *our* place?" Brooks said.

"Three tickets ain't enough to get me that pliable," Smith said.

Brooks pulled a few extra tickets from his pocket. "Good thing I swiped a few more."

"Cheers," Smith said, and they both chugged their boxed wine.

Brooks's jealousy toward the mistletoers didn't last long. A human scream and a parakeet squawk cut short alerted the partygoers to a threat. Everyone in the room turned to the door to see a grizzly bear spitting out green feathers. This was peculiar for a number of reasons. First, bears don't generally live in Manhattan. Second, if any Manhattan bears existed, they should have been hibernating this time of year.

The bear thought so too, and it was as cranky as anyone awoken from a deep slumber. The bear was almost four feet high at the shoulder, and it lumbered into the room with a series of raspy snorts and a rumbling roar.

Gasps and shrieks came from guests around the ballroom. More experienced Reticent agents weren't particularly phased. That is, until a second bear followed the first into the room. Then a third. Then a fourth. Then a fifth. A pack of grizzly bears in a room full of intoxicated, unarmed agents. It was the perfect setup for a massacre.

"Come on, people!" shouted a voice.

It came from the back of the room, where a sober agent threw open the emergency exit doors.

Outside, there were more bears. Lots more. Before the agent could shut the door, one rammed its way in. It bit into the agent's arm and threw him to the ground. The bear thrashed the agent from floor to wall and back, over and over until he was bruised all over and bleeding out on the floor. Finally, the bear tossed his dismembered arm aside. It landed on one of the DJ's turntables, soaking a copy of Michael Bublé's Christmas album with blood.

After that grisly murder, the room filled with panic.

One agent grabbed a full box of wine and threw it through one of the room's thin windows, shattering it. This carved a path for some to escort their spouses from the building. Until one of the weirdly intelligent grizzlies got wise and moved in front of the window, blocking anyone else from escaping. Two grizzlies posted up at each entrance, while the others began mauling.

Agents tried to protect their significant others in any way they could—by having them climb atop the bar, hide under a table, whatever seemed like it had the slimmest chance of saving their lives. Dozens of calls were made, both to Reticent HQ and to 9-1-1.

Brooks and Smith didn't have anyone to protect but themselves. They scouted the room for anything that might kill a bear.

Smith's eyes darted all around. "*Why* do they not let us

bring guns?"

"Because of the incident in 1991," Brooks said. He eyed a cleaning cart tucked to one side of the room. "Maybe we can make them drink bleach?"

Smith stared at him.

"Yeah. I know." Brooks sighed. "*I know.*"

"We're gonna die," Smith said calmly.

They were backed against the ice bear, trapped by two approaching grizzlies.

"Wait," Brooks said. "You think we can topple the ice bear?"

Smith didn't follow. "Why?"

"We pull the tablecloth out from under it, the bear falls onto the bears... maybe?"

"Or it falls onto us," Smith noted.

"We'll scoot under the table, and if not... it's better than getting eaten by a bear?"

"*Is it?*" Smith hadn't exactly done a cost-benefit analysis on being mauled versus crushed.

Brooks had, however briefly. "Yes."

"You ever done either?" Smith asked.

"Don't have to to know which I'd prefer," Brooks said. "Do you need to drink piss to know you'd rather have a glass of wine?"

Smith shrugged, and took the tablecloth in his hands.

They grabbed the fancy red tablecloth under the ice bear and pulled as hard as they could. Their combined strength was good enough. The tablecloth slid—first a little, then all the way across the table.

As the ice bear's feet hit the table's edge, Brooks and Smith dove under the table.

The ice bear crashed through one of the grizzlies and hit the floor, shattering into thousands of pieces. Bits of ice and bear gore flew every which way, including under the table where the detectives were positioned.

The falling statue missed the other grizzly, but something strange happened. The bear stood in a daze, then calmly and quietly turned to exit the ballroom the way it had entered. Other bears followed suit, dropping the human meat in their jaws or casually yawning before leaving the area.

Brooks spotted something in the middle of the floor, right where the ice bear had landed. A bronze amulet, engraved with some sort of Celtic symbol, and text that read "Deae Artioni."

Smith couldn't read that, but he fielded a guess. "Bear god?"

"Bear *goddess*," Brooks corrected, like a know-it-all.

"You're un-*bear*-able," Smith griped.

Brooks ignored that. "Whoever furnished that ice bear didn't carve it. That was Artio the bear goddess, frozen in ice. She must have been alive in there. When the ice started to melt, she started summoning bears—"

His well-read explanation was interrupted as a faint sound came from one corner of the room. A random agent began clapping. Then another. Soon, the entire ballroom erupted into applause for Brooks and Smith's accidental ingenuity.

Burroughs and her friends hurried over.

Smith spoke before she could. "If you tell me you made a bet about the bear, I'm gonna strangle you right here."

"I was going to say good job," Burroughs said.

Agent Smirnova was very drunk. "I was going to say... here's my number." She handed Smith a slip of paper with some illegible smudges.

"Thanks," Smith lied, before dropping the slip to the ground behind him.

❧

Wet with bear viscera, Brooks and Smith once again rode the elevator down to their office. Even accidental legends had to fill out mandatory paperwork.

"Your place?" Smith asked.

"Yes. Please. It's going to take forever to clean the grizzly blood out of these clothes, and I want to get a head start." Brooks was the only one with an in-unit washing machine.

Smith grinned, then pointed at the corner of his partner's mouth. "Speaking of, you've got a little something on—"

"That's not as cute when it's bear guts," Brooks said. He wiped his mouth on his sleeve, hoping he hadn't contracted some bloodborne ailment.

"Okay. Cute's out," Smith said. "How 'bout heartfelt?"

Brooks eyed him with suspicion. "What?"

"I don't want to stay with you tonight," Smith said.

"*Okay.* Your definition of heartfelt is—"

"I wanna move in with you," Smith said.

Brooks blinked a few times. "Seriously?"

"Yeah." Smith took a step closer and brushed a bear tooth off of Brooks's shoulder. "If we got eaten by bears tonight, I'd have gone out not knowing what it's like living with you. I wanna know."

Brooks grabbed Smith and kissed him. First, one excited peck. Then another. Soon they were passionately making out in the elevator. Again.

The elevator opened too soon. Again.

Brooks and Smith didn't fake a fight. They turned and stared down an intern, daring her to say something.

PSYCHICS ANONYMOUS

Like most people who find themselves in Ohio, Brooks and Smith were there against their will. More troubling, neither man knew why. They woke up in a disheveled hotel bed, outside Cleveland.

"Who the *hell* are you?" Brooks hopped out of bed and paced, looking for his missing shirt.

Smith sat up in bed and squinted at the younger man. "Edward Smith. Nice to meet you too."

"Arturo Brooks," Brooks obliged, before snapping. "I don't remember anything from last night. What the hell did you do to me?"

Smith eyed his shirtless body. "Hopefully something filthy."

"Excuse me?" Brooks complained, spotting both his shirt and a duffel bag on a nearby chair.

"I don't remember anything either," Smith said.

"Oh, that's convenient," Brooks huffed. "Do you live here, or—"

"I don't even know where 'here' is," Smith said. He flipped through the room service menu on his nightstand. "*Cleveland*? No, I'm not from fucking Cleveland. New York via Indiana. You?"

"Staten Island, born and raised."

"Okay, so how'd we get here? You see any keys?"

"Um..." Brooks rifled through the duffel bag. "No, but I have an... FBI badge?" A look of alarm took over his face.

"Christ, wonder what you were busting me for," Smith said.

Brooks gave him a sideways glance and pulled another badge from the bag. "You have one too."

"We're working together, then," Smith said. "Huh."

Brooks looked at the badges a little more closely. "They're fake."

Smith pretended to brush sweat from his brow. "Thank fuck I'm not a fed."

"You're not taking this very seriously," said Brooks.

"Not the first time I've woken up in a hotel with no memory of the night before."

Brooks tried to find a response, but before he could there was a knock at the door.

"Room service!"

Each man glanced at the other before hurrying to the door. There, they found a standard room attendant, rolling a metal cart.

"Can I come in?" he asked.

Smith lifted the lid from the room service tray, half expecting a dismembered limb or a bomb, and not sure why he expected those things. It was neither. Just a plate of bacon and eggs. He lowered the lid.

"Who ordered this?" Brooks asked.

"Uh..." The room attendant scanned the receipt in his hand. "Edward Smith?"

"Used my real name," Smith said, yanking the receipt out of his hand. "Couldn't be up to anything too shady."

"Were you working here last night?" Brooks asked.

"Uh... No. I do morning shifts," said the attendant.

Smith grabbed the room service cart and shooed the attendant out the door, sans tip. He eyed the receipt. Charged to a credit card ending in 6248.

Smith grabbed his wallet from the nightstand and rifled through it. "Driver's license, thirty bucks, and a condom. No credit card ending in 6248."

Brooks noticed something more alarming on Smith's nightstand. "You have a gun."

"No permit for that in my wallet either," said Smith.

"Were we drugged and robbed?" Brooks wondered. He tossed a duffel bag onto his side of the bed and began looking through it.

"Thieves that don't take money, guns, or jewelry?" His watch was still around his wrist, and Brooks's cross necklace was still around his neck. "I don't know about you, but I don't feel drugged."

Brooks came up empty on the duffel bag front. He threw his hands in the air. "Who could have altered our memories?"

They began spitballing.

"Master vampire," suggested Smith.

"Mage," said Brooks.

"Mind slugs," said Smith.

"Trickster," said Brooks.

"Witches," said Smith.

"Glawackus," said Brooks, then, "Why do we know these things?"

"I got a feeling earlier when I opened that breakfast. I thought it was going to be—"

"—a bomb or a dismembered limb or something?" Brooks finished. "Me too."

Smith came to a conclusion. "We're professional... whatevers. Come to town, pretend we're the FBI while we try to find... something."

"I feel like it's something obvious," Brooks said.

"Yeah. Mind... people," Smith suggested. Words eluded him.

"People with ESP," Brooks offered.

Smith snapped his fingers. "Those! We're professional monster people and we came here looking for ES-People."

"We must have found them..." Brooks put a hand to his chin, in thought. "Where?"

"There's no case file or anything else in that bag?" Smith asked, moving to take a look inside.

Brooks blocked him. "No. Nothing else."

Smith raised an eyebrow and pushed past Brooks to root around in there himself. In addition to some clothes and the FBI badges, there was a bulk container of Kirkland Signature lube from Costco, and a double-sided dildo.

Smith scoffed. "That's it?"

"Do you think we're a couple?" Brooks asked.

"No. I don't date and if I did... wouldn't be you. Sorry."

For a moment, Brooks was more annoyed with that statement than he was concerned about figuring out what was going on. "What's that supposed to mean?"

"It means you're high strung. Now focus."

"Okay, you're right..." Brooks pondered. "Maybe the front desk has seen us."

The woman working at the front desk hadn't, but she was kind enough to let them know they'd paid for parking, which meant they brought a car, wherever it or its keys were. While Smith lamely tried to get the woman's phone number, Brooks perused a stand of tourist brochures for Cleveland's finest tourist attractions: the Rock and Roll Hall of Fame, the Cleveland Zoo, and the Cuyahoga River, which had the distinction of being the world's only river to catch on fire over a dozen times. There were also brochures for events: a *Drew Carey Show* fan convention, a monster truck rally, a Lebron James summoning circle—

Brooks's eyes went wide. "Eddie..."

Smith, who'd been making no progress but thought he

had, turned around, annoyed.

"Look at this," said Brooks.

He handed over a brochure for the ESP & Healing Faire. Its location: across the street, in the Sponsorship Available Events Center.

Smith scoffed. "Real telepaths don't go for that woo-woo bullshit."

"Not usually," said Brooks, "but I don't think it's a co-incidence we can't remember who we are and we're right across the street from people who claim to have ESP. If nothing else, whoever did this wants us to think it was that faire, which means someone there might know some-thing."

Smith didn't argue with that.

The ESP & Healing Fair was as embarrassing as the detectives thought it would be. The tiny convention center had parking for maybe a hundred cars, and over half the lot was empty. Inside, booths were spread far apart to make it look like they took up more than half of the beige-carpeted room. Guests were nearly as sparse as booths, and vendors shilling protective pendants, aura-cleansing soaps, and healing crystals were desperate to win their attention and earn back their booth fees. As such, Brooks and Smith found themselves on the receiving end of a barrage of sales pitches.

"—crystals to enhance romantic rendezvous—"

"—thrilling book about psychics in the Ohio Valley—"

"—these orbs can also be used to repel mosquitos—"

"—experience the world of enchanted socks—"

Most of these they were able to ignore. They weren't sure what they were looking for, but each man had a sense that he'd know it when he saw it.

Sure enough, Smith spotted something at one vendor's booth: a simple black shoebox, bearing a slit in the top. On the front of the box were two words, scrawled on with purple glitter glue:

Donation Bin

Smith cozied up to the booth and inquired. "What are the donations for?"

"Non-extrasensory percepting children of families with ESP," answered the woman behind the booth. "The funds primarily go toward mental healthcare." She herself, she explained, had a cognitively unenhanced sibling who'd committed suicide.

"The rest of you didn't see it coming?" asked Smith.

Brooks started to snicker, but covered his mouth. "You're *awful.*"

The woman stared at Smith with hatred in her eyes. "Think before you speak next time, or you might find yourself unable to think at all."

"Kay..." said Smith. "Tell you what, I'll give you..." Smith pulled out his wallet, to count his money. There, on one fold of the trifold wallet, was his previously missing credit card. He squinted. On another fold, an ID card for The Reticent. He slid it out, revealing a photo of himself and Brooks tucked behind it. He handed the ID to Brooks.

"The pharmaceutical company?" Brooks wondered. Then he noticed the picture. "We *are* dating." He sighed. "I must be awful too."

Smith grunted. "Fucking psychics."

With that, the room became quiet enough to hear voodoo doll pins drop. Every vendor in the place—and half the patrons—turned to stare at the detectives.

"What did you say?" asked a woman selling tarot cards.

"That word is a fucking slur," said a man selling bespoke cloaks.

"What, *psychic*?" Smith sputtered.

"People with extrasensory perception!" screamed a woman who—until the slur was uttered—had been performing a palm reading.

The man who'd been seated for the reading stood and took a few steps toward Brooks and Smith, his palm bleeding from a fingernail's sudden fury.

"Words hurt," he said.

Brooks turned to Smith. "What is happening right now?"

"Words hurt," said a crystal seller, who also rose to confront them.

Soon, everyone was standing. Soon after, they closed in on the detectives.

As small as the crowd was, it was still much larger than two people. Trapped in the middle of an aisle in a space getting smaller and smaller, Brooks and Smith exchanged bewildered glances.

The crowd chanted, as one. "Words hurt. Stop the violence. Words hurt. Stop the violence." As they moved with intention, the crowd developed a faint purple glow.

"Oh my God," Brooks said. "Apologize to them."

"Fuck them," said Smith.

"That's probably what you said yesterday and then they did this! And now we don't know anything about The Reticent or why we're dating or—"

Smith moaned. "Do I have to?"

"Eddie!"

Smith held out his hands, directing the crowd to calm. "Everyone! Wait!"

For a moment, they stopped chanting.

"I am... deeply sorry if anyone's feelings were hurt."

"That's not an apology!" one person with ESP screamed.

"Come on," Brooks said. "Like you mean it. Not like you're a celebrity who did blackface."

"I'm an idiot," Smith declared, for the crowd. "I'm a dumb piece of shit who didn't know the P word was offensive. You've all educated me. I'm sorry. I'll do anything I can to make it up to the... extrasensory percepting community, including making a donation to the... non-extrasensory percepting children of families with ESP."

That disingenuous attempt seemed to be enough for the crowd.

Think before you speak next time, or you might find yourself unable to think at all.

Those words repeated in Smith's mind a few times, and then everything became clear. He and Brooks exchanged smiles. "You back?"

Brooks nodded, then started chuckling.

"What?" asked Smith.

"How many times have I told you to watch your language?"

"Not enough, I guess." Smith shook his head. "Sorry. I'm sure the last 24 hours have sucked for you."

"Because I'm *high strung*?" asked Brooks, throwing his partner's words back at him.

Two could play that game. Smith smirked. "Because I'm *awful*. Let's get out of here."

TROPE ME, DADDY

You're in a forest, and there's a monster somewhere in the trees. You pull out your cell phone, ready to call for help. But the darnedest thing has happened: the battery that was fully charged just a moment ago is now empty. Also, there's no cell service. That's fine. You'll just drive out of there. You fumble with your car keys for a moment before finally unlocking the vehicle. But oh no. Your car won't start. That's weird, since you just had it serviced at that friendly gas station in the next town over. Time to run. Your companion, who wore heels to the middle of the woods for some reason, trips. You, my friend, are trapped in a world of horror tropes.

Tropes are, put simply, storytelling conventions. They could be characters (the Knight in Shining Armor, the Girl Nextdoor, the Chosen One), objects or entities (the Artifact of Doom, the Evil AI, the Megacorporation), or aspects of the plot (the Zombie Apocalypse, the Alien Invasion, the Will They or Won't They romance). It's impossible to create a story without one or more tropes.

That's something a pair of detectives were about to find out...

Brooks and Smith sat on the couch in their living room, watching the end credits of the film *Basic Instinct*, when

Smith lodged a complaint.

"Why's the bi character always fucked up?" he asked.

Brooks pointed out a fact. "*You're* fucked up."

"Yeah. *Everyone is.* I mean in fiction, where there are characters who *aren't* fucked up. Why's the one who is always the bi one?"

"I don't know," Brooks said. "Why's the gay guy either comic relief or dying of AIDS?"

Smith pulled out his phone.

"That was hypothetical," Brooks said. "Please stop looking at that stupid website."

That stupid website was TV Tropes—a famously addictive wiki of media tropes—and Smith had opened it no fewer than six times over the course of the movie. The combination of compelling material and an addictive personality meant Smith couldn't help being fascinated by such topics as Love Triangle, Lie Detector, Noodle Incident, and Too Dumb to Live.

"There it is!" Smith exclaimed. "Depraved Bisexual!"

Brooks turned off the TV. "Congrats. Can we go to bed?"

"And for you..." Smith tapped at his phone. "Sassy Gay Friend. Tragic AIDS Story. Bury Your Gays..."

"*Now* can we go to bed?"

"Wait." Smith didn't look up from his phone.

Brooks rubbed at his temple. "What now?"

"Occult Detective!" Smith read aloud from the screen. "Their equipment consists of digital thermometers, cameras, camcorders, EMF meters, and voice recorders... may or may not work for Creature Hunter Organization. We're a trope!"

Brooks pinched the bridge of his nose. "Please stop."

"Related links... Defective Detective?" Smith tapped the link. "The greatest challenges a detective faces aren't always criminals or cases. Those are a cakewalk compared to managing their personal life. *Heyyy*."

"Eddie, tropes aren't real." Brooks got up from the couch. "I'm going to bed."

"Be there in a sec," Smith said, still engrossed in the website.

Three hours passed before Smith finally made his way upstairs. He tucked in next to Brooks, mumbled something about Counting Sheep, and fell asleep.

Over the course of the next few hours, something went wrong.

Something always goes wrong.

Brooks awoke first, covered in sweat and in a panic for no reason. He jumped out of bed and shook the bedsheets to wake his partner. "What did I do last night?"

Smith yawned in an exaggerated way. He'd felt groggy most mornings of his life, but this was extra groggy. "You were..." He nodded off.

"Eddie!" Brooks huffed and ripped the covers off the bed. "*What did I do last night?*"

Smith yawned again. "What do you mean? We watched *Basic Instinct*."

"Then why am I panicking?" Brooks asked.

Smith's eyes fluttered as he tried to bring the room into focus. When things became clear, he was looking at himself. That is, he was looking at someone who looked just like him. Blond, bags under the eyes, surly. Smith looked down at his arm, which was much tanner than usual. That was enough to propel him out of bed and into the bathroom, where he looked into a mirror.

"We got Freaky Friday'd!" he exclaimed.

Brooks was trapped in Smith's body, and Smith was trapped in Brooks.

"*Why* did we get Freaky Friday'd?" Brooks asked. "*What*

did we do last night?"

Smith had a different question. "Is my voice always that high-pitched or is that you?"

"I don't know. It sounds different when I'm inside you."

Smith smirked.

"*Eddie*. Why are we doing a Freaky Friday?"

"Not a Morning Person. What Did I Do Last Night? Freaky Friday..." Smith put a hand to his chin for a moment before making a declaration. "We're troping."

"Tropes aren't real," Brooks said.

Smith stared at him. "You know what *is* real?"

"What?" Brooks wondered.

"A one-time opportunity to fuck ourselves."

"Oh, for God's sake." Brooks cringed. "That's honestly... gross and weird and... wrong."

"Why? Everyone jacks off," Smith said.

"Yeah, but you don't gaze into your own eyes while you do it," Brooks said.

"I didn't say I want to make sweet love to myself. I'd absolutely hate-fuck me," Smith said.

Brooks shook his head. "What's wrong with you?"

"I'm a man. I can't help it." Smith realized he'd emitted another trope. "Damn. Trope."

"You know what?" Brooks's demeanor calmed. "I'm hungry. I'm going to eat breakfast and then we'll sit down and figure out this Freaky Friday thing."

Smith chased him down the stairs, listing tropes. "One-Track-Minded Hunger. Too Hungry to Be Polite. Skewed Priorities."

"Stop it," Brooks said. "Life isn't a trope."

They made it to the kitchen, and Brooks came to a halt.

"Did you buy groceries last night?" he asked.

"No..." Smith shook his head.

On the counter was a large, brown paper bag, with a

baguette and celery peeking out the top.

Smith pointed at it. "Standard Urban Groceries!"

On the table were two place settings. Each had full glasses of both orange juice and milk, an apple, a bowl of cereal, a plate with buttered toast, and a hard-boiled egg.

"Part of a Complete Breakfast," Smith said, recognizing it from every cereal commercial ever.

Brooks sighed. "Okay. You *may* be on to something with the tropes, but *why* are we being troped?"

"Beats me," Smith said. "Medium Awareness? Noticing the Fourth Wall? Maybe we're characters in fiction and now we've realized it and we're being fucked with."

Brooks had a less stupid suggestion. "Maybe you managed to summon something. Did any of the articles you read last night look weird to you? Any symbols, foreign words?"

"No," Smith said. "I was blasting through 'em pretty fast, though."

"*Quickly*," corrected Brooks. Before Smith could call out the Grammar Nazi trope, he continued. "We should look through your history and check every page you looked at."

"That's uh... gonna take a while," Smith said.

"I know there's going to be weird porn there. It's fine." Brooks started unloading the groceries from the paper bag. He grabbed a carton of eggs and walked it toward the fridge. When he opened it, he dropped the eggs and let out a gasp.

"What?" Smith asked.

"Eddie," Brooks said calmly. "There is a dead body in the fridge."

"Male or female?" Smith asked.

"Female..."

Smith recognized that one. "Women in Refrigerators!"

"Do *not* get excited for that." Brooks gagged a little.

"Vomiting Cop," Smith said. "A crime scene so gruesome it disgusts even the most hardened detective. I'm here for Autopsy Snack Time, myself." He took a bite of an apple.

"It's not the corpse." Brooks hurried across the room and puked into the sink.

"What's wrong then?" Smith asked, still chewing.

"I don't know."

Smith covered his mouth in horror. "Mister Seahorse."

"*What?*" Brooks snapped.

Smith swallowed his last bit of apple. "Morning Sickness. Male Pregnancy. You gotta get my body an abortion."

Brooks rolled his eyes. "I am *not* male pregnant. That's not a thing. You're jumping to conclusions."

"*Also a trope,*" Smith said.

"Wait a minute," Brooks said. "You know tulpas..."

"Yes. I'm an *Occult Detective.*" As such, Smith was well aware that tulpas were basically imaginary friends come to life.

"What if you... turned TV Tropes into a tulpa by believing in it," Brooks said.

Smith blurted more tropes. "Clap Your Hands If You Believe! Reality Warper!" Smith continued the line of thought. "If TV Tropes had a mind of its own, it would just keep spitting out tropes with no rhyme or reason..."

"Like Freaky Friday and Women in Refrigerators..." Brooks said.

"...and Mister Seahorse."

"*I'm not male pregnant,*" Brooks said.

"Is it just us?" Smith wondered.

They ran to the front door and opened it. Outside, the sky was red and an ominous fog filled the air. There were additional portents of doom: dramatic thunder and mysterious howling in the distance. The detectives shut the door and stayed inside.

"It's not just us," Smith said, with sudden angst. He dropped to the floor.

Brooks dropped down next to him. "Are you okay?"

"It's all my fault," Smith said, anguished.

Brooks looked him in the eyes and spoke drolly. "Dark and Troubled Past."

"Ouch," Smith said. "You're right, though."

Brooks patted him on the shoulder. "I'm always right."

"Trope…" Smith trailed off. Then his eyes lit up. "Wait. I know how to fix everything."

"How?"

"Deus Ex Machina." Smith stood and began pacing. "It's when something comes out of nowhere and resolves a story. Like in *Jurassic Park*, when the T-Rex just shows up at the end for no reason, or in *The Stand* when the literal hand of God appears—"

"I know what it is," Brooks said, "but if this thing is a tulpa with a mind of its own, how are you going to convince it to make a deus ex machina happen and disappear itself?"

"I don't know…" Smith admitted.

He awoke in bed, in his own body.

It was all just a dream.

…or was it?

SEXTS IN THE CITY

I'm coming.

> not yet youre not

*I'm on my way.

> way to ruin it

Did you pick a movie?

> yes

Are you going to tell me what it is?

> no
> youll pick up something else if i do

Might do that anyway.

> judgy bitch
> get the food yet?

No. Line out the door.

why?
its a sandwich not an iphone

8 million people. That's why.

hurry up
im hungry
and horny

Always.
Got the food.
Train's down.

Fuck

Gonna try to find a cab.

just uber

...

nm
i see your typing dots
forget i said it

Found one.

You want to fuck a sandwich?

hungry n horny

Stop trying to use emojis.
I know. Believe me, I know.

                                        you get lost?
Traffic isn't moving.

                              you ever sext from a cab?

Yes.
                                                    ...

I see your dots.
I'm kidding.
I haven't.

                                            wanna?

I guess.

                                        ill take it

That's my line.

                                                lol

What are you wearing?

                                                pjs
                              the spider-man ones

Oh my God.
No apostrophes, but you'll hyphenate Spider-Man.

no shirt

Better.

you?

Still in a suit.
That's not changing while I'm in this cab.

damn

You, otoh...

what?

Lose the PJs.

lost em

Yeah?

call me little orphan annie

Why?

its a hard knock life

No.

its like youre in church again

Why?

cuz theres an organ player
get it?
its me
im playing with my organ
i mean my dick
are you breaking up with me now?
should i get my own dinner?
did you die?

Zombies.

you were dead but youre back?

There are zombies.
They got the driver.

bitten?

No. I'm fine.

did they get the sandwiches?

There's a horde.
I'm gonna help some tourists.

did they get the sandwiches???

The sandwiches are fine.

let the reticent send
a team
youre off tonight
youre *getting* off tonight

come on

Hang on.

my face
damn it
just come here
now
please
brooksy
hello?
in case this is the last thing you see
im not just hungry and horny
i want you here cuz i love you
ok?
im highkey gay for you
hello?
starting to freak out
its weird
if youre dead im jumping off a bridge

Zombies are taken care of.
I'm saving this conversation.

fuck you

Soon.

RECIPE FOR TROUBLE

In the early 2000s, Philippi, West Virginia had more opioids than people. That's not a joke. It was the cumulative result of pharmaceutical companies, lawmakers, and doctors alike not giving a shit about the poor for decades on end.

There were lawsuits, of course. Then came bad press. By 2013, the prescriptions had dried up. It became more and more difficult for people in pain to find ways of managing it. Not to mention the addiction aspect. Some former prescribees turned to heroin. Many more turned to fentanyl. One desperate man—coming down hard from dependence on oxycodone—turned to the internet, where there are recipes for everything from gluten-free cupcakes to crystal meth to homemade bombs. That's where he found something interesting. A new drug out of Russia.

KROKODIL RECIPE:
- 100mL paint thinner
- 100mL gasoline
- 50mL Vladimir Putin's sweat
- 200mL Siberian snow
- 50mL Benadryl
- half a medium potato
- dash of vodka
- 1 Adidas tracksuit, burned to ash

Without access to some of those materials, the man was forced to make a few substitutions.

He didn't follow the recipe.

᷇

Smith stood in the kitchen of the brownstone he and Brooks shared, reading the reviews for a red velvet cake recipe. He wanted to do something nice for Brooks's birthday, but he couldn't tell whether the cake was good or not because nobody followed the damn recipe.

"I substituted applesauce for butter. It was okay," read one review.

"Our oven runs hot so I baked for six minutes at 475 and cake was ruined," read another.

The next read: "My ds is gluten-free so I used powdered edamame instead of flour. The cake didn't rise as much as it should have :-/"

Smith shook his head and began mixing the original ingredients together.

Some jingling and rustling came from the front door. Brooks had arrived home early, and he stepped into the kitchen with a surprise of his own.

"What is *that*?" Smith asked.

Brooks furrowed his brow. "What?"

"That haircut," Smith said.

"You don't like it?" Brooks ran a hand through his hair, now in a side-part that swooshed upward and to his left.

"It looks great." Smith's voice lowered. "You should change it."

Brooks laughed. "No."

It wasn't that Smith didn't like it. It was that he recognized the haircut. It was the same one he'd seen on a body in Willowbrook Park years earlier. But since he couldn't say "that haircut means you're running out of time" or "it makes me wish I was dead," he came up with a different objection. "Everyone's gonna hit on you. I won't be able to take it."

"Shut up." Brooks laughed some more, then noticed the bowls and ingredients scattered around the room. "What are you doing?"

"I have no idea," Smith admitted.

Brooks eyed a mixing bowl. "Is that cake?"

"No. It's batter," Smith said.

Brooks got misty-eyed. "You're baking for me?"

"Don't make a big deal out of it. It's probably gonna taste like shit." Smith wiped his batter-coated hands on his pants. "What are you doing back so early, anyway?"

"Haven't checked your email lately, have you?" Brooks asked.

"You know I haven't," Smith said.

"You and I have an appointment in West Virginia."

Smith grimaced. "Seriously?"

"Afraid so," Brooks said. "Something about cannibals."

"Raincheck on the cake?" Smith wondered.

Brooks nodded.

Smith started tossing ingredients back into the fridge and pantry, in places Brooks preferred they didn't go. He brushed errant flour onto the floor, which constituted cleaning up in his mind.

Brooks, meanwhile, ran a finger through the batter and brought it to his mouth for a taste. He gagged a little at its overly salty taste, then started rinsing the bowl in the sink. Leaving town before Smith could finish the cake was for the best, and he would conveniently forget to cash that rain check.

☙

Sometime later, the detectives arrived in Philippi, West Virginia, parked their loaner car on the meterless street for free, and started looking for cannibals.

"What better place to celebrate your birthday," Smith said.

He—like Brooks—was looking down the town's Main Street. For what should have been Philippi's main thoroughfare, there was a surprising lack of people. On a Thursday afternoon, there should have at least been people out to lunch. Then again, there was nowhere to eat lunch. That might have explained the alleged cannibals.

Main Street's dozens of storefronts sat mostly empty. Some had their windows painted over with American flags and half-assed mountain panoramas in an attempt to make them less depressing. It didn't work. The buildings that weren't shuttered were mostly thrift stores, addiction counseling centers, and ice cream shops. The town was a sad reminder that outside of its most vibrant cities, America was a decaying shell of its former self—a rust-covered cornucopia of poverty, drug addiction, and despair. Not that cities didn't also have those things, but they also had good kebabs.

"At least they've got ice cream," Brooks said, eyeing one window. Then he saw a sign. "Never mind. It's Hershey's."

Smith raised a pinkie finger and mocked his partner. "*Ohhh. I'm too fancy for mass-produced hard serve.* Maybe if you ask, they'll have some gold flakes for you in the back."

Brooks shot him an annoyed look.

"Love you," said Smith.

BRAAGRAAGRRRRARRR.

"Uh... you hear that?" Smith asked.

Brooks nodded.

They looked around, but didn't see anything. Main Street remained empty.

Brooks and Smith rested their hands on their guns, which they wore openly at their hips because they were in West Virginia.

BRAAGRAAGRRRRARRR. CRASSSH.

Out of nowhere, one of the painted windows exploded. The detectives barely had time to turn and dodge shards of red, white, and blue glass, let alone realize the glass had been blown out by a monster.

"Shit," Smith said. He was the first to turn and face the window again. Something close to his height grabbed his arm and pulled him close, ready to bite. "Zombie!"

Brooks turned and shot the zombie through the head.

It let go of Smith, who stumbled backward toward his partner.

"You okay?" Brooks asked.

Smith's eyes widened. "Not a zombie."

Zombies died when you shot them in the head. Smith's wide eyes pointed toward the shattered storefront, where the creature continued lumbering toward them. It was definitely a walking corpse, what with its rotting pale green flesh and the bullet hole in its forehead, but not a zombie.

"Crap," Brooks said.

Smith took a page from his partner and shot it through the head. Same result. Instead of dying, it continued walking toward them, now with a half-collapsed skull leaking green sludge.

"Sword in the trunk?" Smith asked, since Brooks had done most of the packing.

"Of course," Brooks said.

They sprinted back to their car.

Brooks had already popped the trunk when they arrived. He kept an eye on the zombie while Smith rifled through their weapons. The preferred sword for killing zombies was a one-handed weapon, about two feet long. Very sharp, and serrated on one side for sawing off particularly stubborn heads.

Smith handed one to Brooks, then took one for himself.

It was a good thing they had two, since the zombie brought a friend—picked up outside of a shuttered addiction counseling center. They lumbered together, BRAA-GRAAGRRRRARRRing all the way. This zombie was female, but something was off about her face.

"Look at her," Brooks said, disgusted.

"Looks familiar," Smith said.

Her pale, decaying face was zombie-esque, but something wasn't right. Next to each other, it became clear that both zombies had the same exact face, though one had been mangled. Both the male and the female zombie looked just like Vladimir Putin, the latter's face slightly obscured by long, blonde hair.

They approached with beady little eyes, looking like they were ready to annex Crimea. Brooks and Smith lined up with their swords. Brooks took the Putin on the left and Smith took the Putin on the right. With a swoosh and a swing, green fluid sprayed everywhere. The decapitations were successful.

Until they weren't.

While Brooks and Smith assessed the scene, the zombie bodies picked up their own heads and began lumbering toward the detectives again. The Putins' heads were alive, and their mouths were chomping.

"Crap," Brooks said, eyeing the street. One building stood out to him. "The cannibal report came from that pharmacy..."

"Let's check it out and regroup," Smith said.

The zombies were very slow, and it was easy to outrun

them. Brooks and Smith darted down an alley and looked for a back entrance to the store in question. At first, they miscounted and broke into the ice cream shop. There was no one inside to notice.

Eventually, they found the correct door.

The pharmacy looked like a war zone. Shelves were toppled, and empty bottles were strewn everywhere. Not one product remained. The pair stepped around a pile of human feces to make their way behind the counter. It would be a good, secure location if they ended up in a zombie shootout. Not that their guns had worked all that well so far.

"Ack!" said a voice. "Don't shoot!"

Already tucked behind the counter was a terrified pharmacist. She sat on the floor in a tattered lab coat, with her arms around her legs. She saw how well they were dressed and made an assumption. "You with the FBI?"

"Something like that," Brooks said. "You're not a zombie, are you?"

"N... no..." said the pharmacist. "Name's Sarah Wolf. I'm a pharmacist."

They lowered their swords.

Smith used his eyes to motion at the trashed store. "What happened here?"

"Oh... that wasn't the zombies. People keep comin' in and trashin' the place looking for opioids," Sarah said. "Every week, we're open for maybe a day before someone wrecks everything."

"Charming," Brooks said. "Are you the one that reported cannibals?"

She nodded. "Some new drug or another has got folks all spun up. People 'round here get real creative. They'll do anything to get high. Just last week, someone came in askin' about getting some Benadryl and givin' it to a

Siberian husky, then mixin' the dog's poop with vodka. Said it was s'posed to create a super high."

"Siberian..." Brooks pondered aloud.

Smith did the same. "Vodka..."

"Do you know their name?" Brooks asked. "The person who came in looking for all that?"

"I'm not s'posed to share that sort of thing," Sarah said.

"Your town is being overrun by zombies that look like Vladimir Putin," Smith noted.

Brooks nodded. "Now's not really the time to worry about HIPAA."

"His name's Terry Walker. He lives down in Hillman Holler," Sarah said.

Brooks pulled out his phone and opened a map.

"How do you have service?" Smith asked.

"I downloaded the map before we came here," Brooks said. But there were zombies, and no time to berate his partner for not following protocol. He turned to Sarah. "Show me exactly where."

After a few points and taps, the address was logged and nav-ready.

Sarah peeked over the counter and out the window, where another Putin zombie passed by. "You really think someone experimenting with drugs could have done this?"

"It's the best idea we've got so far," Smith said.

"Can I come with you then? I'm kind of responsible for gettin' Terry hooked," Sarah said.

"How?" Brooks asked.

"I kept givin' him oxycodone, well after his prescription ran out. I mean, he's a family friend, and—he ain't the only one. Corporate don't send us much of anything at all and everyone's desperate and angry... I know there's no excuse..." Sarah's eyes were wet with tears.

Smith shrugged. "Was that supposed to be a

revelation?"

Brooks nudged him.

Smith tapped her shoulder and half-assed some empathy. "There... there?"

"You can come with us," Brooks said.

The three snuck out the back door and hurried to the car without incident.

Following them was a growing group of very slow zombies. In the rearview mirror, Smith could see six of them. Fat Putins, skinny Putins, and in-between Putins. All Putins.

Brooks plugged in his phone and started navigating.

Their path took them down a road that started asphalt, gradually transitioned to gravel, and eventually became nothing but dirt. The Reticent-provided Pontiac Aztek performed as admirably as it could, grumbling over bumps and holes as it continued grinding out a cloud of dirt.

"What can you tell us about Terry?" Brooks asked.

"He's in his late forties, not sure the exact age. Has three kids from two different marriages. They all live with their moms," Sarah said. "Used to be a mechanic, 'til a convertible fell on him and crushed his right arm. He couldn't really work after that."

"Well, that's depressing," Brooks said.

"No more than anything else around here," Smith said, eyeing their surroundings.

Each home they passed looked worse than the one before it. Back when there'd been asphalt, the homes looked normal—pleasant, even. By the time the group reached the dirt road, the houses were all ramshackle hovels and trailers, with lawns full of used tire planters, rusted out trucks, plastic kiddie pools, and oil drums.

"It's up here on the left," Sarah said.

On the left, up a steep incline, was Terry Walker's place.

It wasn't a ramshackle hovel or even a trailer. It was an old-school Winnebago camper, held in place by its lack of tires. Parked in front was Terry's daily driver: a lifted, late-model Ford F-250, with chrome accents. The truck was—in contrast to the Winnebago—spotless.

"The man has priorities," Smith remarked.

Smith, Brooks, and Sarah hopped out of their vehicle and made their way to the Winnebago.

Brooks reached forward to knock on the thin metal door. It was already open, and it creaked as it flew inward.

Brooks kept a hand on his gun as he called out. "Hello?"

"Terry, you in there?" Sarah asked.

No one responded.

Smith flicked on the light, revealing a sad state of affairs. The Winnebago had green shag carpeting, upon which rested a twin-size mattress covered in a pile of mismatched pillows and sheets, most of them stained. The camper's centerpiece—a kitchenette with missing cabinet doors—provided some clues.

The scant counter space sat littered with beakers and vials, over-the-counter drugs, a shredded pair of Nike sweatpants, bath salts, and what looked (and smelled) like dog poop.

"What's this?" Brooks spotted a slip of paper in the sink. "A receipt from the We Sell Your Stuff on eBay store... looks like he bought an autographed photo of Putin from someone in Moscow."

"Definitely our guy," Smith said, looking at a different slip of paper. "It's a recipe from legitimat-rekipes.ru..."

He handed the printout to Brooks.

"He didn't follow the recipe," Brooks said. "Nike instead of Adidas, poop instead of snow, bits of an autograph instead of sweat..."

"Nobody ever follows the recipe," Smith griped.

"How could this *possibly* make zombies, though?" Brooks wondered.

"Can I see that?" Sarah asked.

Brooks handed her the recipe.

"Krokodil," Sarah explained. "It's homemade desomorphine. Even when you do it right, it can cause gangrene and necrosis, which is—"

"Dead flesh," Smith said.

"Yeah," Sarah said.

"Not a huge leap from dead to undead," Smith said.

"But opioids should knock people out, not turn them into cannibals," Brooks said, suddenly realizing what a waste of time majoring in chemistry had been.

Smith rattled the container of bath salts. "He didn't make an opioid. He made some bastard hybrid of krokodil and bath salts."

"Bath salts are known to produce psychotic behavior," Sarah said. "Even cannibalism."

"Yeah, that's why it's one of our go-to cover stories," Smith said.

Sarah's mouth went agape. "Your wha—"

Smith spoke over her. "What are the odds Terry is still Terry and we can ask him what he did?"

"Not good..." Brooks trailed off.

Out the Winnebago window, he'd spotted Terry. He didn't know it was Terry yet, but he did know there was a crowd of Putin zombies descending on the trailer. Dozens of them.

"Shit," Smith said. He hurried to the door, shut, and locked it.

"The zombie killers are in the trunk," Brooks said. "Not that they work."

All they had were the handguns strapped to their hips.

"Think," Smith said to himself.

He and Brooks began rifling through cabinets, desperate to find anything that might help. Instead, they found two family size bags of Doritos—open but secured with clothespins—and a fire extinguisher.

"This is bad," Brooks said. "I'm trying to check legit-imat-rekipes.ru for any kind of antidote. Nothing's loading."

"Oh, you didn't pre-download the entire internet?" Smith asked.

Brooks glowered at him.

Smith didn't see that, as he was busy eyeing the Winnebago driver's seat. "You think this thing still runs?"

"It has no tires," Brooks observed.

"Yeah, no shit. I'm out of ideas." Smith began pacing. "Maybe exhaust fumes will annoy them or something..."

"You don't have a key either," Brooks added.

"Maybe I can hotwire it," Smith said.

"For what?" Brooks asked. "It *has no tires.*"

"I don't know!" Smith snapped.

"Oh my God." Brooks was taken aback. "You're panicking."

Smith stopped pacing and tried not to stare at Brooks's new haircut. "I'm not panicking. Maybe we can electrocute them, or..."

Brooks tilted his head. "You *never* care about dying."

"It's not about me. *You're* not dying on your birthday."

Sarah interrupted, with an idea of her own. "I can distract them while you two get to your car."

"What?" Brooks and Smith said at once.

"If none of us make it out of here, no one knows about Terry and the website. No one figures out what happened. If you two get out, you can go back to your secret government project or whatever you people do and you can figure out a cure."

It was a decent point, but they didn't love the idea.

"Are you sure?" Brooks asked.

She nodded, opened the Winnebago door, and stepped out into the hot sun. The Putins were baking, and the smell of their decaying flesh made her pinch her nose, even from twenty feet away.

Sarah sprinted along the side of the Winnebago, toward the forest. The zombies followed at their leisurely pace.

Brooks and Smith peeked out the window, counting them as best as they could. There were no fewer than ten, and maybe as many as fifteen. Hard to tell, since they all had the same face.

When Sarah and the horde were out of sight, the detectives sprinted to their car. Bad luck and disappointment greeted them. Between the gravel and dirt roads, all four of the Aztek's tires had popped.

"Shit," Smith said.

While he grabbed their zombie-killing swords, Brooks opened the door to Terry's F-250 and checked for keys underneath the seat and sun visor.

"Anything?" Smith asked.

"No luck," Brooks said, still rooting through the truck.

"Oh, fuck," Smith said. He grabbed Brooks by the arm, pulled him out of the truck, and handed him a sword.

BRAAGRAAGRRRRARRR. The zombie Putins were back. Closing in on them from every side. Among the zombies was a new one. One wearing Sarah's blood-stained lab coat. BRAAGRAAGRRRRARRR.

The detectives needed somewhere they could shoot and swing swords, preferably where it would be difficult to surround them. Preferably somewhere with a good vantage point.

"Back of the truck?" Brooks wondered.

"I guess. Yeah," Smith said.

They climbed up into the truck's bed and stood against the cab wall, where they looked down on the encroaching zombies. A crowd of ravenous Putins surrounded the truck, in various states of decay. Some Putins held their heads in their hands. Some held their rotted-off arms in their mouths. One Putin was completely limbless. It scraped along the ground using its sharp fangs to drag itself along the dirt.

The nearest zombie reached its arms over the truck bed and pulled itself up. This one was shirtless and had a hole in its abdomen, with a three-foot-long strand of small intestine hanging out.

Smith shot the Putin, and it fell backward.

A few moments later, it was crawling over the truck gate again.

Brooks turned to his partner. "Before we start hacking these things to pieces..."

"Goes without saying," Smith said.

They came together for a brief, let's-not-die kiss. The approaching zombie let out a groan. Not the normal BRAAGRAAGRRRRARRR groan. This was the sort of groan a Baby Boomer might make upon seeing a younger person do literally anything.

As the detectives pulled apart, Smith saw something out of the corner of his eye. Something that didn't make sense. He grabbed Brooks and pulled him back into a kiss, this time leaving his eyes open like a weirdo. Another groan.

Brooks pulled away from Smith. "Kind of need to focus now."

The zombie continued toward them. BRAAGRAA-GRRRRARRR.

"No. Wait. Watch the Putin," Smith said.

"Weird kink, Edd—"

Smith grabbed Brooks and started kissing him again.

With both sets of eyes open, the detectives watched the zombie stop in its tracks and shield its eyes with its hands.

The pair pulled apart. The Putin lowered its hands and approached again.

Smith asked a leading question. "How do you defeat a rabid Vladimir Putin...?"

Brooks caught on. "By being gay and holding fair elections?"

He grabbed Smith's arm and gently stroked it, staring at the zombie the entire time.

"Worth a shot," Smith said, as the zombie once again went still and let out a plaintive groan.

"Let's *vote on it*," Brooks said, with emphasis.

The agitated zombie hissed and flailed. BRAAGRAA-GRRRRARRR.

"I *vote* we do gay stuff," Brooks said loudly.

"I also *vote* we do gay stuff," Smith said.

BRAAGRAAGRRRRARRR.

BRAAGRAAGRRRRARRR.

"That's unanimous," Brooks said.

They started making out, as exaggeratedly as possible—basically just licking each other's faces.

It worked better than anticipated, not just holding the Putin off. In a burst of green and pink, the zombie's head exploded, sending sour-smelling fleshy chunks all over the truck bed.

"Gross," Brooks said, coming up for air.

The remaining Putins advanced on the truck. Three pairs of arms dangled over the walls of the truck bed, each ready to hoist a zombie up into the bed.

Brooks and Smith began tearing off each other's clothes. It was somewhat difficult to become aroused during a zombie attack, but their lives were on the line, and it was working. When they entered a zombie's line of sight, it stood in an angry trance, unable to come closer. If it came close enough, it exploded, just like the first.

One by one—with each homoerotic act—the zombies' heads popped and the truck filled with more gore. An ear nibble—POP. Some light groping—POP. Smith's head between Brooks's legs—POP POP POP POP.

Brooks kept an eye on the creatures, since Smith couldn't from his vantage point. All but one had exploded. Even the stumpy fellow, who'd chewed his way up into the truck. POP.

The remaining Putin was stronger than the others—one in a jumpsuit with a nametag that read "Walker." Terry Walker. The original Putin. The man who created this homophobic plague. He ambled along the truck bed toward them, even as Smith went down on Brooks.

Brooks stared into the Putin's eyes.

"Alexei Navalny is a hero," he said as he came.

That did the trick. With one last POP, the Putins were no more.

Smith rose and cleared his throat. "Who?"

"One of Putin's political opponents," Brooks said.

"*Nerd.*"

Exhausted, the pair slumped down and sat on their jackets, in a deep puddle of green goop.

Brooks eyed his naked partner. "You want me to—"

Smith shook his head. "You know, I've never declined sex in my life, but... I think I'm good."

"Oh, thank God." Brooks sighed in relief.

"I knew your heart wasn't in it," Smith said.

Nearby, a little bit of goop bubbled, shooting an eyeball a few inches into the air. It came back down, and the goop settled.

"Happy birthday," Smith said.

THE 3D PRINTER OF DOOM

Rochester, New York. Home of Kodak, Xerox, and a handful of universities, the greater Rochester area fancied itself a sort of discount Silicon Valley. It had all the amenities, from algorithm-obsessed dweebs to gross privacy violations to libertarians who insisted they were against age of consent laws for non-pedophilic reasons.

It also had a serial killer.

That's why Agents Brooks and Smith found themselves at a Medical Examiner's office, picking through corpses. Three bodies had turned up in less than twenty-four hours, each missing an organ. The first—a twenty-something young man—arrived without kidneys. Expecting changelings, The Reticent had assigned the detectives to the case. In the time it took them to travel from Manhattan to Rochester, two more young adults had been murdered: one woman missing her liver and one man missing his lungs.

"Not changelings," Brooks said, his latex-gloved hands wrist deep in the lungless corpse.

Pretending to be an FBI medical examiner wasn't all that fun. As usual, he and Smith didn't know what they were looking for. They were just looking for something weird, whether it be organs turned to stone (gorgon), organs liquified (wendigo), or a parasitic worm burrowing through an abdominal cavity (parasitic worm burrowing through an abdominal cavity). Unfortunately for them, everything but the missing organs was normal.

"The coroner said that each of these people died from missing whatever organ was missing," Brooks said. "They weren't stabbed or shot or choked to death. Toxicology reports aren't back yet, but I'm guessing they were sedated and someone did some amateur surgery."

Smith's hands were wrist deep in paperwork. "They all went to the same school."

"Which one?" Brooks asked, as he removed and discarded his gloves.

"Rochester Institute of Technology," Smith said.

Brooks joined him behind a desk. "Same major? Same classes? Same dorm?"

"Nope. Mechanical Engineering, Sonography, and... Museum Studies?" Smith shook his head. "Two different dorms and one local living at home with his parents."

"They don't have a med school, do they?"

Smith shook his head. "Negative. That was my thought. A rogue doctor."

"Run of the mill cannibal?" Brooks wondered.

As they speculated, the swinging doors to the examination area opened with a WHOOOF. A rolling cart entered first, with a sheet-covered corpse on top. Then came the person pushing the cart: a sweaty, overworked medical examiner.

"*Another one?*" Brooks asked.

He and Smith stood to check it out.

"No." The medical examiner brought the cart to a halt, and wiped the sweat from her brow. "Well, yes and no. I'm pretty sure this one is a heart attack." She pulled the sheet back, revealing a fifty-something man, and continued. "He freaked out when he found *another* corpse with its eyeballs missing. The guy was on the phone with 911 reporting it when he just... died."

"Just the eyeballs?" Brooks asked.

That made no sense. It wouldn't kill anyone, just blind them.

"As far as I know. I haven't examined it yet," she said.

"Where's the other body?" Smith asked.

"Cops are still taking pics," she said. "You can probably catch them if you want."

"Where?" Brooks asked.

"RIT campus. Right in front of the Liberal Arts building."

Right in front of the Liberal Arts building, Rochester Police were finishing up and loading the eyeless body into an ambulance for transport. Brooks and Smith—fake badges in hand—made their way over and accosted the officers for information.

"What happened to this one?" Smith asked.

An annoyed officer who'd been ready to leave the scene answered. "Eyes ripped out."

"Any signs of the cause of death?" Brooks asked.

"You mean other than having her eyes ripped out?" asked the officer.

"Yes, other than—"

"No," said the officer. "I'm thinking whoever's doing this is poisoning the victims, and that's what they're dying of. If those lazy fucks in toxicology would hurry up— "

"Where exactly was the body when you found it?" Brooks asked.

The officer pointed to a spot on the sidewalk. "Just lying there on her back."

Brooks and Smith knelt down to get a closer look.

"What's that?" Smith asked, pointing to a tiny orange

piece of something. Plastic, maybe.

"3D printer filament," said the officer. "It's *everywhere* around here."

"You don't think it's evidence?" Brooks asked.

"No. You can get that shit stuck in your hair just walking through campus."

"Okay..." Brooks said, doubting that.

Smith also doubted it. "Out of curiosity, where's the 3D printing lab?"

"They call it *The Construct*," the officer said in a mocking tone. "It's a *makerspace*." He pointed across campus. "Institute Hall on Reynolds Drive. We already checked it out, though. One of our officers had the same idea. Nothing there."

"We'll check it out anyway," Brooks said.

The officer shrugged and was on his way.

At The Construct, which was as needlessly capitalized as The Reticent, Brooks and Smith found little but 3D printers, laser-cutters, and CNC mills. Rows of sterile-looking tables were laid out in factory-like fashion. The whole area reeked of solder and future mesothelioma lawsuits. Introverted students buried their heads in their work and avoided making eye contact with the old dudes who clearly didn't belong on their campus.

One 3D printer was still running, making BREEEP and CHUGCHUGCHUG sounds as the printing base moved frantically beneath the nozzle. Brooks and Smith went over to inspect the printer, and found that it was printing a human heart. Not a 3D-printed piece of plastic that looked like a human heart. An actual human heart muscle—unmistakable, especially to someone who'd been doing amateur autopsies all morning. Since it contained no blood, the heart was transparent, and it was about three-quarters of the way finished, missing only one chamber and a little piece of the aorta.

"Umm..." Brooks didn't have words for the unsettling organ.

"Come on." Smith grabbed Brooks by the arm and pulled him underneath a shop table. "I'd say someone will be back for that, wouldn't you?"

In agreement, Brooks grabbed a nearby file cabinet and scooted it closer, further obscuring them from view. He and his partner remained quiet, and kept their eyes focused on the printer.

After an hour, no one had come for the heart. Of course they hadn't. The printer was still BREEEPing and CHUGCHUGCHUGing. The detectives were still scrunched.

"We should be shorter," Smith complained, rubbing at a sore shoulder.

"And younger," Brooks added.

Another hour passed, and the sounds finally stopped. The organ was ready.

Within minutes, a young man entered to retrieve his heart. He wore an RIT hoodie, with the hood up to obscure his face, and carried a lunchbox. His demeanor could be described as 'forced casual.' That is, he was in a hurry but didn't want it to seem like he was in a hurry. He grabbed the heart and stuffed it into his lunchbox. A few pieces of ice fell to the floor and skidded toward the detectives.

Brooks and Smith slid out from under the table, guns drawn.

"In a hurry?" Smith asked.

The young man jumped in fright, sending his hood

sliding off his head. That revealed a pale, chubby face and a buzzcut. "Oh man... I'm in trouble."

"Yeah, you think?" Brooks said.

"It's not, um... it's not what it looks like," said the young man.

"It looks like you're yanking out people's body parts and using them to learn how to 3D print new ones," Smith said.

"No, no. I already know how to 3D print any organ you can think of," said the young man.

"What's your name?" Smith asked.

"Um... Chet."

"Where are you taking the heart, Chet?" Brooks asked.

"Um... b-b-back to my room?"

Brooks pointed his gun at the doorway. "Take us there."

Motivated by the gun, Chet took his lunchbox and showed the detectives to his dorm room. The three stood in a dimly lit hallway that smelled like gym socks, as all men's dorms do.

Chet cracked the door open. "Oh man. Can you just... wait 'til I clean up?"

"No," Smith said, pushing it wide open and releasing musty sex stank into the hallway.

"Ugh," Brooks groaned.

It was a dorm room. Two unmade twin beds, their blankets piled upon them. Two desks, each covered in an array of books and bits of machinery. Trashy swimsuit posters on the walls.

Smith pushed Chet into the room first. As he followed him in, he chastised the student for the stench. "You gotta take out your cum rags every once in a while."

Brooks noticed that one desk was much dustier than the other. "Where's your roommate?"

"Out," Chet said.

"*Chet?*" A soft, feminine voice called out from under one of the blanket piles. "Do you have my heart?"

Smith gripped his gun harder. "What the fuck is that?"

"Who's with you?" the voice asked, frightened.

While Smith kept his gun pressed to Chet's back, Brooks walked over to the bed and uncovered its occupant.

Brooks gagged. "Oh my God. *What is that?*"

The room's awful smell hadn't been from cum rags. It was a naked woman, sort of. She was blonde, busty, and had a seam down the middle of her abdomen—jagged bits of flesh fastened together, running from the top of her ribcage to her belly button. Clear liquid with pink tinges leaked from the seam, which appeared to be held together by Velcro. She didn't move. It didn't seem she could.

"That's Printana," Chet said, like he was introducing a date to his parents.

"Printana?" Smith wondered.

Chet brandished his lunchbox. "I gotta put this heart in her or she's gonna die."

"*She's alive?*" Brooks cringed.

"Kinda. Yeah," Chet said. "I think."

"*You think?*"

"Please. I gotta put this heart in... then I can explain."

Brooks waved his gun toward Printana. "*Fine.*"

Chet pulled the Velcro apart with a CRRRRSSSH, exposing more foul-smelling goop.

Brooks and Smith pinched their noses shut to keep out the mix of decaying flesh and hot metal.

Printana's insides looked human. They also looked like they were rotting.

Chet reached in and pulled out a heart that had shriveled to the size of a plum, its surface looking like it had been scorched by acid. He opened his cooler, pulled out the pristine 3D printed heart, and clicked it into place like it was a Lego. Viscous black fluid began pumping through it.

"What happened to the old heart?" Smith asked.

"It dissolved. I, uh... haven't perfected everything," Chet said.

He sealed her up, and Printana was as good as new. She shot up into a seated position and turned to her maker. "Would you like to have sex with me now?"

"No, Printana..."

"Okay then," Printana said. She shut her eyes and seemingly went to sleep.

"So, you made a fuckbot," Smith said.

"She's not a robot," Chet said.

"She's definitely not a person," Brooks said.

"But she is! Those are all human organs. The blood pumping through them isn't exactly real, but there's no microchip in her head or anything. It's all flesh and bone," Chet said.

"Then why does she want to have sex with you?" Smith asked.

Brooks scienced up that question. "Who'd you model the brain after?"

"I dunno, I found the blueprint online," Chet said.

"Let me get this straight," Brooks said. "You found blueprints for a human brain on the internet, and didn't put even a second of thought into printing it out. Didn't worry about the ramifications of human consciousness or anything."

"Um... yeah," Chet said. "Who doesn't want a warm girlfriend to cozy up with?"

Brooks raised his hand, like a smartass.

Smith tried reasoning with the student. "Chet, you made a fuckbot. I get it. I see the appeal—"

"*Do you?*" Brooks asked.

"*I do.* But I don't think it's a coincidence that a bunch of corpses have turned up with organs missing while you're 3D printing new ones," Smith said.

"I didn't do anything, I definitely didn't kill anyone," Chet said.

"Someone did," Brooks said.

"Maybe Printana?" Smith wondered.

Chet defended his girlfriend's honor. "*Printana would never.*"

Smith, not believing Chet to be a threat, tucked his gun away and speculated. "Maybe she knows her organs keep failing, and she's not waiting for you to print new ones. She's going out and extracting them for herself."

"Let's look under the hood," Brooks said.

"What?" Chet asked.

"Open her up again. I want to compare parts," Brooks said.

"Okay..." Chet opened Printana's chest.

Brooks and Smith leaned in to get a closer look. Each organ—from the brand-new heart to the older kidneys and intestines—had filament lines.

"I don't think he's lying," Smith said.

"Yeah. Everything here looks printed—"

Brooks shut up, as he was knocked out.

Smith saw his partner collapse onto the fuckbot. He turned just as Chet jabbed him with a needle containing a tranquilizer.

"Shit," Smith said, before falling onto the pile.

The detectives awoke strapped to the two beds in the dorm room. Brooks was shirtless, for some reason. Printana was nowhere in sight. Between them was a cot with a different body on it—a brunette—and a lab-coated Chet tinkering around in her body cavity.

Neither Brooks nor Smith had a good vantage point. If they had, they'd have seen a grotesque mockery of a human woman. The brunette on the cot was a Frankensteinean monster, just like Printana. But this one was made from real, human organs that pulsed and throbbed and released foul odors.

Smith softly muttered swear words as he tried not to freak out about being bound.

Even if he could have seen his partner's struggle, Brooks had no ability to comfort him. He tried to work on their predicament.

"Where's Printana?" he asked.

"In the closet," Chet said. "She's exhausting."

"*What?*" Brooks asked.

"Do you know how *time-consuming* 3D printing is? It took twelve hours to finish that heart, and she needs a new organ every other day. It's *killing* my social life."

Smith would have loved to make a crack about that, but he was busy panicking and thrashing against the straps that held him to the bed.

"This is Printana 2.0," Chet said, looking down at his creation. "Using the same concept as the 3D printed model, I can create a real human woman from a collection of body parts."

"Congrats, you made a Frankenstein," Brooks said.

"Frankenstein was the name of the doctor," Chet said smugly.

"*I know*," Brooks snapped. "It's a figure of speech."

"I figure I can use your stomach so she can handle spicy food," Chet said.

"Well, that's racist," Brooks said.

Chet glanced at Smith. "And I can use *his* eyes."

Smith complained as he squirmed. "You already stole someone's eyes."

"I know, but I like yours better," Chet said.

"*Gay*," Smith said.

Chet hit him with another injection, a paralytic to stop the squirming.

He brought a similar needle to Brooks's arm, and loomed over him. "You first."

Smith tried to object, but the tongue is a muscle so paralytics also stop speech. He was stuck inside his body, listening as Chet clinked around in a tray of scalpels and revved a sternal saw. He couldn't even turn his eyes, so he was stuck with peripheral blurs of lab coat and metal.

Brooks was in a similar condition, but with a nerd hovering a scalpel above his bare abdomen. He didn't love the idea of being hacked apart. His mind filled with visions of his father and sister's insides spilling all over the ground in Willowbrook Park. He imagined his looked the same.

Brooks's breathing became rapid, but his body couldn't move with it. As a result, the inside of his chest burned as he was compelled but unable to thrash about.

Unable to speak. Unable to move. Unable to do anything but watch as some doofus in a lab coat succeeded at what hundreds of monsters had tried and failed. Killing him.

Brooks felt the scalpel hit. It didn't hurt exactly. Not physically. There was pressure on his skin until the instrument pierced its way through.

The release of pressure was almost relaxing. As his skin parted, it was as though he was melting, like he'd become one with the bed and would soon seep into the Earth.

Then the feeling stopped, and he watched as Chet's white lab coat developed a spot of red. Dead center. Right at the heart. The spot spread, until it covered his chest. Chet fell forwards, onto the corner of the bed, then toppled onto the floor.

Neither Brooks nor Smith saw him land, but both heard the sound.

An hour later, Brooks was able to move. Once that happened, he looted Chet's cart and stole bandaging to cover the inch-long incision in his abdomen. Oddly enough, Printana 2.0 was missing from the cart.

Brooks hovered over Smith, and started unstrapping him.

Smith's eyes shot open. He realized he could speak again. "Brooksy?"

"I've got you." Brooks helped him to a seated position and sat next to him.

Smith was shaking, but he wrapped his arms around Brooks and laid his head against his chest. "I really thought you were dead."

"Nope. You're still stuck with me," Brooks said.

"What happened?" Smith asked.

"I have no idea," Brooks said. "He was cutting into me, and then he got stabbed or something. All I saw was him bleeding out, then he fell to the floor."

Smith pulled away from his partner's chest and looked to the floor, where Chet's corpse lay face down, with a red puddle expanding all around it.

A familiar feminine voice called out from the closet. "If I can't have him, no one will."

They hopped off the bed and made their way over to investigate.

"Printana?" Brooks wondered.

"Yes..." Printana 1.0 emerged from the closet in bad shape, with her 3D printed organs leaking from a gap in her seam.

"Why'd you kill Chet?" Brooks asked.

"He was going to replace me with the real girl," Printana

said. "Not anymore."

"What did you do with Printana 2.0?" Smith asked.

"I finished her," Printana said. She turned and opened the closet door all the way to reveal Printana 2.0, who looked to be about sixty percent Chet.

"Oh my God." Brooks gagged a little.

Smith moved to Chet's corpse and rolled it over to confirm his suspicion. The front of Chet's body had been hacked apart. His eyes, nose, and lips were all removed from his face. His shirt had been sliced down the middle along with his torso, and several organs had been taken out. His pants were unbuckled, and rested a foot or so below his waist. Just below the spot where Printana had removed his genitals.

The patched-together Printana 2.0 sat naked, with all of its new parts. Splashes of blood and guts looked like tattoos all over its skin. Bits of muscle were exposed from where Printana had tried to cram too many into the petite body. One ear appeared to be sliding off the creature's face. Chet's flappy little dong hung from too high up on Printana 2.0's body, bleeding from the tip.

"We're going to be together forever," Printana said.

"Forever," agreed Printana 2.0, in a voice that was almost Chetlike. There was a gargling sound, and some blood leaked from a hole in her neck.

In reality, the Printanas were going to be together until each succumbed to total organ failure, which would take less than forty-eight hours, but they sealed their sentiment with a kiss. They started making out, pressing their bleeding tongues together in a sloppy display reminiscent of melting salt water taffy.

Brooks and Smith had dealt with enough. They left the Printanas to perish, with a promise that they wouldn't murder anyone else. If they broke that promise, the detectives knew where to find them.

"Don't worry," said Printana. "We'll be too busy enjoying each other."

She then slapped Printana 2.0's ass, which permanently shifted to the side of its body.

"Before we go, any chance you know where your schematics came from?" Smith asked.

Printana nodded. "They came from sexbots4u.xyz/isis-$$-arson-16$$"

"Perfect," Smith said.

Brooks had her repeat that, so he could jot it down.

The Reticent would shut down the website within hours.

Outside, the detectives took deep breaths of fresh air. A few students eyed them and scurried in the opposite direction, either because the pair were covered in various goops or because Brooks was still shirtless in the fall in Rochester.

Brooks turned to Smith, who was still shaking a little, and made an assumption. "You really thought I was dead?"

"For a few. Yeah."

Brooks wasn't sure why he was feeling morbid (maybe from being hacked open), but he was. "What if I was?"

Smith's face scrunched. "What?"

"What if I'd died back there? What would you have done?"

Smith answered without hesitation. "I'd order a fuckbot from Etsy."

"Seriously," Brooks said.

"Seriously?" Smith pretended to ponder, deeply. "Order a fuckbot."

While Brooks rolled his eyes, Smith considered his real answer to that question. It was uglier than Printana 2.0.

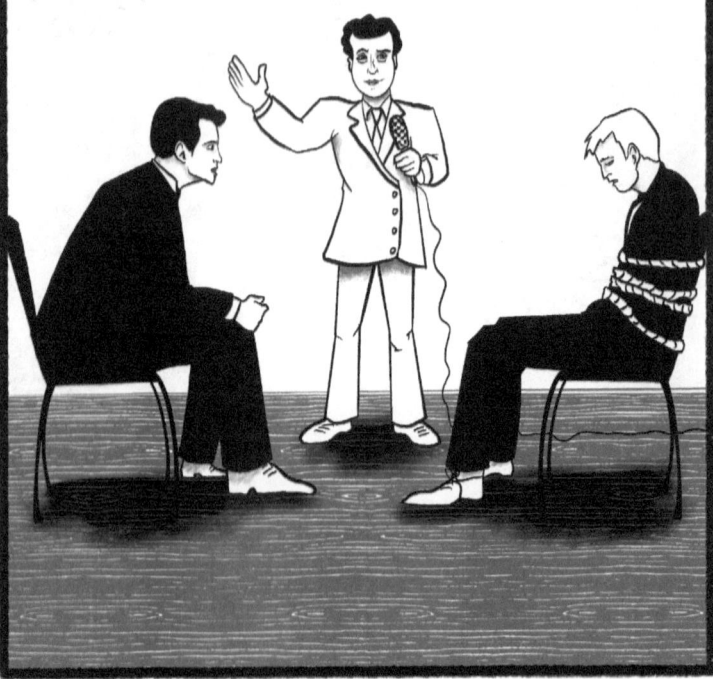

FUNNY OR DIE

The fabulously wealthy don't party like everyone else. For his 50th birthday, Serghei Kunter assembled thousands for a red-carpet event at Gotham Hall, which is a real place in New York City and not where Batman and Commissioner Gordon meet up. It was a semi-exclusive event, and anyone who was anyone clamored to be on the guest list.

Brooks and Smith hadn't done any clamoring, but they were on the list, thanks to The Reticent. There'd been a rumor going around that Kunter was dabbling in the dark arts, and a very public event was as good a place as any to investigate. The couple posed as a much wealthier couple, in Reticent-provided bespoke suits and expensive watches.

Smith tugged at his sleeve, uncomfortable with its proper fit. "It's so goddamn snug."

A server noticed the flagging motion and approached with a tray of martinis.

"Thanks," Smith said, taking one.

"You look great," Brooks said, "but you think maybe you should slow down on the martinis?"

"Why?" Smith scoffed.

"Because you've had like... five? You *might* need your wits about you since we're conducting an investigation."

Smith laughed. "You have no idea how much it takes to get me drunk, do you?"

"That's not really something to brag about."

Smith looked past Brooks. "Oh shit. Two o'clock.

Kunt's on the move."

"For the last time, it's *Kunter*. It rhymes with... mooned her? Spoon fur? I guess it doesn't really rhyme with anything. It doesn't sound like cunt, though."

"The more you complain, the more I'm gonna go all-in," Smith said.

"I know." Brooks's eyes tracked across the room. "Let's follow him."

They trailed the billionaire and his friends down a long red carpet in a long hallway. At its end was the entrance to a small theater. A more exclusive event within the exclusive event. Standing at the door was a bellhop-looking gentleman holding a tray. Each person who entered the theater deposited their cell phone into the tray, then walked through a metal detector.

Since there'd also been a metal detector at the main entrance, Brooks and Smith were already unarmed. Whatever this was, it took security seriously. They deposited their cell phones in the tray and made their way inside.

The room was unimposing, with seating for fifty or so that was half-full (or half-empty, depending on one's perspective). At its front was a stage, where five podiums stood unoccupied. In front of them stood Serghei Kunter, waiting for the crowd to settle in for whatever he had planned.

Kunter wasn't much of an imposing figure. He stood 5'9", with short grey hair that was at least thirty-percent plugs. His eyes were puffy and dark. His lips were thin and set in a permanent smirk. The imposing part of him was his wealth, which he flaunted by having no fewer than three twenty-something women at his side at any given time. All were as tall as him or taller in their stilettos.

Brooks and Smith claimed seats in the back of the small crowd.

Kunter stepped to the center of the stage and spoke, in a thick Eastern European accent. "Thank you for coming, my closest friends. As you know, I am big fan of game shows. When I was growing up in Romania, we get so many American game shows. I loved them. For my birthday, I've gathered some competitors for a very special game I created. This one is called Joke Off."

Smith whispered in Brooks's ear. "I hope they don't joke off all over each other."

Brooks shook his head.

Kunter looked offstage and motioned for someone to join him. "Come on! Don't be shy."

Five uncomfortable men slinked onto the stage and took their spots behind the podiums.

"Please. Give a round of applause for contestants."

The small crowd politely applauded.

Kunter continued. "The rules of this game are simple. You are funny, or you die."

Brooks and Smith exchanged a look.

"Each contestant will tell one joke. If I laugh, they win. If I don't laugh..." He motioned toward his armed bodyguards. "BLAM."

"Oh shit," Smith whispered. "He's not a mage. He's a sociopath. We're gonna watch people die."

Brooks fretted. "There has to be something we can do..."

"He's got a kill squad," Smith noted.

"Then we sneak out and call someone..." Brooks stood to leave, and an usher appeared at the end of the row.

"Remain seated throughout the show," the usher said. It wasn't a request.

Brooks sank back into his seat.

Kunter stepped to the first podium. "First up, we have Barry Birkenfeld. You are from right here in New York, yes?"

An older, balding comedian acknowledged that. "Yeah. I'm just curious. Uh... when you say BLAM... what exactly do you mean?"

Kunter smiled. "Let us hope you don't find out, Barry."

Barry's head glistened with sweat.

"Now. Tell me jokes." Kunter folded his arms in anticipation.

Barry picked up a microphone, cleared his throat, and launched into a routine he'd done hundreds of times. "What is the deal with airline food? It bankrupted my stomach and now my colon has to give it a bailout?"

Kunter stared at him, stone-faced.

One of his goons stepped behind Barry, pressed a gun to the back of his head, and fired. BLAM. Blood and brain shot into the air. The crowd applauded.

"So sad," Kunter said. "Anyway."

He stepped to the next podium, where a very young comic stood in wet pants. "I don't wanna do this, man."

"You want the BLAM already?" Kunter asked.

The audience—aside from Brooks and Smith—laughed.

The comedian shook his head. "I just wanna leave. Can I leave?"

"No." Kunter turned to the audience. "Our second contestant is Matty Lopez. He will tell a good joke, I hope."

Matty swallowed and stepped around to the front of his podium, where everyone could see that he'd pissed himself. His bit required movements. He launched into it. "I'm from Los Angeles. Grew up in Los Angeles. I've been in New York for almost a year now, and the, uh... you know all the bits already. People on the West Coast walk like this." He lazed about the stage. "People on the East Coast walk like this." He stiffened his posture and took on a pompous sneer. "But uh... the thing that gets me most is the difference between the homeless people, right? In LA, the homeless have camps. Everywhere. They've got tents. They've got sleeping bags. In New York, the homeless are always on a stoop or a bench. They're in the middle of the sidewalk. So what I wanna know is... why doesn't New York have any sporting goods stores?"

Kunter wordlessly nodded his head toward one of his goons. The man stepped behind Matty's podium and shot him in the head. BLAM. Blood sprayed across the stage. Some of it splashed the rich assholes in the front row, who exchanged satisfied looks like they were at Sea World being sprayed with water by a playful dolphin.

"Ugh. Heartbreaking," Kunter said.

In the back row, Brooks put a hand to his forehead. "Oh my God."

"I dunno," Smith said. "So far they've kinda deserved it."

"*Oh my God.*"

"Too soon?" Smith wondered.

"Yes. *Ten seconds* is too soon," Brooks said. "How does this not bother you?"

"You might have noticed... I'm a little hard to traumatize," said Smith.

At the third podium stood a blue-collar sort of fellow, wearing overalls and sporting a haircut suspiciously close to a mullet.

"Third contestant is Joe Beckham," Kunter said. "Are you ready?"

"Yeah, man. Let's fucking go," Joe said, coked out of his mind.

"I love this enthusiasm! Good luck, Joe. Tell joke now."

Joe reached into his jacket and pulled out a puppet. It was browner than him, and wore a tiny puppet sombrero and poncho.

"Look who's here!" Joe said. "It's José!"

Then Joe spoke through José, though his own lips kept moving. "Ayyyy, esss-saaayyyyy."

Smith eyed Brooks with a don't-you-kinda-think-he-deserves-it look.

Brooks responded with a yes-but-no-because-that's-horrible face.

BLAM.

Joe didn't get the chance to finish his racist puppet act before he was summarily executed. He and José collapsed into a pool of blood and gore, and the crowd cheered.

Next up was Mark Miller, an edgelord comedian who peaked in the 90s. Before Kunter even got to him, Mark introduced himself with confidence. "I'm Mark Miller, and this joke is gonna kill."

He launched into his rendition of the Aristocrats joke. For those unaware, it's a staple in comedy circles, generally told from one comic to another and meant to be as disgusting as possible. For some reason, he thought Kunter was the right audience. "A family walks into a talent agency. There's a dad, a mom, a son, and a daughter. You know, real apple pie American family. The dad says, 'we have an amazing act, you gotta sign us.' The talent agent isn't sure about it. 'I don't really do family acts,' he says. He says they're too wholesome. He says they're passé. But the dad is really insistent. 'You gotta just see it... let us do the act for you, and I know you'll sign us.' And the talent agent, he has nothing better to do except maybe some coke. He doesn't have any appointments for a few hours, so he agrees. He says, 'show me what you got.' The whole family—dad, mom, the two teenagers—they all start stripping down to their underwear. The son and the daughter kick things off. They start eating each other's assholes. The dad's got no dick 'cause he lost it in a circus accident, but he's got a twelve-inch rubber dildo tucked into his under-wear. He takes that thing, shoves it right up the mom's ass. No lube. She's bleeding onto the floor, her kids are rolling around in it..."

As was tradition for the Aristocrats routine, Mark went on like that for a painful amount of time, describing one horrible sex act after another, until he reached the punch-line. "The talent agent says, 'that's one hell of an act, whad-daya call it?' And the dad—since he's the only one still alive—says, 'the Aristocrats!'" Mark said the last word with flair, and extended his arms wide.

The crowd exchanged confused looks. The edgy non-joke only worked amongst comedians. Usually when drunk. Kunter didn't react. His guard knew what to do, without direction. BLAM. The crowd broke into raucous applause.

"Tssk. Tssk." Kunter approached the final podium, and introduced the last comedian. "Our final contestant. I hope he can make me laugh. Ronan Yost!"

"Good to see you again, Serghei," Ronan said, unboth-ered. He was in his twenties, and wore a nice, crisp suit. He looked like someone who'd have been an attorney if he hadn't gone into comedy. Probably because his parents had both been successful attorneys.

Ronan launched into a routine that famously bombed in any town with fewer than 100,000 residents. "When I was at Harvard, I had a gig with the Harvard Lampoon. And for those of you who don't know, that's the school's com-edy magazine. Well, for one issue, I wrote this fake story about Al Gore and how he'd invented PornHub—y'know because he invented the internet. It wasn't all that funny. Anyway, I wrote the story and I forgot about it. Didn't think about it again. Graduated college. Two years later... two *whole years* later... I'm at a cocktail party and you know who's in attendance? Al Gore. And Al Gore comes up to me, and he says in his Al Gore voice... 'I saw what you wrote in the Lampoon. But I didn't invent PornHub. It's too tame.' And that was the day I learned Al Gore is a *kinky son of a bitch*."

Members of the audience snickered and cackled. Kunter exhaled the slightest bit—what constituted a laugh for him. "I like this. This is relatable content. You win prize."

Brooks and Smith stared at each other in disbelief as the audience around them cheered.

One of Kunter's goons brought in a silver briefcase and handed it to Kunter. The billionaire opened the briefcase to show the audience it was full of hundred-dollar bills.

Ronan approached, nonchalant, to receive his prize.

"This is two million dollars," Kunter said.

"Thanks. Now I have something to toss to some strippers later," Ronan said.

Kunter chuckled. "Wonderful!"

As Ronan left the stage, Kunter returned his focus to the crowd. "Thank you all for coming to my game show—"

Brooks and Smith stood to leave. The same usher from before blocked their path.

"—Before you all go home, I would like to do a second game. This is spur of the moment, but... we have spies in audience tonight."

The crowd booed and turned to see Brooks and Smith, awkwardly standing there.

"Come on down," Kunter said.

"No, thanks," Smith said. "We're good."

"Is not a request." Kunter snapped his fingers, and Brooks and Smith were suddenly on the stage, standing at either end of Matty Lopez's corpse.

Brooks's stomach sank. "The dark magic rumor is true."

"Oh, fuck," Smith said, doing the math that sociopath

+ dark magic = very bad.

"Yes, I'm getting very good at it," Kunter said. He snapped his fingers again and everything cleared from the stage but himself, Brooks, and Smith. "Tell me your names. Where are you from?"

"Eat shit," Smith said.

Kunter's goons stood just off-stage. When their boss glowered at Smith, one stepped onto the stage and punched him—with full force—in the stomach. He doubled over, groaning. The goon remained near him, ready to strike again.

Brooks was more diplomatic, as usual. "Arturo Brooks. I'm from Staten Island."

Smith just groaned again.

Brooks continued, in hopes of sparing his partner another blow. "That's Edward Smith. He's from Indiana."

"Excellent. You two will play a game now." With another finger snap, the detectives were behind two podiums.

"Rather not," Smith said, still holding his stomach.

"We're not funny," Brooks said.

Kunter shook his head. "That's a shame. This will be a quick game then."

Brooks and Smith looked toward each other and locked eyes. Each silently mouthed "I love you."

"Oh. This is interesting," Kunter said. "You two really are a couple. Not just for spying." He put a hand to his chin. "I have a new idea. Have you seen *Newlywed Game*?"

"Yeah..." Brooks said. Smith nodded along.

"Perfect!" Kunter snapped his fingers and changed the set so the detectives were seated, six feet apart, facing each other. "We'll do some trivia."

"What?" Smith asked.

"Glad you ask." The billionaire gestured across the

stage. He was joined by a woman in a long, flowing purple gown and a turban. From her ears dangled two extremely oversized Ankhs. She looked like a 1980s TV psychic that charged $1.99/minute. Another one of Kunter's childhood staples, no doubt. "This is Miss Levi. She has *interesting* abilities."

Brooks tilted his head. "Interesting like...?"

"She's telepath. Reads minds, pokes around in heads. If I ask her, Miss Levi will leave you both drooling on floor." He dismissed the notion. "But we want to have fun, so here's the game. I ask you—" He pointed at Brooks. "—a question about him—" He pointed at Smith. "You get it right, you get a point. Five points, you both walk out of here unharmed."

"And if I get it wrong?" Brooks asked.

"Miss Levi does a torture. You get five questions wrong, he dies." Kunter made a giddy clap.

"Do it the other way," Brooks said, demanding to be tortured to death.

Smith shot him a horrified look. "No."

Brooks wasn't trying to be brave. He was trying to be smart.

Kunter understood that. "Absolutely not. Miss Levi says Mr. Brooks is more forthcoming about his past. You know him too well. This way's more fun."

"*Miss Levi* hasn't said anything," Smith said.

Kunter chastised him. "In my head. Telepath. Pay attention."

The goon elbowed Smith in the ribs, on his boss's behalf. Smith groaned.

"I assume we can't refuse," Brooks said.

"You can if you want a BLAM right now," Kunter said.

"*Great.*" Brooks looked across the stage at Smith. "If anything happens, I—"

"—It won't be your fault," Smith finished.

Kunter turned to Smith. "Oh. If you try to give any hints, you die."

"Figured," Smith said, before muttering "asshole" under his breath.

From nowhere, an upbeat, brassy tune played for the captivated audience. It was something to entertain them while Miss Levi held her fingers to her temples, doing telepath things. As the tune reached its crescendo, Miss Levi strolled across the stage to Kunter, holding a stack of notecards she'd apparated from nothing.

She handed him nine cards—the most he'd possibly need. Kunter reviewed the cards with a grin, and the music petered out.

Kunter shuffled the cards in his hands. "You have thirty seconds for each question. Question One! What is Mr. Smith's middle name?"

Brooks answered. "Lock."

"Correct!" Kunter smirked harder than usual.

In mid-air above the stage, two numbers appeared, as holograms.

1 – 0

"You don't have to do this," Brooks said.

"We'll fuck off," Smith said. "Never mention it to anyone."

"It's fun, though," Kunter said.

"There's plenty of fun that doesn't involve murder," Brooks said.

"True. I wanted to build a superyacht," Kunter lamented. "But that bald bastard Bezos beat me to it, so I learned illusion magic. I'm enjoying myself."

Brooks and Smith shared an apprehensive look.

"Question Two! What is Mr. Smith's Employee ID number?"

"7717812," Brooks said.

"Correct."

2 – 0

"I know what you're doing," Brooks said. "You're going to do four easy ones, then five that are impossible to answer so you can drag this out for the drama."

Smith agreed. "Just get it over with, you fucking psycho."

Kunter grinned. "*Okay.* Question Three. What is Mr. Smith's biggest fear?"

"I..." Brooks didn't know.

"Twenty seconds..."

Brooks gave an answer he knew Smith feared, but that he also knew was in no way the right answer. He mouthed "sorry" before he said it. "Spiders?"

Smith shut his eyes.

A harsh BZZT sound came out of nowhere. The scoreboard updated.

2 – 1

"I'm sorry. Everyone hates spiders, but looks like the correct answer is... he has Merinthophobia. For our audience members, that's a fear of being bound or tied up. I wonder how that happened."

Brooks recalled Smith's insistence on never wearing seatbelts. He recalled his partner's panic when he'd been tied up for Printana parts. He recalled the time he brought home fuzzy handcuffs and was rebuked. The hints were subtle, but they were there. He began beating himself up, mentally.

Two goons came from offstage, carrying rope. The crowd cheered them on, with assorted shouts of "do it" and "tie him up."

"What are you doing?" Brooks asked.

Kunter didn't answer.

The goons made their way to Smith and weaved around him in opposite directions until he was completely bound.

Smith's panic was evident, even as he tried to defy the goons with a "fuck off." His face glistened with sweat in the stage light. His skin reddened. His breaths came quick and sharp. He twisted and writhed beneath the rope, trying to get even the smallest part of himself free.

The crowd cheered as Smith clenched his jaw and forced himself not to make a scene.

"Stop it," Brooks demanded.

"Oh, do you want the easy questions back now?" Kunter continued as planned. "Question Four. What food allergies does Mr. Smith have?"

"Just almonds," Brooks sneered.

"Correct," Kunter said.

3 – 1

Kunter eyed the man struggling to fight off a panic attack with indifference. "Miss Levi, would you remind our contestant what it felt like the first time he had that allergic reaction? I understand it took quite some time for anyone to help."

Brooks objected. "*I got the answer right.*"

"I never said I *wouldn't* torture him if you did. Just that you need five right for him to live," Kunter tapped at the side of his head. "Pay attention."

Smith, who was leaned forward tight against the rope,

shot Kunter a furious look.

Miss Levi approached the bound detective and touched his temple. The moment her finger made contact, memories flooded Smith's mind. Not memories, exactly. They were too vibrant. More like experiences. Smith genuinely felt like he was having an allergic reaction—like his throat was swelling, the inside of his mouth was burning, and his lungs were struggling to find oxygen. He wasn't, but his mind completely bought into the illusion. Audience members laughed at his misfortune.

"Eddie—" Brooks tried to get Smith's attention, to no avail.

"Question Five. What year did Mr. Smith join The Reticent?" Kunter asked.

Brooks glanced from his suffering partner to their host. "1997."

"Correct," Kunter said. "Miss Levi, remind Mr. Smith what he felt like in 1997."

She touched his temple again. In a word, 1997 felt like shit. Drug overdoses and misery and nonstop "Candle in the Wind." On top of being bound and having an allergic reaction, it was basically the world's worst hangover. Not great.

4 – 1

Now that Brooks only needed one more question to win, it was time for Kunter to really bring the pain. He dramatically cleared his throat.

"Question Six. What was the name of Mr. Smith's childhood dog?" Kunter asked.

"That has to be a trick question," Brooks said.

The despondent look on Smith's face told him it wasn't. For a moment, Brooks forgot the crowd and stared.

"You've never mentioned any..."

Smith shut his eyes.

"Ten seconds," Kunter warned.

"I don't know. Spot?"

BZZZZZT.

4 – 2

Kunter tutted. "Oops. That's not it. The dog's name was Jesse. Miss Levi, would you remind Mr. Smith how his pet died?"

Brooks didn't know what was happening in Smith's mind, but he knew it wasn't good. His eyes reddened. His head drooped. He was on the cusp of actually crying, in front of a crowd, no less. Smith hadn't thought about digging the grave for a pet his parents murdered in a long time, and he certainly hadn't thought about how it would affect him if he did. Apparently the answer was... a lot. He shook his head, trying to compose himself.

"Please stop," Brooks said.

There was no humanity to appeal to, neither in Kunter nor in the crowd, which laughed at his plea.

Kunter moved the game along. "Question Seven. The scars on Mr. Smith's left arm. Where did those come from?"

"I don't know..." Brooks stopped acknowledging Kunter and stared at his partner. "Eddie, I'm sorry I don't know..."

Smith wouldn't make eye contact. "It's not your fault..."

"Ten seconds."

Brooks tried. He knew the marks, and that they looked like burns. "The explosion that killed his parents?"

BZZZZZT.

Kunter shook his head. "No. The answer is cigarette

burns."

4 – 3

Miss Levi didn't need prompting to touch Smith's temple and remind him which foster parent had used his arm as an ashtray. As a bonus, she reminded him of other abuses he'd met living in the system. The burns barely registered among the rest of the horror.

Kunter was absolutely giddy to continue, and he wriggled with anticipation. "Question Eight. At what age did Mr. Smith lose his virginity?"

Brooks snapped. "*What is wrong with you?*" Kunter posing this question confirmed something Brooks had long suspected but dared not mention. He didn't want to think about it, let alone posit a guess.

"Ten seconds," Kunter said.

"I don't know..." Brooks hazarded the lowest number he could accept. "Twelve?"

For a brief moment, Smith and Brooks made eye contact. Neither said a word as the buzzer sounded.

BZZZZZZZZT.

4 – 4

"So sorry," Kunter said. "The correct answer is... nine? Oh no." He looked at Smith. "I bet you don't like thinking about that. Miss Levi—"

"*Stop it,*" Brooks pleaded, knowing it would do nothing.

"—would you jog his memory?"

When Miss Levi touched him this time, Smith's eyes glazed over. He became lost somewhere in his mind, unresponsive to the room around him.

Tears flowed down Brooks's face, on his behalf. "*Stop*

it."

"Oh, it could stop very soon." Kunter bounced up and down and clapped. "Question Nine. Win or death! Which prescription drug is Mr. Smith using right now, behind your back?"

Brooks swallowed. "How could I possibly know something that's being hidden from me?"

"Twenty seconds..."

Brooks thought as hard as he could. It had to be for insomnia, and it wasn't any of the benzos he already knew about. Quaaludes didn't exist anymore. There was one, in late-night infomercials that Smith always made fun of. A little too hard, maybe? Brooks struggled to think of the name.

"Five seconds..."

Brooks shut his eyes. "Lunesta?"

"That is..." Kunter shook his head. "Correct. Excellent work, Mr. Brooks."

The crowd booed and jeered.

Kunter hushed them. "Now now. Fair is fair."

5 – 4

Kunter snapped a finger, and the ropes around Smith fell to the floor.

Smith didn't react. He sat there, slumped forward, ready to topple.

Brooks hurried across the stage to him. He pulled Smith to his feet, and put in all of the effort it took to keep him there. Smith was dead weight. Brooks pulled Smith's arm up behind his neck and over his shoulder, so he could walk for the both of them.

Kunter offered them a friendly wave. "Bye! Go on. Get out. Oh. If you ever come here again, or send anyone from your Reticent... we'll do a game you can't win." He made a gun gesture with his hand. "BLAM."

☙

Smith didn't say a word as they made their way through the bustling party and out onto the street. He didn't say a word as Brooks hailed a cab, or during the ride home. He didn't say a word as they shuffled up the stairs to their home. When the front door opened, he wordlessly pressed through and headed for the bathroom.

Brooks heard nothing but retching sounds as Smith evacuated six martinis and a pile of hors d'oeuvres from his stomach. He considered knocking and offering... help? Something? But he knew that would come across as pitying and Smith would reject it.

Eventually, Smith emerged from the bathroom and flopped onto the couch.

Brooks approached from the kitchen and handed him a full glass of ice water.

Smith accepted it with a shaking hand, but dodged eye contact.

Brooks didn't know what to say. You okay? The answer was obviously no. You're going to be okay? Probably not. In lieu of words, he tried putting a hand on Smith's shoulder, but Smith wormed away. Brooks sat there, saying nothing as he tried to think of something—anything—to say.

Half an hour after Brooks escorted his partner home, Smith still hadn't said a word to him. Brooks couldn't take it anymore. He broke the silence with a plea. "Would you *please* say something?"

Smith didn't.

"*Please.*" Brooks went on an anxious ramble. "I can't

imagine how awful tonight has been for you. I really can't. But... I want to be here for you, and I can't do that if you won't talk to me."

Finally—still without saying a word—Smith stood up.

Brooks hurried to his feet to match. "Eddie?"

"I'm leaving," Smith said, evading eye contact again.

"To go where? It's after midnight," Brooks said.

Smith clarified, softly. "I'm leaving you."

Brooks's face scrunched. "*What? Why?* Because I didn't know things you never told me?"

"No. I just... I gotta go." Smith walked toward the door, to retrieve his coat.

"That's it?" Brooks followed, and spoke with a hurt tone. "*Thanks for saving my life. Go fuck yourself?*"

Smith had no energy for arguing. "Something like that."

Brooks grabbed him by the shoulder and forced him to meet face-to-face. "We've been together for *six years*. You don't walk away from that because of one bad night."

"I can walk away whenever and... whyever I want." Smith opened the door.

Brooks blocked the door with a hand and shut it.

"Arturo..." Smith made a rare full-named plea. "Don't take this the wrong way, but I will do *anything* to get out of this house right now. Don't try to stop me again."

The look on Smith's face was that of a trapped animal, ready to lash out at anyone.

Knowing he could track Smith's phone, Brooks let him go.

Outside the door, Smith turned back, just for a moment.

"For what it's worth, it's not your fault," he said.

That wasn't comforting, at all.

☙

Brooks sat in the living room—wide-awake—stalking his partner with his laptop. Smith's phone spent an hour at one bar, then moved down the street to another. After last call, it moved to a 24-hour bodega before moving to an alley a few streets away.

Smith's phone stopped moving in that alley, sometime around three in the morning.

Brooks threw on his coat and followed it.

The alley was dingy, as most are. Broken glass scattered all around. Ugly graffiti covering the walls. Metal bars over what few windows there were. The cracking cement contained half-frozen puddles, their contents a mystery since it hadn't rained or snowed in over a week.

Brooks heard Smith before he saw him. Sloshing sounds and grunting. He rounded the corner of a dumpster to find the love of his life with his pants down, pressing an older prostitute against a brick wall with erratic thrusts. Each time the woman's long fur coat hit the wall, bits of masonry dust sprinkled to the ground. The pair's panting breaths created fog in the cold air.

Brooks grabbed a nearby board and hit it against the dumpster. An echoing CLANG jolted Smith away from the wall and out of the prostitute. She dropped a few inches to the ground, unfazed. He turned around with a red face and a semisoft dick.

"What are you doing here?" Smith slurred the words a bit.

Brooks addressed the woman first. "How much does he owe you?"

Smith objected. "I paid up front."

"You should go then," Brooks told her.

She adjusted her dress and hurried toward the street, her heels tip-tapping along.

Brooks gestured at Smith. "Pull up your pants. I'm

taking you home before you freeze to death."

Smith pulled them up and laughed. "I *am* home."

"*Eddie...*"

"You think I belong in some cozy million-dollar brownstone, with IKEA shelves and walls decked with framed photos of grinning fag—"

Brooks snapped. "No. I don't care how traumatized or drunk you are. You don't call us that."

Smith shook his head and continued. "I'm as out of place there as I was at that birthday party. Kunter reminded me who I am."

"You're not some goddamned alley rat." Brooks stepped closer to him. "You're hurting and you don't want to work through it, so now you're here trying to ruin your own life."

"Fuck off," Smith said, coming up with no better response to what was absolutely true. He knelt down and grabbed a quarter-full bottle of whiskey from the ground.

"Oh. Wow," Brooks said. "I've never been rudely dismissed before." He rolled his eyes. "Your shitty coping mechanisms are going to get you killed."

"They've gotten me this far." Smith leaned against the dumpster and took a deep swig.

"Yeah." Brooks nodded. "They've gotten you to where you're drunk banging hookers in an alley at age thirty-five. You're doing great."

"This is who I am," Smith said.

"This is who you *think* you are," Brooks corrected. "You're not stupid, but right now you're thinking like a drunk idiot."

Smith glowered.

Brooks glowered back, then got an idea. "What's my middle name?"

Smith took another swig and stared at him.

"Humor me. *What's my middle name?*"

Smith rolled his eyes. "Gene."

"What's my employee ID number?" Brooks asked.

In his impaired state, Smith struggled with that one. "85... 9... 1... 66... 1. I think. Where are you going with thi—"

"What's *my* biggest fear?" Brooks asked.

"Wraiths," Smith said, without hesitation.

Brooks shook his head.

"Bullshit," Smith complained. He took another swig and shook the almost-empty bottle.

"It's losing you," Brooks said.

"Already lost," Smith slurred.

Brooks snatched the bottle from his hand. "I'm sorry Kunter hurt you. I'm sorry *so many people* have hurt you. But have I?"

Smith squinted.

"Have I *ever* hurt you?" Brooks asked.

"No." Smith reached for his bottle.

Brooks pulled it farther away. "Then *why are you hurting me?*"

"'Cause I'm a dumpster person. *Like I said...* not your fault."

Brooks noticed a repeated phrase. "You keep saying things aren't my fault."

"So?" Smith snatched his bottle back.

"Not everything is a blame game, Eddie. And... do you think the things that have happened to you are your fault? If you get hurt, it's your fault?"

Smith's silence answered that for him. He finished his whiskey in one long swig, then tossed the bottle to the side.

Brooks continued. "And if I get hurt? That's also your fault? No matter what happens, it's your fault?" Smith's response was more silence. "That's insane."

Smith wouldn't look at him.

"*Eddie*. Having abusive parents *wasn't your fault*. Being bounced around foster care *wasn't your fault*. Being ra—"

Smith wouldn't let him finish. "*This is*." He gestured broadly at the shabby alley around them.

"Yeah. You chose to get drunk and come here. That's on you. But if I can't convince you that you deserve better and bring you home, that's on me."

"You're here because of me. The Reticent, the party, this alley..." Smith dropped to his knees, in the middle of a mystery puddle, and motioned toward the street. "Just go."

"No." Brooks bent down next to him, keeping his own knees out of the puddle. "You take care of me. I take care of you."

Smith practically spit as he responded. "I never fucking asked you to. Let me go."

"Never," Brooks said.

"*Turo*."

"No." Brooks pulled him close, and forced them both to stand up.

Smith mumbled something under his breath. Something like "Nuva lester mollusk."

Brooks couldn't make it out. "What?"

"I've never taken Lunesta."

Brooks's jaw dropped. "I got the last question wrong?"

"I should be dead." Smith swallowed hard. "I *wish* I was dead. Probably why the Kunt let me live... knew I'd hate this more..."

"Eddie..." Brooks held on tight, preventing Smith from dropping back into the puddle.

"Why the fuck do I get bailed out when people are constantly dying around us?" Smith broke away from his partner, bitter. "Fucking... eight-year-olds are getting eaten by werewolves but here I am. Just a big, unflushable piece of shit. I don't want to be here, and I don't deserve to be here."

"Yes you do," Brooks said.

Smith scoffed and lit a cigarette.

"You deserve to be alive. You deserve to be loved," Brooks said.

"Even when I'm out fucking whores?" Smith asked.

"I mean... I'm going to make you get tested for *everything*, but yes. I love you, Eddie. Even when your brain is broken."

"Always is," Smith said.

"You were *tortured* tonight," Brooks said. "In what world would I not forgive you?"

Smith turned the question around. "In what world could I forgive myself?"

"This one, if you try," said Brooks.

"I hate everything about me."

"I know," Brooks said. "People made you feel worthless your whole life. That's not your fault. But if you don't let anyone change your mind... then that *is* your fault."

They stood there for a moment, observing each other's faces.

Smith composed himself and—as always—tried to mask the pain with humor. "At least we didn't get the joke off."

"You would have done okay," Brooks said.

"You'd be doomed, though," Smith said.

Brooks deadpanned. "Two men walk into a bar. That's an OSHA violation."

Smith groaned. "Take me home."

PROPHECY BALL

The Magic 8-ball warmed as it rolled between Smith's hands. This one allegedly worked, and had to be delivered to the Artifacts Division for safekeeping.

He started with an easy question.

"Is my name Edward Smith?"

YES.

"Are you a psychic trapped in a Magic 8-ball?"

YES. DEFINITELY.

"Do I have a twelve-inch cock?"

MY SOURCES SAY NO.

"Can I run an eight-minute mile?"

VERY DOUBTFUL.

"Did I get diddled when I was younger?"

WITHOUT A DOUBT.

"I'll just keep repressing that one..."

SIGNS POINT TO YES.

"That wasn't a question, you cheeky fuck."

BETTER NOT TELL YOU NOW.

"Sorry. Forgive me?"

YOU MAY RELY ON IT.

Smith took a deep breath. "Was the dead guy I saw in Willowbrook Park really Brooksy?"

YES.

"From the present?"

REPLY HAZY, TRY AGAIN

Smith realized that the 'present' was only this exact moment, and clarified. "Was it Brooksy from within the next year?"

YES

"Is there any way to save him?"

OUTLOOK NOT SO GOOD.

CURSE OF THE WEREPIGEON

On a cold November morning in Central Park, bundled-up tourists stood behind a plastic barricade, holding cameras and cell phones, ready to snap photos of the city's newest attraction. Getting the right shot when the sun hadn't yet risen was tricky, but possible. The amateur photographers leaned and stood on their tiptoes just to catch a glimpse of a wing or talon.

Standing two stories tall, the enormous pigeon (nicknamed Pidge by some locals) was discovered when it went on a late-night rampage a few weeks earlier. It first pecked potholes into sidewalks as it tried to scoop up errant french fries. When that didn't satiate its hunger, the pigeon hopped through the park and used its six-foot-long beak to snatch large dogs, zoo animals, and a handful of *Saturday Night Live* writers. People mourned the dogs and zoo animals.

NYPD found that bullets didn't penetrate its feathers. Neither did tranquilizers. Neither did rocket launchers, which for some reason the police had. The pigeon seemed unstoppable.

Luckily for everyone, Pidge was too large and too heavy to fly.

That made way for an opportunity.

The Department of Parks and Recreation enticed the pigeon to a certain area using truckloads of french fries, then fenced it in using twelve-foot-high wooden fencing and barbed wire. They began charging twenty dollars for admission, which granted visitors access to an elevated platform where they could see more than just the top of its grey head sticking out above the fence.

With a VIP pass, visitors could access the platform during feeding time, when they'd witness a dump truck pouring fries through a fence gate. On this particular morning, however, visitors didn't experience the thrill of feeding time because the pigeon was gone.

No refunds were offered.

Across town in Brooklyn, Brooks and Smith were having an even worse time than the tourists who'd paid good money for an absent pigeon. They were seated in their kitchen, arguing—Brooks with a raised voice and Smith with a low, disinterested one.

"It's 10AM," Brooks said.

"On a Saturday," Smith noted.

"It's *10 AM.*"

Smith sipped at a glass of bourbon. "It's Happy Hour somewhere." When that remark didn't garner a reaction, he added, "Never bothered you before."

"You weren't drinking *at 10 AM* before," Brooks said.

"I know what time it is."

"I'm going to keep saying it until you realize it's a problem," Brooks said. "You know what kind of person drinks at 10 AM?"

Smith posited an answer. "Sommeliers who just received a delivery of wine?"

"Sad, broken alcoholics with a dead-end job, three divorces under their belt, and a bunch of kids who hate them. And liver cancer, probably."

Smith grinned. "I only have one of those things. I'm doing great." Noting the serious look on his partner's face, he lost the grin and added, "It's not interfering with my life."

"It is," Brooks said. "Maybe you can't see how slow you are, but I can. You almost got staked by a vampire last night—"

"Part of the job description, Broo—"

"—A *baby vampire* who got turned *two weeks ago*. You're going to get yourself killed."

"So?" Smith took another sip.

Brooks looked at him with a disgust he usually reserved for people who double park. "*So?*"

Smith felt that look. "What do you want me to do? Run a twelve-step and surrender myself to my unloving Creator?"

"I don't know..." Brooks thought something up on the spot. "Go a week without drinking."

"Can I do heroin?" Smith deadpanned.

Brooks stared at him, stone-faced.

"It was a joke." Smith sighed. "Fine."

That was too easy, and Brooks was suspicious. "*Fine?*"

"*Fine.* I'm not interested in fighting you." Smith set his glass down. "When I win, are you gonna get all the way off my ass about it?"

"*Maybe.* If you fail, though..."

"Not gonna," said Smith.

"*If* you do—"

"I'll go to whatever gay little rehab program you want."

Brooks didn't love the choice of words, but the sentiment was acceptable.

"One week." Smith chugged the rest of his drink. "Starting now."

"Good. We just got a case and you're going to need a

clear mind for this one—"

~

When Brooks and Smith arrived at Pidge's Central Park pen, the crowds had dissipated. All that was left were confused NYPD detectives, depressed Parks and Rec managers facing a budget shortfall, and an angry truck driver with nowhere to unload french fries from behind 'CRIME SCENE – DO NOT CROSS' tape.

"Ooh, fries," Smith said, watching as they were dumped onto a sidewalk.

"You *cannot* be hungry," Brooks said. His stomach groaned on his behalf.

On the way to the park, they'd stopped for kebabs, then followed that with a stop for coffee and pastries. Smith had insisted.

"I'm not starving, but I could eat some fries," Smith said.

Thankfully, he didn't start eating french fries off the ground. Instead, he and Brooks approached an officer situated outside the pigeon pen.

"What happened to the bird?" Brooks asked.

"Weirdest thing," said the officer. "No one knows."

"No one knows?" Brooks asked.

"That's what I said, yeah. Pidge was here last night. Come feeding time this morning, no Pidge."

"You suspect any—" Brooks paused for Smith to say "fowl play" but the moment didn't come. "—foul play?"

"Nah, we just put up the tape so tourists would keep out of the pigeon shit. Don't need a lawsuit when someone comes down with some kind of plasmosis."

Brooks and Smith pulled their handy fake FBI badges from their coats.

"Mind if we take a look?" Smith asked.

The officer waved them on. "Be my guest."

On their way to the pen, Smith grabbed a french fry from the top of the pile on the sidewalk, popped it in his mouth, and immediately spat it back onto the pile.

"No salt," he complained.

Brooks simply shook his head and stepped under the crime scene tape.

Inside, the pen looked almost as bad as it smelled. What had once been a nice area of lawn looked like a Jackson Pollock, courtesy of pigeon droppings. A diet of nothing but french fries hadn't been kind to the large bird. Scattered in the poop were an assortment of bones, left over from the pigeon's initial rampage. With the bird gone and its beak no longer a threat, forensics teams pored over the poop, hoping to return any human remains to the appropriate families, or to Lorne Michaels.

Something caught Brooks's eye. Two red smears—about the width of human hands—going up the fence and over the top, right where there was a break in some barbed wire. He approached a cop shaking salt onto some french fries in a corner.

"Did someone fall into the pen recently?" Brooks asked.

"No. Why?" asked the cop, between bites of fry.

"Um... the trail of blood?" Brooks gestured at the fence.

"We think those are talon marks, left over from the pigeon's escape," the cop said. "There's a lot of blood and shit in this pen it's been walking through all day, every day."

The smears didn't look like talon marks, at all. Brooks and Smith had seen enough bloody smears to know. They got closer to inspect.

"Definitely human prints," Brooks said.

"Yeah, but how many humans do you know who can

climb a twelve-foot wooden fence and make it over barbed wire?" Smith asked. "While covered in blood?"

"None," Brooks admitted.

He and Smith looked at each other and made the same conclusion. "Werepigeon."

While werewolves were the most common weremonster encountered by Reticent agents, there had been a few historic instances of other varieties. In the 1960s, a werebear swiftly put a Ringling Bros. Circus competitor out of business. In the 1970s, a weremanatee terrorized the innocent alligators and pythons of the Everglades for over three years. In the 1980s, a vengeance-seeking werecow devised Mad Cow Disease. In the 1990s, a weregallagher disbanded Oasis.

Smith hadn't read any of that history. "Problem," he said. "Giant pigeon's been here for a month. If it was a werepigeon, it should have been one night."

"Not necessarily," said Brooks. "It just has to be triggered by lunar cycles in some fashion. There was a weremermaid case back in '95 where it showed up one full moon and disappeared the next. If I'm not mistaken, that lines up with Pidge. In which case—"

"We'll be seeing another pigeon massacre in twenty-nine days," Smith said.

"Yeah, potentially..."

"We need a list of people who went missing last full moon," Smith said. "Also—"

"The lab results on that blood?" Brooks wondered.

Smith shook his head. "We should go get some good fries."

☙

They did get fries—and burgers—but not until Smith stopped at a pharmacy for some Tylenol. While they'd been scouring missing persons reports in a café, the blood sample from the fence came back one hundred percent pigeon. No match to any human being. That left good, old-fashioned detective work, searching the apartments of the people reported missing. Since approximately thirty-five people are reported missing in New York City each day, it was a tall order.

Most people reported missing aren't actually missing. They're out of town, in a hospital, or too preoccupied with existential dread to check in with a neighbor. As Brooks and Smith went from apartment to apartment, they encountered several of these non-missing persons, all of whom were annoyed to be facing FBI agents over a few simple misunderstandings. The detectives also made their way through a few empty apartments, and several apartments with brand-new tenants who were unnerved to discover they were living in a potential abduction zone.

It was getting late. Just past ten o'clock. Much later and knocking on doors would result in both men getting spit on. Last on their list for the evening was Greg Anderson, a forty-five-year-old accountant with a name as generic as Edward Smith.

Beads of sweat were pouring from Smith's forehead by the time he reached the third-floor walkup. Brooks eyed him with concern.

"You okay?" Brooks asked.

"Yeah, just stuffed."

"I told you not to get the doughnut."

"It's fine," Smith said, wiping his forehead with his sleeve.

Brooks knocked at the door.

No response.

He knocked again, harder.

Still nothing.

He turned the doorknob.

The apartment was locked. Smith pulled a standard-issue lockpicking kit from his pocket and knelt down to get to work. His sweat had returned, and he wiped his forehead again.

"You want me to do it?" Brooks asked.

"No. I'm better at it," Smith said.

"Usually..." Brooks trailed off.

Smith manipulated the tension wrench and lockpick with a slight tremor in his hands. On the first attempt, the pins reset themselves. On the second attempt, the pins reset themselves. On the third attempt—

"Fuck," said Smith.

The pins reset themselves.

"You sure you don't want me to do it?" Brooks asked.

"*I'm sure.*"

After three more attempts, Smith was able to force the lock open. He turned the knob, and the detectives entered the apartment and began rifling around.

There was no one there, but it definitely wasn't abandoned. The television was still on, blaring some news channel. The vegetables in the refrigerator were fresh. The garbage can didn't have the deathly odor of one left abandoned for a month.

"Check this out," Smith called out from the bathroom.

Brooks walked over to the doorway and covered his hand with his mouth. "Oh my God."

In the toilet—or rather scattered all over and around the toilet—were black and white spatters of bird bukkake. Pigeon droppings.

"Think we found him?" Smith asked sarcastically.

"That or we found a pigeon hoarder," Brooks said.

Their answer came when a voice called out from the apartment entrance.

"Is someone in here?" It was male, and nervous.

Brooks and Smith stepped into the living room to greet it. There stood Greg, their missing person, holding a bag of takeout from the sandwich shop downstairs. He was an average-looking man of average build, bundled for the winter, with one exception. Greg Anderson wore no shoes or socks.

"Who are you, and why are you in my apartment?" Greg asked.

For a moment, the detectives didn't answer. They were too busy staring at Greg's unshod feet. He had pigeon toes, in the non-clinical sense. Just above each ankle, scarred human flesh transitioned to scaly, orange bird legs. Instead of five toes, he had four talons: three in the front and one in the rear. The man had enormous, unsettling pigeon feet.

"Um…" Brooks stumbled in disbelief of his own words. "Are you Pidge?"

"No. I'm Greg," said Greg.

"Right, but—"

"Have you always been a werepigeon?" Smith asked. He was ready to get this over with, so he could go home and get something to eat.

"A what?" Greg wondered.

"Have you always had the weird feet?" Brooks asked.

"No. Something happened to—"

Smith hazarded a guess. "Something happened to you about a month ago?"

"Yeah…" Greg nodded.

"You get bit by a pigeon?" Smith asked.

"Pecked," Brooks corrected.

Greg stared in confusion. "You don't think I'm the

pigeon in Central Park, do you?" He gestured at his talons. "This is eczema."

"You remember the last month?" Smith asked.

"Well... no. But I've been here the whole time. I went to sleep here about a month ago, and I woke up here last night. I think I must've been in a coma or something," Greg said.

"A coma where you can survive without food or water for a month?" Brooks asked.

"Stranger things have happened," Greg said.

Smith rubbed at his temple. "Have they?"

Greg couldn't believe what he was hearing. "You think I turned into a pigeon and somehow found my way home... as a bird?"

Brooks nodded. "Pigeons are great with directions. They used to deliver letters."

"Are you cops?" asked Greg.

"No," admitted Brooks, "But—"

"You two are trespassing and harassing me over a medical condition. I want you to leave," said Greg.

Brooks tried reasoning with him. "We'd just like you to come with us. We work for an organization that can run some tests and prove you're not the giant pigeon, or if you are maybe come up with a cure for your, uh... eczema—"

He and Smith stepped cautiously toward Greg.

The man-pigeon leapt into the air and kicked toward them with his talons. Brooks was ready for this, but Smith stared at him, in a daze. As the razor-sharp claws came toward them, Brooks grabbed Smith and pulled him to the floor. From there, they watched Greg prance out the door.

Brooks hurried into the hallway to follow, and Smith lumbered after him. The detectives watched as Greg leapt from an open window at the end of the hall, his bag of takeout still in hand.

They ran to the window, in time to see he'd landed just fine.

Three stories below, Greg made a run for it. They were hopeless to catch him.

"Fuck," Smith said.

"At least we know who it is now," Brooks said.

Smith scoffed. "Imagine *growing talons* and being in denial about it."

Brooks stared at him. "Weirdly enough, I'm not having trouble imagining someone in denial about having problem."

If looks could kill, the world would be desolate. Nevertheless, Smith shot Brooks the sort of look that would kill, if such a thing were possible.

Later that night, Brooks awoke to a sliver of light shining through their bedroom door. He rolled toward where Smith should have been, and found nothing but crumpled sheets.

Brooks's mind went to the easiest assumption: that Smith was downstairs drinking, and that he couldn't even make it one day without breaking their agreement. Grogginess made way for fury. A red-faced Brooks made his way downstairs, ready to start a fight.

Smith sat on the couch, with a laptop on his lap. In front of him, on the coffee table, was what looked like a glass of water.

Brooks assumed it wasn't. He approached and crossed his arms. "What are you doing?"

"Research." Smith looked up from the screen. "Did you know Greg Anderson is the most boring motherfucker alive?"

"Why aren't you asleep?" Brooks asked.

"*Well*—" Smith's voice dripped with sarcasm. "I don't know if you remember, but I'm not great at sleeping. Especially when I've made a pointless sobriety pledge."

Brooks walked over to the coffee table, picked up Smith's glass, and gave it a sip. Water.

"Appreciate the trust, babe," Smith said.

Brooks sat down next to him. "What did you find?"

"Boring, like I said. He's in a bowling league, for fuck's sake."

"What about the person who reported him missing? It was his mom, right?"

"Yeah," Smith said. "Get this. She knew he was missing because he didn't show up for their weekly meetup to watch *Antiques Roadshow.*"

Brooks shook his head. "We should go talk to her. See if—"

"—if she noticed her son was growing talons?" finished Smith.

"Yeah," Brooks said. "If it's a slow onset like it looks, she might be able to give us something."

"That would be a lot easier if she hadn't also disappeared," Smith said.

"What? *When?*"

"A few days after she reported Greg missing," Smith said. "I bet you when we see a list of all the remains found in that pigeon pen... mom's there with the SNL writers."

"Ugh." Brooks uncrossed his arms. "So... how are you doing?"

Smith didn't look up from his screen. "I'm going through contacts of contacts and contacts of contacts of contacts. I'm sure there's somebody in here who noticed the man having talons..."

"Not what I asked," Brooks said.

"Can't sleep. Feel like shit. Same as ever," Smith said. "I'd rather focus on the werepigeon."

"Okay... if you change your mind—"

"You're here. I know," Smith said, with more than a tinge of annoyance.

A week after their investigation began, Smith hadn't found the werepigeon. What he had found was a new number on the bathroom scale, having gained six pounds. He'd succeeded at sobriety, though. At ten o'clock on the dot, he cracked open a bottle of bourbon in the kitchen as Brooks looked on in dismay.

"Cheers," Smith said, raising a glass.

"That's not funny," Brooks said.

Smith's eyes shifted. "Wasn't trying to be."

"All you did was replace drinking with food, and complain about your head hurting all week."

"Uh huh," Smith said. "*And?*"

Brooks responded with a heavy sigh.

Smith took a big swig, then looked his partner in the eyes. "Just do it."

"Do what?" Brooks squinted.

"Break up with me," Smith said.

Brooks stood completely still and stared at him. "Is that what you want?"

Smith turned away.

"*Is it?*"

"No," Smith said, still not looking at him. "What I want is happily ever after with fucking sparkles and rainbows, but there's no universe where this ends that way."

Brooks grabbed him by the shoulder and turned him around. "Why can't there be?"

"'Cause you're you, and I'm... me."

"There's a half-man, half-pigeon running around Manhattan, and you're telling me happily ever after is what's impossible," Brooks said.

"Yeah."

"Bullshit," Brooks said. "When we first met, you told me there are three things that don't exist." He raised his fingers to count as he listed them off. "Aliens. Dragons. Unconditional love."

"Still true, still true, and still true," Smith said.

"I will love you until I die," Brooks said.

"Contingent on me being sober..."

"Contingent on *nothing*," Brooks reiterated. "Until I die."

"Yeah, well that's a pretty likely outcome since *we hunt monsters for a living*."

Brooks stared at him. "Yes... and? You think you're the only one who knows that?"

"The longer we're together, the more it's gonna suck when one of us bites it," said Smith.

"So... give up on life now?" Brooks wondered.

"That's the spirit." Smith pretended to toast.

"That is absolutely deranged." Brooks looked him in the eyes. "You're in a funk. I get it. But you can get out of it."

"I don't want out of it," Smith said.

"Yes. You do." Brooks pleaded with him. "Maybe you don't see it right now because things have been awful lately, with Kunter and Printana... I know it's got you thinking about stuff you had buried—"

Smith set his drink down and offered a sarcastic clap. "Wow. You know what I'm thinking better than I do. Amazing work, detective."

"You know what?" Brooks said. "I don't need that attitude. If you're not going to give a shit about yourself, at least give a shit about me."

"I do," Smith muttered.

"Then show it," Brooks said. "Give me one more week."

"No." Smith paused, in thought. "I'll give you 'til we find the werepigeon."

Brooks had been ready to raise his voice. Instead, he lowered it. "Seriously? That could be three weeks, more if he skipped town—"

"Yeah." Smith grabbed the bourbon bottle and tipped it over the sink. He watched—expressionless—as the liquid funneled down the drain. "Then you drop it."

"I—"

"You'll drop it," Smith said.

Brooks hesitated. "I'll drop it."

The case was taking a lot longer to solve than Smith thought it would when he made that bet. He sat in his home office, poring through alleged Pidge sightings. Most of them were bullshit—nothing more than fantasies concocted by bored minds. Any other day, they would have been Bigfoot or Nessie sightings.

Smith noticed he had a visitor, and griped as he took a sip of water. "Happy birthday to me."

Brooks stood in the doorway.

"Forget the werepigeon for a day," Brooks said. "We can do anything you want."

"I'm good," Smith said, without turning away from his work.

Brooks didn't believe that. "There's *nothing*? Not even some crappy new sci-fi movie?"

"What do you want to do?" Smith asked.

"It's *your* birthday—"

"—and I'm relinquishing control of it," Smith said.

Brooks sighed. "There has to be *something*. I mean, we haven't had sex in like two weeks..."

Smith spun his chair around and faced his partner. "You wanna fuck me? Knock yourself out. Use any hole you want."

"*Oh my God.*" Brooks stepped closer and took a seat on the other side of Smith's desk. He looked across it at a man with deep, dark circles under his eyes.

"We've got *one day*," Smith said.

"And no leads," Brooks noted. "He probably skipped town."

"*One day.*"

"Forget the werepigeon. You never focus on work like this."

Smith looked into his eyes. "Focusing on the werepigeon is the only thing keeping me from putting a bullet through my head."

"That's not funny," Brooks said. "You know how fucked up that is?"

"No. I'm an idiot. I don't know how fucked up I am..."

Brooks noticed Smith rifling through a desk drawer. "What are you doing?"

"Of course I fucking know," Smith snapped. "Let's see. I've tried..." He pulled an empty prescription bottle from the drawer and threw it down on the desk. "Lexapro... garbage." He slammed down another. "Prozac... garbage." Another bottle. "Paxil..." That one bounced across the desk onto the floor. "Garbage."

"Are you—"

"Not done," Smith said, his voice passionless. One by one, he grabbed bottles and chucked them across the desk. "Zoloft... Effexor... Wellbutrin... Vivactil... Doxepin.." The last one bounced off Brooks's arm before making its way to the floor. "It's all garbage. Nothing ever changes."

"Can I do anything to help you?" asked Brooks.

Smith couldn't say "you're a walking reminder of how unfair this miserable world is," so he made his response about his own self-loathing. "That you'd even ask is why I don't deserve you. I guess you could try being more of an asshole like me."

"You're not an asshole," Brooks said.

Smith shrugged. "Booze doesn't help. Neither does gorging on every food under the sun. I'm gonna pretend solving this case will make me feel some sense of accomplishment or some shit, but it's not gonna work."

Brooks considered that. "Only one way to find out."

"Yeah..." Smith faked a smile, poorly.

Brooks tried to help him focus. "So, the full moon is tomorrow night—"

BING. Their doorbell interrupted. BING BING BING.

Both men made their way upstairs.

Smith looked out the peephole. "You've gotta be fucking kidding me."

"What?" Brooks asked.

Smith pulled open the door.

Standing on their stoop were Greg Anderson and a woman they'd never met.

Greg was more pigeon than before—much more. He was almost fully bird. Still human sized, he had a lumpy, feather-covered body, bird legs, and a stubby little tail. One arm had transformed into a wing, while the other—presumably the one used to ring the doorbell—was still a hairy human arm. At the top of this mess were one and a half heads. There was Greg's normal head, and a second pigeon head forming from the back of his neck. The beginnings of a beak poked up into the sky from the top of his skull, while a beady pigeon eye stared from the base of his neck.

He tried to say something, but what emerged from his mouth was a cooing sound.

The woman—much older than Greg but a fully human woman—spoke up. "I'm Carol Anderson. This is my son, Greg. I believe you've met?"

Brooks and Smith welcomed the Andersons into their home, and escorted them to the kitchen, where Greg's uncontrollable poop would cause the least damage.

"Cooooooo, starting to coooo think coooo not eczema," cooed Greg.

Brooks stared at him. "Starting...?"

"We need your help stopping this," Carol said.

"Full moon is *tonight*," Smith said. "You couldn't have come to us some time in the last month?"

"Cooo," Greg said sadly.

"We were hoping it might resolve itself," Carol said. "Which one of you is leading this investigation?"

Brooks nodded at Smith, to encourage him.

"I guess that's me," Smith said.

"May I speak to you in private?" Carol asked.

Brooks and Smith exchanged a suspicious look before agreeing. While Brooks interrogated the pigeon, Smith and Carol reconvened in Smith's office.

"There's no saving my son," Carol said, before they'd even shut the door.

"Aren't you an optimist," said Smith.

"It's a family curse on Anderson men," she explained. "It happened to his grandfather. It happened to his father. They turn forty-five, they turn into werepigeons. If they live, they get bigger and deadlier each lunar cycle. All the others killed themselves at the onset, but... Greg's not the brightest. His father and I never had the heart to tell him about the condition. I've been letting him think it was eczema, just to enjoy what little time he has left."

"So, what... you want me to kill your kid?"

"Of course I don't *want* that, but last month it was just SNL writers. This month... who knows who he might kill."

"Why don't you just tell him the truth and let him eat a bullet?" Smith asked.

Carol stared him down. "Have you ever loved someone, Mr. Smith?"

"Maybe..." His jaw clenched.

"Then you should know sometimes you'll do anything to protect that person. Even if it breaks my heart to lie to him, at least Greg's spending the last days of his life watching *Antiques Roadshow* and feeling normal."

Back in the kitchen, Brooks had a revelation. "Did you know there's actually a type of eczema caused by pigeon mites?"

Without comment, Smith drew his gun and fired a bullet between Greg's eyes. It bounced off as Brooks emitted an "Eddie, what the hell are you doing?"

"Shit, he's already got full pigeon power," said Smith.

"Cooo! Cooo!" Greg swiped at Smith with a talon, ripping a hole in his pants and grazing the skin. The pigeon then hopped through their living room and exited through the window, sending shards of glass and pigeon poop everywhere.

It was well after sunset when the detectives caught up with Pidge. Yes, Pidge. Not a trace of Greg remained. The massive bird—now three stories tall—was in Prospect Park, having left a trail of toppled taxis and kebab carts in its wake. Brooks and Smith hurried toward it, armed with silver bullets, silver daggers, and silver knuckles just in case they were in for some close-quarters combat.

That seemed unlikely. They'd been chasing Pidge through the park for hours, but their legs were no match for its gigantic talons. The werepigeon could cover a football field in the time it took them to take just a few steps.

Smith shouted, trying to get the bird to notice them.

Instead, it ruffled its feathers, cooed, and then raised its beak high. Something—some scent—had caught its attention. The bird sprinted into traffic, on a mission. Traffic was already at a standstill, so no one was forced to slam on their brakes on the bird's account. Nevertheless, several drivers honked at it anyway.

Smith doubled over, exhausted, trying to catch his breath.

"You okay?" Brooks asked.

Smith nodded through wheezes. "Every time we... catch up to... fucking... bird..."

"It has to stop moving eventually. Come on." Brooks grabbed his partner's arm and dragged him into traffic to pursue Pidge. The cars were still stopped, but once again several drivers honked anyway.

CRRAAAAASH

The unmistakable sound of shattering glass led them to their bird. It had pecked through the glass windowfront of a Fish 'n' Chips joint, spreading the smell of fry oil throughout the area. Pidge's head could just barely fit into the restaurant, and it cooed aggressively—unable to reach the delicious french fries it craved. With its head in the window and its tail to the sky, Brooks and Smith were treated to a nice view of the bird's filthy cloaca. It made a

FLRRRRP noise, and a large bone flopped out onto the sidewalk.

Brooks groaned. "Here goes nothing."

He and Smith shot their silver bullets at the bird's hole, hoping to catch it in a vulnerable spot.

All they managed to do was piss it off. Pidge withdrew its head from the building and turned to face the street. It threw its beak wide open toward the sky as it emitted a furious coo.

"Distract it," Smith said.

"What ar—?" Before Brooks could finish his question, Smith was underneath the bird—out of its view—making his way into the Fish 'n' Chips joint.

Brooks's idea of a distraction was psychological warfare. He crossed his arms and shook his head at the bird. "Greg, I know you're in there."

"Cooo."

Brooks eyed the street, where two cars sat tipped on their sides, covered in bird shit. "Look at what you've done. What would your mother think?"

"COOOOO."

"Don't 'coo' me. You're a disgrace."

"COOOO. COOOOOOO."

Pidge was just about ready to peck Brooks to death when Smith emerged, holding an extra-large bucket of french fries.

"Hey!" he shouted. "You looking for these?"

"Cooo?"

Smith set the bucket on the sidewalk and stepped toward his partner.

"Eddie? What—"

"Trust me."

The werepigeon scooped up the bucket in one quick motion, then emitted a plaintive coo. It wasn't enough food to satisfy a creature of its size—not even close. The plaintive coo quickly turned to an agonized coo, which turned into gargling sounds. The bird flapped wildly, as if it were attempting to take flight, but it just spun in circles.

"COOOOOOOOOOOOO! COOOOOOOO—crrk—CRRK—"

It fell to the road, dead.

"What did you do?" Brooks asked.

Smith grinned. "Silver french fry. Couldn't penetrate its feathers, so—"

"—kill it from the inside. You're a genius."

"I'm an idiot," Smith corrected. "Lucky for us, werepigeons are idiots too."

He picked up a fallen café chair and seated himself to catch his breath, which was visible in the cold air.

Brooks did likewise, seating himself next to Smith. He eyed some tourists snapping pictures of the dead bird, then turned to face his partner. "It's too bad Greg didn't come to us sooner. We might have been able to cage him, let The Reticent research a cure—"

"I get it," Smith said.

Brooks settled in his seat. "I wasn't being passive aggressive. I was actually talking about Greg."

Smith had never looked so defeated. "I'll go to rehab or whatever."

"You will?"

The high of defeating the werepigeon had lasted about thirty seconds. Smith knew there was nothing he could do to make himself feel better, but if he could convince Brooks that his rehab suggestion had helped... that would make *him* feel better.

"You deserve at least that from me," he said.

Brooks shook his head. "For the last time, Eddie... it's not about me. If anything ever happens to me, I want to know you'll be okay."

"Yeah..." Smith remained unconvinced. Arturo Brooks was his world, and the world was ending. But he channeled his inner Carol Anderson and prepared to lie his ass off.

WATERCOOLER

Half a dozen Reticent agents sat in the sixteenth subfloor break room, their eyes glued to the forty-five-inch television mounted on the wall above the coffeemaking supplies, next to the fridge. It wasn't often one of their company's cases happened out in the open. They hadn't seen press coverage like this since the Goblin King—a case that coincidentally involved the same two agents.

On screen, a camera on a helicopter captured the scene below.

Two suited Reticent agents—Brooks and Smith—stood in Astoria Park, negotiating with an orc. Their voices couldn't be heard from the helicopter. Nor could their faces be seen. But everyone in the break room knew exactly who they were.

At over six feet tall, each detective only came up to the orc's waist. It was a huge, hell of a green creature with warty skin and a severe underbite. In its left hand was a large wooden club, crudely fashioned from a tree trunk.

Something one of the detectives said pissed off the orc. It slammed its club to the ground.

The headline below read:

NEW MEN IN BLACK MOVIE FILMING IN QUEENS? RESIDENTS PERPLEXED

The agents in the break room looked on, in awe.

"Those guys are legends," said one.

"Were you at the non-denominational holiday party two years ago?" asked another. "They defeated a *demon bear*."

"Everyone knows about the demon bear," said a third, smug agent.

On screen, Brooks and Smith continued negotiating with the orc. One of them gesticulated while the green monster nodded its head in consideration.

"I heard they're fucking," said an agent, making it weird.

"No way. Agent Smith got caught sleeping with his last partner. Agent Burroughs."

"She's hot," said a pervy male agent.

Two women rolled their eyes.

"No reason he couldn't do both," said the weird agent.

One agent had gossip for the group. "Agent Stephenson said they heard from Agent Gutierrez who heard from an intern that Agents Brooks and Smith were making out on the elevator."

"I heard they were fighting on the elevator and the intern had to break it up," said a different agent.

"Lovers' quarrel?" suggested another.

"You know they live at the same address," said the smuggest agent.

"In *two different apartments*," said someone else. "It makes sense. They do research all night. If you got the workload these guys got, wouldn't you live near your partner?"

"No," said that agent's partner.

"*Please*. There are no apartments. It's a total sham. They're fucking."

The agent pointed to the screen, where she perceived evidence of such. As the orc brought its club down with force, one of the men pulled the other out of its path.

"I heard Agent Brooks got committed once," said a nosy agent.

The agent next to them gasped. "What for?"

"Beats me."

Another agent butted in. "You know Agent Smith went to rehab?"

"No," said the agent who knew about the committing. "What for?"

"Beats me."

On screen, the frustrated orc had gotten its club wedged in the ground. It knelt forward, pulling and pulling but seemingly unable to free its weapon. Shots were fired at the only place bullets could penetrate the orc—its eyes. Suddenly blind, the creature stumbled forward and fell onto its own club, impaling itself. From there, the agents in the break room tried to determine whether Brooks and Smith were making out or simply talking. They longed for high-definition.

"I've got it," exclaimed an agent.

"Got what?" asked several.

"They're fucking, right? Maybe Agent Smith went to rehab for sex addiction, then Agent Brooks got committed because he couldn't deal. Because, uh... I dunno..."

"Because he's in love," suggested one.

"Right!" The first agent continued speculating. "He's in love, but it turns out Agent Smith is just a sex addict. Now they're both trying to remain just work partners."

"But it won't work," said a voice from the back of the crowd.

"Of course not."

"Agent Smith will realize it's not just sex he's looking for, and that he loves Agent Brooks. And Agent Brooks will realize his partner loved him all along—"

"It's like a rom-com!"

"*Or*—" said a voice entering the room, "—it's none of your goddamn business."

"Oh shit," said the agent who'd been coming up with a dramatic scenario.

Smith and Brooks stood in the doorway, staring at the trashy gossipers.

"You all should really check whether you're watching a live broadcast," Brooks said.

In the uncomfortable silence that followed, he and Smith poured themselves coffee.

As they turned to leave, Smith reached over and squeezed Brooks's ass.

That would give the group something to talk about.

THANKS FOR READING!

If you enjoyed yourself, please leave a review.
If you enjoyed the characters, check out the books in
the Brooks & Smith series:

Time Binge (Book 1)
Time Purge (Book 2)
A Genie Ruins Everything (Book 3)
Fun Times in a Dystopic Hellscape (Book 4)
Oops! All Zombies (Book 5)

Also by the Author:
The Bedazzlers
F*** Around and Find Out

To find out when new books are released,
sign up for the mailing list at martina-fetzer.com:

www.ingramcontent.com/pod-product-compliance
Lightning Source LLC
Chambersburg PA
CBHW020517260626
47156CB00006B/2039